The Power

Jannus said: "I can clear the Circle of Valde in under an hour. I'm no Screamer, but they'll hunt me or flee me within an hour in spite of anything you can do. Some may not survive it, and none will return as long as you hold me. How will the balance between Circle and Crescent rest then, Lady Ketrinne?"

"I discover you are a perilous guest," observed Ketrinne. "Do all Newstockers take such power from their Screamers?"

"It's not the Screamers," he corrected her. "There's enough desolation in the least child of your household to cripple twenty troopmaids. But it scatters. Newstock's the same. They'd have to go to the Valde for that—if the Valde'd tolerate them . . .

"Learn how to focus, how to hold it long enough to make a weapon of it. . . ."

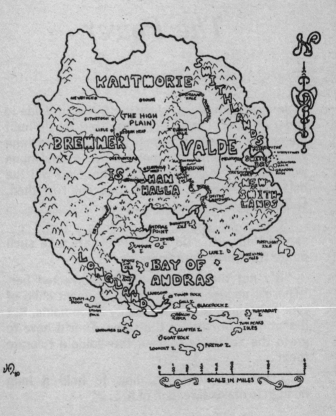

KANTMORIE

THE HIGH
PLAIN

BREMNER

VALDE

HIGH
LANDS

ISLANDS

SLETTE
BAY

NEW
SMITH
LANDS

ISHAM
HALLA

LONG LAND

BAY OF
ANDRAS

SCALE IN MILES

CIRCLE, CRESCENT, STAR

*The Second Book of the
Strange and Fantastic History
of the King of Kantmorie*

by
ANSEN DIBELL

DAW BOOKS, INC.
Donald A. Wollheim, Publisher

1633 Broadway, New York, N.Y. 10019

This book is dedicated to my mother, Barbara Waterman, who taught me about how people do and don't get along, and why.

FIRST PRINTING, MARCH 1981

1 2 3 4 5 6 7 8 9

DAW TRADEMARK REGISTERED
U.S. PAT. OFF. MARCA
REGISTRADA. HECHO EN U.S.A.

PRINTED IN U.S.A.

Table of Contents

I:

OFF THE CLIFF

"Go ahead, admit it," Dan Innsmith challenged, slapping the gate shut behind them and bouncing down the steps to the wet street. "You think the same as me. Ashai Rey's a tyrant, a house afire, a rabid stoat. An't the less true for the fact we take his coin, even if a few more hands warm it on its way to us."

The other young man shrugged his collar higher up his neck, squinting into the drifting mist, and stuffed both hands into his jacket pockets. His name was Jannus. Moving with his friend toward the hazy lights of the riverfront, he replied mildly, "My saying so won't make it any the truer, then."

Dan had been arguing with his uncle, their host, all through the daymeal. Solvig Innsmith was Duke Ashai's man, and refused to hear a word against him. So of course Dan had to *say* that word, and thump it into the table. Innsmiths were like that.

But Jannus wasn't a redheaded Smith but a dark Bremneri: he seldom committed himself until he had to. He wasn't about to denounce Duke Ashai, called the Master of Andras, for the sake of casual table talk, whatever his own feelings in the matter might be.

The street couldn't be trusted. Typically, the two young men chose each a separate wariness. Jannus watched the actual pavement, avoiding in his longer strides the holes and the stones heaved crooked by the first thrusts of frost. Dan Innsmith watched whatever moved: lounging guardsmen, drawcarts, cats springing to windowsills, children thieving

9

from stalls, a wheelbarrow overturning into the flood ditch, two whores with bead-plaited hair quarreling with abrupt gestures in a doorway, laden peddlers wearing their shops on their backs. Dan ducked and sidestepped a flying wad of vegetable peelings tossed out of a window above. The wad missed Jannus too: for when Dan shifted, Jannus moved with him, easily and automatically. But Dan, craning to spot the window, put his foot in a hole and limped the next few steps damning Quickmoor, its Crescent, all of Bremner, and Ashai Rey together to a parched and chilly afterlife.

"You know it," Dan persisted as they turned into the Crescent proper, a perpetual dangerous fairground twenty blocks long and four blocks wide at High Street, its center, fronting the docks and the river. "Ashai's as dangerous as wildfire. You're just too damn Bremneri to say so in three plain words."

"I do hear you." It was a Watertalk phrase, a Bremneri phrase of the riverstocks, evasive and noncommittal. Before Dan could react, Jannus added, "Quickmoor's a Bremneri riverstock too, and you shouldn't forget it. Whatever is said will put you up before a Truthsayer almost as quick as it would have in Newstock. What you *think*, that's still your own affair. But put words to it and you'd better be ready to answer for it."

"Who's going to haul you up before a Truthsayer, then: me? Old Solvig? Just what—"

"Oh, let it *be*, Dan. . . . You just go on and on. Duke Ashai never begged your good opinion, or mine."

Rising above the confused hubbub of the Crescent was a woman's voice, singing. Jannus could catch only the words, "Days of fire, days of ice," and then something that ended in "sleeping." This being Bremner, it probably wasn't a love song; but then again, this was the Crescent, the freeport, where all commodities could be bought or at least rented, so there were love songs to be sung, on demand, for a price. The plaintive sound was lost under the wheels of a passing drawcart and Dan's voice muttering, "You, you're his lucky pocket piece. He treasures *your* good opinion. Else why get Lady Whore—"

"Don't *call* her that."

"—to send clear to Ardun for you, tell me? With scribes ten to the copper here in the Crescent, she sends clear to

Ardun for you, you being so famous and all, scratching contracts and lading sheets on a strap desk at two coppers the page. Surely, for a fact."

"With me, she got you," Jannus pointed out, which stopped Dan for a minute.

"That's true," he admitted. "I'd not have set hand to Ashai's work else. That's true."

Officially, Dan was contracted only to Jannus, who in turn was contracted to the Lady Rayneth—whom Dan persisted in naming, with malicious accuracy, as "Lady Whore." Rayneth ruled the turbulent Crescent district with her gift for organization and about threescore guardsmen. The wages of these guardsmen, beyond what they could extort, were paid by the Andran Duke Ashai Rey, Rayneth's patron. The duke was currently occupied far to the south in trying to get his conquest of a jutting chunk of seacoast called the Longland Spur properly tidied up before winter. Claiming the arrogant title "The Master of Andras," Ashai was nearly halfway to earning it. Five of the Isles of Andras were now under his sunburst banner. Quickmoor, Jannus thought, was just a trinket Ashai had pocketed idly, passing through on his way to somewhere else. An upriver harbor, a freeport at Bremner's southern border, might just be handy to have someday, Ashai might well have thought. So Rayneth had been chosen and mortared neatly into place on a foundation of guardsmen, overlooking the Crescent.

Some people saved string.

Nor was Ashai tight-fisted about maintaining what he collected. The dictionary, the project for which Jannus and Dan had been brought across the continent back into Bremner, had been the Andran's suggestion. Left to herself, the Lady Rayneth would probably have kept happily stuffing entry-slips into random barrels until she died, whereupon her successor would have had an enormous bonfire. Instead, her pack-rat collection was to become the world's first printed book, in this, the 26th of the month called Fading in the year 874 a.k.—after Kantmorie.

Jannus's job was deciphering and ordering the entries; Dan's was inventing a press to reproduce uniform pages.

Though Dan would theoretically have walked fire for the chance at such a project, he'd never had handfasted himself to Ashai Rey—no matter at how many removes—in defiance of his father, patriarch of the Free Smith Clan of Ardun, had anybody but Jannus been involved. The Innsmiths had already split once on that issue, when Solvig Innsmith had accepted Ashai's commission and taken his family with him. On Jannus's say-so, however, Dan had cheerfully walked away from family and clan, that were water and air to any Smith, to live and work among foreigners.

Apparently still thinking on this same point, Dan remarked, "Can't argue that. But it's a fine thing when you won't speak your mind in plain words to me, even if you wouldn't back me up against old Solyig. I don't need a box to keep a secret. An't I to be trusted, then, tell me?"

"Some things are just private, that's all," responded Jannus uncomfortably, attending to the paving stones. "I don't see how what I think of Ashai Rey matters at all—to him, or to you, or to anybody. If you can't be satisfied without something to nag me about, pick something worth the trouble. You just go on and on like a creaky mill wheel."

Dan grunted—an offended, unreconciled noise—and stopped trying to keep pace with Jannus's longer strides, letting the distance between them be his comment.

The harbor, no new sight to him after nearly five months here, was always changeful and worth the watching. Since it was past sundown and daymeals were mostly over, the last of the produce barges were casting free of a nearby wharf and being either poled or sculled toward the Is shore; shadowy, flat, and low on the opposite side of Erth-rimmon, with the sky gray above it.

Except for such barges, the occasional dinghy or raft, and the one-man coracles that Fishers made, all the craft seen in Quickmoor were Andran. Andrans were the watermen, controlling all commerce up and down the vast length of Erth-rimmon because they held the sea, controlling all traffic across the Bay of Andras. Everything that didn't move on its own feet, moved by water; and the Andrans had the ships. Moored out at the floating ends of Quickmoor's long, hinged piers were steam packets, stubby barge haulers, and the high bare-masted silhouettes of sailcraft from the sea, all creaking and groaning restlessly. Most were in the process of being loaded or unloaded by squads of shirtless dockers. Cargo booms at each dock's hinge point bent or swiveled like deliberate storks, high as the mastheads.

The sight of so much purposeful activity made Dan more sharply aware of his own galling idleness. Walking faster, he caught up with Jannus, saying, "Damn Longlanders. Two mortal weeks, I been waiting for those letter slugs now. Jannus? I've run out of things to put my hand to in the meantime. Just sit and watch the press sprout mold and the wood warp. Two mortal weeks. Why couldn't he be satisfied with his Five Isles, tell me? Why does he have to go and war on the Longlanders, that never did him no harm and that make the only decent glass or clay or ceramic to be had since the fall of Kantmorie?"

Jannus, who'd been attending to the voice of the street singer, responded, "I expect he forgot your letter slugs, when he planned on taking the Longlands. I expect it just slipped his mind."

Dan pivoted, hands solidly on hips, confronting him. "Fine for you! You, with Poli and your children about you, what do you care? Me, I'm stuck here with no family but Solvig's, and can't bear *them* more than once a tenday, and have to haul you along to keep me from doing murder, and wait, and tinker, and wait some more. . . . You put that hand on me and I'll bust it for you," Dan threatened, and Jannus let his arm drop and regarded his friend quietly, without anger.

"Dan, maybe you ought to go home for a bit. You need your family about you. I can't be family. I wouldn't know how to even begin."

"Never mind that," responded Dan roughly. "I can live with all you outlanders well enough, so long as I have my proper work to put my hand to. 'Go home for a bit?' Don't talk trash. It's a good month to get there, even with no war closing the Longlands harbors, and more to get back. . . . It'd be first thaw before I could get back here, or the first week of Greening. No, you get me my slugs and I'll be blithe enough. . . . You're Duke Ashai's pocket charm, to keep him from the cold steams: you send him word. Get my slugs here within a tenday or else I swear by the Wheel I'll quit altogether. I'll go home. I mean it."

The ultimatum took Jannus by surprise. He said, "But two seasons' work . . ." but didn't finish the thought, frowning unseeingly off toward the slanting convergences of a baycraft's rigging, where lanterns were hung.

The idea of asking a favor of Ashai Rey, of involving himself that closely with the Andran duke and his doings, of being in Ashai's debt, made Jannus feel heavy and cold. He tightened both arms against his ribs reflexively, hunching his shoulders inside the damp jacket, and made himself think about it.

Asking and getting, he thought, were two different things. He could ask, and Ashai refuse to spare time from his pressing military concerns for so trivial a thing. And if he'd tried, he was sure Dan could be talked around again, persuaded to wait or else devise some other way to produce what he needed. . . . All Dan really wanted was some dramatic gesture of loyalty and concern anyhow; Jannus understood that plainly enough.

But what if Ashai *did* turn aside, and did as he was bidden?

That didn't bear thinking about. Jannus had no desire to discover whether he could command storms, or the tide.

"I'll ask Rayneth—" he compromised, without turning, but Dan interrupted, "Tried that. The Lady Whore . . . your pardon, the Lady Rayneth, flashed about a twentyweight of rings at me and said she'd not trouble the Master of Andras with such a matter at such a time." Dan's rendition of Rayneth's haughty manner was heavily sarcastic.

Jannus fisted his hands inside his pockets, frustrated and feeling colder yet. "I want to stay as clear of Duke Ashai as ever I can," he said slowly. "This contract, this dictionary, that's one thing: it's work I'm fit for, and I could bring you into it. No, that made sense enough. But I want to stay clear out of his way. I let him be and he lets me be—"

"*Nice* of you. It's his commission to begin with, his money paying me to sit and twiddle my fingers, and he's the one holding it up. You're entitled to tell him so, ain't you? Any other foreman'd do the same. And likely get dismissed for it," he added, chuckling. "Go on, send word. Then he'll drop the commission and we can all go home."

"Can't send any word until the sun comes up . . . *if* it shines tomorrow." Jannus was referring to the heliograph system Andrans had introduced along the southern length of Erth-rimmon, beyond the river-link maintained among the riverstocks by their troops of empathic Valde. "I've got till tomorrow, anyhow. And I want to find out what Poli thinks."

"She wouldn't know a letter slug if it bit her."

"Suppose I *was* dismissed from the contract, with the cold just coming on. Maybe you have enough cash put by to get back to Ardun, but there's seven of us. I won't walk the width of Han Halla swamp twice in this life. And with the girls. . . . I'd want to ask her what. . . . Do we have to settle this here? I'm soaked through."

Abruptly Jannus started on down the street in long impatient strides, like someone beginning a journey. He didn't care if Dan kept pace or not: Dan knew his own way back to Rayneth's household. But before he'd gone a block he heard Dan yelling his name. Dan was excited, hollering, "Come here!" Looking reluctantly back, Jannus failed to see the Innsmith. He kept going.

A scruffy child, wearing only a man's heavy shirt with the excess sleeve rolled around his wrists like sausages, came racing crookedly among the people and drawcarts to intercept Jannus's course. "News!" he cried, tugging at Jannus's left sleeve, dancing barefooted in the puddles. "News, for a copper!"

The Crescent was full of such roofless folk in the warm seasons: errand runners, spies of small intrigues, sellers of trivial secrets. Resignedly searching for the required coin, Jannus said, "Cry your news, then."

"I'm Blind Ella's boy," replied the child, hauling at Jannus's arm, pulling him toward the shop side of the street. "Ask Ella."

Blind Ella was a street singer, the one he'd heard: he'd recognized her voice. He and Poli had talked with her more than once. Following less reluctantly, Jannus made his way through a crowd gathered around a fistfight and saw the singer perched on a barrel under a canvas lean-to where firebrick was piled out of the wet. Light from a tavern window shone on her back as she spoke with Dan, making the fabric of the heavy shawl around her shoulders look like graven stone. Like most women whose intimate company was for rent, she wore her hair uncovered and braided into two thin plaits in front that swung with the weight of ceramic beads. Ella's were three on a side and bright green, indicating that her preferred customers were Bremneri farmstead men.

Spotting Jannus, Dan hurried to meet him, saying, "It's a shipment, under Ashai's seal—"

"Mistress Ella," Jannus greeted the woman, who turned

her scarred, sightless face toward his voice. "How does your
evening pass?"

The stiff, shiny skin of her cheek tightened with her smile.
"The better for a mug of ale to warm me," she suggested, ex-
tending a hand. Jannus laid in it two copper coins which she
rattled briskly like dice, then handed to the child crouched in
the folds of her voluminous skirts. At once the child darted
off. "See the fine errand runner who's come to me?" she inquired with satisfaction. "I'm teaching him how to play the
marapipe. And he steals only one coin in five for his share,
scrupulous as a cargomaster."

"There's a shipment," prompted Dan impatiently.

"Jacko One-hand, the Lady Rayneth's doorkeeper," Ella
began obediently, still facing Jannus, "came up in a drawcart
a little while ago and asked if you'd passed. He'd gone to the
factor's household and missed you there, it seems, and was
trying to find you on your way back home. He said a shipment had just docked but the cargomaster was under orders
to release it to nobody but you—"

"Under Ashai's seal!" put in Dan jubilantly. "My slugs!"

"No. It can't be," contradicted Jannus, more sharply than
he realized. To Ella, he said, "What ship?"

"*Windfoam*, out of Camarr. Under Duke Ashai's banner.
At Butcher Street pier, Jacko said. So, is the news worth the
price?"

"If it's my slugs," rejoined Dan warmly, "you'll sleep soft
for a tenday and only open your mouth to put something in
it. Come on," he demanded, grabbing Jannus's elbow and
starting away.

But Jannus knew how to stand still when he wanted to;
and though Dan was by far the stronger, and of equal weight
though a head shorter, Jannus didn't move. Dan wasn't
braced for resistance and lost his grip. He stumbled a step before he wheeled about, scowling. "*Now* what is it? You coming, or not?"

"If I have to take delivery, I'll need somebody to swear to
who I am. Solvig would be best—any sailmaster of Ashai's
would know him. Ask him if he'd do me that kindness. I'll
meet you at the pier." When Dan had trotted off, Jannus said
quietly to Ella, "And what news of the war?"

"Well, there's talk that the Master of Ardun, Domal Ai,
landed a cargo of food and weapons at Cape Storm, and

Duke Timath's men sank one of Duke Ashai's baycraft by keeping it from shelter in tidestorm—"

Jannus nodded, adding the rumors to the pattern that, half unwillingly, he kept in a corner of his mind. The six remaining Andrans of power were giving some aid to the Longlanders, sinking the occasional ship, but had not as yet made up their minds to unite and oppose Ashai in force. But they'd have to, sometime soon: Longlands commanded the mouth of Erth-rimmon. Controlling it, Ashai would have absolute domination of the western half of Andras Bay and control all traffic up and down Erth-rimmon, charging whatever tolls he pleased. He would be Master of Andras in fact as well as in name.

The boy returned with a mug of hot ale which he held against Ella's hand, releasing it only when she had a firm grip. Jannus noticed that the ale was a good three fingers down from the top of the mug; if Ella noticed, she said nothing, but gathered the child against her side with one arm around his shoulders while she drank.

"Oh, and another thing," she said suddenly, raising her burn-shiny face. "There's a gang of Bremneri youngsters— farmsteaders and riverstock boys both—were taking daymeal at the Red Rooster, you know, near Water Street corner? Twoscore or more, my boy counted. Bonded to Duke Ashai, to fight in Longlands for him."

"*What?*"

"Seems strange for Bremneri to be fighting in an Andran quarrel, but seems he paid good coin to indent them. . . . Poli's not poorly, is she? Or one of your girls? It isn't often you're about just on your own."

"What?" responded Jannus, this time vaguely. "Oh, no— all's well. Innsmith meals have a way of turning into yelling contests about whose grandfather's cousin stole whose hammer. Poli can't abide anything that sounds so much like a blood feud, even when she knows none of it means a thing. . . . Bondboys, you said. Are you sure they were Bremneri?"

Hastily finishing a swallow, Ella laughed. "Such a mix of Watertalk and farmstead 'nowt' and 'gi'way' I never heard under one roof in my life. Some Lislers, even, making witch signs against a Valde troopmaid—" She nudged the boy, who performed a flipping gesture, thumb and little finger extended, which Jannus recognized. "Upriver folk," she continued, "all of 'em. Most scarcely grown to their Naming, I should think."

Jannus found he had only another three coins with him. Taking Ella's hand, he folded the coppers into it. "For the rest of the news," he said, and left the protection of the canvas reluctantly.

Butcher Street was about eleven blocks north, back past the Innsmiths' compound. Jannus eyed drawcarts being pulled along but reflected he'd spent every coin he had; and not even Lady Rayneth's marker would get him credit in the Crescent. So he settled to walking—more slowly and carefully than when he'd had Dan to make folks step aside and give way. Nobody stepped aside for Jannus; and a collision would mean a fight, nine times out of ten, especially after nightfall.

He wasn't used to watching out for himself in a crowd. When he and Poli were abroad in the Crescent even the drunks took pains to get clear: nobody in possession of any sense at all would cross a Valde, even one who was no longer a troopmaid. It wasn't just that the whole troop might well join in, or that any troopmaid could stand an untrained man on his head; Valde, whether troopmaid or freemaid—all Bremneri ordinarily had any chance to see—were sacrosanct. They enforced the Summerfair peace on which all nations' commercial lives depended, acting as Fair Witnesses to validate the annual contracts made there; and troopmaids guarded and dueled for the riverstocks and their contentious Ladies. So all local governments, but most particularly those in Bremner, reserved their severest penalties for the harassment of Valde. Therefore if the troopmaid didn't hit you with a dagger-dart and the troop didn't swarm, some local judge would have your head. Valde were seldom molested.

It was uncomfortable, Jannus found, to be walking alone. He thought about turning back to Rayneth's household for Poli. He rehearsed how he'd explain to her, imagining her replies. He imagined, too, the feel of dry clothes.

Meanwhile he was yawning. Tiredness seemed to have dropped onto his every motion. A tender, feverish feeling grew in the tendons of his hands, the bones of his face.

His body was afraid. It was offering him bribes, threats, and distractions to stop short of Butcher Street dock, to keep itself from being walked over some irrevocable cliff. Sensible, predictable body, he thought with a kind of wry fondness.

Undissuaded at being caught, the body contributed a feeling of hollowness and immense lethargy, arguing in many silent voices that it was not a good night for walking off cliffs or calling down lightning. Tomorrow would be so much better, or the next day. . . .

Not unkindly, Jannus let his pace slow to a stroll. Sliding levels of cloud had parted to reveal a moon just past the full. It lit the flat landscape across the river as though the horizon were no more than a room and the moon, a newly trimmed lamp glowing in the middle of it.

He was coming to the thin end of the Crescent, where the high earthen levee surrounding the Inner Households bulked close above a scatter of crooked roofs. The Crescent was temporary—scoured all but clean by each annual thaw flood—and under this moonlight, its makeshift construction was more than ordinarily plain. Badly trimmed wood stuck out at corners, and doors were no more than canvas curtains. What night life there might be here was not to be seen on, or from, the street.

Butcher Street, when he came to it, was no more than an alleyway running dead into the weedy slope of the levee, which looked like a landslide ready to dump itself and its anklet of shacks headlong into the river. The street had no name sign or anything to mark it save the pervasive smell of offal and of the livestock pens out of sight behind a sagging board fence. Everything was shut, dark, deserted.

The long dock, by contrast, was lamplit and busy as noonday. On the downriver side, a baycraft was moored; on the right, the upriver side, a paddlewheel packet. They looked rather like a stork courting a duck. The packet's foredeck was barely arm's reach above the water, even its wheelhouse well below the deckrail of its deepwater cousin. Each ship showed on its bow the rayed sun sigil of Ashai Rey. Jannus had expected to see it, though he'd checked each of the ships he'd passed, just in case. But there were, as best he could determine, the only craft of Duke Ashai currently in port. Naturally, they'd moor near each other by preference, to simplify the transfer of bay-bound goods.

And there was considerable transferring going on. The main cargo boom was in use, its crew chanting a count as they guided its motions, raising a net fit to hold a haystack from the packet's deck and turning it, swaying overhead, toward the waiting hands of the *Windfoam's* lading gang, grouped together amidships to center the load over the open hatch. Goods for local delivery were being heaved onto a line of two-man flatcarts under the directions of two well-dressed men, probably merchants.

It was easy to tell the locals from the ships' crews by the length and style of their hair. Landsmen, Jannus included, tended to have hair cut on the soup-pot principle: whatever stuck out under the pot was cut off. Watermen were reputed never to cut their hair, instead plaiting it in one long rope down their backs. There was a joke about that which ran, "How do you tell a rat from an Andran?" The response was, "The Andran has a longer tail."

It was a Bremneri joke.

Thus the roundheads moving on the pier—carters, laders, and merchants alike—were Bremneri and identifiable as such at a glance. As were the cluster of youngsters peering over the bow rail of the *Windfoam. All* Ashai's goods were gathered here, crated and indentured alike.

Among all the dark heads on the pier, the two copper-haired Innsmiths blazed under a hanging lantern. They hadn't seen him yet, standing motionless by the unlit alleyway that was Butcher Street. Dan, predictably, was pacing, occasionally flinging his arms out to punctuate some remark of frustration or impatience. His uncle, Solvig Innsmith, some thirty years his senior, was a more deliberate man and stood stolidly clear of the bustle, exchanging civilities with one of the merchants. As Duke Ashai's resident agent, or factor, Solvig was a considerable personage in the Crescent, and knew it, and looked it. From shoulders as wide as a bargefront hung an expensive wool cape, maroon with a blue border—not the dress of a retiring man—and at the edge of the road a closed drawcart waited on his return, balanced on its shaft-props. Solvig didn't grudge hiring a drawcart to come three blocks, but he didn't mind standing in the wet, either. In profile his face was very like Dan's, short-nosed and ruddy, with a jaw like the half of a melon clapped solidly under an imposing moustache Dan had yet to cultivate. Red Smiths, visible in any company.

An adequate audience for cliff-walking, Jannus judged, and

yawned compulsively three times in succession. He rubbed the back of his neck, then lifted his head against the hand's pressure, feeling a remote amusement at his body's continuing arguments for inaction.

He could recall being this frightened only a few times before in his life—only once, since the protracted terrors of childhood. And this situation, at least, was quite straightforward, sane, and certain: he knew precisely what he meant to do, and the main alternatives of what might come of it. You walked off the cliff, and either you flew free or you fell.

It was very simple.

He sneezed.

Dan spotted him then, and came running. "Where've you *been*, in the name of the green world?"

Jannus let himself be hauled out onto the pier—it was easier than pushing himself—and while Dan went off to fetch the *Windfoam's* cargomaster, Jannus thanked Solvig for coming.

"You'd not have found a Valde or a Truthsayer abroad in the Crescent after nightfall," nodded the Innsmith in reply.

Dan had found the cargomaster, who displayed an expanse of embroidered violet waistcoat and had a young Fisher clerk in tow wearing a strap desk and carrying an open casket of scrolls whose ribbons and tapes fluttered like tiny banners. A second Fisher hurried behind, opening a large umbrella. "Good even' to you, Factor," said the Andran to Solvig. "Hope all's well with your family. . . ."

"Well enough, thank you kindly."

"This the Bremneri, then?"

"Jannus Lilliason of Newstock in Bremner," confirmed the Innsmith formally, "now under the seal of the Lady Rayneth. Jannus." Solvig nudged him sharply, drawing his attention away from the crowd of boys looking down from the bow. "Show your marker."

"Oh." Jannus unfastened the looped toggle at the jacket's throat and fished for the cord he wore around his neck. The small leather pouch of personal things he closed a fist around protectingly, then held up the scrap of mark-burned leather that was Rayneth's token. Satisfied, the Andran nodded and had the girl with the strap desk make an appropriate notation on a scroll weighted with a seal of yellow wax. "Come take delivery, then," he said to Jannus, rerolling the scroll and

sliding it into an ivory tube as they ascended the steep gang-
plank, Dan foremost, the Fisher with the umbrella precariously trying to keep at the cargomaster's side.

The shipment pointed out to them consisted of two knee-
high kegs set against the outside wall of a cabin. Ashai's yellow seal secured the top of each cask in three places.
Stencilled across the top was an inscription Dan recited
jubilantly: " 'Amando Potter and Sons, Norby Hill, Duncove,
Longlands!' I knew it! My slugs!"

"It's a wonder you got them at all," remarked the Andran,
popping the shut ivory tube into the Fisher girl's casket.
"There's been fighting around Duncove for a . . . since the
end of Summerfair, now I think of it. It's a wonder the goods
were made at all, much less casked and delivered. Duke
Ashai was very particular about the conditions for delivery,
when he had them brought aboard."

"Saw them on board himself?" inquired Solvig Innsmith,
mildly surprised.

"Did," confirmed the Andran. "First time I'd seen him up
so close. He's not so lame as I'd heard tell. My brother's with
the fifth Camarr troop, and my lord duke knew it and told
me he was well and had been promoted to tenner. An't it
something, that he'd take thought for a thing like that?"

"For a fact. Ashai takes care of his own, always has," declared Solvig pontifically and pointedly; he used the exact
words scarcely an hour before during the daymeal argument.
Dan met his kinsman's provocative stare that dared him to
say something *now*, and shrugged peaceably, grinning, all ill
will dissipated. Solvig grunted in satisfaction, his views vindi-
cated.

While the others continued talking, Jannus drifted unre-
marked toward the bow. The Bremneri boys were attended
by a bored Andran marine sitting cross-legged on a coil of
rope, cracking nuts. A thick pole, the sort called inelegantly a
belly-buster, was propped against his shoulder, a crooked elbow holding it in place.

The boys paid little attention to either the marine or Jannus, still absorbed in their inspection of dock and street. They
seemed cheerful enough, lounging and poking at each other,
enjoying the unaccustomed leisure, the novelty of travel, even
toward a foreign fight. Not one looked over seventeen.

"Flat, isn't it?" Jannus remarked at random, recalling his first journey past the Kantmorie escarpment into the southern marshes. Some of the boys looked around then. "Bonded, I hear tell," Jannus said. "Riverstock-born, most of you?"

"Who wants to know?" retorted one by the rail, reacting to the direct question with hostility and suspicion that marked him, at least, as a child of the riverstocks, raised under the scrutiny of Truthtell.

A direct question was a threat in the mode called Watertalk, with Truthtell waiting to weigh the anwer. And a flat question in a man's mouth was an insult, making the one addressed a servant's servant, oppressed by underlings.

Only the riverstock women had the so-called gift of Truthtell, and not all of them. Not all—only too many.

"I've been out of Bremner so long I've forgotten my manners," responded Jannus easily. "I'm Jannus Lilliason, Newstock-born." He surveyed the faces turning toward him and again noted one he'd singled out even from Butcher Street—set apart because the boy had been shaved bald, a common enough punishment for major insubordination, banishment being the final penalty—one suffered eventually by obedient and rebellious alike, once they'd grown to their Naming. Once they'd fathered a child, they were allowed to select a name to carry off to the farmsteads with them, or wherever they might find to go. Even the prospect of indenture might be attractive, to a riverstock boy near his Naming.

Hearing him name himself, two boys muttered together a moment. Then one said, "Heard of you. You're the one as went to the Summerfair and pacted with a Valde."

"It is wondered where you're from," asked Jannus, in the proper oblique manner of Watertalk.

The boy said he was from Sithstock and that Ultreena was still Lady there. Then another boy, with a thick inland accent and no self-consciousness about direct questions, put in, "Did tha'? Pact wit' a Valde? No, y'never. Tha'rt all liars!"

The group snickered at that, mostly stock-born, then, considering the thought of lying a hopeful, uneasy joke.

Jannus said, "I never heard of Bremneri bonded to Andrans, for fighting before."

"Nur I," agreed the farmsteader readily enough. " 'Dentrunners come to Overwater whilst I was in wit' harvest barges. Says I, 'tis a chance to see more'n the thick end on a sow 'fore I die, and good coin at the end of it. What's she *like*? The troopmaid?"

The snickering was louder this time, but Jannus wasn't really inclined to take offense. He knew how little the Valde were beloved by the boys in the riverstocks where they served; he and Poli were the lone exception proving the rule. "We get on well," he answered mildly. "There're five children to us now."

"Must be *good*, then, isna'?" suggested the grinning boy.

Looking past him, Jannus remarked, "I hear there're Lislers among you."

"I'm one," said a thickset boy with projecting ears. "And the baldy one, yon's, another."

The shaved boy raised his head and scowled at Jannus. One of his eyes was swollen shut and there were other purple bruises to mark a beating not many days past.

"Didna' want to go and be bonded," explained the first Lisler. "His da made him come. We owe the Duke Ashai a debt, us Lislers. Wasna' for him, we'd all have starved, long since."

Jannus nodded: everybody knew about Lisle. It was an outlaw riverstock which men had wrested from its Lady, with great slaughter of its defending troopmaids, about eighteen years ago. Any ship or person dealing with Lisle was immediate anathema to all the other riverstocks, forbidden food, fire, salt, and shelter. Only through Ashai did Lisle trade for what it needed to maintain itself. Lislers would do much, Jannus imagined, to keep the duke's patronage and good will.

"I'm a Named man," burst out the shaved boy fiercely, in his own behalf. "I got t'right to say and do as I will. Hadna' the right to sell me off to some Andran 'dentrunner, he didden'!"

"He's your da, Named or no," shot back the other Lisler hotly, "and Master of Lisle, besides. You was always quick enough to take t'cream of that before, to puff yoursel' over t'rest on us. So you take *this*, bitter wi' better."

Grayhawk's own son, a gesture indeed, to ingratiate himself to Duke Ashai. Jannus had heard fathers often were choice of their sons, among folk where the one could know the other. Jannus made his choice then.

He asked directly, "How are you named?" for Lislers would not be bound to Watertalk civility. The bald boy muttered what sounded like *Sparrowhawk*. Jannus recalled the odd names Lislers took. "Can you read and scribe and count?"

The shaved boy, Sparrowhawk, met his eyes sullenly. "What's it to you?"

"I'm of a mind to buy your bond. Can you do what you're told?"

"What d'y want me for then, wi' your witchwife and your—"

Jannus reached through the group and plucked Sparrowhawk into the open. The boy looked startled and made a move to duck back among the rest, then halted, indecisive. The marine was getting up, flipping his staff to a balance point. They'd have to be quick, now. Sparrowhawk knew it too, saw Jannus waiting with no friendly expression, the marine coming toward them, and suddenly slid around behind Jannus, accepting his protection.

To the marine, Jannus said curtly, "Come here," and started back to the Innsmiths and the cargomaster. The marine changed course uncertainly to follow, casting glances back at his charges. Sparrowhawk kept on whichever side of Jannus he figured would be farthest from a blow, the expression on his bruised face warily speculative.

Jannus said to Solvig, "Lend me a copper."

Solvig blinked a moment at Jannus, the shaved boy, and the waiting marine, then reached inside his cloak to find a pocket. "What for?"

"I'm buying his bond."

Solvig's hand stopped moving. "For a copper?"

Jannus merely nodded.

"The indenture price," mentioned the cargomaster awkwardly, feeling a situation building around him and not liking it, "was five hundred, and a thousand bonus after two years."

Jannus looked to Solvig, who slowly withdrew his hand and made a great business settling the folds of his cloak: he wanted no part of such a gesture. Jannus looked to Dan and found the coin already extended, Dan's green eyes bright with mischief. Taking the coin, Jannus passed it to the cargomaster, who refused to close fingers about it, let it fall to the deck.

"I'd best fetch Mickell," said the cargomaster to Solvig apologetically, and hurried off.

Mickell, called sweating from the hold, was the ship's sail-master and owner, and clearly only Solvig's presence kept him civil. "The bond isn't for sale," he told Jannus bluntly. "It's Duke Ashai's to sell or not—not mine."

"I do hear you," replied Jannus formally. "But I think he'll take my price. Send on the sunflashers in the morning and ask. Meanwhile, I'm taking him with me—to the Lady Rayneth's household. I'll be there, when you get the answer."

"That's fair enough," remarked Solvig, willing to commit himself at least that far. To Mickell, Solvig said again, "That's fair enough." Deliberately stooping, he retrieved the coin and handed it over to the sailmaster, who took it.

"As you say, Factor. But who'll stand to the price, should the lad run off by morning?"

Judiciously, reading Jannus's expression, Solvig said, "I'll stand to it. He an't going to run off. And if he does, it'll be me to be answered to."

Jannus nodded slightly, accepting the condition.

"Well, then," said the sailmaster, sourly enough, and pock-eted the coin before starting toward the open hatch.

Dan was swinging one of the casks to his shoulder, but Jannus told him to let Sparrowhawk carry it. Dan looked du-bious—the boy was slat thin, for all his height—but handed the keg over. Sparrowhawk wrapped both arms around it, watching Jannus for directions. Jannus managed to get the other cask under one arm, thinking that he was lucky there hadn't been three, and led the way down the gangway cleats. "Is there one of those carters with room, and headed our way?" he asked Dan, who turned aside to find out. To Spar-rowhawk, struggling along at his right, Jannus said rapidly, "As soon as we pass the bow, do what I do."

"All right," responded the boy, as quietly.

They came to the bow of the ship, level with the tangle of mooring cables. Then Jannus took his cask into both hands and heaved it as hard as he could into the open water be-tween the piers. Sparrowhawk's keg struck the water with an enormous splash only an instant later.

Tugging his wet sleeves back over his wrists, Jannus turned resignedly to face Dan's uncomprehending fury.

Shortly after breakfast, word arrived from Solvig that Duke Ashai had replied with an undecorated permission for

Jannus to keep Sparrowhawk at the price named. And shortly after that, Jannus was summoned to the audience chamber—actually, more of an office with lewd murals—on the upper floor of the south wing of the household, from which the Lady Rayneth was accustomed to direct her affairs.

Waiting his turn, Jannus shared the anteroom with the managers of two bawdhouses who were discussing the apple harvest near Stone Lake, in which they apparently had a financial interest; three woodwind players nervously rehearsing in a corner, apparently hoping for a week in one of the better eating houses in High Street; an oddscaller occupied in counting his betting slips, methodically licking the thumb to turn each one, and, when he reached the last, shaking his head and beginning again at the first; and a pigtailed waterman asleep with his legs stuck out where the succession of clerks and scribes passing to and from the inner room invariably tripped over them, not quite spilling their armloads of ledgers and scrolls.

A sparse collection, as those things went; in two days, at week's end, the place would be packed until midafternoon.

Jannus had taken a place near the rear, expecting he'd be there quite a while. Rayneth seldom kept anybody waiting except for disciplinary reasons, and Jannus anticipated being left an hour or two to contemplate the sin of jeopardizing the Lady's standing with her patron by offering the duke public affront without asking her permission beforehand. But he was called out of turn, to the obvious dismay of the oddsman, who'd gotten up, expecting to be next. So he was in worse disfavor than Jannus. Jannus didn't envy him his wait: one of the musicians, the flute player, kept breaking into the upper register with a squeal and then looking perplexedly at his instrument. Jannus remembered just in time to circle the outstretched legs of the snoring waterman providing the hapless flute player with bass counterpoint.

There was no tirade. Instead the Lady Rayneth inquired in minute detail about his progress with her bins of word citations, saying she regretted that she'd lost touch with the project the last tenday or so, being occupied with overseeing the construction of a dueling barn behind one of her warehouses.

"You can't expect people to fight in the rain," offered Jannus politely.

"Exactly!" commented the Lady, with a glitter of rings brighter than her smile.

The astonishing shower of ornaments which descended on Rayneth's person each day in the shape of rings, bracelets, beads, brooches, and hairdos incorporating feathers, three colors of silk ribbon, and entire spools of wire had nothing to do with vanity. It was Rayneth's sensible practice to awe her subordinates so she equipped herself with every ounce of finery her limbs could support. As much of her as showed above the desktop was encased in slabs of fabric stiffened with embroidery and lumpy with enough pearls to have dowered a fair-sized troop of Valde. As an ordinary precaution she kept within reach at all times two flat-faced bodyguards it was bad manners to admit noticing.

Her face was that of an intelligent goat: long, sly, and melancholy.

Her age Jannus guessed to be somewhere between thirty and forty. She was in her twelfth year of rule. As an administrator she had only one major lack, as far as Jannus had been able to observe: like many people of self-won power, she delegated poorly. When he'd first arrived she hadn't trusted him to decipher correctly her private system of abbreviations, much less her incredibly tiny and precise handwriting, and had insisted he work in a corner of the office and recite each notation to her aloud. It'd been a month, four long tendays, before she'd trusted his competence enough to assign him a room to work in—only three doors away, it was true, but still beyond her immediate supervision. It was to her credit that she'd managed to leave him alone for a whole week: Jannus was quite sure her inclination had been otherwise.

Still inexplicably cordial, Rayneth asked whether she should send him extra clerks to help him keep ahead of the press once printing began. Jannus declined, explaining that he'd stopped sorting and transcribing for the time being and was just pinning the completed entries in order on large corkboards for transfer to the press room whenever Dan was ready for them. It didn't somehow seem the time to mention the probable delay occasioned by the letter slugs thrown back, as it were, in Duke Ashai's face; if Rayneth chose not to mention it, Jannus was certainly not about to.

"Who'd you buy your corkboard from?" Rayneth demanded.

Jannus quoted her the name and the price, which she noted with a critical eye, directing, "Don't reorder without telling me. I'll get a price quoted from a factor for a woodmiller, later this week. And I'm sending you two helpers tomorrow. Don't waste your time with pins. That's not what I'm paying you for. Let the clerks do the pinning."

"Lady, I do hear you."

Rayneth produced from the drawer a packet tied with string and poked it across the desk toward him with an expression both challenging and guilty. "Is there still time . . . ?"

More entries. Jannus took the packet, promising to fit them in. Privately he hoped they were past the middle of the alphabet.

"Duelists' terms," she explained. "I thought I knew dueling, but there's another whole set of terms, it seems, for every work a man can contrive to put his hand to and talk about. Do you ever . . ." she began, then answered herself, "Of course not, you're a riverstock man. The Valde do the dueling there. Now, I want to know when the first sheet's to be printed. I want to see it."

"I'll tell Dan."

"Then that's all. No, wait. There's one other thing. I'm changing my quarters for the time being. The ground fogs are making me hoarse as a crow, so I'm taking rooms on this level, down the corridor. You must be cramped, the seven of you, in those two rooms with the marks of the root bins still in the walls. You can have northwing, first level, while I'm not using it. I'd have to keep fires going in there anyway, to keep the damp out. So you might as well have it. The children should like the garden, I'd think."

Jannus accepted the offer with suitable thanks and took his leave considerably bemused. Transparently, the Lady Rayneth saw no need to antagonize someone with such unexpected influence with the Andran duke. What was more, if claiming a weak chest as a pretext to offer better quarters was all that was needed to purchase a little goodwill, she considered it well worth it. The Lady Rayneth was nothing if not pragmatic.

He went downstairs to his erstwhile root-bin quarters back by the kitchen and found the removal already underway, wicker bales of clothing and personal paraphernalia being stacked in the hall by three of Rayneth's servants: older

women who nevertheless plaited beads into their hair to the
number of a hundred or more, asserting that they'd retired
from active prostitution only because few could meet the
value they were accustomed to set on themselves.

It seemed a harmless enough fiction, and he always be-
spoke the women courteously, though he told no outright lies.
There were a few Truthdeaf women born into every generation, even in the riverstocks; and back among the
farmsteads, few with Truthtell were allowed to survive infancy. Truthdeaf women, whatever their origins, were more
likely to take up the Crescent's unique profession than those
who inherited the "gift"; but one could never be sure. Truthtell was less easy to spot than Andrans.

One woman straightened from tying up toys in a kerchief
to tell him Poli and the children had been sent off to the
garden to keep them from getting underfoot. "There's not
much here: we'll have you settled before midday and you'll
scarcely know a thing's been touched."

Jannus thanked them and took his bemusement down the
corridor past the storerooms, servants' quarters, pantries, and
the erstwhile laundry that was Dan's workroom, to the center third of the building that contained the front entry hall
and the big Evenhall, where the household took the daymeal
together. The entry hall was the absolute territory of Jacko
One-hand, an all but toothless veteran of the Crescent alley-
ways, forceably retired from the trade of pickpocket and
chokey, who now monitored the household's comings and goings with the care once given to assessing the capacities of
drunks to defend themselves. He too reported that Poli and
the children were in the garden. Jannus nodded and passed
on to the doors of northwing.

He'd been prepared for opulence, for anything up to and
including furniture made of the jewel-like *plarit* whose secret
had been lost with the Teks of Kantmorie, or colored glass in
every wall. Instead, his chief impressions were of light and of
quiet.

There were, predictably, no windows in the outer wall,
where some thaw flood might have forced an entry; but instead of the high slit-windows on inside walls found elsewhere
on the lower floor, these rooms had tall casements of plain
clear glass fixed in white lattices. The baseboards and ceiling
strips were also painted white, and the walls, a uniform gray-

green, without the graphic murals that decorated the walls of the audience chamber.

The furniture was plain in line and decoration, but highly polished. Jannus hoped idly that a chamberer or two would continue to look after the rooms: Poli had never been fully reconciled to living shut within four walls, much less tending whatever inanimate objects she happened to find dwelling there. Jannus had served in his mother's household in Newstock enough years to know what went into polishing several rooms of maple furniture, into tending around ten oil lamps and their chimneys and wicks every day, into maintaining the fireplaces he saw in each room and keeping the firebrick cupboards filled to feed them.

Poli's idea of a fire was breaking sticks over her knee and piling them into a cone burning hot enough to boil water in a kettle hung from a tripod, while she skinned a rabbit.

Jannus touched a tabletop gently, spread-fingered, then bent quickly to breathe on the mark and wipe it away with his sleeve. Well, Rayneth had known perfectly well that they had five three-year-old children when she offered the apartment. Jannus trusted she'd have the sense to have anything she was especially concerned about removed. He wasn't about to worry over it.

There were five rooms in all: two bedrooms in the center, their fireplaces sharing a single flue. The left-hand room had no window, but curtained door arches and two large framed mirrors kept it from being gloomy. Jannus suspected it was generally used as a robing room; the bed didn't match the other furniture, and depressions in the rug showed where something large and square had been moved out, probably the wardrobe he found in the room beyond. That room was full of chests and cabinets, many with doors standing ajar from the haste of their emptying. Circling through the archway, he found the adjoining room devoted to a large ceramic bathtub, with pipes that disappeared into the ceiling. Jannus grinned: he hadn't met indoor plumbing since he'd left his mother's household. The Lady Rayneth knew how to put her money where comfort mattered.

The windows of the main bedroom stretched all the way from floor to ceiling, were in fact doors opening onto the protected garden walled between the building's three faces. On the east was the looming hill of the levee, here so heavily

planted with shrubs and small trees that it looked like a
thicket and almost completely obscured the enclosing wall he
could glimpse about halfway up the dike. The trees were all
bare-branched but the shrubs remained vivid, some still in
late bloom in the warmth held by the sheltering walls. Small
explosions among the shrubbery, branches quivering suddenly, informed Jannus that his children were chasing each
other, out of sight in the miniature forest.

The center space was dominated by a water garden: a pipe
descended from a suspected roof cistern, plunging into the
grass to disappear for about fifteen paces, then poking out of
a bank, disguised as a dripping stone. The drip descended in
plinking steps to end in a moss-shouldered tank under the
arching haystack outline of a gnarled cotton willow. Beyond
was a low hill of ferns. The grass was still green wherever it
wasn't submerged in drifts of multicolored leaves.

Poli sat at the edge of the tank, trailing one hand idly in
the water.

Standing in the casement he'd opened, Jannus looked from
the room behind him to the secret garden, invisible from at
least the other lower-level rooms, with only this one entrance.
The Rayneth who'd made the apartment, he knew, after a
fashion: she was the Rayneth who'd spent a lifetime harvest-
ing words and their meanings in pedantically precise script,
who kept scrupulous account of the costs of everything, who
loved above all things order and clarity. But the Rayneth
who'd made this garden he'd never met or even suspected.

Giving up her apartment was a simple bribe and understood and accepted as such. But to have surrendered the
garden which that apartment alone commanded, even with
winter coming on—that, Jannus felt, was another thing entirely. He regarded the garden thoughtfully, for in his experience every gift had its price, or its cost, eventually. He liked
to have some idea beforehand what that cost might be.

But it was a beautiful garden, uncontrived and inviting.

He should have gone upstairs to his stacked corkboards
and his sorted bushels of notations in Rayneth's minuscule
fly-leg script. But the temptation of the warmth and light was
too great. He found the grass as resilient as a good wool car-
pet, just the way it looked, interrupted here and there by
strategic stones nudging through the turf to make the ground
pleasantly uneven and channel rain toward the tank. He

settled down beside Poli, finding a bare willow root placed just right to be a backrest.

"The Lady Rayneth likes one of us," said Poli, continuing to tease at a fish with a leafless willow whip, "and I don't think it's me."

" 'For a fact,' " Jannus rejoined, Dan Innsmith's phrase. "It's because I'm such good friends with Duke Ashai, and all."

She looked around, wordlessly inquiring how he felt about the gift. In reply Jannus arched his eyebrows, rolling his head to survey the willow canopy, the tan cement of the facing wall, the thicket where the children played at pursuit and escape.

His glance rested last and longest on Poli herself, seated in a balanced crouch, the angle and poise of each limb just as it should be, the weight as ready to spring as to settle. She remained for him profoundly exotic. Knowledge only revealed to him the extent and detail of difference. Her hair, the wild silvery fluff of all Valde, was bright against the mound of ferns beyond; the wide gray eyes were more still and calm than the shivering surface of the pool; the unlined repose of her face was the heritage of a race which had never needed to learn to communicate emotion by any system of twitches and smirks because they knew it directly, with a sense as immediate as sight.

But it wasn't sight, or hearing—although some called it that rather than by its proper name, *marenniath*. The nearest word would have been empathy. Valde—all Valde, men and women alike—were empathic, perceiving emotion and the body's life with unique immediacy. Nor was the *marenniath* much like its feeble grandchild, the Truthtell inherited by the women of the Bremneri riverstocks; it was more basic, less focused or discriminating, underlying all other senses.

Born with *marenniath*, born to the attitudes and habits and expectations produced by that unique sense in Valde culture, Poli had lost it. She'd been *sa'marenniath*, unhearing, for nearly four years—just a month less than they'd been married. So she was twice exotic, unique even among Valde, who not uncommonly declined and died from any wounding of that sense, at once so intimate and so diffuse, linking them with the ebb and flowing of all life, vegetable or animal, within their range. But Poli had survived it, just as she'd survived ten years' troop service in Newstock; no more like him on that account, perhaps, but not part of some vast, complex interconnectedness from which he was excluded, either.

Jannus wondered what the garden was to her—denatured and depthless as something painted on a wall? or tended, tame, with the phantom fingerprints of human manipulations rustling each leaf of grass or artful boulder? Or were the air, the openness, the privacy enough to *be* enough, for her, as they were for him?

Poli touched his hand lightly, the softest of comments—generally she had no need of *marenniath* to follow his moods and often, it seemed, his thoughts—and then made her own deliberate survey of the garden. "It's tidier than Han Halla," she conceded judiciously, faint enough praise, glancing swiftly aside to catch his reaction.

"Fewer snakes," he contributed.

"Drier," she offered, cupping a palmful of water and letting it trickle down into the pool, then abruptly shaking the last drops off her fingertips with pretended fastidiousness.

Full of laughter and contentment, Jannus leaned back into the comfortable curve of the root. It was then that two dripping watermen arrived, escorted by Jacko, saying that Dan had told them to come to Jannus to be paid. Dan had hired them, it seemed, to dive between the docks for the two casks of letter slugs which were now safely retrieved and being unpacked and tenderly dried by Dan and his helpers in the south-wing workroom. And Dan had sent them to Jannus for their wages.

Jannus couldn't help laughing.

The men's appearance in the garden was so singularly inappropriate, and their truculence so woebegone and unhopeful, that Jannus went cheerfully enough to find where in transit his cash box was and, without argument, paid them what they claimed Dan had promised—no small figure for a morning's work. Jannus didn't mind, figuring it meant Dan would be fit to live with for a while, at least until his next fit of homesickness.

When he returned to the garden, Poli was ducking in and out of the bushes of the embankment in pursuit of the children. Presently one appeared, scrambling into view on all fours, then came pounding across the grass at a chub-legged charge and grabbed Jannus's leg to hide behind. Poli stopped a few paces onto the lawn, then wheeled to continue the hunt, calling, "Midmeal," meaning he should keep track of the one while she flushed the rest out of their cover.

The one holding him was Sua, the only cotton-headed one, craning back to stare up at him with eyes as black as a weasel's, or his own.

He said, "There's a snake in the pool."

The child giggled and hid her face against his knee, replying decisively, "No."

It came on them so early, the Truthtell of the part-blooded. Winding fingers in her feathery hair, lest she suddenly decide to dart away, he suggested, "Ship in the pool? With lanterns and banners and masts and tiny little sails, going to cross Han Halla to Ardun-town, all under the—"

"Noooo!" Sua crowed, chuckling harder, rocking from side to side and gripping the fabric of his pantsleg with both fists.

Before he'd exhausted an impromptu list of improbable occupants for the pool, Poli had delivered to him Amalia and Fealis—Mallie and Alis—the latter snuffling piteously, having run into a sharp twig. Mallie advised sensibly, "Spit on it," and proceeded to demonstrate.

"Snake in the pool," offered Sua provocatively, plopping herself down on Jannus's right foot, both arms wrapped around his leg, her head turned almost backward to face her sisters.

"Is not," replied Mallie firmly, undistracted from her spit treatment of Alis's forehead.

Sua bounced sulkily, singing with a wandering tunelessness, "Snake in the pool, *green* snake, eyes like the mooo-n—"

His ease in the company of his children was of relatively recent date. He'd been only eighteen when they'd been born, all five together, intimidating in their strangeness, the plain unnatural *number* of them, in spite of Poli's assurance that even six at a birthing wasn't uncommon among Valde. Jannus was no Valde. They'd upset him profoundly.

During their infancy he'd felt toward them a kind of anxiety near terror. Their cries and rages and hungers seemed unfathomable and threatening, demands he could neither interpret nor respond to.

Poli had been of no help. Her effortless adaptation to motherhood had served only to make her more alien, him more desperate.

Seeking some more comprehensible model, he'd become practically a fixture in the Innsmiths' household, incidentally cementing a friendship with Dan, the one nearest his own age and, untypically for an Innsmith, still unmarried. He and Dan had shared a Newstock upbringing—Dan among his numerous family, Jannus in the isolation of his mother's household. Jannus escaped to the Innsmiths in Ardun partly as a means of avoiding the demands he felt unable to meet, but more as a quite deliberate effort to learn how families behaved—what they did, how they acted and reacted, what they found to say to each other, how either anger or affection could be permissibly expressed. Smiths, he believed, were born knowing those things, as Bremneri were not.

Riverstock children were raised in groups segregated from the rest of the household until they were old enough to be of use. They knew their mothers merely as names and their fathers not even as that. Jannus still had no idea which of the previous generation of Newstock-born adolescents had sired him on Lillia, that adolescent's assigned pactmate, before being thrust out at Naming. Jannus had been around young children before, but as one of them: without relationship or affection. And being among Innsmiths only served to show him the extent of his own ignorance and incapacity. He saw what they did but never came to understand how they knew to do it.

It'd been the children themselves who, in growing, mended things. Their childish self-absorption freed him. To his diffident approaches they responded with a like offhandedness, not anxious or even especially interested in him as long as he was there, part of the familiar, predictable furniture of their lives. Only Sua, most like him in temperament, persisted in clinging fretfully, grabbing for reassurance that was never quite right, or enough; that rapport remained the most awkward and uneasy. Toward the rest, his feeling of threat faded into an uncritical acceptance which put slow roots into the dark levels and spread its network of relationship imperceptibly across the gaps.

"Swimming in the pool," sang Sua, "swimming in the shadows. . . ."

Poli appeared with the last pair skipping alongside, surrendering as fairly caught, and they all went inside.

In midafternoon, about the ninth hour, Jannus and Poli scrambled the last paces and reached the top of the levee. On his knees already, Jannus found an easy position by simply rolling over onto his side: the hill was steep, and he was completely winded. Too unself-conscious to be smug, Poli stood avidly looking outward, plainly enjoying the height for its own sake.

And it *was* a novel perspective, Jannus had to admit.

They were above all the rooftops and the myriad chimney pots. The Crescent, its name visibly suitable, reached with a score of dock-fingers into the sliding slate water of Erth-rimmon. The river easily freed herself from the faint tugging at her fringes and flowed away southwestward around a bend. Erth-rimmon looked chilly and far broader than from street level, although the far side looked much the same: reeds and tussocks and wandering slow pools out into the gray distance where cloud and ground-fog met indistinguishably.

"Come on," Poli called, kicking through the tall brittle grasses, "or we won't get the whole way around before dark."

The top of the levee was broad enough for a house to have been built on it—tens of scores of houses, in fact, for the dike circled the Inner Households completely around, pierced only by the High Street gate. Walking the footpath they found worn into the grass, Jannus tried to imagine how long it'd taken to heap the levee, the innumerable baskets of earth dumped every day for generations to hold off tidelift and flood on the west, and the swamp from north, east, and south.

"How old do you suppose Quickmoor is?" he said to Poli, whose only response was attentive listening. "Six hundred years? Eight hundred, at most. Since the Rebellion and the fall of Kantmorie, for certain. If the Teks had had any hand in the making of the city, they'd have heaved up this hill in a day and fused it solid and waterproof as glass from a flier in a couple of hours. It's hard for me to imagine a hill being built by hand—the work of it, after the Teks withdrew. . . ."

Their course had brought them past the last edge of the Crescent and the last of the paved roads. For a hundred paces, perhaps, the dike was washed by the shallows of Erth-rimmon herself—stones had been tumbled down, there, to make a breakwater—and then the path brought them overlooking the primordial swamp itself: Han Halla, unchanging and pathless, filling half a continent between the High Plain of Kantmorie and the sea.

Stopping and squinting, Jannus could just discern the edge of the High Plain, suspended over fog and lower cloud like a long black thunderhead far to the north. When Poli halted and turned inquiringly, Jannus pointed and she looked with him. "The High Plain. The edge of the Wall. Cliffhold. The Broken Bridge."

One of the great artifacts of the lost Empire of Kantmorie, that bridge, which had once spanned Erth-rimmon from clifftop to the marshes of Is, and he'd been asleep during his only opportunity to see it, coming downriver by steam packet with Poli four years ago. "Before the ice closes in," he remarked, "I'd like to buy passage upriver to see it, the bridge. Dan's seen it, you've seen it—everybody but me."

Poli regarded the Teks and all their works with loathing both racial and personal: in the millennia of Empire, Valde had been kept by Teks as slaves and pets; and it was on the High Plain that she'd become *sa'marenniath*, maimed by the inspoken violence of the deathless, shambling army of Teks ravening after a final death, specters of horror and agony intolerable to the *marenniath*.

After one long look her attention returned to Jannus. "If you like," she responded indifferently. "I can see the Murderlands well enough from here."

She continued along the path, and he turned too, accepting the justice of her revulsion even though he did not share it. For him with the death of the last Tek, something supremely exotic—terror and wonder, foulness and exquisite beauty— had departed as well, leaving the lowlands safer but duller. Baskets of earth dumped tirelessly, year after year, instead of fliers and *plarit* bridges and encapsuled selves who might, at their whim, wear fur or wings or curious shapes of their own devising.

"Han Halla," said Poli, pointing in her turn—a slow hand sweeping like a caress over the mosaic vista of reed canes, low trees, and interlacing streams and pools, all fading by degrees into a glimmering mist where a trio of white herons rose with deliberate wing strokes, tiny as moths. "Full of such a singing. . . ."

The wistfulness was of memory, perhaps of regret: the daysinging of Han Halla was, like Han Halla itself, interdicted by her loss of the *marenniath*. Nobody without the ability to sift the subtle singings of plants could survive an hour's walk into Han Halla: no one who could not discern pool from sinkpond, and find the fog-hidden sun by sharing the plants' awareness of its angle. Not Jannus, and not Poli—not anymore.

" 'There's a snake in the pool,' " murmured Jannus, recalling Sua's tuneless song. Walking the width of it once with Poli guiding him, from Quickmoor to Ardun, even he had not been immune to its enchantments. Now, to him, it chiefly looked like a wet place excellently suited to one's getting lost and drowning.

"I tell you what," he proposed lightly, strolling at her side. "You be the Queen of Han Halla, where you can't go, and I'll be the King of Kantmorie, that's dead."

Poli cuffed him across the head, not all *that* lightly, and broke into a run, increasing her pace each time he began to draw level, until she was racing at full speed. In that fashion they completed the second third of the circuit, the sun red in their eyes, their long shadows flying behind them.

Poli stumbled to a halt in the grass alongside the path and flopped down. Seeing her stop, Jannus at once broke stride and wandered the distance remaining, breathing in great gulps and holding his right side where a pain jabbed with each breath, alternately bowed forward and staring blindly at the sky in the effort to take in enough air. Lowering himself by degrees for fear of falling, he lay flat on his back while the earth seemed to pump and resound beneath him. It took him several minutes to gather the energy to grope for her hand. Finding her elbow instead, he settled for that.

Predictably, she recovered first and sat up, clasping her hands around her knees. Jannus made himself move, levering himself into a position where his knees provided a backrest against which she leaned heavily, bonelessly relaxed. Himself, he wasn't ready even to sit up yet.

"Little run like that," he started, and had to cough. "Little run like that . . . and you just fall down. Newstock troopmaid. First Dancer. Disgrace." He tipped his head back and shut his eyes, still concentrating on breathing. "Why are we out here?" he asked, because it somehow had become time to ask.

For a while she didn't speak; but he could feel her con-

sidering, sorting, in the way her head and neck shifted. "That
Lisler you took from the *sa'farioh*, Ashai. . . . When we
were changing rooms I saw him, in Dan's place. The door
was open. And he saw me. He. . . ."

"What'd he do: yell, hide, or both?"

"He made *that* . . . at me." Her hand lifted, shaped the
wardsign of Lisle whose folk knew no Valde directly and
called them witches or worse.

Poli had been a prisoner, once, in Lisle: he could imagine
how this unexpected echo would have upset her. Reaching for
her hand at an awkward angle, Jannus said, "He's sixteen
and ignorant as a brick. He'll learn."

"*I* don't want to teach him." The voice suggested a great
weariness rather than anger, as if the prospect of learning
and being learned by still another ignorant Bremneri were
tedious beyond describing. "Let him believe in witches or
cold steams or curse-knots or anything he pleases, I don't
care. . . . And the children. Each day they're more different,
each from the other." Her free hand opened in a scattering
gesture. "One laughing while another's crying, each closed to
the others. . . ."

"Closed to you," he deduced softly, seeing that it must be
so. He hadn't thought about it before.

"They're not Bremneri," she formulated slowly. "There's
no word for what they are. Bremneri, the women and the
men both, are closed." The hand turned into a fist, shook as
if in threat. "It's the way they're raised—the riverstocks
where women and the Truthtell rule, the farmsteads where
the men do, and the troopmaids in between, hearing it all and
keeping it that way because it's our fault the Truthtell ever
came into Bremner in the first place—"

"We don't have to sort all that out today, do we? I'm no
more a Bremneri than you are a Valde, in most ways."

"Even you. Even you're heir to the fear of being fully
seen, known, spied upon. You can be easy now, because I'm
sa'marenniath and you think you can forget about it. But it's
there, all the same. But ours aren't Bremneri anyhow." The
hand opened to its farthest spread. "They're separate. They're
not Valde either. But at least when we were in Ardun, we
were on the border of Valde. And there are the Awiro Valde,
the Unpartnered, across the river in Lifganin. They were

close, in reach. In three years ours will be old enough to run free with a *hafkenna*, a childpack—"

"They're not Valde," Jannus responded. "Six is too young for a . . . an ordinary child to go without care."

"Some of them will have the Valde growth. We're quicker than you, ready to have children in turn in nine summers, ten. . . . Sua, she's already a full hand taller than the rest. And Mallie is shrewder than some Bremneri children twice her age. Maybe Mallie will have the growth, as well. Don't ever forget, they're not riverstock children, with nothing but the Truthtell left of the Great Pacting between Bremner and Valde. They are full half-blooded. But here we are, in Bremner, where Valde are just troopmaids and men make signs against us. . . ." Again the hand moved in the wardsign, heavily, and dropped.

Jannus twisted until he was propped on one elbow, able to see her face. "First thaw, we'll go home. I promise. If running with a—what? childpack? in Valde is possible for them, or if they can ride with the Awiro and their herds, then that will be the way of it. But the freeze will come down before I'm done with my wretched corkboards you dragged me away from, and then there's no passage until thaw. For now, we've got better rooms, and the Lady Rayneth *likes* us. . . ." he offered, joking, but watching her eyes. "If it's important to you, we'll go now. Before the cold comes down. I can walk off that cliff too if I have to."

Poli's expression was blank, inward, as she consulted with herself. "We can winter here," she said finally, making Jannus imagine a snowbound shack. That's what the new quarters were to her, then: a furnished shack with a nice view of a counterfeit of Han Halla just good enough to make her hunger for the thing itself.

"Then that's what we'll do. But are you sure, now, Poli? Once the freeze comes down, nothing moves on the river, and I won't walk Han Halla again for *any* manner of cause."

"We can winter here," she said again, deciding, and looked around her, apparently noticing the flattened sun, barred with clouds, leaning toward the level swamps of Is. "We'll be late."

"Let's cut through the Inner Households. Scare them out of their tiny minds."

They helped each other up, Poli judging, "We can do that, Arlann' Wir knows us. . . ."

They crossed the rim and started descending, one sideways step at a time, clutching bushes.

As it happened, Arlanna Wir, leader of the Quickmoor troop, was waiting for them in the basin's twilight, standing beside an arch. The cross-strapped harness she wore over tunic and tabard was filled with rows of dagger-darts; her bow poked unstrung from its case, however, and her quiver was capped. Thus she looked like what she was: a soldier but not, at the moment, a threat.

She and Poli had answered the Troopcalling at the same Summerfair, though they'd served in different riverstocks, so they were roughly the same age, about twenty-five.

"Burn bright," she greeted them as they approached.

"Burn bright, Arlann'. We're just cutting through," replied Poli casually.

Jannus inspoke a satiric query whether the dread Lady of Quickmoor had sent her out to capture the invaders. Though he knew nothing, firsthand, of the *marenniath*, yet he'd learned to shape and pattern his attitudes, his *farioh*, to communicate after a fashion in the inspeaking mode in the days before Poli was deafened, and since had practiced the discipline among the Valde who were often abroad in Ardun. He'd been told that, chiefly, he was loud.

But he'd made himself understood well enough, by the glance the troopleader gave him. "After a fashion," she replied. "I was sent to get you-both. We heard you-both above," she went on, tilting her cottony head—closely shorn, in the manner of troopmaids—at the slope they'd descended. "I was on my way to the Crescent gate when you-both decided to come down, saving me the walk."

"And it seems the Lady Ketrinne has word for us. . . ." Jannus found himself automatically falling into the Watertalk of his childhood, where a direct question was the worst of bad manners. Inwardly, he concentrated on the fact that he was muddy and scraped and more than a little lame from the unaccustomed exertion, and that he wanted to go *home*.

"You-both can take the daymeal at the household, if the audience is too long," Arlanna Wir assured him, saying next to Poli, "The Crescent woman will see that the *ena'ffrì* . . . children? . . . are—"

"It's late, for an audience," Jannus cut in. "Can't it wait till morning?"

"I was sent to get you before the ninth hour," Arlanna admitted, and glanced again at the levee, meaning that she'd been reluctant to intrude, interrupt.

And Jannus noted the singular form of address. To Poli, he remarked, "Maybe Ketrinne wants to give me a garden too," whereupon she leaned against his shoulder, lazily amused.

"No need," Arlanna replied to some inspoken comment of Poli's. "I'll have Rora go and make sure all is well with the *ena'ffri*, if. . . . All right," she concluded after a pause, having sent the troopmaid about that errand.

Jannus wondered what Rayneth's household would make of that—a troopmaid of the Inner Households stopping by to check on the children. Sparrowhawk might throw a fit.

"The Lisler," remarked Arlanna, without favor, guiding them into the maze of overhung passageways that led, presumably, to the Lady Ketrinne's household.

Her quickness to interpret his casual speculation returned to Jannus the beginnings of a hard caution he'd almost forgotten, or thought he had: the distrustful wariness of male Bremneri among Valde. The feeling of being spied on, examined without consent. As Poli had just reminded him, it was his heritage. It could be lulled to sleep, perhaps, but never lost. He found that a discouraging reflection.

He set himself to clear away things personal and just observe. He'd never been among the Inner Households before.

The convoluted flow of one building into another, replete with buttresses and arched walkways passing above, he found typical, though more crowded than was common. Distinctive too was the habit of having the entry doors at second-story level, with an outside staircase. The first floors were windowless and mostly faced with brick, though the floors above were the ubiquitous sand-colored concrete. The novelties, he judged, were secondary defenses against flood—or perhaps they predated the building of the encircling levee.

"I don't know. Long ago," responded Arlanna, then turned away to adjust the set of her bowcase. In anyone but a Valde, Jannus would have described her manner as fidgety.

Frowning slightly, he looked to Poli and nodded questioningly at the troopleader's back. Poli responded with a wide-eyed disclaimer, meaning that she wasn't responsible, wasn't fretting Arlanna about the children or some such. Puzzled, aware that the small exchange might as well have been shouted for all the privacy possible, Jannus returned his attention to his surroundings.

The narrow street sloped, he noticed: probably to a central drain somewhere that would exit through the dike; otherwise the basin would be flooded with every rainstorm. A person could find his way in this warren, he thought, by minding the slope of the paving stones. If one needed a way out, and had no guide. . . .

Firmly he put that idea away too. It implied he was theorizing about escape, which wasn't tactful. But he didn't forget about the slope, either.

"It is thought you spent your troopservice in Sithstock," he said to Arlanna, with unaccustomed formality.

"Yes. I was of the Sithstock troop in the year that Lisle was taken." Another uncomfortable subject, one that need not have been brought up: Jannus had only been making conversation.

"And so you decided to take a second term, as leader. I've heard tales of the taking of Lisle. It's scarcely in link-distance of Sithstock, though—I hope you were able to keep clear of the worst of it."

"I lived," replied the Valde bleakly. "This is a better place to serve," she added, in a deliberately lighter tone. "We-all are into the third year of the term, and I have lost only two—one to heartsickness—"

Poli was nodding. She knew how that happened, the shared and reechoing loneliness and despair that burned out, destroyed, those troopmaids unable to endure it.

One was unusually few, Jannus mused, to be lost so. The current Quickmoor troop must have excellent morale, and good rapport with the Bremneri here, for the initial shock of exile and isolation to have taken so mild a toll.

Meanwhile Arlanna was continuing, "—and one to the dueldance. It is isolated, this place. There are few feuds, city against city, and the Crescent shields us against much of the tradestrife others must endure. It's why the Lady Ketrinne,

and the Lady Baillen before her, have let the Crescent and
that woman continue. Left, now."

She led them into an enclosed passageway that sloped up
toward a heavy door set into grooves. The ramp was for
carts, the door constructed for the easy delivery of goods:
they were being brought in the back door, the serviceway.

"It's nearer," explained Arlanna briefly as she and a troopmaid inside heaved the wheeled door far enough along to admit them.

As the door rumbled aside it occurred to Jannus that not a
living soul knew where they were. And after the Crescent
gate was shut, along about the eleventh hour—about now—
nobody would come or go without the consent of the
Quickmoor troop, one hundred ninety-eight strong.

Arlanna turned, facing him with no readable expression.
Suddenly she remarked, "Rora says the *ena'ffri* are in the
foodplace, kitchen. The . . . the Smith? . . . is playing with
them. The Lisler is there too," she added in the same flat tone
she'd used before.

"Did she go in?" More directly, Jannus changed that to,
"Do they know we're here?"

"Yes," Arlanna replied steadily, to both questions,
pointedly not disputing the conclusions he'd been coming to.

He wasn't surprised to find that three more troopmaids had
come silently behind and now blocked the bottom of the
ramp. Reading his altered stance and looking in turn, Poli
drifted two balanced steps left, putting herself between Jannus and Arlanna, the wall of the passageway at their backs.

The two actions, threat and response, were as smooth and
coordinated as a dance figure, clear as speech.

The next move should have been a feint, to draw Poli forward while the three below darted in to separate them. But
Arlanna did not feint, letting the first figure remain six long
breaths, until the suddenness had gone out of it.

"You would not like waiting outside," she warned Poli,
emphasizing both her power to separate them and her un-
willingness to do so.

Poli didn't reply, but her weight settled back on her heels.

Arlanna winced fractionally, struck by inspoken anger and
accusation. "I do what I can," she protested, but without
apology. "And what I must."

Reconstructing her actions, Jannus decided that was proba-

bly true. Directed merely to fetch him, Arlanna had first
delayed, then warned them in subtle ways quite clear in retro-
spect, so they'd not be taken entirely by surprise. She'd even
gone so far as to send a troopmaid into the despised
Rayneth's household, on her own authority, to see to the children but also to insure that Poli remained with him, protect-
ing him by her presence from any of the cruder forms of
maltreatment. That, she might yet have trouble justifying to
her Lady.

Within the limits of her orders, she'd shielded them already
in a number of ways, juggling her divided loyalties as best
she could.

"We'll thank you later," Jannus told her rather sardoni-
cally, and passed through the door's opening with Poli watch-
ful and tense at his back.

The audience chamber was supported by Valde. Carved
each out of some white wood dulled to ivory with smoke and
time, the figures stood poised against the walls at intervals of
about four paces. On their upreaching fingertips was balanced
a sinuous window of opalescent blue-green glass winding the
length of each wall—representing, Jannus supposed, Erth-rimmon and her Riverstocks buttressed, maintained, by the service of untold generations of troopmaids.

Each figure was depicted as open-eyed, but the lids enclosed only blank pupilless curves, as if the carved troopmaids were blind to what they upheld and whatever might
pass before them in this chamber.

Jannus judged that interpretation was likely his own. To
assume the ancient carver had even suspected how the troopmaids would come to enforce the division between the sexes
in Bremner which their gift of Truthtell had begun was to
impute a bitter irony Jannus suspected to be a more sophisti-
cated and recent taste.

Predictably, the jewel and fruit of all this service was seen
to be Quickmoor itself. Already circled in its protective dike,
it was pictured in a large round window high on the wall opposite the door. Surrounded by rough-looking waves with tops
politely bent, as if bowing to the city, and improbable fishes
peering out in awe, the Circle of Quickmoor was supported
by a total of five carved Valde: one crouching beneath, two
in profile with one knee bent, the other leg extended, to hold

the supposed globular weight, the last two upright and full face in the reaching pose of the rest.

Quickmoor clearly was their especial care, surrounded as it was by all those dangerous, deferential waves. Successive Ladies of Quickmoor had doubtless found this hall reassuring.

Perhaps a score of wooden benches in two tiers with a central aisle down which he, Poli, and their attendant troopmaids followed Arlanna, were to hold the throngs of folk appealing for the Lady's notice. At this hour, all were vacant, though an apple core and dropped white florets of popcorn attested that the chamber could be lively enough at other times.

Under the round window was a dais, five broad steps high, and upon the dais, a free-standing partition of blackwood panels with pierced ivory grillwork: the Stranger Screen, half the basic and indispensable furniture of any Bremneri audience hall. The other half stood on the tiled floor a few paces from the dais, at the end of the runner of dyed rush matting: a ponderous low-backed chair fashioned from a block of stone whose nature was concealed under peeling green paint.

Jannus laid his hand on the cold arm of the Guest Seat, thinking with inconsequent amusement that he knew why Guest Seats were green, and the reigning Lady unseen, by tradition: he doubted anyone in the hall, or in all of Bremner for that matter, could have claimed as much.

The traditions were a faroff reflection, a forgotten memory, of the Circle of Power deep in Downbase in Kantmorie on the High Plain, where no living man but Jannus had stood for the better part of a thousand years.

He settled himself in the chair. Poli perched, subtly disrespectful, on the arm, one warm hand resting on the back of his neck.

The troopleader, Arlanna Wir, went on to the outer edge of the dais before turning: the post of a prolocutor, who would speak for the Lady. Jannus didn't like that. It was customary for a male, usually an adolescent page, to serve that role whenever a man occupied the Guest Seat. That a Valde was to be prolocutor portended the most searching kind of inquisition.

Two troopmaids advanced to seat themselves on the lowest step of the dais. The harness of one was smooth, without dart loops: she'd be the troop's First Dancer, most formidable of its fighters, reserved for dueldances against other Valde and exempt from lesser conflicts. The function of the other troopmaid was less obvious. She was unusually thin, with vague staring eyes that seemed to focus on nothing in the scene before her. Jannus was reminded forcefully of the expression of the ranks of wooden Valde against the walls.

The troopleader intoned, "You are Jannus lar-Poli, Lillia's son—"

"Her son, scribe, and prolocutor for three years," broke in Jannus in the most bored of tones, pointing out that he knew audience ritual backward and forward and wasn't about to be awed by ceremony. "I'm Newstock-born. I've had dealings with Lisle in that I got Poli out of there four years ago when the Lislers kept her to serve them as Fair Witness, Truthsayer. It is hoped my contact with Lisle does not put me forever beyond the Lady's notice." That, not part of the ritual, was a club of ironic sarcasm. He went on, "I have never contemplated harm to Quickmoor or the Lady thereof until this hour, nor, by my will or with my consent, has anyone under my sole control or authority. . . . It is noticed there are offered no courtesy meats nor anything to drink. As we are being kept from our daymeal, the omission is doubtless unintentional, audiences being unusual at this hour and the hall pages perhaps not notified."

Poli's knuckles bumped his head softly, congratulating him on his choice of approach. Arlanna was silent, discerning the will of the Lady Ketrinne, concealed behind the Stranger Screen. Jannus heard soft retreating feet on the matting, at the rear of the hall, then a door shutting.

Arlanna said, "The matter will be attended to. The Lar Haffa Poli, at least, is my Lady's guest."

Well, that was ominous enough. Facing the issue directly, Jannus said, "It is wondered what cause for complaint the Lady Ketrinne finds with me, who never set foot into the Circle of Quickmoor until this hour."

"My Lady has seen a service you may be to her."

The *be*, used rather than *do*, jabbed Poli into saying, "He is not *here* to be of use. He is under nobody's hand but Rayneth's, and that by free contract!"

"And through the woman Rayneth to Ashai Rey, called the Master of Andras. What you did last night, Jannus, was it by her bidding?"

Jannus leaned back in the seat. He saw it then: inadvertently he had involved himself in the inner power struggle between Circle and Crescent, and this was the result. He'd called attention to himself. Ketrinne's attention, at least.

He was annoyed with himself, not for taking that first step out of the protection of anonymity, but for not having foreseen Ketrinne's interest and taken precautions. Elda Innsmith, Dan's father, would have put it that the Fool-Killer had finally caught up with him.

"No," he replied with rough brevity. "Rayneth knew nothing about it."

"Did *anyone* suggest to you such a defiance might be profitable? The Innsmith, the duke's factor?"

"Nobody whatever. I acted on my own intention and will."

The thin little troopmaid stirred then, lifting her dazed face toward Arlanna, who held a post of listening. Jannus murmured to Poli, "What's that one?"

"*In'marenniath*, I think," she said. "An . . . open one. They don't often come for troopservice, the Haffa *in'marenniath*. More often they join the Awiro at the Summerfair Troopcalling. . . ."

That made sense. A preternaturally sensitive Valde would find contact with the blaring uncontrolled *farioh* of outlanders extraordinarily painful. One volunteering for troopservice, and the right to marry if she survived it, would likely be assigned to Quickmoor, the quietest of the Riverstocks. The inquisition was to be at a deeper level than any he'd ever had to face. He began to feel not only spied upon, but surrounded.

"A private spite," announced Arlanna, after her silence. "An anger, against Ashai, whom you know well. Why?"

So much, they'd pulled out already, without a word or anything directly inspoken! Jannus set himself to be aware only of last night and now, as if nothing else existed, had ever existed. They had Ashai from him already, they—

"Duke Ashai had done me a favor, unasked." He recreated within himself the currents of the past evening: Blind Ella, the disbelief and indignation, the wish to reject and the fear of the consequences of doing so—let them occupy his whole concentration. "A matter of materials ordered from Longlanders, needed to continue the work I've contracted for to the Lady Rayneth."

Arlanna's lips parted, making him aware that his uncon-

sidered designation of the ruler of the Crescent was unaccept-
able within these walls. Likely they'd have preferred Dan's.
But Arlanna forbore to interrupt and said nothing.

Good, he thought; detail was good, the surface of things.
Let them be sifting Dan and his miserable letter slugs.

He went on, "In spite of the war and confusion on the
Longlands Spur, by all reports, Duke Ashai had these materi-
as completed and delivered under his own seal. The cargomaster called it a wonder. I wanted no wonders performed
for—"

"Why not a favor to the woman Rayneth?" demanded Arlanna, as if directed to find how well his belief was founded.
"Why not a favor to the young Innsmith, the toolcrafter? Or
even to the factor, the old Innsmith?"

"The shipment could be released to my hand alone. Not
Dan Innsmith's. Not Solvig's. Mine."

Arlanna waited while the screened Lady weighed that, then
at length signaled her to proceed. "Why would you not be
glad of such a mark of Duke Ashai's attention and regard
for you?"

I don't need his good regard, Jannus inspoke, a clear burst
of feeling, before he jerked himself back to just Ella, and the
night, and Dan's maddening refusal to let the subject of
Ashai drop after the daymeal argument. He laid his hands on
his knees and looked hard at the pattern the tiles made between the chair and the dais. Details, meaningless patterns,
three fingers' worth gone from a new-bought glass.

"Ashai is a dangerous enemy. An enemy for a nation, not
a man. But his friendship can be just as dangerous, to someone like me. Anyone whose reach won't extend to Ashai himself will aim at what's lower, in reach. Dan's wonder, the
letter slugs, might have gifted me with this audience as easily
as my throwing them away. I don't want Ashai, or his
friends, or his enemies. I go my own way. I have to. I can't
afford to take sides. Ashai should have known better than to
single me out that way. I told him so."

"Throwing the casks into the river would have done that.
Why take the Lisler, as well?"

"I was angry," he said simply.

"But you disliked seeing Bremneri bonded to him. Why?
And why take a boy from Lisle, the only Bremneri town that
openly honors Ashai and serves his will?"

Jannus looked up toward the screen, thinking that a Bremneri should understand that, easily enough. . . . "The Lady's a Bremneri. She knows the tension of the balance between the riverstocks, where Truthtell rules by means of the Valde, and the farmsteads, where men hold power over themselves and what is theirs. I'll set you an example, Lady. Take a stick fit for digging, or for a good staff, and send it to an armscrafter. He'll harden it and weight it and put a head on it of bronze or of stone, and when you receive it again it's a spear, fit for a spear's work. I disliked what I saw to come when a troop, five troops, ten, of grown bondboys returned to us hot from the forging of the Longlands. Lisles, all up and down the river. I wonder that the upriver Ladies agreed to the indentures."

Greedy. They saw only a way to dispose of boys at a profit who'd soon be lost to them by Naming in any case. The indenture gang received none from *me*."

The reply, in a high-timbred voice suggesting youth, came from behind the screen. The Lady Ketrinne had been moved to direct speech. One custom broken, she broke another. With a rustling of fabric she left her place and appeared on the dais.

She was indeed young, no more than twenty. Under the heavy, concealing headdress all women of the Inner Households affected, her brow was wide and unlined. The expression and stance were utterly assured, with no doubt of her own authority and control. She wore her city's colors, red and saffron, which marked her troopmaids too—the red a deep wine-colored gown, the saffron in bands at hem and sleeve and on the undecorated tabard she wore beltless, hanging in one long panel before and behind.

Placing a cushion on the floor, she seated herself on the dais, feet tucked under neatly. This hall was her place of judgment: she'd have seen fingers or hands struck off, lashing administered, monies great or small awarded, this claim validated and that dismissed, all on her sole word. Quickmoor was noted among the Riverstocks for the severity of its punishments, a result perhaps of its mixed and cosmopolitan nature.

The face confronting Jannus showed all this. The eyes said, *Do not dare to make me angry, for there is no one's hand over you but mine, to do as I will.*

"You didn't like the indenture," summarized the troop-leader, while the Lady watched, "and you told him so. Why?"

Jannus shrugged. "I wish me and mine left alone. I've seen one Lisle. I would not see another."

"Why?" interjected the young Lady Ketrinne. "Have you such great loyalty to the riverstocks, then?"

"No more than most," admitted Jannus steadily. "I think another balance will be found, in time. But a war of men against women would be an angry thing to see, Lady. I could not watch Ashai do this thing to us, with our own stupid consent, and do nothing at all."

"You think he does this with purpose, then?" demanded Ketrinne gravely, as to an equal.

"Lady, I think Ashai Rey does few things without purpose. But I do not claim to know his mind."

"So you showed him that you, at least, did not consent." The next question slapped at him unexpectedly: "How did you dare?"

"I was angry," Jannus said again.

Arlanna challenged, "You knew Ashai would take the price you named, even to a clipped copper. You knew you could insult him with impunity, publicly."

"How could you *know* that?" demanded Ketrinne.

"He had done me one favor. I looked for—"

"No!" Ketrinne cut him off with a chopping motion, slapping the tiles. "You *knew*. Or you would not have dared. How could you *know*? I *will* be answered!"

"Ashai owes him obedience," supplied the frail troopmaid suddenly, speaking for the first time. "There is . . . a debt, I cannot discern . . . he is hard to sort. . . ."

"And so." Ketrinne folded her hands in her lap. "And what manner of debt could Duke Ashai, called the Master of Andras, owe to such as you?"

Forced another step back in his resistance, Jannus cast fire and drowning pits, suffocation and solitary death at the *in'marenniath* troopmaid to distract her, disturb her concentration. All three Valde reacted. But the *in'marenniath* troopmaid crowded against the First Dancer, crouching as small as she could.

Arlanna snapped, "Stop that."

Jannus just looked at her levelly. She could not prevent

him, unless she rendered him unconscious or got the vulnerable troopmaid out of range. Or let him go.

None of these could she do. She couldn't silence him without going through Poli, which she'd already refused to do. Nor could Ketrinne order her to. Valde were sacrosanct, not to be harmed except by their own consent; that law was the life of the riverstocks. And Arlanna herself had seen to it that Poli was beside him here. The standoff was of her own making.

Jannus also meant to do what he had to, what he could. The little *in'marenniath* would have to leave, or else take her chances.

Impatient with the unheard duel that to her was only silence, Ketrinne demanded, "What debt does Ashai owe you?"

"I *believed* he would not act against me, over such a little thing. But I didn't *know*. There were two ways it could have gone. He'd accept my request, or he'd order me killed. I thought it was worth the chance—"

"A service," blurted the little *in'marenniath*. "A service done a greater than Ashai, someone Ashai answers to, is. . . . I cannot sort it, Lady—" She twisted anxiously, appealing first to Ketrinne, then to the troopleader, reacting to their impatience or disapproval, more immediate to her than Jannus's inspeaking. "There is dark, and dream, and being greatly afraid, a place like this but . . . unlike somehow, confusion and pain—I do not know how to connect them, Lady—"

Ketrinne patted the air placatingly. "It is enough that he holds a debt strong enough to compel Ashai Rey. Be at ease, Sellah, I am content with you. . . ."

The thin troopmaid subsided, huddling against the First Dancer as if she'd have hid, or escaped, had it been permitted her.

Ketrinne then named to Jannus the use she'd seen for him. "You will send to Ashai a direction that the woman Rayneth cease to receive his support—in money, weapons, favor, all things, of whatever kind. And I will keep you safe within the Circle of Quickmoor, where he cannot reach you to cancel the debt *that* way, and so must honor it."

Oddly, Jannus felt like smiling. He was not the only one in

danger of the Fool-Killer. "Lady," he replied gently, "his reach is longer than you imagine."

"No one passes the Circle without the knowledge and consent of my troopmaids," the Lady declared, between indignation and arrogance. "Would he abandon Longlands and set a siege about us, just for you, or for a bead-headed whore? I think not."

"Lady," piped the *in'marenniath* tremulously, "he thinks you are a baby, and do not know what—"

"Enough!" Again, the chopping gesture. Undertaking calm, Ketrinne propped her chin on two fists, considering him, meditative. "I am young, truly: only two years old in the rule of a city. I have not seen Lisle, nor the Thornwall of Valde, nor the Summerfair. I sold none of my boys to the indenture gang not because I could see the spear in the stick, but because I would not give what was mine to Ashai, in whatever guise. Make me wiser, then, Jannus Lilliason of Newstock."

Jannus found her determined humility, her lack of personal arrogance, unexpectedly appealing. She deserved a proper warning.

"You could not keep out his agents, if he were minded to send any," he told her bluntly. "They would pass your troopmaids like breath, or slay them, unknowing, where they watched."

The Lady Ketrinne frowned at his certainty, unwilling to credit it, unable to name it false. "Do you believe the chat of Ashai being a mage, then, a wizard? That's foolishness, like the Lislers who name the troopmaids witches. How would these agents pass? As ghosts, or by some spell? You cannot believe that."

"As a wind of fire, or as a deadly poison shaken onto a breeze. I don't know his limits, but those things at least are not beyond him. He holds what remains of the weapons of Kantmorie."

"So fearsome an adversary, and he's been in unsuccessful siege of Longlands almost two seasons, now? You are too much in awe of Fisher gossip. He is a man, like other men. His agents cannot pass through solid walls or locked doors. And Kantmorie is dust, and less than dust. Nothing survives, after such a time. Walls will keep you safe enough."

"And what of me?" demanded Poli suddenly, with the unabashed aggressiveness that had once made her First Dancer, in her time. Jannus could just make out the thin pale line slicing from brow to temple, one of her keepsakes from those days. She went on, "Do you propose to shut a Valde Lar Haffa up in a walled box too, as long as it may please you? And the children?"

"If I must—" confirmed Ketrinne hardily.

Arlanna broke in, "Lady, you cannot."

"*Cannot?*" flashed Ketrinne.

"You cannot hold a Valde unconsenting," said the troopleader earnestly. "It was done in Lisle, to their great shame. You cannot do it."

"And what is to stop me?" the Lady inquired of her troopleader in an ominous tone.

"Lady, I would," answered Arlanna, with visible reluctance. "I would withdraw the troop. We would winter in Lifganin and I would see them assigned elsewhere when the thaw comes."

The little *in'marenniath* was all but sobbing while Ketrinne meditated on the fate of a Bremneri riverstock without Valde to defend it or duel for its honor.

"All right," Ketrinne said at last, admitting that one threat at least had power to compel her. The intense black stare she kept on her troopleader said she wouldn't forget it quickly, either. "It seems I cannot keep you, Lar Haffa Poli. You must see to your own protection, and that of your children. If you would not be parted from him, then that is your concern and none of my compulsion. Stay or go, as you will."

"If I am abroad in your household, look to yourself, Ketrinne," said Poli flatly.

"Take care," the Lady warned, while Jannus took Poli's arm in a light grip whose import was the same. If Poli lost her temper, she might yet bring the Quickmoor First Dancer into it. Willingness to fight was consent to be fought with. Poli could forfeit her own protections, and his with them.

But Poli would never tolerate imprisonment for either of them. What she threatened, she'd do.

Jannus said, "You're dickering for a dead cat. You can't keep Poli. Neither can you keep me."

Ketrinne surely heard the conviction humming under his words but replied nevertheless, "I think I can. Who is to stop me?"

This time, Arlanna was silent.

Jannus said, "*I* can. If you force me to it."

"You mislead yourself. While Reyneth rules the Crescent I will keep you here."

"There was a time," Jannus remarked in a meditative, conversational tone, "I gave nightmares to half the Awiro Valde in Lifganin. I'd think I could manage to make life very unpleasant for a few Quickmoor troopmaids. . . . How many did you say you'd lost to the heartsickness, Arlann'? Two?"

"One. One only," replied the troopleader softly, braced, with no choices she could take. It was up to Ketrinne.

Jannus inspoke the image of a pit and a trapdoor, and his hand on the rope that would pull the latch. The image itself wouldn't reach them, but the intent, the attitude, would. The image just helped him focus, concentrate. "Have you heard of the Newstock Screamers, Arlann'?" he inquired, softer still. He visualized a rock slab poised over a doorway, himself inviting her through, a rope in his hand. "Have you been told how everything in the household would stop while the whole troop hunted the creature down and silenced it? How sometimes it went on for days, and troopmaids had to flee two days' run into the backcountry to be free of it, and even then some died afterward, from the horror? Did you know that of Poli's troops fewer than thirty survived to receive their bridestones? Would you like to know how Poli became *sa'marenniath*?"

As she had done by the outside door, Arlanna winced away, leaning against the Stranger Screen. She said, "I have heard of the Newstock Screamers. . . ."

The *in'marenniath* had gone as pale as the carved figures and even the First Dancer looked uneasy. With any luck Jannus felt he might push them into a mood echo, a sympathetic resonance among the three of them, each reflecting and amplifying the others' dread and spiraling it toward panic.

He let himself enjoy their fear, enjoy the power to hurt them if he chose. There was still that in him that could savor the chance to injure a troopmaid—he was not Newstock-born for nothing—and for once he could acknowledge it, indulge it with the full force of his will. He let himself remember indignities and humiliations almost twenty years old, suffered before the indifferent stare of some Newstock troopmaid, throwing the antipathy at the three before him with all the crude inspoken power he could command.

Poli was safe, *sa'marenniath*. There was really nothing to prevent him.

"No!" Arlanna jerked back and the screen tipped over, smashing into the stone chair it had hidden. The ivory panels shattered, strewing the dais with a snow of sharp particles. The screen flopped, broken-backed, over the chair.

But Ketrinne didn't budge, impassive, maintaining her challenge.

Some final reluctance made him tell her, "I can clear the Circle of Valde in under an hour. I'm no Screamer, but they'll hunt me or flee me within an hour in spite of anything you can do. Some may not survive it, and none will return as long as you hold me. How will the balance between Circle and Crescent rest then, Lady Ketrinne?"

"I don't believe you," rejoined Ketrinne somberly, waiting.

So. His belief alone wasn't enough to make her surrender. He'd thought not.

Unconsciously tightening his hand around Poli's arm, with the obscure intention of shielding her from what she could not perceive, Jannus set himself to recall the worst days on the High Plain: the torment of heat, fear, and exhaustion, the days and nights he didn't dare sleep for fear of the dreams always scrabbling at the edges of his waking consciousness, his despair at finding Poli's *marenniath* scorched away by the surrounding horror, herself cut off from him, unable to help or even touch his isolation, as he'd felt then; the Teks themselves, the Deathless, the Screamers, marching toward Down on a false promise of ending, savaging each other for food as they moved so that the way to Downbase was paved with half-gnawed bodies—manform, beastform, some shapes that were the dreams themselves trudging steadily under the sun.

It was his own pain he threw at the Valde, raw and ugly as an unhealed wound, summoned up clearer than memory. It was like forcing a river through a funnel. It was as much as he could do to hold his balance and keep the torrent directed outward. It had shape and direction only in the instant he was touching it. Before and after it was roiling chaos, suddenly no more his than was the air he breathed. He was only the focus, the funnel, the burning-glass.

Ketrinne cried out, "Enough!" when the frail *in'marenniath* collapsed soundlessly and slid forward unheeded by the First

Dancer, who rose holding a long shining knife drawn from somewhere. The First Dancer jerked free of the troopleader's attempt to grab her, stepping forward, stalking. Jannus didn't see her.

He didn't see Poli pluck a dagger-dart out of the air with an overhand slap or reverse it deftly in her hand, moving to block the First Dancer's path. As an afterthought Poli kicked him, not chancing to look back.

A second kick broke his concentration. The First Dancer's advance faltered, was forgotten in her concern for the little *in'marenniath*. She and the troopleader bent over the sprawled figure. They cradled and lifted her between them and carried her away down the aisle.

The Lady Ketrinne was left alone, brooding on the edge of the dais.

Distractedly Jannus undertook the effort of banishing what he'd called up. He imagined himself with handfuls of mud, mortaring up a furnace. It disappeared, part by part, the heat hardening the barrier. Finally he didn't see it any more.

There was dried mud on the palm of one hand. He stared at it, shaken. For an instant, image and reality interpenetrated. Then he caught hold of the memory of climbing the dike—just a fact, without resonance—and, making sense of the smudge, wiped it slowly against the front of his shirt.

"I discover you are a perilous guest," observed Ketrinne, watching him recollect himself. "Do all Newstockers take such power from their Screamers?"

"It's not the Screamers," he corrected her tiredly. "There's enough desolation in the least child of your household to cripple twenty troopmaids. But it scatters. Children don't hold it, not long enough to hurt anybody but themselves. Newstock's the same. They'd have to go to the Valde for that—if the Valde'd tolerate them. . . . Learn how to focus, how to hold it long enough to make a weapon of it. I never tried such a thing on purpose before," he reflected, realized, feeling that wondering perception, too, wither into a fact even as he tried to examine it. The sense of touching the living forces of awareness itself was slow to leave him.

"Hush," Poli murmured, leaning over the chair back. "It's none of her affair. Don't let it bother you."

Ketrinne was saying, "I would not be unfriends with you

on account of this . . . duel. What would you ask, to heal things between us?"

Trading. Value for value, or for debt. It steadied him.

"I want no trouble with Rayneth," he said, thinking out loud. "I'm not taking sides, and I don't want her to think I have. I don't want to draw any *more* attention," he added fervently, "if I can help it. So just forget this. Whatever may be between me and Ashai, that's my concern. I know it's next to impossible to keep anything private when troopmaids are involved, but try. What they're not asked, they don't think to repeat. Let it be over."

"I understand." Absently the Lady Ketrinne brushed flakes of ivory from one sleeve, then the other. "I will do what I can. Poli Lar, what would you have?"

"The daymeal that was promised," said Poli at once.

"Certainly! I am remiss, not to mention half-starved myself. . . . How fares Sallah?" she called past them, the clear young voice echoing among the benches and the rows of graven troopmaids.

"Lady," returned Arlanna's voice, softer and lower-pitched, "I ask your leave for her to go into Han Halla for perhaps a tenday, and Lora with her, to keep her company."

"They have leave. And you?" inquired Ketrinne solicitously.

"Lady, I have known the taking of Lisle. Screamers can do me no great hurt after that."

So even the Valde hadn't understood. They'd heard only a shouting darkness they didn't comprehend, and called it *Screamer*—as they'd done in Newstock, knowing nothing of Teks, caring nothing so long as the intolerable torment was silenced. The High Plain was a fresher corpse than they suspected; Poli knew, but Poli didn't care.

"This audience is mine," Ketrinne was saying to her troopleader down the length of the hall. "No one is to say one word about it, inside or outside the household. Is that clear?"

"Lady, I do hear you." The troopleader withdrew.

"Lisle," muttered Ketrinne, climbing to her feet, taking up the cushion to replace it on the chair. She saw the broken screen then, looked around vaguely, and tossed the cushion aimlessly aside. "It is wondered why you chose a Lisler to keep, you with no great fondness for Lisle. One supposes a meaning in it."

The oblique mode turned it into merely a conversational question, no longer a demand.

Jannus rose as well, feeling it would have been easy to go to sleep right on the floor, or on one of the stone benches. His exhaustion vaguely puzzled him. "Well, he was the only one I could find who didn't want to go. That's all. And I felt sorry for him."

Stepping down from the dais, Ketrinne said, "Come on, we'll eat in the Evenhall like civilized people. After the fires go out, this place is like a cave." She folded her arms tightly and shivered.

As they went together along the aisle, Jannus asked suddenly, "How old is Quickmoor, do you know?"

"Seven hundred fifteen years," replied Ketrinne as unceremoniously. "The Circle was finished a hundred fifty-nine years after the Fall of Kantmorie. This wing was finished eight years later, in one sixty-eight. It's about the oldest part of the complex, they say." Glancing idly about the walls, she became meditative. "The Valde hold Bremner in their hands. That's true. I never knew it as I do now." They passed out into the corridor. Still musing, Ketrinne said to Poli, "Why do you do it? I know, the bridestones and all, but such stones can be had ten to the copper, down on the coast. One needn't serve ten years, and likely die, for such a trinket as that. Why the whole construction—troops, Summerfair, dueling, and all? Why do you do it?"

It was the first time Jannus recalled ever hearing the question voiced. He remained silent, letting Poli answer it if she chose.

"It's the price of the Truthtell," Poli said presently.

"The Gift? But we didn't buy it, it was the Great Pact, the marrying after the Rebellion."

"We do not call it a gift."

"And for *that* the troopmaids come?" rejoined Ketrinne incredulously. "For a pairing-off of folk eight centuries dead and gone?"

"The Truthtell is among you still. And not all Valde pacted to Bremneri are—"

"No, not all," agreed Ketrinne, with a quick sideways look

that bracketed them both. More soberly, she commented, "Then *that's* the Gift: the pity of the Valde."

Poli didn't deny that interpretation. "It has its uses to us, the troopservice . . . but none that could not be served more simply, with less cost in lives and sorrow."

"Then there'll come an end to it. Pity doesn't last forever. Even Kantmorie ended, at last." Ketrinne started down a staircase, biting on a knuckle. "I must think on this. What *can* be lost, *will* be. It has come to me that I lean too hard upon my Valde. I must look to my walls."

In the middle of the night, a conversation:

Poli remarking sleepily, "I didn't know you could do that."

Jannus, reflexively pulling the quilts farther over his head, saying, "What?"

"Drive them into a mood echo like that."

"Didn't either. Little stalk of an *in'marenniath* made me think I could. Sallah. Easy to hurt."

"Lucky you didn't kill her."

A grunt, probably affirmative.

She poked his shoulder. "A great farspeaker was lost in you, born Bremneri. You know that? Jannus? . . . What'd you give them—Lisle?"

He rolled over on his back, blinking at the moonshadows. "That's your nightmare. I didn't mind Lisle all that much, once I knew I could buy you clear. No, I gave them the High Plain. That's *my* nightmare. I'll never go through anything *that* bad again."

She made the wardsign, fending off ill fortune and witches, and watched his smile.

He said, "And that's the last I'll hear of Dan's wretched letter slugs, too. Dan's pleased, Rayneth's pleased, Ashai likely thinks I'm odd, but isn't seriously unhappy, and Ketrinne . . . she's. . . ."

The thought unfinished, he was asleep. Poli settled her shoulder and adjusted the quilts without disturbing him.

Half an hour later Sua woke them, screaming incoherently about a snake in the pond. They scarcely got back to sleep before firstlight. Sua was always the slowest to adjust to any change: the strange quarters had upset her. Resignedly Poli reflected that she should have expected it.

II:
THE LOST BOY

The last of the month called Fading passed uneventfully, and the sole notable event of Frostdark was that actual printing was finally begun. But on the Sixth of Waiting came the news of the lost boy, and everything changed.

It was bitterly cold in Han Halla and overcast, though the sun had been shining when the four of them left the Crescent. As always, Han Halla kept its own weather. The mud was stiff underfoot but the cold had yet to penetrate its deeper layers. Jannus found that a good hard step—for instance, jumping from one rough tussock to the next—was likely to land him on his back as the mud skidded out beneath his foot.

The pools were frozen, but barely so. Each plant stem still had a tiny collar of water. The ice sheets they broke in walking were so thin Poli couldn't pick one up. It broke under its own weight and the shard left in her fingers slipped and fell, lubricated by its melting.

Every few steps Jannus glanced back to make sure the bonfire was still in sight. In spite of the horns and the whistles and the shouts, he was sure more would be lost, searching, than the one they'd all come out to find.

It was Dan's turn to blow the whistle. He emitted long doleful hoots at intervals when he wasn't swearing or stumbling. Like all of them he was bundled in four or five layers of sweaters, with a red plaid coat and a bright orange muffler—visibility was important—and he claimed he couldn't see his feet, much less watch his step. The back of his coat was muddy and had a clot of burrs sticking to the shoulder.

The three of them, along with Sparrowhawk, who'd finally made up his mind to stay with them rather than join a haphazard collection of pages and 'prentices, were part of a line stretched quite a distance along the margin of Han Halla to search for the lost boy. Rayneth had turned out the whole of the Crescent by promising five hundred coppers to whoever found him. Since the reward would be spread thinner, the larger the group, most teams contained no more than two or three. It served to scatter them farther but was also more dangerous: three times already Poli had caught a more urgent note in the surrounding shouting and they'd helped to haul out someone who'd gone through the frozen surface of a sinkpool.

"Who is it?" Sparrowhawk asked, hanging onto a branch to step gingerly down a lattice of ice-glazed roots. "That we're looking for?"

The branch broke, but Dan was near enough to grab him before he fell.

"Damn. Near lost the whistle. What's it matter? Lovely day to go for a stroll in the swamp. Everybody's doing it. . . . Is it worse in the winter, Jannus, or the summer? What do you think?"

"This will do," responded Jannus, using his staff to crack the ice and test for bottom before stepping into a channel barely arm's length across.

"But how'll we know him if we find him?" Sparrowhawk persisted.

A root collapsed under Poli's foot. Sparrowhawk, momentarily closest, caught her arm to steady her, then snatched his hand back as if regretting he couldn't make the wardsign in mittens. Poli stared at the broken root, and the shape and angle of the tree above it, memorizing this hazard too. She seldom walked into the same sort of difficulty twice. From her had come the information that the ropy plants with alternate branches and spiky seedpods most often grew beside sinkponds and that a smooth curve of mud with a hole at the side was the top of a marsh-chuck's burrow, deep enough to break your knee if you stepped into it, even if the chuck didn't object and bite you to the bone.

She was learning Han Halla all over again, the way Blind Ella liked to learn faces on first meetings.

"Anybody who's mud from head to foot and clutches you like a brother hollering 'Ale! Beer!' in a downriver accent, that'll be him," remarked Dan, which was as good an answer as Sparrowhawk was likely to get.

The description they'd heard was very vague—not even a name. All they knew was that some Andran boy, not a local, had gotten himself lost in Han Halla and Rayneth had put up a reward.

"Somebody stuck," decided Sparrowhawk, listening. "Over that way."

Jannus's automatic check showed the bonfire no more than a paler place in the luminous blur of mist. "You stay here," he directed Sparrowhawk. "Dan, when you—"

"I'll make a link," Dan agreed, understanding at once. As they picked their way toward the right he called back, "Lisler, don't you budge or I'll come back to haunt you, you hear? Rope, that's what we ought to have. Rope."

"We'll remind you next time," remarked Poli, teasing, free of the constraint of Sparrowhawk's presence.

"May the cold steams get you, saying such a thing. *Next time*! Ain't reconciled myself to *this* time, yet."

Poli went up a crooked tussock higher than most, both arms out for balance. On top, she put out a chill-reddened hand. Jannus laid the end of the staff in it and used the staff to climb up beside her.

"Here's where I stop," announced Dan, below. "Just lost sight of the Lisler."

"Come on up anyhow—you can see better from here," said Poli.

"If you say. . . ." responded Dan dubiously.

They stood, absurdly crowded, on a space the size of a bushel basket while Poli listened. Presently she shook her head.

Dan yelled, "Somebody in trouble out there?" He yelled twice and blew the whistle, but was answered only by unintelligible shouts and splashes far away. Banging spit out of the whistle, he said, "Maybe the Lisler mistook—"

"You find him?" came Sparrowhawk's eager voice, and Sparrowhawk himself, out of the indefinite opaque glow.

Near enough to read the three uniform glares confronting him, he faltered, "I thought you'd. . . . You blew the whistle."

"Who wants him more'n me?" inquired Dan rhetorically. "No, I don't need your motherless *stick*—"

In two long steps he descended, caught his balance, and started for Sparrowhawk, who backed away along a narrow tongue of reeds and yellowish sedge.

"Dan! Dan!" Jannus shouted. "Think where you are!"

Dan hauled up short, gave Sparrowhawk a last baleful look, and said, "I can see where we came through the canes. Or somebody did. Stay put."

His form receded, faded into the luminosity, though his heavy steps were still audible. He stopped. "All right. I can see the fire from here. Come on."

Poli went down first, then Jannus. Sparrowhawk hadn't moved. When Jannus looked toward him, Sparrowhawk directed, "You just go on. I'll look wi' those 'prentice lads."

Of the four of them, only he had never been in Han Halla before. He didn't know what he was proposing to do.

Jannus said, "You come here to me. Right now."

"You're fixing to hit me."

"What of it? I bought your bond. You contracted to do what you were told, and you moved when you'd been told to stay put. Isn't your word worth anything?"

Jannus figured that inlander's taunt would strike at Lisler as well. But Sparrowhawk sullenly refused to move.

"Let the Fool-Killer come for him," called the Innsmith's voice, off to the left. "Won't stay, and then won't go."

"Thought you'd *found* him!" complained Sparrowhawk. "You had the witch wi' you—I thought you'd find him sure!"

Poli scuffed at the edge of an ice plate which fractured into sliding, floating layers. Then she trudged off toward the tongue of reeds. Without saying a word she walked down the raised spit, took Sparrowhawk by the front of his coat, and towed him behind her like a goat.

"You let him be," she told Jannus, passing. "He's sixteen and ignorant as a brick."

"I do hear you. You'd best tell Dan, though."

"We're going back. That's enough of Han Halla for one day."

Following, Jannus heard Sparrowhawk plead, "Leave me go, Mistress. Leave me go. I won't run, I swear."

"Dan?" Jannus got a whistle hoot in reply. A few paces later he distinguished Dan's blocky outline, faint as smoke, beyond a thicket of spiky naked bushes.

Poli directed Dan, "You let him be. We're going back."

"Yes, Mistress, anything you say, Mistress," said Dan, and let them pass before falling in behind, carefully avoiding doing anything that might push the youngster into another suicidal excursion on his own.

Sparrowhawk's coat had been released but he walked as if he didn't know it, keeping the same distance behind Poli's right shoulder. Presently he said, "You really quitting? You're going to leave me off and come back, ain't you. You ain't really quitting."

"We're really quitting," rejoined Poli distinctly, without looking back.

"But you can *find* him! Is it that you don't want to? Then why come out to begin with?"

Poli wheeled then, with one foot ankle-deep in a pool. "Once and for all, there are no witches. *Say* it!"

Sparrowhawk backed a step, but Jannus was there, though Jannus took care not to reach out or move suddenly.

"There are no witches," Poli declared again. "Only people. I can drown in a sinkpool as quick as you, and look just as foolish doing it. All I have to guide me is some experience and what sense I was born with. I've been yearning to come into Han Halla for seven long months and haven't set foot in it until today because *it's . . . too . . . dangerous.* Now, can you understand *that*, Lisler?"

"Yes'um," agreed Sparrowhawk hastily.

"You'd better." Poli jammed her hands into her pockets and moved on, ducking under a bowed limb. "Chuckholes," she warned briefly, and, a few steps later, "Sinkpool."

That was the sum of their conversation, as they returned to the bonfire.

The fact that a Valde was giving up seemed to have dispelled any enthusiasm Sparrowhawk had for joining another team and continuing the hunt. While they wandered around the bonfire, warming one side at a time, the boy stayed close to Jannus and made no attempt to drift away. Dan, habitually the only one who carried any money around, went into a roped-off triangle near the foot of the dike, where hot cider was being sold. "You got to come in," he reported loudly. "She's scared we'll run off with the mugs."

Holding the hot mug with care against beard and cheek, Jannus looked pensively over the nearer frost-rimed clumps and out into the fog. Moving to his side, blowing on the surface of her scalding cider, Poli proposed softly, "*I* will if *you* will. . . ."

Jannus thought about it, warming the other side of his face. "No. You're soaked. We both are."

"It isn't that lost boy that bothers me as much as those fools in the sinkponds," she remarked, chancing a sip, looking pleased.

"That too. You take the mittens."

She tucked them under an arm, preferring for the moment to wrap her long fingers around the surface of her mug.

Dan wandered up, saw how they were looking out, and said at once, "No. Not me. Missed by midmeal and half a day's work. I'm done."

"Who's going to help you?" Poli asked lazily. "They're all out there. All except the Inner Households folk."

"They're the only ones around here with any sense, that's plain enough. . . . Drink up, Sparrow," advised Dan heartily, as the boy joined them. "We're going to go wading some more."

"But *she* said—"

"Ah, witches don't know everything, didn't she just tell you?"

They went out, all told, three times. They hauled nine people out of sinkponds, steered eleven who'd been foolish enough to lose sight of the fire, watched a broken leg being set by a drawcarter who seemed to know what he was doing much better than any of them did, drove away a man and a woman occupied in beating and robbing another man, and failed to persuade four chattering, blue-lipped 'prentices to go home. They found a wheel with six spokes missing, a good fishing pole that looked brand new, a lantern Dan cut his foot on in spite of heavy boots and three pairs of socks—that was their last foray—and, unpleasantly, a skeleton, all intact, picked clean. Sparrowhawk wanted to collect the skull but

Dan wouldn't let him. They left it where it was, frozen into the mud.

They went around the dike's south curve into the Crescent and reached the arch over the household's gate as the bell within the Circle was striking its tenth stroke.

"If you don't see me for the daymeal," remarked Dan, limping with Sparrowhawk toward the southwing, "don't figure I'm lost and come looking for me. I'll be asleep."

Jacko, turning from fastening the outer door he'd opened to admit them, asked hopefully if there was any news. Jannus just shook his head, following Poli toward the left-hand door.

Jacko's voice, saying, "The Lady told me she wanted to see you the minute you came back," caught Jannus in the doorway. He sagged against the doorframe.

"Can't we not get back for another hour or so?"

"She'd have my other hand for that. Sorry."

Jannus reported to Poli, "Says he's sorry." Of Jacko, he asked, "What's it about? No: you don't know. All right. Where is she? No," he told Poli, who was waiting just inside, tacitly offering to go with him, remain cold and filthy to keep him company, "not this time. Rayneth doesn't keep troopmaids—I won't need a keeper to get me out again. Really." Visibly relieved, Poli drifted toward the inner rooms. "Now, where?"

"Her rooms. Her new rooms."

Upstairs. Resignedly, Jannus went across the entry hall to the staircase and hauled himself up by dragging the bannister toward him, fumbling with the fastenings of his coat. He shed the coat and two of his sweaters on his way down the corridor, which seemed oppressively hot after a day outdoors, just letting them lie where they fell. He'd collect them later.

One of the invisible bodyguards unfolded from his chair and rapped on the door behind him. It opened a crack, shut again. Then Rayneth herself came into the hall carrying a tumbler full of something cider-brown which she handed to Jannus while steering him inside. Seeing him glance about for an appropriate place to sit, Rayneth said harshly, "Anywhere. It doesn't matter. You," she directed the other invisible bodyguard, "out."

Jannus figured that the bodyguard's chair wasn't likely to be the most valuable and chose that to lean into. That gave him a view of the chunks of mud leading from the door to his guilty boots. He sighed, crossing one ankle over the other, reminding himself that it was Rayneth's own fault if he hadn't taken time to get cleaned up.

And indeed Rayneth seemed to have no attention to spare for such things as rugs, mud. She remarked, "I sent Rabb after you but he kept missing you at the fire. Nobody can find anybody in Han Halla."

That didn't seem to call for comment. Jannus took a swallow from the glass and almost choked. It was brandy. He wondered if Rayneth had mistaken the bottle in filling the glass. So-called strongwine was prohibitively expensive: he'd tasted it perhaps four times before in his life. He held the glass out and studied it dubiously, conscious of having eaten nothing since sunup but part of a sausage and half a roasted potato, thinking that if he drank a water tumbler full of brandy he'd very quickly be incompetent even to get safely back down the stairs.

But, then, there were always the invisible bodyguards. The Fool-Killer also came for those who rejected luck merely because it was unexpected. Privately saluting the bodyguards, Jannus sipped more decorously.

Rayneth, having walked to the outer door, circled back to the window, each time seeming on some urgent errand that failed to materialize. She was pacing. Belatedly, Jannus noticed that though the rings and bracelets were all in place, her hair hadn't been done today. It was just pulled straight back and tied at the nape with what looked like yarn. That fact made him sit up straighter and pay attention.

"Nothing's happening out there," Rayneth exclaimed, and stared at him for confirmation.

"Nothing of any use."

"He's *there*. I know he is."

"Maybe he's hiding," suggested Jannus, with careless sarcasm.

She halted her circuit of the room briefly, again staring. "What do you mean by that?"

"Nothing in particular. We looked. We didn't find any lost people who weren't looking themselves, for the reward."

Seeing her listen, the particular *way* she listened, Jannus suddenly knew for a fact what he'd always wondered about: whether Rayneth was Truthdeaf. Bead-girls generally were—

farmstead-born, never touched by the heritage of the Great Pact. But Rayneth had Truthtell. He was certain.

Nevertheless Jannus drank again from the glass before folding his hands around it. The certainty woke no sense of threat in him: the ceremony, the familiar, hated audience ritual, the prolocutor, were all missing. It was only Rayneth, after all.

"You're tired and disappointed," remarked Rayneth, abruptly cordial, "and here's this woman going on and on and saying nothing, practically running around the walls like a mouse." She looked to the window, and in its light her face was drawn, anxious. "Well, it's been a bad day for me too, Jannus. After a bad night. Bear with me a while. About a month ago you visited the Lady of the Inner Households. Did you part on good terms?"

"She didn't give me any gardens. . . ." rejoined Jannus, pointedly enough. But he wanted no second inquisition, this time over his meeting with Ketrinne.

Reading something of this in his face, Rayneth said, "It's not just another Quickmoor intrigue. I need a favor from her. From Ketrinne."

Jannus thought about that unhurriedly. "It depends on the favor," he commented finally.

"I want the Valde troopmaids to join the search."

"No chance. I'm not popular enough for that. I don't know anybody who is."

"You could try."

" 'Tisn't worth the walk. Send that bunch of troopmaids into the craziness out there, those homebound downy chicks? And leave the Circle naked? Ketrinne'd have to be shy most of her wits to agree to that."

"There has to be a way, a price."

Jannus set the glass back on his knee, saying, "Then I don't know what it would be, short of you setting out downriver in your shift, barefooted, and her with the keys to your household."

"It might come to that," she retorted, shooting him a look. "He *has* to be found!" she exclaimed, circling the table distractedly, shoving in chairs. "It's the Crescent, the household, everything, if I don't find him. And if I'm out barefooted in my shift, my lad, you'll be right behind me. So you'd better

quit finding this funny and help me think. It's a long walk
back to Ardun of the Rose."

Ashai. Duke Ashai had threatened her with the complete
withdrawl of his patronage unless she succeeded in locating
this boy.

"It's a long walk back to anywhere," he responded heavily.
"You'd best tell me, Rayneth. And open a window. I'm going
to sleep, just sitting here."

Working at the stiff latch and pushing the casement into
the last of the daylight gave Rayneth time to make up her
mind. Leaning against the sill, she said, "It's Ashai's private
page. He knows all sorts of things that mustn't get out. He's
run off."

"From Ismere?" rejoined Jannus skeptically, rubbing a
sleeve across his forehead as the chill air reached him.

"From Longlands. Duke Ashai keeps him close at hand.
An . . . agent of my lord duke lost him in Han Halla, south
of here. He'd come part way by schooner but jumped ship
when he was discovered. The agent followed, but lost him in
Han Halla before pursuit could be organized."

"How far downriver?"

"Between the second and third flasher towers—about
twenty miles as the light goes, or thirty-five river miles," admitted Rayneth reluctantly. Answering his next question before he asked it, she added, "The fourth: two days ago."

"Then one gets you a hundred he's dead. If he *could* have
made Quickmoor, he *would* have. . . . There're a few Fishers in Han Halla, around the edges: might *they* have taken
him in?"

"That's being checked. But I need the Valde. Could Poli
ask . . . ?"

"Poli might cross the street to see Ashai hanged, but then
again she might want to buy a sausage instead. I'm the only
friend Ashai's got in our family, such as I am, such as he
is. . . ." That was incautious. Jannus leaned to set the glass
down on the rug, then pushed a spread hand through his hair.
Finding he still had the knitted cap on, he pushed it back,
taking no notice of where it fell. "And if Poli herself was lost
in Han Halla, the troopmaids would just huddle and try not
to let each other get too upset about it. I've seen them do it.
That time she was in Lisle. They just left her there. Served

ten years with her, and all they could think of was to get clear so they wouldn't have to listen when Greyhawk had her killed. That's true."

Rayneth nodded. She looked odd without the immense birdsnest construction of hair framing her face—older, and more vulnerable. "Come on," she encouraged. "You thought of the Fishers. Think of something else."

"Well, there're the flasher towers themselves. They'd be shelter of a sort."

"Only the first and fifth are on the east shore. He's not there, nor been there."

"How do you know he's still on the east shore at all? Fishers downriver have those little one-man coracles, and they're back and forth all—"

"No. The river's being watched."

"For forty, fifty miles? It isn't possible."

"All the same," responded Rayneth positively. "Fishers wouldn't dare shelter him against Duke Ashai, and they've been warned now to send word if the boy's sighted. Assume he's still on the east shore, in Han Halla, and almost certainly alone."

Jannus rolled both hands over, a gesture of helpless frustration. "Then he's dead. You know Han Halla. What if he *is* dead? Even Valde couldn't locate a corpse for you, not unless they tripped over it by happenchance."

He suddenly thought of the skeleton they'd found, but had to dismiss the possibility of its being the runaway's remains. It'd been picked clean, and moreover had been in the mud undisturbed at least since the freeze came down, two days ago. Poli had said so. Some other unfortunate wanderer, but not the boy. The times were wrong.

"If he's dead," Rayneth was saying, "then I won't find him and the Crescent will have some other Lady."

"That doesn't seem fair."

She smiled then, wanly. "Whatever made you suppose my lord duke was fair? He serves the Rule of One—" She stopped, seeing his reaction. "What is it?"

"That phrase . . . isn't in the word citations."

"Perhaps I overlooked it. It's familiar enough, among Anrans. It goes back to Kantmorie."

"I know."

"I thought you did," said Rayneth, the remark calm and much too pointed, as if they shared a secret.

Unaware that he was scowling, Jannus retrieved the glass and deliberately finished the last of its contents: both announcing and enforcing his disengagement from this discussion. But Rayneth merely fetched a bottle from a cabinet and refilled the glass, deftly adapting to his vague efforts to move or cover it, remarking blandly, "Some think better, and some stop thinking altogether. Which kind are you?"

"*I* don't know. . . ." he sighed, a surrender. Fair or unfair, the problem was his as well as Rayneth's. His immediate fortunes depended on hers, that was true enough. Besides, he owed her something for the garden; and he couldn't really be indifferent to her any more than he could to Ashai Rey. "*You're* Ashai's lucky pocket piece: did his patronage ever extend to providing any Fathori wine?"

That *was* a secret, coercing her in turn. Reluctantly, she said, "Once, it did. . . . All right." Rayneth went into the room beyond and was absent some minutes. She probably had to go through five layers of locks to get at it.

Hardly anybody had heard of Fathori wine. It was ancient and rare, with unique properties. Jannus half recalled, half heard, a child's voice explaining tersely, "*A focuser, not a relaxant.*"

That'd been Lur, one of the last Teks alive in the world.

A Screamer, a deathless Tek of Kantmorie, whom for two seasons Jannus had numbered among the odd collection of people he cared about. The collection included Ashai Rey, who was not, strictly speaking, a person at all. Ashai had no *farioh*, no self-singing that a Valde's *marenniath* could hear. Ashai differed from Lur principally in that he was still alive; but there were other differences as well. . . .

Rayneth returned and exchanged the tumbler for a thimble-sized glass whose contents were straw yellow, waiting until his hand adapted to the different size and weight of the container.

"Don't spill it," she warned anxiously. "It's the last."

"I know. It's always the last."

The Wood of Fathori had once stood opposite Quickmoor, on the west side of the river. A wonder that hadn't been forgotten in all the years between, a forest grown from seed and inhabited by creatures unimaginably beautiful and strange created by Teks to decorate it, Fathori had been incinerated during the Rebellion. The word survived, a memory of something wonderful and lost that made people view with contempt the Is marshes that steamed where Fathori had bloomed long ago; and, for those that knew, there remained the secret hoarded treasure of its wine.

Having emptied the tiny glass, Jannus sat for a while resting his head in his hands. He was thinking about Lisle, which was where he'd tasted Fathori wine before. Ashai had had some. Lur had been there, bodied as a child, and Jannus had been intent on bargaining with Ashai Rey to intervene with Grayhawk for Poli's release.

Sparrowhawk, Grayhawk's son, might even have seen them there. He'd have been twelve or so. It was odd to think of it. Jannus now had for a bondboy the son of the man who'd kept Poli prisoner and fully intended to kill her. She hadn't been able to tell the Lisler if Ashai was speaking truth or not, because Ashai was *sa'farioh*, like a Tek; and Grayhawk had been furious, after all the trouble he'd taken to capture a Valde, to find her useless.

Of course, Grayhawk hadn't any more idea than Poli'd had then of what Ashai was, why she couldn't hear him. . . .

Jannus looked up finally, feeling the cold from the window against his side. He was being watched by Rayneth and by a large slate-gray bird that surely hadn't been there before. It was perched, hunched, on a chair's high back, its tail feathers touching the table. It was an alver, a kind of large hawk, though this was by far the largest he could recall having seen, not that he'd seen many at such close range. Generally an alver was a drifting dot against the clouds. Some people trained them to hunt small game and waterfowl. But not Rayneth. What it was doing here Jannus couldn't even conjecture.

He looked to Rayneth for an explanation, but she showed no inclination to offer one. So he studied the bird again. Hawks' eyes were reputed to be sharp; but he never remembered being watched by any creature with quite such intentness.

It wasn't a stuffed bird—that he knew intuitively, though it hadn't moved since he'd become aware of it. He wondered if it'd flown in the window, but realized that was impossible. No bird with a wingspan twice a man's height was going to fly, horizontally, through a space a quarter that wide. Besides, he'd have heard it.

The bird's presence was a puzzle, one he felt was set for him to solve.

The inner door, opposite, was ajar. Before, it'd been shut. So Rayneth had gone into the next room and . . . carried back the bird? That seemed absurd, but once he looked, he could see talon marks on the fabric of her left shoulder. She'd let the alver grip there, while she brought it in, no more than the sound of footsteps, her interminable pacing, to have alerted him.

The bird had been in the next room, then, while they'd been talking. Rayneth had gone away, first for the Fathori wine, then for the alver.

Disliking its unwavering inspection, Jannus stared back. The alver disengaged casually and began to straighten the feathers on top of one wing—on what, in a man, would have been a shoulder.

He'd seen it do that before. The memory popped up, just as if he'd always known it. There'd been a big alver preening itself just that way on the wall of the ruined garden in Lisle, that time he'd met with Ashai Rey. He didn't even remember noticing it particularly, having at the time many more urgent concerns. But the memory was there, clear and unmistakable.

This, then, was Ashai's agent, which could overtake a schooner and locate a boy on board, and then lose him under the fogs of Han Halla. Thus bodied, such an agent could then hurry on to Quickmoor and deliver an ultimatum, with Ashai's own authority, to the Lady of the Crescent and have it unquestioningly accepted.

A Tek.

"I give you greeting," said Jannus—steadily, he hoped. "Where are you based? How may I call you?"

"Based from Down," replied the bird in a harsh, scratchy voice, "but Fourth in Debern Keep before it was abandoned. Ethologist, tenth-level aptitude. You may call me Bronh."

Bronh; the word meant *up-floating*, used of light in air. Sometimes it meant sunrise, or sunset, or a new-lit fire and the sparks and smoke ascending. A good name, for a Tek bodied as a bird. Jannus vaguely recalled Lur telling him that the runaway Teks of Debern Keep, planters of Fathori, had the custom of regarding themselves as female, rather than indifferently androgynous, like most Teks. And what an ethologist might be he had not the least idea.

"I'm most glad to see you, Bronh. I didn't think any Teks remained alive."

His ignorance apparently deserved no comment. And even the impersonal rudeness of Tek manners was delightful to Jannus because it was so characteristic, and so familiar.

Shaking her wing back into place, the Tek remarked abruptly, "It's not a page that's lost," both unblinking marigold eyes watching to see how he'd react to being informed he'd been lied to.

Any other time, he'd have been furious. But once a Tek was involved, all the rules were changed. "So?"

"It's Pedross," said the Tek. "Ashai Rey's son."

"That's the problem, you see," commented Reyneth, spreading her hands apologetically, appealing.

Jannus got up and yanked the window shut, and latched it. "Then we'll have to find him. In Han Halla. But I swear I don't know how."

Poli noticed the boy as she was getting out of the tub. The window was steamed, but her eye caught a flick of motion outside. With the corner of a towel she wiped a little peephole and looked out, uncomfortably conscious of the cold of the window against her thoroughly scrubbed skin.

The boy was kneeling by the pond and methodically washing his face and arms, though he must have had to crack the ice to do it. His hair was an odd straw yellow shade—by no means unknown but fairly rare, usually suggesting some Smith blood somewhere. But the boy was lither, less boxy, than any of the big-boned Smiths she'd ever seen.

There was no way into the garden from the household except through the bedroom casements, and he surely hadn't come from there. He must have come over the wall near the top of the dike, which was hidden by the shrubbery. And there he was in the garden, taking a cape out of a strapped blanket roll and trying to shake the wrinkles out, his poorly cut hair falling over his eyes. He slapped at it in a vaguely annoyed way, looking very sober and intent.

Wrapping the towel around her, Poli made wet footprints

on the carpeting on the way to the robing room next door. Her warmest tunic, filthy from her day in Han Halla, lay in a heap on the bathroom floor. She found a brown tunic and slipped it over her head. Groping for the sleeves, she padded back to the bedroom fireplace and pulled on trousers she'd worn yesterday, a fresh pair of wool stockings, and a pair of kidskin latch-boots. Rubbing at her wet hair absently, she went around the unmade bed to look out the casements, less impenetrably steamed than the one in the bathroom.

The boy was still there by the pool, wearing the cape. The blanket roll had disappeared. He'd probably cached it back in the bushes.

Poli was only slightly more interested than if she'd seen the same boy, from a window, down on the street. She hadn't any particular sense of owning the garden, so felt no sense of intrusion or trespass. If he was there, he plainly meant to come in, and the only door was the one whose latch was under her hand.

So she opened it.

Seeing her almost at once, he hurried across the frozen ground, skidding a little and catching himself, until he was just within reach. He had a polite way of standing, as if he was used to waiting to be noticed without fidgeting. He looked about Sparrowhawk's age. The top of his head was level with Poli's chin.

He said, "You're Poli lar-Jannus." He said it as if it were a special secret, or he'd just discovered it all by himself. "Is Jannus here?"

"No. The Lady wanted him."

"The Lady Rayneth?" he clarified, and Poli nodded. "Is he coming back soon?"

Jannus had been gone about an hour, Poli guessed. She hadn't been keeping track. She said, "I don't know. Before the daymeal, I would hope."

"I'd like to talk to him. May I wait until he comes back?"

Poli let him in, glad for the excuse to shut the casements again. When she turned, he'd gone into the front room. She found him looking about him brightly.

"Is all this yours?" he asked, surveying the room, Rayneth's furniture. "It's very nice."

He was in no haste to get closer to the fireplace, so either he didn't mind the cold or else he hadn't been out in it very long before she saw him.

"Are you hungry?" she inquired. "I have to go fetch the children now. I don't expect there'll be a proper daymeal today. I can bring you something back."

"Only if you're having something too." He didn't seem anxious about that either. "They are selling sausages and cider out past the dike. . . ."

Poli categorized him then as some boy of the Inner Households who'd heard of the search and escaped his pacted mistress to join in and try for the reward. Why he should want to talk to Jannus probably involved trying to enlist his help in avoiding punishment for the forbidden excursion, since Jannus would be known to be on fairly good terms with the Lady Ketrinne. Nothing stayed secret very long in a Bremneri household. Poli forgot about him, circling through the corridors to the far end of southwing, where the kitchen was.

After their midmeal nap, the children often stayed in the kitchen playing with the household's other children—four boys, three girls, all older. The cook, Arabet, was willing to keep an eye on them during the midmeal cleanup and the paring and peeling, but insisted they be called for before the daymeal preparations were too far advanced.

The crowd of children was by no means a *hafkenna*, a childpack—their movements were too random and self-willed, lacking the unanimity of shared mood; nor was there any adolescent boy for them to flock around and follow. Nor could any true *hafkenna* have had four boys in it; not in Valde, where scarcely one child in ten was male. Another translation of *hafkenna* would have been *brotherchasers*. All the same, it was as close to a *hafkenna* as Poli could contrive in this foreign place.

Perhaps, as Jannus had said, they were still too young. But they were as large as household children almost two summers older, and as able. They'd not be too young much longer.

Except for its troop of sentinel cats, who attended to their business of hunting, grooming, sleeping, and watching just as usual, the kitchen seemed as deserted as the rest of the household. Alone with the children, Arabet was enjoying her unaccustomed leisure reposing in her own particular chair beside the smouldering hearthfire, her stockinged feet propped on

the fender, slowly stirring a cup of tea. At the near side of
the hearth was a nest basket underneath a table. Beside it the
three—Alis, Ami, and Liret—and two Bremneri children
were folded in the chin-to-knees crouch only a child's torso
allowed, huddled as close to the kittens as Muff, the mother
cat, would permit. Poli spotted the two, Mallie and Sua, in a
far corner trying to cajole Ink, First Cat of the household
troop, from his preferred napping place atop the pie cup-
board. Four more Bremneri children were gathered underneath the largest table playing some sort of game with
smooth flat riverstones laid in lines, arguing about whose turn
it was. Several peered up with sober jam-smeared faces before
returning to their occupation.

Declining Arabet's offer to tea, Poli located the sweater
Liret had shed and one of Ami's shoes, while the three clambered out of their lair to report the kittens' recent doings and
recite the names they were considering for each. Perched by
Poli on the big table to be re-shod, Ami wanted to know if
children were born blind too. Alis proudly announced she'd
licked all the jam off Ami's face—indeed it was the sole clean
one Poli could see—but that Liret wouldn't cooperate. Meanwhile a wooden creak gave Poli just enough warning of Mallie's attempt to scale Ink's cabinet, by means of a drawer,
while the cat peered over the edge, yawning skeptically. Poli
lifted Mallie just as the child was setting her foot on the
drawer's pile of clean towels. With her free hand Poli secured
Sua's wrist and led the two around the big table, where she
finished lacing Ami's shoe, then got all five out the door, Alis
still trying to make Liret hold still to let her face be licked.

As always Poli was struck by each child's separateness
from the others. Even among the three there were cross purposes, disputes. Sometimes Poli wondered if there was anything of Valde in them at all.

Fretful at any interruption or change, Sua lagged and
twirled at the end of Poli's arm, complaining of the cold in
the passageway. "Why aren't there fires out here? I *say*,
why—"

"Can we see Dan?" Mallie interrupted, tugging left toward
the workroom door farther down the corridor.

If there was time, they often stopped to visit the Innsmith,
who, homesick as he was, loved the children's company. If

her five had been a *hafkenna*, which they weren't, Dan would have been its focus if he hadn't been too old and too preoccupied with machinery the rest of the time, which he was. But the yearning and the closeness were there, nevertheless, on both sides—Poli didn't need the *marenniath* to know that: just her two eyes.

But she said, "Not today. Dan's tired."

"I wouldn't bother him. I'd go ever so soft—" Mallie demonstrated tiptoe stealth, hopeful. The three began creeping too and shushing each other. Ignoring them, Mallie proposed artfully, "Can we see the Sparrow, then?"

They all hated the Lisler, sensitive to the antipathy between him and their mother. But where Sparrowhawk was, Dan could be found.

"No. You're all over jam—"

"I'm not!" asserted Ami.

"—and you're going to have a bath. I've—"

Just then Sparrowhawk came into the corridor, he and the children confronting each other with a silent, recoiling chill; then he said to Poli, "Mistress, I don't know what else to do. His foot won't let off bleeding."

Escaping Poli's loose hold, Mallie flashed past him through the workroom door, and the three after her. Since there seemed no use holding just Sua back, Poli let her go and followed to see what was the matter.

Beyond boxes and pillars of paper bales, Dan was sitting on the edge of his cot with his left foot in a pan of bloody water. When he raised his head Poli could see every freckle clearly: he was that pale. As the three clambered around and on him, expecting their usual rough welcome, Dan trapped them against his sides, two under one arm, one under the other, and held them squirming there while he offered one broad hand to Mallie, who alone seemed to have caught the adults' concern and had stopped by his knee, looking anxiously from the basin to his strangely waxen face. Dan gathered her close too, patting her, saying, "Here, kitlet, ain't a thing for you to be. . . . Here, Mallie, no great harm done. . . ." To Poli, he added, "*Told* the Lisler not to trouble you with it, but he—"

"Wasn't nobody else about," rejoined Sparrowhawk, without apology.

Poli paid no further attention to them, making a thick pile of quilts and bolsters at the foot of the cot. Having had some experience of wounds, she felt exasperation that neither man'd had the sense to prop the leg up, get the blood draining away from the cut. And then, to soak it in warm water, that would keep it from clotting . . . ! She got the three out of the way—much subdued, they backed a few steps against a crooked pillar of paper bales and whispered—and made Dan lie flat with the injured foot elevated on the quilts.

He objected, "But it'll make a mess of—"

"Keep still. Lisler, you know where the linen press is? Sua, you show him. Fetch a clean sheet and two little towels. Liret, you go tell Arabet . . . no." Poli realized the cook wouldn't hand over a sharp knife to a child. "Lisler. After you bring the linen, tell the cook I need a boning knife."

"I'll go," said Mallie, and pounded off.

Poli patted the foot dry with an edge of a quilt. The wound was a puncture, not a tear—an oozing line about four fingers wide across the instep. Delicately she spread the edges of the wound, to check for glass, but found it deeper than she'd supposed, since the foot had been protected by boots and several layers of wool socks. The cut bled freely but without the rhythm of heart-pressure, which at least was one good sign. . . .

"I figure it must have been a shard of *plarit*," Dan remarked tiredly, staring at the ceiling. "Underneath the busted lantern. I never seen it, scarcely felt it. But *plarit's* the only thing I know can cut to the bone like that. . . . Except that there was just mud underneath, not frozen stiff, I'd likely have stepped it clear through before I noticed it. How—"

"Hush up." Poli made a pad of Liret's sweater and pressed it firmly against the sole. "That'll take stitching to close."

"*Plarit*," repeated Dan fretfully. "Damn all Teks, leaving their junk scattered all across the lowlands. . . ."

Mallie reappeared carefully carrying a knife, point-down and at arm's length. Briefly wondering what persuasion Mallie could have used, Poli accepted the knife. Mallie waited, mutely pleading to be told some other way to help, but just then the Lisler returned with the linen and Poli was occupied cutting a sheet into narrow strips while the Lisler held the fabric taut for her.

When she had a temporary pad of toweling tied in place,

Poli rocked back on her heels, sorting what was necessary and what was possible. Before the wound could be properly bandaged it had to be stitched, and before that it had to be packed with arrowleaf salve or powdered healall to stop the bleeding and bond the depths of the cut together. But she thought it hardly likely the herbalist would be calmly tending his shop while all sorts of profitable injuries were going on out in Han Halla, not to mention a chance at the reward for himself.

A pot of burn unguent that Arabet kept by the stove was the best the household had to offer. For anything more serious, the herbalist or a bone-setter was sent for. Poli decided the most likely source of what she'd need would be the Inner Households: as a conscientious troopleader, Arlanna would be sure to keep a supply of wound salves, freshly made up, always at hand. And Arlanna would have the anesthetic dallis-root paste, used to coat the points of dagger-darts, as well, which nobody but a Valde knew the trick of making. Poli would need that too, as she did the stitching.

She'd have to go herself. There was nobody else she could have sent on that particular errand, even if there'd been anybody to send. Surely the Lisler wouldn't do. Nor was Sparrowhawk fit to watch the children. They disliked each other too much.

Jannus would have to see to that.

Beckoning the Lisler to her, Poli showed him how to keep an even pressure on the pad and told him not to remove it even if the blood soaked through. He should add another pad and then change *that* if he needed to. "Mallie, you see that nobody frets at Dan or the Lisler. Sua, you see that nobody gets into Dan's things here. You three, you sit on that crate and keep still. Yes. Liret, you let Alis clean your face. Your da will come and fetch you in just a while." To Dan, she said, "Don't fret. Stay still and I'll be back as quick as I can."

She found Jannus's coat by the head of the staircase and spotted two of his sweaters in heaps against the molding farther down the long corridor, marks of how thoroughly disgusted he'd been at Rayneth's ill-timed summons. It occurred to her then how long he'd been gone—almost two hours, she guessed, with mild surprise. It must indeed have been urgent, to have kept him so long. That, or trouble. . . .

As she should have expected, Rayneth's two personal guards would not admit her to Rayneth's quarters. But they wouldn't even pass word inside that she was there. Poli wasn't used to being naysaid, and, in a complex involuntary process not unlike finding one's balance in the instant of falling, she estimated the configuration of each man's position, reach, and alertness, knowing just what moves she'd have to make to get past them. The two chairs figured as weapons. The sequence rested, ready, in her bones, scarcely noticed except as a general sense of confidence and calm.

"Jannus," she said, just loud enough to penetrate the door to the room beyond.

He opened the door within two breaths, comprehending the obstructing guards with a quick glance and moving aside to let her pass, each motion economical and controlled. His manner surprised her, considering how tired he'd been. It wasn't even a morning face. It was one she saw seldom: only when she called him from some task that had utterly absorbed his attention and he turned that same humming intense alertness to whatever he found around him.

"Dan's stepped on *plarit*," she told him, noting indifferently Rayneth's displeasure at the interruption and the fact that Ashai Rey's alver was perched on a chair. The size and the wing bars were distinctive. Probably another Tek. There'd been birdforms on the High Plain, she recalled.

"You'll be going to Arlann'," Jannus responded, grasping that conclusion as if by the same unthought process with which she knew the opening sequences of a fight before anyone had stirred. "What should I do—watch Dan, or our five?"

"The five. The Lisler can watch Dan. Get the five away from the machinery or they'll be into everything—"

As he reached out for the edge of the door, turning with her, Rayneth protested, "But we haven't decided—"

"You've set a watch around Circle and Crescent both," he replied, "and I don't see—"

Poli didn't wait to hear the end of that but strode back down the corridor. Catching up his coat at the top of the stairs, she swung it behind her, poking to find a sleeve, as she jogged down to the entry hall. The coat was still wet, but so was hers. Her latch-boots weren't really fit for the street either but she didn't want to delay to change them.

She found the streets all but deserted in the last light, scraped by a chill breeze that set her shivering until her haste warmed her. Turning presently onto High Street, in sight of the Crescent gate, she inspoke her need in clear sequences to alert the troopmaids who'd be on watch there. They'd relay to Arlanna; with luck, Poli wouldn't have to go any farther than the gate and she could save an hour or so that way. Seeing one of the sentries stand clear of the gate pillars, Poli waved, hurrying again to come within breathtalk distance.

The first two steps Jannus took with as much care and self-doubt as if he were descending a ladder backwards. Each foot settled on the stair matting, heel first. Ankle and knee locked. He knew because he checked.

At the fourth step it seemed safe to let go of the bannister. The feet managed without supervision. The lamp-thrown shadows of the ceiling flickered and shifted.

The last eight steps he took in two long easy strides, landing light, grinning. Slinging the sweaters over his shoulder, he gave the tall slope of the staircase a happy, measuring look. He could have walked down the bannister.

He could have juggled coals or stepped off a roof and taken no hurt at all. It was a very strange feeling.

He'd expected the Fathori wine to cancel or at least moderate the effects of the brandy, but it'd done nothing of the sort. Like oil and water compatably layering, each influence had proceeded independently. The body was almost anesthetized, communicating little beyond sensations of floating and ease. Within, unhindered by distractions, the freed mind found a separate balance and spun, gathering momentum— an utter concentration without need of focus or object.

Except for the intensity, this was nothing like duel-trance—Poli's name for what he'd done to the little *in'marenniath*. That had been all heat and hurting intention. This was cool and effortless. It looked outward. Even looking in, being aware of the state itself, was looking out. There didn't seem, somehow, to *be* any in.

He wondered if being a Tek was like this; Teks who put on or discarded bodies at will—or had done so, until the bases had been starved of the power broadcast from Downbase and had become sterile nests hatching no more bodies for Tek redes to animate. But if Teks were like this, he wondered why he'd never seen one laugh. Even Bronh, by far the sanest Tek he'd encountered, seemed to take no joy in wings. Perhaps it was that, after centuries, Teks took this state as much for granted as the seeing, sight. But somehow Jannus found that difficult to believe.

He found the workroom dark and funereally chill. Bumping into a snuffling child, he swung her up onto his shoulders so she could light a splint from the flame of one of the hall lamps. It was Mallie, he discovered, and trusted her to hold the burning splint while he returned to the workroom, located a lamp near the toadlike bulk of the press, and bared the wick. She touched the lamp alight neatly enough, asking, "Should I blow it out now?"

"For now. Till we get the fire laid."

Sua demanded, "Can I light the fire? Mallie lit the lamp." She stretched toward the smoking splint Mallie held high.

"Mind the table, Sua." Jannus steadied the rocking lamp and eased Sua away while he looked past piles and boxes to locate Dan. "Teks left you a surprise, Poli said."

To Sparrowhawk Dan said something Jannus didn't catch, apparently asking for water, because the Lisler left the foot of the cot to fill a glass. Lighting a fire seemed at the moment more constructive than making conversation, so Jannus busied himself about that. He tried to get the other three children to help but all they wanted to do was huddle close and hold onto him with small cold hands. So he draped his sweaters around them, tying the sleeves together, and let the three snuggle against his side while Sua relayed fuel bricks to Mallie, still perched on his shoulders, who put one into his hand whenever he raised it. To avoid argument he relit the splint himself but let Sua carry it back to the hearth.

He asked Mallie if she wanted to come down now but she declined by wrapping her arms around his forehead and laying her cheek against his hair. "Mind the doorway, then," he advised, and steered the sweater-bound three ahead of him into the entrance hall, Sua hanging onto his wrist.

He noticed that the doors to the Evenhall, opposite the outer door, were still shut and the corridors were empty of the usual comings and goings from the kitchen, suggesting that this evening's daymeal was to be an improvised affair. He'd fetch something, he thought, after he got the children settled.

For him to manage all five children alone was generally like trying to herd fish. But their long, odd, parentless day, and then finding an adult injured and strange, had depressed and likely frightened them. They wanted the reassurance of being close and noticed, and seemed glad to be going back to the familiarity of the northwing rooms. They dashed inside the instant he had the door open. Then Sua's voice cried indignantly, "It's *our* fire! You leave it alone!"

A strange boy straightened beside the hearth, dusting his hands lightly, saying, "Mistress Poli gave leave for me to wait here."

"Wait for what?" Jannus slowly lifted and swung Mallie around to stand on her own feet.

"I'd like to talk to you," said the boy composedly. The downriver accent was slight; Jannus noted it automatically.

The front room wasn't nearly as dark as the workroom, what with the windows and the firelight. But the stranger had his back to both, so Jannus could see little more than an outline, except for the distinctive fair hair too yellow for a Valde's. But even the outline, the self-assured way the boy stood—without fidgeting or awkwardness—was noted and interpreted. The thought came, *audience manners*, while Jannus lifted shade and chimney from the fat ceramic lamp on the table. He was just screwing up the wick when the boy materialized at his elbow proffering a flaming splint.

Well trained, the thought came, adding idly, *ring marks on the fingers, but no rings*, as the light flickered and steadied against the wall. *Sold? Hidden?*

It'd been in his mind to go around to the kitchen to find out what directions Rayneth had given about the daymeal. But there was no rush about that. It could wait a while.

Disentangling Alis, Liret, and Ami from the damp sweaters, he sent them to fetch the blue quilt out of his and Poli's room. Mallie was sent for a washcloth, wet but squeezed, and Sua went to find the comb. Meanwhile Jannus took two of the high-backed chairs and put them, backs facing, between the table and the fireplace. Over these he draped the quilt the three hauled in, making a tented space, covered and enclosed, into which the three immediately wriggled like cats discovering an open drawer. He smiled slightly to himself: there was a satisfaction in guessing right. From a crock on a high shelf he added to their refuge a large handful of toffee wrapped in twists of waxed paper. The toffee, he laid like bait just outside the quilt overhang and, after a moment, saw a grimy fist snatch and withdraw. So that was all right too.

He let Sua dive into the quilt cave once she'd surrendered the comb, but kept Mallie. He settled in the armchair by the left corner of the hearth and drew Mallie into reach between his knees. Methodically he cleaned her hands of firebrick dust, her face of sticky smears. "Jam tarts?" he asked her softly, but she was shy in the stranger's presence and wouldn't answer. As he ran the comb through her thick, straight hair, finding no tangles of any consequence, he could feel her weight rest more heavily against his leg as the familiar routine stroked her into calm. He smoothed the hair back from her brow and said, "Alis."

"I'm clean!" objected a voice, piercingly treble, from the cave.

"*Fealis*. . . ." Their full, proper names, seldom used, had a special weight. Alis peeked out under a fold, met his eyes, and resignedly elbowed out. But Mallie didn't go under. Collecting a toffee as her due, Mallie curled up on the rug between the armchair and the hearth and leaned against his leg, patiently unwrapping her prize.

The boy had remained near the table, waiting like an experienced page, watching without intrusion. Jannus had been aware of him every minute.

Having sufficiently established that the children and his own routine had precedence, Jannus held a bit of Alis's hair to tease out a snarl without pulling her and remarked, "You're not local."

"No." Thus invited, the boy took a hearth stool from near the firebrick cabinet and sat down at the other corner of the hearth, where lamp and firelight gave Jannus a good view of his face and showed how awkwardly he'd cut off his waterman's braid; the long hair at the crown kept trying to hang across his eyes from the center parting. "I'm from Blackrock Isle," the boy volunteered, and from under the quilt came Sua's unmistakable uncomfortable giggle the same instant as Alis flinched and Mallie looked up.

"Hold still, or it'll pull," Jannus told Alis calmly, working at the snarl. He'd learned two things: that the boy was lying, and that he was not *sa'farioh*, immune to Truthtell, as Teks were. Teks and one other. He was an ordinary human boy. "That's one of Duke Ashai's five, isn't it?"

"The Master of Andras is regent there, yes," confirmed the boy, lacing his fingers together between his knees. "I'm one of Duke Ashai's folk."

Interestingly enough, that brought no reaction from the children. Jannus nodded, giving Alis a nudge, and said, "Sua." Best to have her under his hands, in sight, rather than making those prompt noises while two more flinched from the undertone of conscious falsehood. Jannus wished Mallie would decide to join the others in the cave but wasn't disposed to make her move. She'd been the most upset about Dan's being hurt and Jannus thought she ought to stay any place she found comfort.

Locating a fresh place on the washcloth, he started on Sua, the daughter he and Poli each thought of as most like the other. "What does Duke Ashai want with me, then?"

"Me, probably," responded the boy, with a tense, tentative smile. "I've run off. Can you keep me here?"

"Why should I do that?"

"Because I have nowhere else to go," replied Ashai Rey's son simply.

Again, no reaction from Sua. Mallie only leaned around the chair and rolled over to stretch for a second toffee. Jannus's hands paused while he revolved and weighed the boy's statement.

"The Lady Rayneth is beholden to the Master of Andras," he said finally, "and I hold her marker. She'd not permit any of her household to stand between Duke Ashai and what's his."

"Rayneth doesn't matter," asserted the boy confidently.

"Easy to see you never worked for day wages," Jannus commented mildly. "In the Crescent, in this household, Rayneth matters. As long as I'm contracted to her and carry her marker, Rayneth matters."

"She didn't matter before," replied the boy boldly, then challenged, "Buy *my* bond for a copper."

Sua jerked and made a pained noise, but that was because Jannus had dug her with the comb. Her hair was densely curly and fine, like Poli's: he had to go slowly and take care.

Patting the hurt place absently, Jannus remarked, "So you heard about that."

"It's why I came. I never had a place to run to before, so I never ran. But you crossed him, and he let you. Nobody has ever done that before."

Sua's quiet said the boy believed it; but Jannus thought the statement preposterous. "Domal Ai's crossed him, and the other baymasters, time and again."

"And he's paid each back, ten times over. Sent for Secolo, his chief of security, and set the revenge going, all in the same hour. But not you. When he heard about the casks, he laughed." The boy turned toward the fire, and his sharp-boned face became at that moment very like that of his father. He continued, "He put me in charge of those letter cubes, you see, after the contract was found. He always has all contracts and business papers collected and analyzed when a town's taken, to see what volume of trade has been common there. . . . And he happened to see that contract, because it specified delivery to Quickmoor. Everything involving any of the other isles, or Quickmoor, or Lisle, he always wants to see himself. And he told me to see the contract was fulfilled if I had to roast . . . if I had to watch old Potter every minute for a tenday. I had to report to him every evening on exactly what had been done, and he kept the area free of fighting and looting. So I knew it was important. He saw the cubes were packed properly, and sealed them with his own seal, and saw them stowed aboard *Windfoam* himself. . . . And then you threw them away." The boy was silent a moment, as if reliving the enormity of that announcement. "And when he was told, he laughed. He has different laughs. Most aren't pleasant. But that was . . . was just a *laugh*, as if it were the funniest thing he'd heard in a year. And he told Secolo not to bother about it because it wasn't worth the trouble. And even Secolo Ai was surprised and asked him again what should be done about it. Then he called Secolo a dullard and deaf, to boot, and wondered if he should put somebody in Secolo's place who could *listen*, and Secolo got out as quick as I've ever seen a man go who wasn't running."

Clearly, the boy had enjoyed seeing Secolo thus discomfited.

For Jannus, too, the anecdote had its memorable points.

Not until Sua began to fidget did he recall the task at hand. He finished with her quickly and released her to dive back into the quilt cavern. He didn't at once summon Liret, but instead sat back and put one hand lightly on the top of Mallie's head as she half dozed against his leg. She roused and he stretched both legs out before him more comfortably, crossing one ankle over the other. Then Mallie leaned back again.

"It seems strange," Jannus remarked, "that Duke Ashai would speak so to this Secolo while you were there."

Pedross's face was fair enough for the flush to show plainly in his cheek and neck. "Nobody notices me."

"You're good at waiting. I saw that right away."

"I practice," commented the boy, without inflection.

"Look here, now." When the boy turned, Jannus said gently, "I can't keep you. You're not a keg of letter slugs or a Lisler in disgrace at home. Rayneth's desperate to find you— if you're not found within a tenday, the duke will take the Crescent from her. If she knew you were here now, she'd have me flogged, or worse. And I couldn't protect myself from that, much less you. I expect you know she's had the whole Crescent out looking for you in Han Halla."

With a wan mischief, the boy responded, "*I* helped look for me. I ate sausages and heard all the news."

"Then you know what you've set going. There're some that went out today who won't be back. My friend Dan Innsmith cut his foot—I don't know how bad it is yet, but he's hurt. And then there's Rayneth. It's not fair she should lose everything because some boy she's never seen took a notion to run away. . . ."

"I can't help that!" burst out Pedross unhappily. "I didn't mean anybody to be hurt."

Mallie's head stirred under Jannus's fingertips, but he decided not to pursue the matter. "Just the same, you're the cause. You're too sharp for my hands. I couldn't hold you. You'd have done better to run to one of the other baymasters—"

"And be a hostage? Alive as long as I'm useful, then put out of the way? Or, more likely, handed back to my—my lord duke to buy some favor?" Flushed again, the boy challenged, "Is that what you'll do?"

"You were right this far: I don't want Ashai's favors," re-

joined Jannus steadily. "If I had to give you away to protect
me or mine, I'd do it. But there's no need. . . . From where
I sit, I'd think the best thing would be to let yourself be
found."

"And go back? To what Duke Ashai would do to me for
defying him?"

"He's too fond of you to do you any real hurt. Besides, I
don't see that you have a whole lot of choice."

"I *can't*. You don't understand. I . . . killed a man," said
Pedross tensely, watching Jannus's face to read his reaction.
"Getting away."

Jannus turned toward the fire. "By mischance, or on purpose?"

"On purpose. He'd killed my mother."

"Then that's—"

The boy broke in, "I killed Duke Ashai."

Mallie shifted, making a sleepy, inquiring sound.

Jannus and the boy both looked at her involuntarily, then
caught each other looking.

"I don't care what your Truthsayer hears," the boy asserted
wildly, "I *did* kill him. I stabbed him out on the foredeck
during the third night watch and tumbled him down into the
sea when the tidestorm was making. Just like my mother told
me she'd done. *But he didn't stay dead for her.* And he won't
stay dead for *me*. He's not a man. I don't know what he is."
The frantic look fading, Pedross's face showed a settled, bewildered misery. "He uses a stick. That's because he smashed
his right leg in a fall and couldn't reach a bone-setter for
weeks. I've seen men who remember it. Lislers. He swam
Erth-rimmon to Lisle with a smashed leg. Only it isn't. I've
seen him bathing, and it's as whole and sound as the left. In
his private quarters he lays aside the stick and moves as
freely as any man. But when he goes out, he takes the stick.
And he limps, just a bit, because everybody knows smashed
legs don't heal without *stiffness*, without a mark. . . ."

Pedross drew air hissing through his teeth. "She told me
she'd killed him, she was laughing and crying so I was afraid,
afraid somebody would hear. She wasn't supposed to see me
any more, but she came in and told me how she'd killed him
and we'd be all right now, we'd go away. . . . And the next
morning there he was, just the same, the cut throat gone the

same way as his smashed leg. She just . . . she just folded into herself and went with him, and I never saw her again. I was twelve." The boy's haunted look changed into something angry, defiant. "And what does your pack of half-blooded Truthsayers say to *that*?"

Roused by the sharper tone, Mallie stiffened, blinking anxiously up at Jannus. He patted her shoulder, settling her back against his leg, telling her with touch there was nothing she need fear.

"You're not surprised," the boy realized, accused.

"I'm tired. I spent all day hunting you through Han Halla," Jannus evaded, and changed the subject. "There's a blind street singer called Ella who can find a place for you, for a day or two. She's dependable but I wouldn't have much to do with the boy she keeps by her, were I you. The Crescent folk don't know who they're looking for, but Rayneth does. The Crescent won't be safe for you. You're too conspicuous. And Bronh's here."

Pedross shot him a narrow, surprised glance full of wariness. "The valkyr?"

"Is that what they're called in the isles? Alvers, they call them, up here."

More cautious yet—absurdly so, considering what he'd been saying about Ashai Rey—the boy asked, "How do you know the valkyr's name?"

"She told me. Which is more than you did, Pedross Ashaison." The boy didn't dispute the name; that game was finished. "Bronh has changed bodies a few times," Jannus mentioned, an oblique suggestion but as far as he was willing to go.

"That's different. Bronh's a Tek. *He's* not. *He's* something else. But Bronh won't tell me," the boy added dispiritedly. Then he had a hopeful thought. "But if Bronh talks to you too—"

"It's past time I fetched something to eat. You can stay the night, anyhow—whatever harm's to do has been done."

"Do *you* know—?" the boy persisted, the fair face open as a child's.

"I don't even know what manner of man *my* father may be," evaded Jannus roughly. He pushed himself up from the chair slowly enough to give Mallie time to shift her support.

He lifted a fold of the quilt and tossed the washcloth inside.
"Liret, Ami, wash your faces or I'll be in trouble when your
mam sees you." Their giggles contradicted him.

Poli dumped her bundle of ointments on the long table and
let the coat slide to the floor. There was a place laid for her
flanked by two covered dishes, but the rest of the daymeal
had been cleared away. She'd lost all track of the time.

Jannus brought a pitcher from the hearth, where it'd been
put to stay warm, and poured the mug at her place full of
fragrant spiced ale. Poli drank half of it still standing, leaning
on a chair back. He'd put the children to bed, she saw, but
the boy was still there, perched on a stool near the fire. Poli
wished him gone. She was too tired to deal with strangers.

"Dan?" Jannus prompted.

Poli dragged a chair out and investigated the covered
dishes. One held kidneys-and-something in a stiffening brown
gravy; the other was apple crumb and raisins. And there was
a heel of a loaf wrapped in a cloth, the leftovers of yesterday's baking. Poli pulled off a fist-sized piece of bread and
drew the kidney dish closer as she slid into the chair.

"I didn't need the dart paste after all, to do the stitching,"
she answered him, chewing between phrases. "He never
stirred. The cut's packed and stitched and bandaged. He'll
make the blood back in a day or two." She held out the mug
for refilling. "But the bad time will be in a fiveday or so
—when he wants to get up and won't be told he can't. He
mustn't set weight on that foot for a tenday. A halfmonth
would be better. But how to make him do it is beyond
me. . . ."

"What'll happen if he walks on it?"

"At the best? Split the flesh from the stitches, start it
bleeding again. At the worst, keep the muscles and cords in
the foot from joining right and lame himself for life. You recall Mene, who's troopleader now to Overwater."

Mene, who'd shared Newstock troopservice with Poli, had
been lamed that way. Jannus said he remembered. He rested
a hip crookedly on the table edge, balancing the pitcher on
his knee.

"You know the one everybody's been looking for in Han
Halla?" His look directed her glance to the boy by the
hearth.

Poli jerked her eyes back to her dish. "What's Reyneth about?" she muttered angrily. "*He* was never lost." She recalled, confirmed, his indifference to fire and food. And Jannus, who had yet to change clothes, was by far the more grimy: the boy's ill-trimmed hair shone like new brass. Still low-voiced, she demanded, "Was he ever in Han Halla at all?"

"Pedross? How did you manage in Han Halla, all alone?"

Addressed, the boy quit pretending he wasn't there. "I have Tekcloth underclothes, that hold body warmth, and waterproof leggings. It wasn't too bad."

Poli asked him, "How could you go, unguided?"

The boy looked uncomfortable, reluctant. "I have a way of knowing my directions."

"How?"

"Your pardon, Mistress Poli, but I'd rather not say. Even Bronh doesn't know I have it," the boy added, with a glance at Jannus.

"There's more to it," Jannus put in quietly. "Pedross is Ashai's son. The alver's a Tek, hunting him."

Poli set down her dish with a thump. "And he came hunting *you*. What sheep's nest *is* this?"

"Dan's letter slugs again. He thought I could shield him from Ashai."

"Well, you can't," she responded, reinforcing it with a stern glance. "You cross the *sa'farioh* in any matter that touches the Rule of One and you're dead." She was all but quoting him, a fact he acknowledged with a hand lifted and dropped. "You took some trouble to tell Ashai to keep out of your affairs."

Again he admitted her point. "And I ought to keep out of his."

"Is there a choice?"

"No," he responded, slower than she would have liked. He wandered across to the armchair by the fire and stretched out there, setting the pitcher on the slates. "But he can stay the night, at least. . . ."

"No." She twisted around to face him. "Not even one night. A cat can't kitten without somebody mentioning it to Rayneth an hour later. This is still a Bremneri household. You should know better."

"But everything's upside down here now," he argued, appealed, as if it would be safer if they both were foolish together.

Poli scraped the dish with the last crust of bread. The boy, she noticed, was keeping still, letting Jannus argue for him—which Jannus seemed willing enough to do. Poli didn't like it. He'd talk himself into something yet, if he wasn't careful. She said, "If you found a snake in the bedcovers you'd want to make room for it. Or that alver."

"Bronh. Well, yes. . . . But what's the harm—"

She set both elbows on the table and folded her hands. "Are you going to take him out the door? Jacko knows he never came in that way. Or back out through the yard, the way he came? In the broad daylight, he's going to scramble off the Circle hill, plain as a hen on a tabletop?"

"I'll take him out in a hamper. I can row him across to the Is side and at least leave him clear. A man can walk the west shore of Erth-rimmon, and nobody will expect—"

"You're not afraid," Poli interrupted, the realization and the words coming together.

"No. . . ." And then again, "No," the second time mildly surprised and thoughtful. "And I should be," he agreed with her.

He considered himself a cautious man, Poli knew, but he wasn't. On impulse, quite heedless of consequence, he could do the most preposterous things—hide a Screamer, or set himself to cross Han Halla unguided, or pursue a Valde freemaid going to her Summerfair briding. In certain moods he could walk blithely off a roof; and this suddenness in him Poli distrusted profoundly.

But this once, she felt, she'd stopped him short of the edge, made him look over and doubt himself. And, believing himself a cautious man, he retreated with reluctant good sense.

"The body's asleep, just the head awake," he muttered, then turned back toward her soberly. "You call it, then."

"I say he goes now."

Discreet, quiet, the boy Pedross had been following the argument, only his eyes shifting from one to the other. He said abruptly, "I don't understand. Why can you insult the duke in public, and know Bronh, who won't talk even in Secolo's presence, and be told who *I* am, when the duke doesn't even dare risk admitting I'm missing for fear some other baymaster will catch me for a hostage, and yet. . . ."

"You mean, how come I can call down lightning but can't light a splint for fear of burning my fingers?" supplied Jannus, with a wistful self-mockery. "It doesn't make any sense. That's just the way it is."

"But why are you the exception?"

"That's just the way it is," Jannus repeated, and smiled vaguely at the fire. "I'm the king of Kantmorie." When the boy just stared, Jannus looked around at him again. "I really am. I stood on the Sun Circle and called the Rule of One down on myself, to end the bases and the deathlessness. I'm master of all the sand on the whole High Plain and all the dead bases. I hold the Rule of One, just as long as I don't try to *use* it. Ashai Rey, who serves the Rule of One, is answerable to me. Sure he is. Just as long as I don't *ask* him anything, anything that matters. Because his answer would be the thin side of a knife. King of Kantmorie. . . . For that and a tenpiece you can hire a drawcart to go three blocks in any direction you choose."

Recovering from incredulous astonishment, Poli snapped, "The head's asleep too, and I wish the mouth was! What's possessed you, to tell *him* such a thing?"

"Who else is there to tell?" he rejoined, with that same restrained bitterness. "Who else would care?"

"But what—" the boy began earnestly, but Poli shoved back her chair and hauled the boy off his stool, declaring, "*Now* I said, and *now* I meant. You get out of here!"

She dragged him to the garden doors and shoved him outside, turning the latch and slapping the bolt home for good measure. For a moment she could see the pale blur of his face through the frost on the pane. Then he turned and there was only dark.

Jannus hadn't moved from the armchair. Poli settled on the hearth slates, right in his line of vision; he accepted the change and contemplated her without altering expression.

She said, "Now go tell Rayneth what you've done. And that alver."

"Why?"

"It seems to be all you've left undone. You might as well smash the thing properly while you're about it." She couldn't remember the last time she'd been so furious at him.

"Ah, Poli. . . . I want to help him, and I don't dare. I don't dare even try. I want to help Rayneth, and the Longlanders, and even *Ashai,* may his leg rot off. . . . And I don't dare even to lift my hand. I'm a plain Bremneri stock-born scribe and I can't even use the leverage of *that* for fear the ice will break if I take a step. And then you tell me I'm not afraid *enough.* Maybe you can tell me how to live like that. Because I swear *I* don't know. . . ."

This near him, Poli realized what his casual steadiness had kept her from even suspecting. "You're drunk."

"Not so much as I was. Mostly tired, now." He rubbed his eyes slowly with the back of one hand. "Ashai had no business raising a human child. He's even worse at it than I am."

Poli's anger was disrupted by a powerful complicated sadness that twisted and wrenched at her. One strand pulled inward—the sharp awareness of how separate he was from her, in spite of all love and outreaching; how she was shut among the cold outsides of things, until even his surface could deceive her, until he seemed as remote and inert as furniture. In her mind she repeated his complaint against the intolerable, *Maybe you can tell me how to live like that.* For if he could *not.* . . .

And another strand, compassion and a piercing protective fondness, pulled outward, knowing that particular piece of furniture very well indeed. She thought of herself and Jannus as two adjacent stones on a riverbed, rubbing and adjusting until at last there would be no lump that did not meet a hollow, nothing that did not fit. If not water into water, as Valde marriages were made with the blending of the *marenniath,* then stone upon stone, and acceptance of the slow, sometimes hurtful process of the mutual wearing away.

The two strands' pressure came to a balance and she ceased to be aware of them. She asked softly, "Were they awful, the five?"

"No, I used them for Truthsayers, as a matter of fact. But Pedross caught us at it. . . . Mallie's very upset about Dan, though. It scared her, I'd guess. She was hanging on worse than Sua, afraid I'd go off and be hurt too, or some such."

Poli laced both hands around his left arm above the elbow. With utter gentleness she said, "Don't get hurt."

For answer he leaned forward and kissed her on the brow and then, less lightly, on the mouth. In the quiet room, with no sound but the tiny periodic tinkling of the coals cooling at the outer edges of the heap, they put aside what separateness they could for a little while before falling into sleep as into deep water.

Since strategy dictated that a line of retreat be chosen before going into an engagement, Pedross found his way across the garden to the hollow where he'd hidden his pack without scarcely a wasted step. The moon was well up, but this was the sixth day of waxing week; the thin right-handed curve gave scarcely enough light to see by.

The air within the contained space was still. A sound like a soft blanket shaken alerted him instantly. He pulled his sling strap from under his belt and charged the sling's pad with a ceramic ball warm from his pocket, three more balls and a knife, blade up, ready in his left hand. He could have changed hands easily—naturally left-handed, he was ambidextrous with all weapons because it confused an opponent and because the choice hand or arm might always be injured.

When he wasn't immediately attacked he slid his left wrist carefully through his pack's carry loop, otherwise motionless, crouched low against the screen of brush. But his face and hair would be visible, he realized, at quite a distance even in this light. No use crouching, then. He'd been seen.

"Good even', Bronh," he said, making no special effort to speak softly. Except for the northwing, there were no ground-level windows on the inner sides of the walls.

"He wouldn't keep you," remarked the valkyr's raspy voice from about the middle of the garden: the cotton willow beside the pool. Automatically Pedross calculated distance and angle. "I could have told you that."

"He says he's master of the High Plain; could he make you claim you hadn't found me?"

"Nobody can make me do anything," said Bronh.

"Not even unlame Ashai?" Pedross returned, jeering.

"Not even he. There's always an alternative."

That was what she always said; and the last alternative was always death. She couldn't be compelled; Pedross envied her that. And nobody could be used as a hostage against her.

Pedross knew that now. Once he'd thought Bronh was his friend. Now he knew better.

It was, momentarily, a standoff. He couldn't move without Bronh following, but Bronh couldn't call help without giving him time to disappear. Han Halla wasn't more than five minutes' run away, around the curve of the dike. And even Bronh's eyes couldn't penetrate the mists to find him there.

Pedross considered his options, meanwhile saying, "And how *is* my father?"

They'd had no conversation at their last meeting, down-river: Bronh never talked in front of anybody but him and Ashai—and Rayneth and Jannus, it now seemed. . . . Bronh had just drifted in, level with the top mast, in a balanced open-winged curve that brought her near enough to identify him. Distance had made him imprudent enough to suppose that after nine days' steady travel he was safe from immediate pursuit. And attack on Ashai should have bought him at least a little time. Besides, he'd been planning it, yearning toward it, for so long it'd have been all but impossible for him to have left without that blow struck. And it'd been good tactics, he assured himself: demoralize leadership, block communications, at least temporarily.

He said, "I trust he's *quite* recovered?"

He'd all but severed the head before toppling the corpse over the rail. He wanted to be absolutely certain, without possibility of mistake.

"He is unchanged."

"I'll bet he is. Bronh, he's been *dead!*"

"No. Not for the smallest part of an instant. He never should have taken you into the war. You're too young—"

"I've been imagining things, then. Like my mother," said Pedross harshly, trying to discern the bird's outline against the crosshatch of bare willow whips. By careful listening he'd harrowed the target to a small space.

"She's an unsophisticated and fanciful woman, Pedross—you know that. She's even terrified of me, claims I'm some sort of a spirit of the 'Old Ones' crawled up out of a grave. And I'm just a plain Tek. Away from Downbase, I'm as mortal as you."

That was a good long speech, focusing the target area even further. Pedross spun the sling quickly and loosed. By the sound, the ball had hit only wood—drilled in or glanced off, he couldn't tell which. He'd already recharged the sling, and sent the next ball a bit to the right, covering the target square as quickly as he could throw.

Again there was the soft blanket-sound of the huge wings cupping air. He'd at least drive Bronh aloft. Pedross dragged the cloak's hood up to cover his betraying hair and shield his face, as long as he kept his head down. He eased almost soundlessly into the continuous thicket.

The brush stretched unbroken up the dike to the wall he'd scaled, coming in. Either Bronh would wait there, watching for him to climb the wall where she could catch him with one hand, at least, occupied and perhaps even make him fall . . . or else she'd go for help at once, to cut him off. The wall was the one barrier between him and Han Halla.

Breathing in soft, controlled exhalations as he moved uphill, Pedross tried to listen for the beat of the valkyr's wings; but, except for the thrust or rising or the last strike of descent, her flight was soundless. Unable to determine which alternative she'd chosen, Pedross saw his only chance was to make for the wall as quickly as he could.

He was a bit surprised to see the line of his rope hanging where he'd left it. It seemed that Bronh hadn't detected him until he'd come out, or she'd have taken the rope to delay his retreat. Sheathing the knife, he tugged hard on the rope twice, then, satisfied, began climbing as he heard movement in the brush farther down the hill.

She'd gone to give warning, then: but the men behind were stumbling among the bushes and would never reach him before he—

The rope parted. He fell about his own height and, in spite of himself, tumbled backward and slid on the icy slope. Suddenly much more urgent, Pedross rolled to all fours and scanned the blank cement face of the wall—without footholds or handholds, with no trees of any size anywhere near it. Nor could he run and jump, the way he'd done on the other side: that had been downhill.

For an instant he thought of circling back down to the pale light of the windows but the thought that the whole place might now have been roused against him made him discard the idea. He began moving quickly along the wall toward its south corner, the one nearest Han Halla.

He had one advantage, that the men would be under orders not to kill him, but to catch him. They'd have to get their hands on him and, in turn, come within his reach. His close-combat training would be likely to surprise them. He smiled tightly, shifting his bundle to his right hand to leave his left free. Most people were right-handed, and that would give him the advantage. With the corner at his back. . . .

But he couldn't afford delay. Rayneth would have put men into the street, too, to try to intercept him on the other side of the wall. He ran, keeping his head low because Bronh would be back any moment, spotting for the pursuit.

He stumbled over a fallen limb, caught his balance, and took two more strides before whirling back. The limb was almost too heavy for him to budge, but he managed to heave the narrower end high enough to pivot it parallel to the wall, scraping through the intervening bushes. Long enough, he thought, and thick enough, maybe—a good fork about halfway up. . . .

He hunted a rock to brace the butt end against, kicking the ground, groping. With the ground frozen, it was hard to tell stone from dirt. He heard a man's voice and thought they'd probably seen the rope. They wouldn't be immediately certain he hadn't already gone over: a grown man could have jumped and reached the rope above the cut, and they'd be slow to allow for his size. Being misjudged he'd often found to be an advantage.

But he could have wished himself larger to handle the limb. He dragged the butt end to the niche he'd located, then lifted the smaller end and got underneath it, his feet braced crookedly, working his way toward the crotch, the limb gradually lifting toward the vertical. When he had it nearly straight up, and before it started to wobble, he gave it a shove toward the wall. The top of the limb scraped down, broke, and scraped again, coming to rest at a steep angle about halfway up the wall. It seemed solidly wedged. It would have to do. The men would be coming toward the noise, and coming fast.

Jamming his arm as far as it would go through his bundle's carry-strap, he scrambled up the leaning limb. At the fork he balanced, one foot where the wood was broadest, the other stretched as far up the thicker branch as he could step.

Bronh dove at him then, catching him across one shoulder

with the stiffened edge of a wing. But he wasn't taken by surprise—tactically he was at his most vulnerable, and Bronh's advantage greatest, so she *would* attack then—and grasped the smaller branch a moment to steady himself. Then he threw his weight forward on the bent leg and, using the instant's purchase before his foot began to slip, sprang upward. He got both elbows over the edge of the wall. With a sideways hitch, he was lying flat on the top.

He rested a moment to recover from the strain of hauling the limb. Bronh was no longer much of a threat. Unless he was off balance, or couldn't use his hands, the valkyr wouldn't close with him. He rotated the shoulder she'd struck: it felt as if he'd been solidly caned. But the valkyr's hollow bones were more fragile than his: probably she'd taken more damage from the blow than he had. It might slow her down.

The far side of the wall was still short of the crown of the dike. The remaining slope looked dry and hard, clumped with bunches of dead grass. Cautiously, Pedross raised to a crouch to look along the outer side of the wall. He saw no motion. He was tempted to go along the top of the wall, like a cat on a fence, but didn't dare risk Bronh's sweeping into him. Poising his bundle, he tossed it as high on the hill as he could, then went belly-down on the wall and swung his legs around. For a moment he hung by one hand, just time enough to kick clear of the wall, and dropped cleanly.

Scooping up his bundle, he trudged up the rest of the hill and discovered a path, almost luminous in the moonlight, that wandered away among the tufted mounds of grass. Then he went faster, a controlled jog that didn't risk tripping. He passed by the south corner of the wall and left it behind without any sign of pursuit. Jannus had said the household was upside down; perhaps Rayneth hadn't been able to rouse a full pursuit at that hour. Anyway, he thought he was well beyond them now. He could swing into Han Halla and spend another damp, chilly night—Tekcloth, for all its lightness, wasn't *that* comfortable—and calculate what his next move should be.

Bronh's voice, disembodied but near, called, "Get off the dike!"

He glanced up involuntarily, but he couldn't see the valkyr. He saw something else. Four Valde were paralleling him on the inside curve of the rim, outlined against the sky. They were outpacing him, their course slanting gradually uphill toward the path.

Pedross was confused and alarmed. Rayneth wasn't a proper Lady, couldn't command troopmaids, and yet there they were. Had Rayneth made an alliance . . . ? He got a ball out of his pocket and charged the sling without breaking stride. Then, stopping suddenly, he whirled the sling and loosed at the head of the leading Valde. She cried out and fell. He fished out another ball and had the sling spinning when something sharp hit him in the left side. Reaching down, his fingers touched the stiffness of feathers. Some kind of a small arrow or dart. He hadn't thought they'd risk hurting him. He checked that the ball was still in the fold and began whirling the sling, standing side-on to present the smallest target. The sling cord slipped from his fingers, sling and ball arcing away together. He heard, felt, a rushing in the air all around him and collapsed into unconsciousness as the first of the Valde reached him.

Pedross was prepared to resist inquisition or even torture, if need be, but not the ordeal to which he was subjected early the following morning.

He was wakened, heavy-headed and disoriented, and marched through a seemingly endless succession of passages, staircases short and long, open and enclosed, and across the cold floors of large halls with painted walls, where the feet of his escort of troopmaids seemed loud. The place to which he was brought was noisy with people sitting on rows and rows of wooden benches, busily chatting, arguing, and exchanging food from hampers they held on their knees. None took any notice of him. Almost all were women, wearing large boxy headdresses over starched caps. The few bared heads belonged to smooth-cheeked adolescent boys whose unsmiling rigidity of expression contrasted sharply with the informal gregariousness of the women. He saw no children and no men—not even one.

He'd heard of the Bremneri practice of bedding the half-grown sons of their contemporaries but hadn't much thought about it before. Clearly, the boys found little to be delighted about in the arrangement.

The Valde found room for him on a bench near the right-hand wall and then just left him there. The high headdresses all around him cut off his view of the raised dais he'd fleetingly noticed at the far end of the hall. The one woman he ventured to address turned on him with such a ferocious scowl that he stared at his feet and pretended he hadn't spoken. Miserable and bewildered, he spent one hour, and then another, feeling less like a prisoner than a piece of forgotten baggage. He occupied himself with contemplating the elongated flat-breasted females sculpted in three-quarter relief in a line along the wall, speculating in detail on what this hall would look like in flames or invaded by fivescore axemen.

Suddenly at the end of his aisle there was a Valde who pointed at him. He followed her and was directed to a cumbersome stone seat all alone in the middle of an open space before the dais, empty except for a hinged wooden screen. A boy about his own age, standing on the first step to demonstrate his superiority, began bombarding him with questions: first, demanding his name and his place of origin, then asking him about his relations with Lisle and whether, by a complex formula, he'd ever contemplated harm to Quickmoor or its Lady. Suspecting his answers to those would be unlikely to please Bremneri, Pedross tried to interject questions of his own. Strategy dictated he capture the initiative. The boy ignored the interruptions, merely reciting the questions again in a bored sing-song tone.

Then for no discernible reason the boy walked off to be replaced by a Valde—whether one of his escort or another, Pedross couldn't tell, since they all looked alike. The Valde asked him the exact same questions, right from the beginning. She, too, ignored his demands to know why he'd been attacked, why he was being held. In frustration, Pedross refused to say anything at all. Thereupon the boy returned wearing a glove and carrying a skinny twig with a few withered leaves at the end. With this ludicrous weapon he lightly touched Pedross's right hand. And while Pedross was wondering what *that* was about, another Valde joined the first on the dais and the questions began all over again.

As the first Valde asked his name, Pedross noticed a stinging where the twig had touched him. Slowly a welt appeared and his eyes began to smart. When the Valde had repeated the same question three times, the boy touched him again with the twig, on the same spot. This time, the touch was like

being struck with a rod of fire. Pedross recoiled, snatching his
hand against his chest. The pain expanded from hand,
through elbow, to shoulder.

Pedross was almost relieved: pain he knew how to deal
with. After his immediate shock, he laid the arm back on the
chair's arm and managed to ignore it after a fashion.

The system became clearer. If Pedross offered an answer,
any answer at all, the boy did nothing. If he refused to speak
after three repetitions, the twig descended on the sensitized
skin, each time more painful than the last. Pedross's eyes and
nose began to flow, so that he had to use his sleeve to clean
himself, humiliated to think they might believe him to be
weeping. The answers he gave were random and sometimes
insulting, but he answered.

And then the questions changed. Why was Rayneth anxious to find him? How had he injured Ashai Rey? Who in the
household had turned him out, and why? What was the alver's importance?

Specific question followed specific question, spiraling in
with incredible accuracy no matter what sort of response he
made. When he didn't answer, the twig spread fire up his
arm.

Even Rayneth could not have supplied the information that
supported these questions. Slowly it came to Pedross that he
himself was supplying it, that he was being probed and sorted
beyond the level of speech. When the boy took the twig
away, Pedross understood that it was no longer needed, that
his speech or his silence had become equally informative.

He thought of covering his ears to block the questions but
discarded the thought. That would only make them tie his
hands down to the chair, making his helplessness more apparent and leaving him weeping and beslobbered like an in-
fant. He'd rather remain free.

There was more than one way to stop listening. His head
hammered and, about every fourth breath, he sneezed. His
right arm was swelling and felt as though it were submerged
in scalding water. Pounding aches discovered to him joints he
hadn't known he owned. He heard questions about Lisle,
about Longlands, about the relationship between Ashai and
Rayneth, about his mother. Or, more accurately, he heard
those words embedded in the surrounding noise. The interrogation made progressively less sense. It faded into the

oblivious chatter from the benches behind, continuing undiminished. He *made* it fade—though that wasn't hard. He'd been sick once, when he was about five, but he didn't remember it very well; *this* felt more like the aftermath of a very thorough beating.

His memories of *that* were a lot fresher.

A beating, followed by a horrendous hangover, he amended, as though he cared. He wondered if he were dying, as if it mattered.

Eventually they either found out all they cared to or else he so thoroughly ceased attending that they decided continuing would be unprofitable. Troopmaids got him up flights of stairs—gently or ungently, he was past noticing—hanging onto him not because they feared his escaping but because his eyes were swollen almost shut and he stumbled from step to step, head hanging. They pushed him against some horizontal surface and he fell back on it. But he discovered he couldn't breathe at all on his back so he pushed up on one elbow, coughing and choking.

Somebody was peeling back his layers of sleeve—the woolen one, and the silvery Tekcloth one he wore next to the skin. Sensations of wet and stickiness came faintly through the scalded, swollen skin. His arms braced on either side to keep him upright, he continued to concentrate on sipping air in the intervals between prolonged bouts of coughing. Presently he was aware that the room was empty again.

Quite a long time passed before his breathing eased at all; but once the coughing spells stopped, improvement was rapid. Squinting at his arm, he found that, under a layer of drying salve, the redness was already gone and the swelling less. As he felt steadier, he worked his way across the long narrow room to the window, halfway expecting to find it barred, but there was only a simple latch. He found himself looking out, level with the top of the dike, into a sky featureless with rain. But he watched the motion of the clouds for a while and guessed the window faced southwest.

No bars were needed. Sticking his head outside, he saw tile roofs far below and counted six levels of windowsills between his window and the place where the nearest roof connected to the tower wall. Above him, there were two more levels; the watchposts would be up there, overlooking the dike into the country beyond.

The freezing rain felt good on his face.

The city had a terrible defensive position. No walls except the one wall that was the dike, protection against water and nothing else; too long, too broad, to be held long, and then providing an ideal mount for enemy catapults hurling stones or firebombs. Archers on the height could shoot down into the city and need no more protection than shields from any return fire, which would be weakened, shooting uphill and blind. Buildings were as interconnected as a rabbit warren, so if one was taken or set afire, all were in jeopardy. Quickmoor: built after the Rebellion in naive confidence that there were no enemies but the one enemy, the Teks, who'd retreated behind their force-field Barrier to sulk, unintentionally locking themselves in, on the High Plain, as well as shutting the lowlanders out. Or so Bronh had told him once.

The door opened, shouldered aside by a young serving maid balancing a large tray which she carefully lowered to a tabletop. "You're better," she remarked. "I was worried. I never saw anybody react to fireweed like that." Busily she took a pitcher and a washbowl from a cabinet, then set about laying the table for a solitary meal.

Pedross was surprised to discover he was hungry. He washed up, the back of the right hand still slightly tender.

As he was eating, the servant suddenly whirled to shut the window, exclaiming at the cold, as if she'd restrained herself as long as she could. Pedross had scarcely noticed, protected by the Tekcloth.

"By whose order am I kept here: Rayneth's, or the Lady's?" he asked, and got a hard look in reply.

"You don't ask questions here," she said stiffly.

"I meant no offense—I only want to know."

"Then put it decently."

"How?" he responded, in honest bewilderment, and by her expression realized he'd done it again.

"Say 'It is wondered,' " she directed, going to stand by the brazier and trying to rub the chill out of her forearms.

"It is wondered," he repeated dutifully and then had to think how to phrase what followed. "It is wondered whether Rayneth commands in this, or the Lady."

"The woman Rayneth commands nothing within the Circle of Quickmoor."

Pedross broke off a piece of bread and chewed on it, meditating. Of course, a serving maid didn't know all that passed, but she was his only current source of information. "Will I—" he began, then corrected it to, "It is wondered when I will be brought before the Lady."

The servant looked around curiously. "You've just *been* before the Lady. Didn't you know?"

Questions, plainly, were permitted her. That let him know that in a Bremneri household, he ranked below the kitchen help. But there was no sneer in the girl's voice, only surprise, so he judged her innocent of intent to give offense.

"No. I didn't see her."

"Of course not!" she rejoined, with a laugh. "She was behind the Stranger Screen."

Pedross shook his head slightly, marveling at inlanders' queer customs. He'd had little to do with Bremneri, although of course his studies under Secolo had included them. "It is wondered what sort of person the Lady is."

"Ketrinne?" The girl appeared to consider, her head, with its weight of headdress, tilted to one side.

She was not, Pedross was now recovered enough to notice, an ill-looking girl—rather the reverse. Large, bold, dark eyes under a broad forehead, mouth generous without being overwide, dark definite brows that were quick to lift or frown with each shift of mood. The arms were nicely round, the figure under the loose overdress unguessable but at least not gross or, judging by the arms, too skinny either. She was taller than he, and somewhat older, but that should be no barrier, Bremneri tastes being what they were. He speculated on possible advantages in bedding her.

"To look at, you mean?" the girl went on. "She's a great Lady, tall and solid as a pillar of the Audience Hall, with a nose like a hawk's, so fierce you scarcely notice the warts at all, or that she lost four teeth, poor thing, in a fall, though it does make her whistle a bit when she talks. Her eyes are very fearsome too—I'd hate to have her notice *me*—though of course they're not as sharp as when she was younger, and she does tend to doze off during audiences. I expect that's why she didn't notice sooner how badly you were taking the fireweed. You must have thought she meant to kill you. Do you hate her very badly for how you've been treated?"

That query was just a bit too ingenuous to be entirely in-

nocent. And certainly Pedross didn't intend to outline any of
the possible revenges he'd been cobbling together, awaiting a
suitable opportunity. So he answered her roundabout, saying,
"If it's true the woman Rayneth has no say here, then the
Lady Ketrinne may be my best friend in all the world, and I
hers, if she's willing to take the risk."

"What risk?"

"My father, the duke, will know soon where I am and will
want to have me returned to him. But I came to Quickmoor
hoping to find someone to shelter me from him. Perhaps it
was Ketrinne I was seeking and didn't know it. Perhaps
Ketrinne could be persuaded to see advantage in keeping me
rather than just handing me over for the privilege of being
spared by the terrible Master of Andras. . . ." He glanced
up at her alertly, wondering if she had access to the Lady, or
was the sort to spread useful gossip. "It's a pity she's so old,"
he added absently.

"Why?"

"Well, for one thing, she'll want to think and argue and
talk to a score of counselors before doing anything, and by
that time it will be too late."

"For what?"

"To try to put this city in anything approaching a defensi-
ble condition, to begin with. I've seen better built places
taken in half a day, in the Longlands."

"You mean she should look to her walls, if she means to
keep a young alver like you caged?"

"I wouldn't be an alver," rejoined Pedross, with sudden
harshness. "I wouldn't fly away, even if I could. I want good
strong walls between me and the Master of Andras."

Again, the girl considered. "If he waits too long, the river
will be frozen. And then, you could be here until thaw, before there was any danger." Her tone suggested she found the
prospect not without its attractions.

"But if he comes, the siege of the Longlands will collapse.
He—"

The girl had glanced sharply aside, through the open door.
"I'm late," she announced hurriedly and began snatching
crockery onto the tray, looked down at it a moment, and
started empty-handed toward the doorway. "A page will
come for this. Tell him whatever you wish to make you more
comfortable. . . ."

The last words reached him from the corridor. An arm in an orange-yellow sleeve reached past the opening to catch the edge of the door and swing it quietly, firmly, closed.

As the story reached Jannus that morning, the lost boy, Pedross Ashaison—Jacko, the doorkeeper, named him so without hesitation—had been found. The folk of the Inner Households had found him, cheating all the rightful searchers of the reward. He'd just wandered over the dike in the middle of the night and the troopmaids had grabbed him. The Lady Ketrinne was keeping him to spite the Lady Rayneth, who wasn't going to stand for it.

The Lady Rayneth, Jacko announced with satisfaction, was going to fight.

The guardsmen were out already, with orders to collect at least ten walking bodies apiece, with a promised bonus for every proven fighter thus enlisted. The Lady Rayneth and Goren, her guardsmaster, had been nose to nose since sunappear, planning.

"For a fact," responded Jannus blankly, finding the sole good news in this recital the fact that his name wasn't in it.

He'd been on his way to see how Dan was. He continued toward the workroom for much the same reason a stone resumes an interrupted journey downhill. What the search for the lost boy had metamorphosed into, a full-scale armed confrontation between Crescent and Circle, was quite beyond his reckoning. Once inside the workroom door, he just stood, trying to sort it out and understand what he should do.

"You got that stick?" demanded Dan's voice from the far side of the press.

"What?" responded Jannus, rousing.

"Who's that?"

"Dan, you utter fool. Don't you know you've got no business being up?"

"It's business I'm up for," rejoined the Innsmith—his idea of a joke. "You seen the Sparrow?" Dan appeared around a stack of paper bales, balanced on his good leg and a crutch. "An't even a smudge on it," he announced, waggling his bare toes to display the spotless bandage.

"No, I haven't seen him."

"By rights, I need a pair of these. I sent the Sparrow out to buy me the wherewith to make a proper pair: this began life as a broom. But that was a good hour ago, first light." Dan leaned against the press to rub an arm across his sweat-shiny forehead.

"Then a 'dent gang's got him."

"*What* 'dent gang, tell me?"

"Rayneth's. She's raising about six, seven hundred people to attack the Inner Households. That's three-to-one odds, against the Quickmoor troop. It's going to be a shambles," observed Jannus morosely.

"*Why*, in the turning world—? No, don't tell me. I got to set down."

Jannus went to him then, stooping a little so Dan could get an arm around his shoulders. "Can you make it across to northwing?"

"In a minute. Just let me set here a minute," Dan requested, easing his weight onto a low stack of paper. "An't so dizzy I can't listen. . . ." he hinted, after a moment.

"Well. . . ." Jannus tried to think how to begin. "You recall Pedross, Duke Ashai's son?"

Dan grunted affirmatively, adding, "*Heard* of him."

"He was the one Rayneth was hunting in Han Halla, under threat of losing Ashai's patronage. Now Ketrinne's got him, and Rayneth's going to try to get him back. It'll be a shambles. The tale is he's a prisoner, but I don't believe that. He's running from Ashai, and Ketrinne's given him a place to stand, to spite Rayneth and Ashai together. That's how I read it. Circle against Crescent, and Pedross in the middle, like snatch-the-sack."

Dan raised his head, a glint in his eye. "Pedross. You sure?" When Jannus nodded, Dan commented, "Then he an't the only one in the middle. Solvig's having fits, about now."

"Solvig? Why?"

"Because he's sworn to Pedross," explained Dan, with the serenity of savored mischief. "He's been Ashai's factor, making no distinction. But the fact is, he handfasted himself to Pedross, for the form of the thing, rather than serve Ashai himself. . . ."

"I know. Ashai approached Elda first—"

"—and my da would have none of him. But Solvig took Ashai's ring on the form that it was Pedross he'd be serving and not Ashai. Now he'll be in a forked stick, if Pedross has split with his da. If he sides with Pedross, Ashai will have his

skin. But that's what he's sworn to. And if he sides with
Ashai, he's oath-broke, and Pedross will be Master of Andras
someday and well able to manage his own revenges. How
old's the boy now, you know?"

"Fifteen, sixteen—Sparrow's age or thereabout."

"Too old for a runaway, too young for a rebel—just
barely. Or maybe not. Civil war in Andras? But then why
would he run north?"

"Well," said Jannus uncomfortably, awkwardly, "the fact
is, he ran to me, actually. He thought I could protect him
from Ashai. On account of the business about the letter slugs
and all. . . . Poli put him out. I expect that's when the
troopmaids got him, while he was trying to get back into Han
Halla. . . . I *know* it's preposterous," Jannus burst out,
feeling heat in his cheeks, "but it's true all the same."

"Well now," said Dan mildly, setting his hands on his
knees, "ain't that a thing. Rayneth know this?"

Jannus just shook his head.

Dan studied the floor, perhaps savoring the fact he'd finally
been trusted, relied upon, the way he'd always wanted.
Presently he glanced up, remarking, "So what is he, then: a
runaway, or a rebel? Has he sworn feud with his da, or—
What?"

Jannus had kicked a leg of the press explosively. "The
hair! I looked right at him and never thought. Yes, blast all
blind fools, he's sworn feud, all right. Hacked off his braid,
the way Andrans do, and sworn feud against Ashai. Blast!
And all I had the sense to see was that he was trying to hide
the fact he was a waterman."

"So it ain't Rayneth we got to worry about so much as it is
Ashai," commented Dan succinctly. "He'll be down on
Quickmoor like a landslide if Pedross ain't returned to him."

"Just leave the Longlands war to take care of itself while
he surrounds Quickmoor, that he could put in his pocket and
not feel the bulge?"

"The Spur's a place. This is *family*," Dan instructed him
primly.

"Ashai's no Innsmith. Who knows how he weighs such
things?"

"What use is the Longlands, or anything, to Ashai, without
anybody to have it after him? Son or no, Pedross is his heir.
He'll come. I'll give you odds."

"I don't know. Anyhow, Pedross is more than the sack in the middle, then. If he's sworn feud, he'll make alliance with Ketrinne, and she's—I don't know, ambitious, maybe—enough to pledge herself to it, hoping to force Rayneth out."

"And he's got Uncle Solvig and his Family to call on, besides."

"Maybe—if he knows. Or if Solvig tells him. What a mess. What's to be done?"

"Like anything else—duck, run, or fight. Can't duck and the 'dent gangs won't let us run. So we fight. You got a side you like?" inquired Dan quizzically.

"No! I've been trying so long *not* to take sides, and now *this*—!"

"Ain't no justice. Come on, I can manage a bit more, now."

With Jannus supporting him on the right and the crutch on his left, Dan made his way slowly across the entry hall and into the front room of the northwing apartment. Jannus helped him into the armchair near the fresh fire and, with Poli's help, kept the children from leaping all over Dan while Jannus propped the Innsmith's injured foot on a cushion on the bench.

"I've got to talk to Rayneth," decided Jannus abruptly. "There's got to be some way around this thing—"

"What thing?" asked Poli, trying to pry Mallie away from Dan's knee, which the child was hugging with determination, refusing to be budged.

"It's about Pedross. I've told Dan—the bones of it, anyhow—but it's come all unraveled since last night. And it's going to get worse. Dan, you tell her."

When he reached the second floor, the position of the two invisible bodyguards, about halfway down the hall on the left, told him Rayneth was using her office to confer with her guardsmaster.

"Tell Rayneth—" Remembering his manners, Jannus changed that. "Tell the Lady I'd like to talk to her. It's important."

The men exchanged glances. The nearer one said, "She wants you, she'll send."

"Tell her I'm here. I have news she ought to know," Jannus improvised, without the least notion what the news might be.

The nearer bodyguard—a noted no-rules wrestler, Jannus had once been told—hitched one shoulder indifferently and went into the anteroom, the only way in since the office's outside door was always kept locked. Faintly but unmistakably came Rayneth's raised voice berating the intruder, who reappeared an instant later, red-faced. Jannus took himself out of reach, but retreated only as far as his room full of corkboards, where he lit a lamp and poked about aimlessly for about a quarter of an hour, trying to concoct some pretext Rayneth would heed. The two youngsters, Alan and Sann, who generally helped him, were absent—filling somebody's quota of walking bodies, no doubt. If he wasn't careful, he'd be doing the same, and Poli too. Being the ruler of the abandoned High Plain wouldn't even exempt him from conscription in a petty internal city feud.

In frustration he took up a pen, trimmed it, and wrote on a blank word citation slip:

> *The Rule of One.* Tek origin, First Millennium or earlier. Refers to the belief that the ideal in governance is undivided and absolute power held by a single individual at a time. Practiced by Tek rulers from the earliest days of Empire until the Rebellion (3703-3862), when the High Plain was in chaos until 871 a.k. An incompetent Bremneri scribe, Jannus Lilliason, was then accepted to the kingship to provide nominal sanction for the termination of all functional bases but one and thereafter did nothing at all of note; after which the Rule of One passed to Pedross, the second Master of Andras, and became altogether meaningless. See also Empire of Kantmorie, Downbase, Andras, deathlessness, Tek.

He threw the pen across the room. Then he ripped up the slip.

Hearing men's voices arguing loudly down the corridor, he slid off his stool to investigate. It was Solvig Innsmith, standing hands on hips facing the locked office door and shouting, "—have this house down around your ankles by sunappear tomorrow, and don't think I can't! You get out here before I get to the stairs or I'll go home for a hammer!" He came down the corridor toward Jannus, round heavy jaw clamped grimly tight, looking straight ahead.

"What's wrong?" Jannus inquired and was granted a brief glance in passing.

"Those motherless guards walked in and took eight of my young folk from their breakfasts without so much as a by-your-court'sy—" Having reached the head of the stairs, Solvig paused ominously, then stepped down.

"Solvig—" called Rayneth, bursting into the hall, hanging onto the office door as if she'd just managed to get it unlocked and open. "Solvig, wait!"

Ponderously Solvig looked around, deciding whether to let himself be recalled.

"It was my orders," Rayneth said rapidly, "but you should have been told, it's just been so frantic—"

"Since when do you have the right to collect chunks of my family, woman?"

"It's for Ashai, as much your concern as mine, but you should have been told, I do apologize for that. Come in, you'll understand when I've told you—"

As Solvig glowered past, Jannus drifted in his wake as inconspicuously as he knew how and slid by when they stopped to argue just inside the doorway. Goren, the guardsmaster, was facing in the other direction and didn't see him at all.

Leaning against a cabinet full of ledgers, Jannus had a splendid view of Solvig's face as the Innsmith realized Pedross was involved in the matter. Except for two rapid blinks and a judicious expression, the Innsmith listened to Rayneth's tale of Pedross the captive—and, to be fair, Jannus admitted it was possible she believed it—without giving any sign more revealing than a quick glance at his right hand, which bore the seal ring of Duke Ashai Rey.

"This is all craziness," Jannus exclaimed suddenly, surprising Goren and annoying Rayneth and Solvig. "Rayneth, you claim the respect due a Lady of a Bremneri riverstock, and then you can't think of any better way—Listen!—any better way to settle a dispute than to throw a mob into it. In the Inner Households, they call you—"

"I know my name," Rayneth said, in a deadly voice.

"Solvig, you know the riverstocks," Jannus appealed to the Innsmith. "Did you ever see a thing settled by conscripting everybody in sight, like a rolling panic?"

"They duel," commented the Innsmith, delivering a judgment.

"Their Valde do," said Rayneth, like a curse. "Shall I send my troopmaids, Jannus? Or has Poli volunteered to be my First Dancer?"

The edge on her voice was dangerous. Before she could push that thought any further, Jannus said, "Cry challenge, and then negotiate terms, like any other lady of a riverstock. Don't you have any duelists that you'd back against a Valde, one to one? Goren, for instance?"

Goren's broad, lined face remained impassive. He merely waited for Rayneth to tell him to throw Jannus down the stairs, which no doubt he'd do competently and without excess motion. Jannus didn't like him either.

"She'd laugh," snapped Rayneth, betraying how the thought of such laughter stung her. As she'd said, she knew her name, the one Dan liked to call her by and likely others even cruder.

"With a chance to spend one troopmaid instead of many, would you laugh, if you were Ketrinne?" Jannus rejoined, with increasing confidence. "What's to be lost? Surprise? You think they don't know already the hive they've tipped over?"

"All right," said Rayneth slowly. "You go call challenge for me against the Lady Ketrinne."

Even though he'd half expected it, Jannus felt a chilly lurch of unease. "Don't you want somebody—"

"It's your idea. You're acceptable in the Inner Households, even if they don't give you any gardens." She showed a few teeth, throwing his remark back at him. "I'll give you until the seventh hour. And if she laughs . . . keep out of my sight, that's all."

"Lady, I do hear you."

As he descended to the lower level Jannus heard someone following. It was Solvig Innsmith, who said, "I'm coming. The Lady Ketrinne won't laugh at *me*. And I recall one other time you spoke for me and mine, in Sithstock. You were as much use as curtains in a henhouse."

"Please yourself," responded Jannus, turning toward northwing. "Come in by the fire while we get ready."

"*We*?" repeated Solvig, but Jannus made no answer.

Dan was playing spiderweb with Mallie, both hands laced with a complicated lattice of string which he was just in the

process of transferring to Mallie's tiny fingers when Jannus
and Solvig came in. Typically, Dan made sure the transfer
was complete before responding to his kinsman's surprised in-
quiries about what was the matter with him; and even as he
answered, his eyes followed Jannus, alert for news.

"Rayneth's consented to try a formal duel first," Jannus remarked, pausing by the table where Poli and three of the
girls were finishing porridge and honey. To Poli, he added, "I
get the treat of telling Ketrinne." She pushed back her chair,
as aware as he of how risky such an embassy might prove to
be. He advised, "We'd best dress fit for an audience."

"What I wear doesn't matter," she responded.

"Just the same." He wanted to feel at no disadvantage, at
least none that was avoidable.

His wardrobe these days was meager, compared to that at
his disposal as his mother's principal audience scribe; but he'd
always had an eye for good cut and style born, perhaps, from
the awareness of being looked at, inspected, which was his
heritage as a boy of the riverstocks.

He chose a collarless white shirt with sleeves slightly flared
at the wrists. It was summer-shear wool, a bit too thin for the
season, but he'd prefer to be chilly to looking like an upended goods-bale. A dark brown sleeveless vest was as close as
he could come to a tabard, and plain enough to pass for
formal. The trousers were dark, black and brown interwoven.
He was poking under the bed for his boots and not finding
them, when Poli told him Dan had thought Jannus might
need them and had scraped off all the dried mud and polished them. Jannus padded back into the front room, where
both Innsmiths were enmeshed in spiderweb lattice: Solvig
with the more competent Mallie, Dan being patient with
Sua's frustration at a botched transfer. No Innsmith could
keep his hands off a child even if it meant trading surly remarks over the children's heads. Jannus traded a nod of
thanks for Dan's self-congratulatory grin and collected the
boots, which probably hadn't been so well tended since they
were made. But that'd been in Ardun, a freeport under Andran control, where folk were less fanatically conscious of
their appearance than in Bremner.

When he and Poli had tended each other's hair—she'd
chosen a silver-gray tunic over dark green trousers, Newstock
colors, a subtle reminder that she'd been a troopmaid in her

time—Jannus took off the cord he always wore around his neck and, on impulse, opened the small pouch the cord supported and shook its contents into his palm.

It was a clear green jewel about the size of a small hen's egg, faceted all over. When he let it dangle from its fine-linked chain—an extravagance which had cost him several months' earnings: a cord would have done as well—the stone sparkled and flashed. He'd never worn it openly before, for a number of prudent reasons. But he slipped the thin chain back over his head, the stone resting in the middle of his chest.

Catching Poli's dubious glance, he said, "It's mine. I can wear it this once without the sky collapsing." Poli turned away, reaching for her cape, disinclined to argue.

The jewel had no value to anybody but him. He suspected its material was crystal or some Tek glass whose structure could be coded. But to him it was precious, and only in part because of its total uniqueness; into its substance were impressed the essential identity patterns, the redes, of all the Teks alive at the hour of its making. Bronh would be here, and Lur, and all the mad remnant of the Empire of Kantmorie imprisoned, latent, in this single jewel; and it was a matter of absolute indifference to anyone but himself whether he kept it or smashed it or tossed it into Erth-rimmon. The redes would never be recalled or given flesh again. The bases were lifeless, all save Downbase itself. But the jewel remained, and he treasured it.

This once he would wear it, the tangible heritage of Kantmorie to which he was more truly heir than Pedross, though the boy be flesh of the flesh, bone with bone, with the first Teks ever to step down onto the High Plain.

Besides, it looked impressive.

When, carrying their overcloaks, he and Poli returned to the front room, Dan was inspecting another token: Ashai's seal ring. Dan handed it back to his uncle with a quizzical expression; Solvig rubbed it on his shirt and replaced it on his thumb, his mouth set grimly. Jannus supposed they'd been talking about Pedross.

"*You* look fit for a Fisher funeral," commented Dan cheerfully, hitching back in his chair.

"You ready?" inquired Solvig, his earlier impatience visibly diminished. "I got a drawcart waiting. It's raining."

The three of them crowded, knee to knee, in the leather-covered box of the drawcart, the Innsmith facing backward as their host. The two carters lifted the shafts off the props and started with the usual rough jerk that settled to a smooth trotting pace as the cart gained momentum. After one brief glance Jannus dropped the window flap, and Poli did the same on her side, so that they rode in near darkness as well as silence.

There was only a brief delay at the top of High Street, while the gate wardens determined whether they were to be admitted; but on a normal day, there would have been no delay at all. Traffic normally passed through the gate, unquestioned by the troopmaids, during daylight hours.

The carters delivered them before the broad stairs of what must have been the right building because Arlanna was waiting for them under the protection of a broad portico. Jannus noticed that Solvig stepped down to the road and started up toward the troopleader without sparing the dripping carters a glance, nor did they seem to expect immediate payment. Jannus's own experience was otherwise.

Seeing him smiling to himself, Poli looked inquiringly but he only shook his head and followed Solvig.

Jannus had expected to be shown to the audience hall but instead Arlanna conducted them to a good-sized parlor full of plants—the first time Jannus could recall seeing things growing indoors, except for mildew—which gave the chamber more the feel of an arbor than of a room. Some shrubs nearest the windows were even in pale gold flower, as was a vermillion trumpet vine hanging above them.

Jannus thought that, on the whole, he preferred Han Halla kept outdoors, where it at least could be ignored some of the time.

Handing their damp outerwear to a servant, who put down a tray of wine and glasses to receive the garments, they found chairs not too obscured, one from the rest, by assorted fronds and stems, and made themselves comfortable. There were plants painted on the walls too, in stylized curves and curlicues parallel to ceiling and floor, and outlining the doors.

Through the farther of these doors Ketrinne came hurrying, her feet noisy in wooden-soled clogs, dressed improbably in the same sort of coarse woven tan smock, covered by a bib-front starched apron, as was worn by the girl serving the wine. A lock of black hair had escaped the band of her cap behind; Ketrinne poked it back into place nonchalantly, taking the wineglass offered her and clacking across the tile floor to stand as near the fireplace as she could without singeing herself.

Jannus had risen as soon as he recognized her, then Solvig more slowly and only because Jannus had.

"How is Dan Innsmith today?" Ketrinne inquired of Poli, sociably including Solvig in the conversation by adding, "Your son?"

"Mother's sister's son's son," Solvig corrected, unsure if it was permissible to sit down again, deciding to do so anyhow.

Jannus remained standing. Like Pedross, he knew how to wait. Moreover, he guessed that whether or not it pleased Ketrinne to be unconventional, she'd not tolerate anyone else being so, especially if it slighted her dignity.

Poli was saying, "Better this morning. We are obliged to you for the salves."

"If I'd known what would be boiling in the Crescent today, I might have been less generous. We may need them ourselves." In spite of the cutting edge on the remark, Ketrinne seemed in a thorough good humor, excited and animated. Her dark eyes flashed as she turned to face Jannus, saying, "Is it Rayneth you've come to speak for, or yourself?"

"Both," Jannus replied, mindful of Arlanna, quiet beside the far door, behind a small thicket of leaves like large spread hands. "I want this settled with the least hurt to everyone." He paused to give her time to weigh that, sift the undertones for the jarring copper taste of deception. Then he continued, "Lady, the Lady Rayneth calls duel against you for the possession of the boy Pedross."

She almost laughed. Though surely forewarned by Arlanna, Ketrinne found the declaration freshly preposterous, it seemed, in the moment of intention's becoming act. She busied herself having a chair fetched and put exactly at the angle she wanted it, and seated herself, arranging the unfamiliarly voluminous smock and apron neatly across her knees. Then she was able to face him again with decent soberness. "Rayneth has no Valde," she pointed out.

"Nevertheless she has duelists, who will fight Valde soon enough if you won't accept the challenge."

"Fairly said," Ketrinne observed, judicious.

Solvig put in, "Pedross. He's here?" and Ketrinne reacted with instant displeasure at the overbold phrasing.

"It is wondered," substituted Jannus, with heavy politeness, "whether the boy Pedross is a prisoner or a guest."

"A bit of both." Ketrinne sipped wine, composed again. "He is not disposed to leave, in any case. Nor will he, as long as Rayneth is in the Crescent. You may tell your Andran duke that, Factor Innsmith."

"I would like to speak to him," said Solvig.

"No," replied Ketrinne, very definite.

Solvig sighed, removing the seal ring from his thumb and placing it on the table at his side. "Give him this for me, then, and say that I and mine are at his disposal."

Ketrinne leaned forward to pick up the ring, turning it until she saw the engraved sun symbol on its signet stone. "What's this mean?"

"I'd be obliged if you would just tell him what I said," replied Solvig, folding his big hands before him.

"I do hear you. I will do as you ask." Ketrinne bounced the ring twice in her palm speculatively, then tucked it in a pocket. "Arlanna Wir, what says Lora to a duel without trance, without time for preparation and against a stranger, and *sa'marenniath*, besides?"

Since Jannus had last seen her, Ketrinne took her troopmaids less for granted as if freshly aware that nothing bound them to her but their own consent, that she possessed nothing they either needed or wanted. Toward her troopleader, Ketrinne's manner had become almost deferential. And when Arlanna indicated she'd prefer to speak to her Lady aside, Ketrinne rose and went with her toward the window without hesitation.

That wouldn't last long, Jannus judged. Ketrinne was not one to endure charity gladly, or know herself at the mercy of that same charity she had no power to enforce—not for very long, if there was any alternative. But as long as there was none, he felt she schooled herself well; and only a Valde would truly know how thin that deference might be, or what lay under it.

As Ketrinne returned from the window, her clogs made almost no sound, as though she were controlling each step with inordinate care. She stood a moment with her hands laid on the back of the chair she'd been using. Abruptly she said, "I am given a condition not of my choosing which must be met before I may accept challenge. Lora, First Dancer, will have choice of her opponent." Against Solvig's immediate contemptuous snort, probably visualizing Lora selecting a palsied crone, Ketrinne raised a hand indicating she was not through. "Lora chooses you." Expressionless, Ketrinne looked straight at Jannus.

Poli's face and pose became very still, which meant she was very angry indeed.

"You know why," added Ketrinne, still addressing Jannus, her tone as quiet and careful as her steps on the tiled floor.

And Jannus expected he did know. If Lora had to fight somebody all alone, some deaf stranger, she'd have the most satisfaction in cutting to pieces the one who'd hurt the little *in'marenniath* during that memorable audience. Too, he wasn't altogether a stranger.

"With what weapons?" Jannus inquired steadily, directly.

Arlanna, approaching, said, "You may have choice of weapons, being the less experienced one."

Discarding all edged weapons, what was left? Jannus looked over at Poli, requesting her advice. But Poli ignored him, demanding, "Will Lora Wir fight *me?*"

The troopleader responded, "It would be too difficult for her to fight another Valde, without the rapport of dueltrance. She will have her choice or nothing. It is her right. She did not come into Bremner to duel Bremneri."

"Neither did the troopmaids at Lisle," Poli snapped in return. "Lora should be less particular, considering the other choice—three troops' worth of Crescent folk coming over the dike."

The troopleader merely repeated, "It is her right."

"For myself," observed Ketrinne, "I would tell the woman Rayneth come and be damned to her, with her mismatched herd of potboys, carters, and trulls. Except that the Quickmoor troop is only three years into its service, and I'd have to wait seven more years to get another. I must be sparing of those I have. I will surely have need of them. Yet I mislike such a pairing—mislike it nearly as much as you, Mistress Poli. Riverstock man against troopmaid; it has bad echoes that could last as long as Lisle's, whatever the outcome of this one duel. But what am I to do: call the minor

households out into the streets? The ladies would never tolerate it, when there is all but a full troop here to stand between
them and the mob. I have few choices."

Jannus has been cataloguing weapons, having decided he
was willing to risk a broken bone or two for Sparrowhawk,
and Solvig's conscripted kin, and even Rayneth. For the
troopmaids, too, who'd inevitably be hurt in an assault that
could well turn as ugly as the memory of Lisle, of which
Ketrinne, too, was so sharply mindful.

"Belly busters," he said, deliberately choosing the gutter
term. "A pinned fall to win. Two hours after nightfall—
where? The edge of Han Halla, beyond the east side of the
Circle," he decided. There, where the bonfire had been, and
the roped booths, the footing should be solid enough.

"And will Rayneth be bound by the result?" asked
Ketrinne.

"If she agrees to it at all, she will. Her word's good. But
we all know I'm not what she had in mind for her champion
in arms: if she won't take me for her duelist, you'll know
soon enough," Jannus commented dryly. "But we'd best get
back, or she'll start without us."

Following their Valde guides through the maze of passages,
Poli remarked, "I knew a few things about stick fighting
once. I think there's time to teach you enough to keep you
from getting your head broken."

"That's a kindly thought."

Walking behind them, Solvig said, "Think I got a couple of
nice sticks you could use for practice, that'd make good
steady crutches for Dan when you were through with them.
If it suits you, we'll go to my place first and fetch them."

Like himself, Jannus observed, Solvig had too many con-
flicting loyalties and could tangle himself in contradictions
trying to reconcile them. Solvig shouldn't be trying to help
him, but hadn't fully realized it yet. Jannus accepted Solvig's
suggestion as another kindly thought although he knew that
once Pedross was in a position to make his wants and prior-
ities known, the Innsmith could become Jannus's enemy.
Doubtless Solvig would regret it a good deal, and take pains
to see to the welfare of Poli and the five afterward, but were
he directed to see that Jannus stopped complicating the situation, he'd do it. Beyond a general friendliness and an inordinate respect for contracts, his given word, and his kin, Solvig

Torvesson Innsmith hadn't a great many scruples: one reason he and Elda, Dan's father, had split the Clan between them and parted company some years ago.

That was why, Jannus thought with a passing sadness, he himself was fond of so many people and trusted so few.

They descended the long slope of steps toward the waiting drawcart.

"You know," Jannus remarked to nobody in particular, "I'd like to push her through just a small tree. Lora, the First Dancer. I really would," he said, mounting the step of the drawcart behind Poli, and laughed.

"You've always been a Lisler at heart," she rejoined, untroubled. "That's why you collected the Sparrow."

"And that could be true, too. Maybe he's my brother. Who's to say otherwise? Not the Lady Lillia—if she'd pacted with a lad who'd grown up to be Grayhawk of Lisle, she'd surely not admit it. But then again, she wouldn't know what might have become of him after his Naming, my father. That's likelier. Likely enough she'd not know him now if she saw him."

"Keep your mouth off your mother, lad," advised Solvig firmly, the cart tilting as he climbed in. "Ain't never any profit in that once you're weaned."

Jannus made no comment, bracing for the initial jerk, then settled back, his mind still on Newstock. It seemed to him that it was to Newstock he must turn for weapons rather than the High Plain, as he had done before. Absently he reached inside his cloak and tucked the redstone through the slit of his shirtfront, where it rested, a cold lump, until his body heat finally warmed it. He was thinking about Newstock, and First Dancers, and duels, and the redstone was no part of that.

It was odd to imagine fighting a Valde. In spite of his flippant comment, he wasn't at all sure how he felt about it. Poli's loyalties, he suspected, were less confused: without any inner reservations at all, she'd spend the afternoon happily teaching him the best ways to crack a Valde's head and avoid being cracked in return.

Breaking the silence, Solvig wondered, "What was she dressed like that for, tell me?"

Poli replied caustically, "Making an impression on someone." She knew Bremneri.

"Not on me, that's sure," Solvig responded. "Looked like
we caught her on her way to milk goats. Skinny twig of a
lass. . . . Don't look old enough to be put in charge of raising bread, to me."

"Pedross, that you're under seal to, is about sixteen," Jannus reminded him pointedly.

Solvig wiped wet off his face with a slow, unhappy scrape
of his palm.

By the time the girl in serving costume came back, Pedross
had decided on his revenge. The troopmaid in the corridor
must have caught some of his intent because he heard soft
talk outside before the latch moved, and the troopmaid came
in first as though to protect the girl from attack. Pedross
spared them an uninterested glance, sitting calmly cross-
legged on the floor under the open window.

He said flatly, "You're the ugliest girl I've ever seen."

The girl checked, looking startled, furious, confused, in an
instant's sequence.

For he was lying.

He continued deliberately, "Your hospitality would shame
a pig. I presume you've been playing twiddle-fingers with
your Valde so long that you don't know how to behave
around a man."

That one succeeded in insulting them both. The troopmaid,
getting the fuller sense of it, shifted balance, leaning slightly
forward; the girl went bright red. As she whirled to leave,
Pedross told his third lie: "You're a serving maid."

She checked again and looked back; then she laughed out
loud and turned fully, amused and rueful. "Well countered,
Pedross."

"I thank you, Lady," replied Pedross moderately. "You
were right, I scarcely notice the warts at all."

"Enough, enough," said Ketrinne, waving all such returning ghosts away.

"And if you dozed off during any of my audience, I'll be
glad to repeat any part of it as many times as you like. Without compulsion."

Ketrinne bowed her head before that, gracefully with-
drawing from the contest. "Now, O honored guest, would you
consent to accompany me?"

"O Lady who graciously abases herself to serve her guests with her own hand, I delight to continue in your company."

That brought him a sideways glance, as she tried to sort irony from seriousness. He unfolded without using his hands and rose, all one motion. They went into the corridor together at a strolling pace.

The troopmaid remained behind—at Ketrinne's order, he had to assume, and took it as a tacit sign of their new relationship of hostess and guest.

They descended several levels by means of a spiral stair, then crossed a broad hall, went through several chambers or short, broad hallways—he couldn't tell which—into what were apparently Ketrinne's own quarters. It was less the nature of the furnishings that told him than Ketrinne's manner, once they'd entered—at once comfortable, kicking her feet free of the noisy clogs on her second step past the door, and shy, looking around for a chair to offer him as though the problem of seating a visitor were a new one and unforeseen.

He solved that problem by going on to lift a drape and look out the window to orient himself. After a moment his survey fixed on a break in the dike spanned by two tall pillars supporting shut iron gates. The gateway would be the outlet facing the riverside, he judged, with some sort of panels that could be slid into place in flood season to complete the circle.

Behind him, Ketrinne said, "Do you always prefer open windows?"

"It's the Tekcloth. I don't feel the cold."

"Then open these, if you wish. I can get something warmer."

"It doesn't matter," he responded, but she was already gone into a farther room. There was a brief flurry of maids and pages—collecting the clogs, tending the fire, arriving suddenly either from the corridor or one of the several adjoining rooms and giving him swift neutral glances before whisking off in another direction. When the room emptied, Pedross saw his bundle had been deposited on a side table. Inspecting it, he found it rolled a bit more neatly than he'd left it. Inside were his knife and sling, and his compass box, the one irreplaceable item. He carried the box to a windowsill and idly confirmed that the room looked westward, toward the river.

"What *is* that?" inquired Ketrinne as she returned, soft-footed. "Some Tek thing?"

"No, it's new. It finds north. See now. . . ." He'd looked up to find her busily brushing plait-crimps from a mantle of thick shining hair that fell to her waist, which was also visible since she'd changed from smock and apron to an embroidered pearl-gray robe that was far from shapeless. "See how the point moves?" he commented, a remark that suddenly seemed altogether idiotic except that it brought her beside him to see that the point did, indeed, move.

He left the compass box forgotten on the windowsill, himself turning to follow a different pole.

He was mildly surprised, and a good deal flattered when he came to think about it, to discover her a maid in truth. She made no great matter of the inevitable pain and accepted him with an enthusiasm that was more than sufficient substitute for technique. As they lay together in the ebb time, comfortably talking and petting, he said, "I'd have thought you'd have your choice of bedmates."

"I do. And I chose to have none." She rolled over on her stomach, clasping a pillow, and flung her hair aside so she could see him. "I came young to the rule of the Circle and at the first, I wanted no added challenges to my authority. And then, I grudged the time of making and bearing a babe, with so much to be done that needed my whole energy. Touch-loving, I have heard it reported, requires a great deal of energy," she added, mock-solemn, and kicked up one bare foot, then the other. "Is that true, O my guest?" she asked slyly.

"You are the Truthsayer, O my Lady," he rejoined.

"I would prefer to test such reports for myself. . . ."

It was even better than the initial encounter.

Entwined with him and half dozing, she shivered all down the length of her body. Thinking her cold, Pedross slipped carefully free, reached a quilt from its rack at the foot of the bed and spread it over her, tucking it close at hip and shoulder with a spontaneous solicitude. Waking more fully, she lifted one side of the quilt for him, teasing, "No Tekcloth longclothes to keep the cold from you now."

"And no screen for you to hide behind." He stretched out beside her again, accepting the quilt more for the companionship than the warmth since the truth was that he felt no chill, the room's air being well heated and the ceiling low.

She asked, "How did you know me?"

He commended her self-control, that she'd managed to hold that question, unhatched, this long. For answer, he marked with a forefinger an accusing cross upon the relaxed round of her left palm, then turned the hand over to draw a line across the smoothly trimmed ovals of nail. He placed his hand beside hers to show the dirt, ingrained beyond the powers of mere cold water, around each nail. She touched the hard pads of callus on the inner ridges of his palm, inquiring, "How did you acquire these?"

"Rowing. Weapons training. Cable, rope. . . . Climbing. Winching in nets. Setting sails. Hull scrapers—"

"You *are* ill used," she interrupted, to stop the list.

"—drawshaves, saws, mallets. . . ." he appended, laughing at her. "But I didn't have to be forced to it. I put my hand to whatever I find. My mother was part Smith. Tresmiths of Camarr. . . ."

"Oh—" As if reminded of something, Ketrinne reached past the head of the bed, then dropped something cold into his hand: one of his father's executive seals. As he examined it, Ketrinne explained, "Solvig Innsmith, the duke's factor these last few years, bade me give you this and say that he and his kin were at your disposal."

Pedross tightened his fist around the ring, elated. "How many in his family, do you know?"

"About eighty, ninety people. They have a household toward the north angle of the Crescent."

Belatedly Pedross realized he'd asked a direct question and not been reprimanded, though there *had* been the least hesitation before she'd responded. He didn't care, merely glad to be exempted from that crippled phrasing. "What does he want for it?" he inquired matter-of-factly.

"He hasn't stated his conditions yet. But it wasn't a suitable meeting for bargaining. . . . And you, Pedross, what do you want?"

"My father dead, and myself the Master of Andras, not necesarily in that order."

"Not a runaway, then: bait."

"Just so," he responded, appreciating her quick grasp of the situation. "For your support, if we win, I offer: firstly, a half share in all the bay surcharges for five years—"

"Ten."

"Seven. Let me finish, woman." He shoved her gently, and she smiled, looking at him under the dark of her lashes. "Secondly, the rank of First Companion for five years, or until such time as you bear me a male heir, whichever comes first; at which time, either companionate status or marriage, irrevocable. If marriage, then the Isle of Camarr as your bride-gift. If companionate status, then maintenance of your own household to the number of one hundred—"

"No. I would return to Quickmoor."

"Then the right of toll over all my craft docking here. . . ."

They were a while settling the details. Pedross was aware that he was not the only one who'd been planning terms ahead of time. Ketrinne had a clear grasp of both his potential resources and the value of her present support. But eventually they arrived at a mutually satisfactory arrangement.

"Rayneth wants you," she told him then. "I've agreed to a duel to settle it. Otherwise, she'd have sent half the Crescent over the Circle, the way she threw them into Han Halla yesterday. I can't spare the troopmaids that'd cost me. I'll need them all, and more, when Ashai comes."

He understood the suddenness of her invitation to intimacy a little better then, realizing the bond had been forged in defiance of a threat of parting. "When will it be?"

"Tonight. About the fourteenth hour. You know Jannus. It's to be him against Lora, my First Dancer."

"To the death, or the win?"

"Only the win. A pinned fall, only sticks. I don't like it, any part of it, but. . . ."

But she'd had no acceptable alternative. Pedross understood that. "Will he fight a Valde?"

"You mean because of Poli? She was there, she didn't naysay him," she remarked, considering. "I've thought sometimes that they're like the way it must have been in the beginning, in Bremner. . . . But that's just moondreaming. She's *sa'marenniath* and he's lived almost all his life under the Truthtell with enough dark-heartedness somewhere in him that he could half kill one of my troopmaids, just hearing it. . . . I didn't want to bring that kind of anger into *my* bed," she commented, a sudden personal revelation sparking off as she continued to revolve the question. "Will he fight? All I can say is that he means to. But he has no training, and his anger won't help him against a First Dancer. Fire feeds fire. But Rayneth's no fool. She'd not have agreed to it if she thought there was no chance at all. If Rayneth should win, I'll have the Crescent down around her feet if I have to, to get—"

"I think not." To soften his disbelief, he went on, "Bad tactics. Don't waste on the Crescent what we'll need when Ashai comes. And there'd be no time, anyway. Once Rayneth had me, she wouldn't keep me prisoned in the Crescent, risking that I'd escape or be rescued while in her charge. I'm too sharp a blade for *her* hand. She'll hustle me onto shipboard, and into someone else's responsibility, as quick as ever she can. No time for a rescue, Lady—even if it weren't poor strategy."

"Lora will win. So there's no need of arguing about it," Ketrinne rejoined, rather shortly, and, pushing back the cover, swung her feet to the floor. She stooped to catch up the robe and tied the sash with her back still toward him, remarking, "The personal room's over there," and pointed with an elbow. "I had some clothes laid out for you there."

Sensible, he thought, but hardly subtle, that forethought. "Any chance of having a hot bath brought?"

"Hot water's in a tank upstairs. Just turn the top handle. The bottom one's cold."

When he'd washed and dressed—predictably, the clothes fit him well—he returned to find her sitting at a dressing table engaged, with visible determination, in rebraiding her hair. She had one plait done: the part in the back was crooked, and the completed braid had wisps sticking out and was loose and bulgy in some places and tight in others. But she was doing it herself, refusing to call in her troop of personal maids and tiring-women to interrupt their privacy. Strained, it was, and a bit awkward at times, but privacy, and theirs, all the same. Pedross stood watching her struggle with the task for a moment, unexpectedly touched.

"Call your maids," he suggested gently. "I'm not shy."

"I *am*," she retorted crossly.

"Then let me do it. I'm a waterman: I know how."

She lapped two more strands, then let the plait fall.

He undid the first braid and what she'd done of the second, then made the parting run a true line from brow to nape. He found the actual braiding harder than he'd expected: the ends of the strands kept counter-braiding and tangling

because they were so long. He had her hold the partly completed plait while he brushed out the twined strands lower
down.

"What became of your mother?" she asked, and he was
startled because that had been in his thoughts—recalled,
probably, by the business his hands were about.

"She's dead. My father and . . . and his companion, they
claim she was only sent away. That she's still alive. But I
don't believe it."

"Can't you get a Truthsayer?"

"Against my father, and he unwilling?" Pedross chuckled,
grimly derisive. "There's never been a Truthsayer or Fair
Witness anywhere *near* my father. He makes no point of
keeping them away. After all, there's little occasion for Valde
or Bremneri women to be in the Isles of Andras."

"How does he manage his business, then, with no Truthsayers?"

He thought, but did not say, how quaint he found her
parochial assumptions. "If anybody was caught lying to him,
he'd have them skinned. And that's not just a manner of
speaking—he has a woman who's been trained in it, and has
no other chore but to skin things. Birds, beasts, they're stuffed
and treated until they look all but alive. People . . . are just
skinned. No one but a fool would dare lie to Ashai."

Ketrinne contemplated this alternative to Truthtell.
Presently she said, "But why were you parted from her at
all?"

"She wanted to keep me from my training. She shouldn't
have tried to interfere. But she loathed my father and so held
the harder to me. I understand that now, but . . . it doesn't
change things. She shouldn't have interfered, but he shouldn't
have hurt and frightened her so. And he surely should never
have had her killed. Because that's what he did. I know it, no
matter what he and Bronh say. She'd have gotten word to me
somehow, if she were still alive. She'd have sent me word."

Mechanically his hands continued to lap and twine the
strands with an even pressure, producing a braid as smooth
and uniform as mooring cable.

"What manner of man *is* he, then?" inquired Ketrinne
softly, with awed repugnance.

"I don't know. Yes, I do," he contradicted himself suddenly. "He's a man who knows everything there is to know about power. *That's* what he is. Hold this, now."

While she tied the end of the first braid, he began the second, making sure the initial twists lay flat to her head and wouldn't pull, later. He remarked, "You know what he wants the Longlands for?"

"There's been talk he needs stable coast ports. Or, perhaps, control of the mouth of Erth-rimmon."

"A market," he told her. "A year-round market, to replace the Valde Summerfair as the hub of the trading world. Each craft to have a guild and each guild, a city. Longlanders already are the finest glassmakers of the five nations, and nearly the finest shipbuilders. When we have it there'll be woodworkers and masons, metal crafters, builders of all sorts, and schooling all the year, not just hired scribes—everybody able to read and write and count, keeping their own records, their own accounts. A market: a new nation. I wonder if he'll drop it to come after me?" Pedross remarked dreamily, gently shaking out the counter-braid, the reverse image of the pattern he was making. If the two met, they'd undo each other completely. "Where do they keep your pins? I'm almost done."

When he'd looped the braids into a coil and fastened them securely, Ketrinne went off to bathe. Pedross poked through the bed cover to find the ring. It was too large to fit any of his fingers. He cut a length of cord from a ball in his pack so he could hang the ring around his neck, but didn't immediately do so. When Ketrinne, gowned and headdressed and adorned with a small splendor of rings and ornaments, came out to join him, he was sitting in the windowsill, spinning the ring to wind and unwind around a forefinger. He remarked, "Likely you're right, and your Valde will win. But it's always a good practice to have a fallback or two. Can you get this Smith—"

While he tried to recall the name, she supplied, "Innsmith. Solvig Innsmith."

"Can you send for him? Not a Valde—that'd be noticed. Some page, dressed so he won't show he's of the Circle. On foot."

"It's almost time for the daymeal. . . ."

With conscious patience, Pedross responded, "Can't it wait?"

"I only meant that the Innsmith may not wish to come until afterward. Daymeal's often the only time a whole household is gathered together; I've been told the Innsmiths make quite a ceremony of it."

Pedross used his knife to scratch the character *P* on the inlaid sun-circle on the seal's face. Then he handed the ring to Ketrinne, remarking, "He'll have to interrupt his routine. Send someone trustworthy."

Gathering cord and ring into her palm, Ketrinne replied, "We are all Bremneri here. I'll send someone who fears me. . . . Now we must be public for a while, Pedross. The ladies minor are all gathered, most anxious to see what we go into this duel for. Can . . . anything be done about your hair?" she added, with hesitant delicacy.

"No. I've sworn feud, and that's the sign of it. Unless men go bonneted, in Quickmoor . . . ?"

" 'It is wondered,' " she corrected him, with even more care.

Yes, back to crookbacked courtesies again. "It is wondered,' " he sighed. "If they can bear my appearance, I can bear their manners. By all means, let us be public. There'll be time enough for us to be private again, afterward."

With eyes modestly downcast, she reached for his hand.

At the edge of Han Halla, the din was deafening. Every few paces was an oddsman crying his rates. Shouldering through the crowd were vendors with strap trays of almost every kind of food imaginable. Off to Jannus's left there was even a brazier, more or less stationary, from which were being sold collops of pork skewered on green splints and adding to the fog greasy, fragrant smoke. A beer keg passed by, carried shoulder-high on a trestle. All these vendors were in full cry too. Folk standing side by side shouted gaily to each other, so fragments of personal conversation surfaced on the flow of the noise in strange counterpoint.

By unspoken agreement the Crescent people had the ground and the Circle folk the hill. The side of the dike looked like an upended melon patch, only the round, pale, torchlit faces visible under the white margin of their headdresses. It seemed the boys of the Inner Households were not to be permitted the demoralizing spectacle of a riverstock-born man fighting a troopmaid. At least Jannus could see none, past the open corridor maintained between the two groups by the guardsmen and the troopmaids.

At the end of the corridor nearest the dike was the dueling ground itself, a space about twenty paces around punctuated by cressets full of burning branches that flared and spat sparks on the people below. The rain had diminished to a thin, icy drizzle that would probably become sleet before morning. The air was still. Breath hung like puffs of thistle-down, gradually fading.

It was a setting as utterly unlike that of a proper dueldance as Jannus had been able to contrive. He'd have fought in a lightning storm, had there been one available, or on stilts. The more unnatural the duel's surroundings, the better he judged his chances.

At either end of the cresset-ringed space was a bonfire and a canvas pavilion to shelter the principals. Jannus, Poli. Rayneth, and Dan, who was sitting high in the drawcart that'd brought him, together with Blind Ella, who'd begged shelter because she'd feared being jostled or trodden on in the crush, shared the outward shelter. The inward one, close by the dike, had benches in it but was as yet occupied only by a lone troopmaid—probably Arlanna, though at that distance it was hard to be sure.

"She's not coming," predicted Rayneth morosely, tugging at a guy-cord bracing one of the posts. "I should never have agreed to this."

"Then she'll forfeit," Poli pointed out sensibly, "and you'll have won. Don't be foolish."

"Why couldn't *you* fight the troopmaid, if they wouldn't soil their hands with Crescent-born folk?" rejoined Rayneth disagreeably, gesturing in a flash of rings and a clang of bracelets.

"She wouldn't have me."

"That would've been too obvious," snapped Rayneth, the implication clear. "Oh, this is insanity! To be turned out of my place on the strength of a scribe's arm . . . !"

Jannus reassured himself that he'd promised her nothing more than to try. He wasn't responsible, either, for arguing her into accepting him. The Innsmiths had managed that unpleasant task.

The nearest oddsman, Jannus noticed, was offering twenty to one in a hoarse bellow. Jannus hoped this demented free fair would demoralize Lora, the First Dancer: it certainly wasn't doing *his* confidence any good.

For whatever reason of his own, Solvig had volunteered to report to Rayneth Ketrinne's terms, so Jannus had been spared that choice explosion whose shouting voices could be heard a floor and a wing away. Presently Rayneth had appeared above them, up in the gallery of the Evenhall where Poli was demonstrating for Jannus the moves of attack and defense, with exaggerated slowness, in a slant of multicolored light from the high west window against which the Lady's watching outline was silhouetted. After overlooking the proceedings for a time, Rayneth had come down one of the curved staircases that linked gallery to hall, each step definite, her eyes promising confrontation. But Dan, peaceably knitting to amuse his fingers, had deflected her with a remark about odds; so she'd argued with him instead.

Jannus heard most of it, since he wasn't outdoors. Their voices bounced off the underside of the gallery almost like singing. Dan pointed out that the Inner Households numbered above ten thousand souls: three times what the Crescent could muster. "You scare them bad enough, they'll quit depending on just their troopmaids to protect them and come out against you themselves. You scare them bad enough, Lady, and they'll just scrape you off the Crescent into Erthrimmon like leaves into a ditch."

Rayneth's response was that the Bremneri of the riverstocks had never turned over a hand in their own defense in forty generations, and why should they begin now? They wouldn't stand against a howling mob, she declared.

But Dan had countered with the example of Lisle where everybody—lady and scullion, householder and page—had fought bitterly, with whatever came to hand, when the farmstead men attacked. "You send a mob roaring up High Street, they'll fight, Lady, to keep what's theirs. Will they trust you to take just Pedross and leave, do you think?"

"Just a small mob, then," suggested Rayneth, and Dan laughed, the sound reverberating up among the high rafters and ceiling braces.

"You match the troopmaids less than two to one, they'll slice your mob to pieces and feed 'em to you. Don't talk trash, Lady."

Rayneth responded with something of which only the sibillants were audible, and Dan said, "Well, there's that. But he's not about to be scared of one, either. And who else you got that can claim that, tell me?"

Poli told Jannus to take up the other staff then and he was able to ignore the voices behind.

Poli's tutoring was largely silent. She taught his reactions and his balance, bypassing speech for the most part. She gave him time to learn the staff's reach and weight, and how it vibrated in his hands from a blocked chop. Then she led him through a routine of six-stroke sequences, blow and counterblow, and the lunging jab that was so hard to parry. He must stand side-on, she taught him, so he could lean away from the jab or pivot for a backhander.

Eventually he began to anticipate her moves, beginning to counter before her stick reached his, catching the rhythm of the thing. And once he tricked her into an open stance with a feint, which gave him inordinate satisfaction. She promptly restored his proper sense of proportion, once they'd slid on the padded knuckle guards, by running through the six-stroke exchanges again at full speed, a discouraging revelation.

As he'd tired, Poli had begun teaching him responses to position cues. She'd assume a stance and direct him in one or two good ways to strike at her in that pose. He set himself to memorize the cues but, whether because of the prolonged concentration or something as subtle as the angle of light, he found that exercise unsettling. He'd gone through the motions promptly enough, but with an uneasiness he couldn't identify. Each image of her, poised as if in stopped time, had seemed a mute word of intimate and perilous import, strange as a scene revealed by lightning.

As he waited now in the pavilion, sitting on one of the drawcart's propped shafts while Rayneth fretted, the cues recurred spontaneously, uncalled, like erupting shards of dream. His arms tensed to the proper responses but there was warning and unease, the feeling of something amiss. It would have been easy enough to put some name to it—the clamor, or the oddsman's pessimistic calling, or plain bodily dread of being hurt. Surely there were enough causes for gloom without groping after smoke, yet the conviction persisted that it was something altogether different. . . .

"There they are," Rayneth crowed suddenly. "Is that the boy with her? Is that Pedross?"

"He wasn't on display this afternoon," said Poli, which sounded like an answer but wasn't.

Jannus was grateful that Poli would answer for him, and Dan deflect argument, so he could be alone. He reached for the knuckle guards and worked his hands deliberately into the padded leather.

There was no yawning, no preposterous sudden tiredness; the body, it seemed, was willing enough to do this thing. And he'd agreed to it, accepted it as necessary. He even thought there was a chance he could so seriously disrupt the Valde's concentration that he might have at least one clear strike at her if he kept his wits about him.

Peculiarly, the prospect bored him.

At least it felt like boredom—just plain dull uninterest. It didn't make any sense at all. Maybe he needed to be hit a few times, he thought with annoyance, to spark his enthusiasm.

The first into the ring were the two Ladies, confirming the terms of the stakes and inspecting the staffs to determine they hadn't been weighted or set with needle spikes or some such. Jannus moved when the Valde did, advancing a few paces inside the cressets. Conscientiously he tested the footing, finding it wet and spongy but not especially slippery beneath the thatching of grass. The ground was near enough to the dike to drain fairly well, it seemed, though it appeared flat enough to the eye. Reminding himself of the plan he'd made, he inspoke a reflection on any woman stupid enough to volunteer to be First Dancer with seven years of her term yet before her. A troopmaid would have to be almost suicidally desperate to do that. She'd never survive her term.

If Lora heard him, she gave no sign. Likely the tumultuous *als'far*, the crowd's chaotic manysinging, drowned him out. And, almost by definition, First Dancers hadn't the most sensitive, tender, or compassionate natures. Otherwise, they wouldn't be First Dancers, accustomed to duel to the death.

He tried to gather up his uglier memories of Newstock troopmaids but, though accurate, the images refused to resonate for him the way the High Plain had done. They were flat, merely facts. Newstock seemed very far away.

Anyway, she was a First Dancer, not some tender *in'marenniath* troopmaid. It would take more than the spite and resentment of a long-ago Newstock boy to shake her composure.

There seemed to be some dispute over whether body armor was to be allowed. Jannus had been given some to wear—two stiff leather shells that buckled at the side, the sort guardsmen wore—whereas Lora wore over her trousers only a short-sleeved suede tunic that provided no real protection. The Ladies decided against body armor. Poli came to undo the straps for him, leaving him abruptly chilly in the thick sweater he'd used mainly to make the armor fit better.

Lora accepted the staff handed her, gazing across at him impassively. It was like being regarded by a tree.

"What's the matter?" Poli asked, bringing him his staff.

He found the proper position for his hands, with slightly more weight on the right side, right hand knuckles-down in its guard. He said, "I don't know. I wish this was over and done with."

"You'll be fine," she rejoined with a reassuring squeeze. "This will be the first duel Lora's fought with sticks, and the place is all wrong for her. It's evener than you think."

The two Ladies had separated and were returning to their respective pavilions. When Poli followed Rayneth, the dueling ground was left to him and the Valde.

There was some traditional gesture of greeting or acknowledgment customary when duelists first came in reach of each other: a touching of weapons. Jannus ignored Lora's beginning motion of such a greeting, just holding his staff level, standing with his left shoulder toward her, left leg slightly advanced. Decisively, her motion changed. Her upper arms tensed and the stick leaped toward his face. Instead of fending the blow, he ducked, her stick scraping over the back of his head. Meanwhile with a sharp forearm push he clubbed her solidly in the side just above the hip.

Her stick reversed, coming at the side of his neck. He deflected it but was hit hard on the back of his left hand. He almost lost his grip in spite of the protection of the knuckle guard. He'd let her get too close. She hit him three times on the upper arms in rapid succession, once near enough to his elbow to make his whole arm spark.

In guarding against his crooked return stroke she was, for a luminous stopped-time instant, in one of the cue positions. With a sudden effort of will, he responded. It was too late for

him to change the stroke's direction but he brought his left
hand forward, spinning his staff end for end. His staff struck
hers, knocking it up, and the left point jabbed like a shovel at
her torso.

The push was a bit short. She'd leaned away from it, but
had to back a step to keep her balance. He had time to
revolve his hands again, bringing the longer right end of his
staff arcing down from overhead like a poleax. She blocked
the descending club by dropping to one knee and flinging
both arms upward, staff braced horizontally. The two poles
met with a resounding crack. His rebounded with a shock he
felt all the way up his arms into his spine; hers turned vertical, its base braced against the dirt, the top slanted slightly
back to protect her from a side-slash while she was in poor
position.

Jannus rocked back slightly to keep his stance and balance
fresh and flexed his hands in their guards, renewing his grip.
There was a pause.

And that was wrong.

In a dueldance there were no pauses. It was motion interwoven from first touch to ending, gaining momentum and
speed as it proceeded. And here he was flat-footed, and she
kneeling and off balance, stopped dead, staring at each other
like one stranger watching another stooping to tie a bootlace
in the road.

The dull unenthusiasm wasn't just in him, then. She felt it
too. She couldn't be so influenced by his mood; not a First
Dancer, not with all that hot emotion being shouted at them
from all sides. She was going through the necessary motions.
She hadn't come into Bremner to fight Bremneri, but other
Valde, who could make even of death a shared celebration,
with meaning and resonance. Not to trade blows with such as
him, standing bored and uninterested still, unwarmed.

This apathy wasn't merely an absence but a force; capable
even of muffling partisanship, interest, and even his dislike
for being whacked with a club while several thousand people
screamed at him. Nobody could be as indifferent toward a
Valde as he felt now. And yet—

She came up at him then with a one-handed sidewise fling
of her stick, without needing to change her position. The
stick's end caught him solidly across the forehead and the

bridge of his nose. Stunned, he managed to stumble away and guard himself after a fashion as she came after him, the ends of her staff whirling in rapid alternation pounding him faster than he could block. For a moment she was facing him, feet planted but side by side: another of the cues, recognized without thought, almost without sight. His body replied at once with a lunge, the staff held level, then speared forward when the body was fully extended, with the momentum of the lunge behind it. The blow had connected, he could feel that much as he jerked upright in anticipation of a return stroke that didn't come.

She was down, already swiveling to bring her staff up but stopping as she found he'd been slow to seize the chance to pin her.

He didn't want to pin her, he discovered. That would have ended things. He might never get another legitimate chance to smash a Valde as nearly flat as was in his power.

Emotion had finally escaped the smothering layer of apathy that had deepened and broadened in its attempt—*his* attempt —to keep safely hidden what it concealed.

For the emotion was hatred.

He hated her stupid unreflective face, blank as a sheep's, and her sheep's willingness to lean to the strongest wind though it drive her over a cliff; he hated the troopmaids, all the years and generations of them, for holding the intolerable balance in Bremner that distorted everyone it touched. He hated her for *making* him hate her, for forcing him to such lengths to *avoid* hating her that he'd risk his body, his beliefs, and his loyalties rather than recognize his own ferocious willingness to do her hurt.

As if released from some constraint, the Valde sprang up then and drove him retreating around the ring of stinking cressets. When he had the least opportunity he swung at her with the full length of his staff, striking her guard with such force that after a while he needed only to threaten to shift his grip from the middle third of the staff to make her check in her pursuit and brace herself.

Sometimes her attack put her in one or another of the cue positions, and he saw in her clearly then what he'd seen all along: Poli, ten years younger, at the beginnings of her troopservice in Newstock, with the accompanying shadow of himself at eleven frantically deflecting the ambient hatred and distrust by transmuting it into fascination, into hopeless self-destructive yearning for acceptance into the strangeness, by the strangeness, to destroy its power over him.

Jannus saw each pose, felt with entire comprehension its poignant resonances, and tried singlemindedly to break her teeth.

She took to making double circles in the air, holding the stick like a long, unwieldy sword. Out of these looping figures the staff would cut at him so suddenly he scarcely ever could move fast enough to protect himself. She caught him twice in the left arm that way, and once in the ribs as he was trying to lean away. The advantage of reach, added to her superior skill, was too great: he was forced to use his stick sword-style too, though it felt clumsy as a broom to him that way and his wrists lacked the strength to wave the staff around in continuous whizzing figures, as she did. He just had to try to block her stick before it hit him.

Each time he succeeded, the shock of the two sticks meeting, full force, came nearer to tearing his staff out of his hands altogether.

The only consolation was in knowing the Valde took the same risk: he already knew that, stroke for stroke, he could hit harder than she if he'd time to get braced. And she was tiring too. He could see the effort in her arms a bare instant before she started her strike. He took a blow across the face that finished the job of closing his left eye and another squarely in the kneecap—she'd left his legs mostly alone because the downstroke would have left her open to his strong overhand chop—watching for that signal of strain in her arms to come once when he wasn't either in mid-step, turning, or recovering from being hit.

When it finally came he struck at once, not at her, but at the staff end, swatting it aside and down into the trodden mud. He jumped on it with both feet. Of course she yanked at it and overturned him, but the footing wouldn't stand her pull. She hadn't been out here all day yesterday, as he had, and misjudged how much sideslip the ground would stand. As he fell, his staff finally escaping him entirely and pinwheeling away out of sight, the Valde's feet skidded from under her. With a frantic groping twist he rolled onto the remaining staff and held it down with his weight against her attempts to wrench it free.

Less than the staff's length apart, they confronted each other, sprawled in the matted grass. Continuing to pull at the staff, she wasn't ready when it was jammed suddenly into her midsection. Jannus rolled away, the staff in his possession.

He managed to stand, hanging onto the upright staff like a barge pole, swaying. The Valde was propped, leaning back on one arm, no steadier. Then, appallingly, she threw herself around, locked ankles around the pole, and toppled him again. But her palms were clumsy in the guards and she was unable to catch hold of him or the pole. He scrambled hastily away, dragging the staff with him. Regaining his feet, he crutched himself a safer distance off and scraped the mud out of his good eye until he could see her plainly. She was gathering one knee beneath her, her bowed back undefended against the blow the crowd was screaming for. But he held onto the staff, sure that if he let go he'd either fall or else she'd grab it as it came down and the push-pull business would begin all over again.

He shouted at her, "Stop it! Just stop it!"

Perhaps she heard. At least for a moment she stopped moving.

He would have liked to feel sorry for her, but he didn't. He felt as if he'd fallen eight or ten times down a rocky hill and had finally hit bottom. He wanted her to get out of his sight so he could stop hating her. He didn't even know her. Troopmaids had no right to make of him a man who could hate strangers with such violence.

He felt that troopmaids were an abomination, a bane worse than the Truthtell, a heartsickness become a way of life. He was sick of it, the waste and hurt of it all.

"I don't want you dead," he shouted, inspoke, against the mob's clamor. "I want you gone. Just get out!"

The First Dancer of the Quickmoor troop struggled upright, still strong enough to move unaided. In four halting steps she was among the crowd at the base of the slope, abandoning duel and dueling ground without a glance.

New shouting, hysterical and confused, broke out all around—he couldn't mistake Rayneth's triumphant hoot approaching from behind—but he continued to lean on the pole and stare balefully into the dark where the Valde had disappeared. He wanted her gone.

As the crowd overran the dueling ground Poli was buffeted and stepped on, and some people, seeing her only as a Valde, even struck at her. She'd have struck back, but the crowd moved so confusedly and quickly that she wasn't always certain who'd hit her, or else they'd passed beyond her reach before she could turn.

It was nightmarish, ugly, chaotic.

She couldn't see Jannus at all.

Her arm was grabbed firmly. She kicked out and roughly wrested her arm free before recognizing the Lisler, Sparrowhawk. He held up both hands, disclaiming harm, then cautiously slid an arm around her back to deflect the people pushing from behind.

Leaning closer, he said in her ear, "You'd best get clear of this."

"Jannus—" she started to protest.

"I'll find him. Come on."

Slowly managing to turn, Sparrowhawk led her against the current of shoving people, shoving and shouting himself, until they found a bit of clear space in the lee of Dan's cart. People were moving all around them still, coming right through the pavilion in spite of two guardsmen's efforts to make the crowd veer around it.

Dan leaned down and gave Poli a hand as she stepped from a shaft into the open body of the cart, Sparrowhawk steadying her from behind. He stepped between the shafts and leaned as close as he could to the cart, which rocked from people bumping into it. Precariously crouched on the edge of the seat, Blind Ella held onto the siderail and Dan's arm, looking frightened.

"I seen him," Dan remarked loudly, bending so he could be heard. "They picked him up and turned toward the Crescent before I lost sight of him. If they don't drop him, he ought to be all—"

"But he's hurt," Poli interrupted fiercely and stood up, balancing on the seat and the front partition to look over the moving heads. A clod of grass and mud struck her in the shoulder, but she caught hold of Dan and didn't fall. There was nothing to see, though. She eased down again, frustrated.

Sparrowhawk tugged at her sleeve to get her attention. "The farther they go, the more spread out they'll be. I'll find him. Soon's this clears, you go on home. I'll send word there, or bring him, if I can."

"Send word," directed Dan. "He'd as soon not go back to the Household just now, I expect. Scare the kits," he explained, and Sparrowhawk nodded comprehension. "You need cash, Sparrow?"

The Lisler grinned broadly. "I won enough t'buy my bond, my own self!"

"Fine for you," responded Dan, so dryly that Poli guessed he'd bet the other way, with the majority. "But you'll have to corner your oddsman first, you and a few hundred other folk. Here." He handed down a small string-necked pouch, advising, "Keep track of it. Ella's boy ain't the only one's been working the crowd."

Having promised to beware cutpurses, chokeys, and pickpockets, the Lisler stepped over the shaft in one quick motion and elbowed an opening.

Poli thumped at the side of the cart in a fury of impatience. "Where's the carter?"

"Chasing an oddsman," Dan replied. "Settle down, Poli. Ain't a thing we can do till this clears. Damnation. Look at that, now."

"What is it?" Ella asked anxiously.

"Lady Whore's clearing the dueling ground, or anyhow about a score of guardsmen are. Has Ketrinne backchallenged, or what, tell me?"

Moving outward from near the middle, a solid ring of guardsmen were pushing the people back, leaving a widening patch of empty space behind them. The crowd's motion became less headlong as people were turned back; and a lot had left. Poli thought she could get through now.

"I'm going," she told Dan abruptly, and he spared enough attention from the dueling ground to ask *where*. "The Household." Grudgingly, she'd accepted that for her to be abroad in the Crescent tonight was to court an endless succession of fights. "Can you manage?"

"Couldn't pry me out with a stick. What's she about, then?" he wondered aloud, adding absently, "You take care, all the same."

Poli pulled her hood up to make her less instantly identifiable as a Valde and then dropped carefully to the ground. The guardsmen had finally succeeded in clearing the pavilion: she

reached the back edge and made her way past the bonfire
and among the standing people without attracting notice.
They were all looking past her in the other direction and,
once she was beyond the foremost, Poli found enough gaps to
weave through at something like a normal walking pace.

There was a main plan and a fallback. Pedross squeezed
Ketrinne's hand once as the glittering bolt of fabric that must
be Rayneth came charging from the other pavilion a step or
two ahead of the mob. Pedross set himself to look as young
and stupid as he could contrive. As an afterthought he
slapped quickly at his hair to bring a ragged fringe down
over his eyes, then was still again.

The fallback was dangerous. He hoped he wouldn't have to
use it. It'd mean his escaping alone into Han Halla without
shelter and keeping clear of pursuit until Ketrinne's troopmaids could locate him. All it would take would be one black
sinkpool, or a bad wetting in this freezing weather, and he'd
not live to be found. It was really a terrible plan. But one
had to have a fallback, after all.

Rayneth seized his arm and dragged him upright, demanding shrilly, "This him? Name yourself, boy!"

"Pedross—"

From the other side Ketrinne grabbed him too, objecting
that a pinned fall was to win, and there'd been none. It was a
feeble argument. Leaving the dueling ground meant forfeit
according to any custom known to man, as Rayneth was
shouting contemptuously directly into Pedross's ear.

Meanwhile a cuirassed man was proceeding in a rough
body search of Pedross, who was firmly pinioned between the
two shouting women. Pedross snuffled and hung his head,
noting that the man was right-handed and that the cut of the
leather cuirass would make a groin kick unprofitable. There
was a broadknife, almost a sword, scabbarded at the hip; that
would have to be disposed of. The man's hands poked at
Pedross's sides and back. Then the man stooped to check for
weapons concealed in a boot top. Pedross resisted the impulse
to knee him in the face. It wasn't time. The crowd was still
too thick, swirling exuberantly all around them.

A Valde, the troopleader, edged into the tangle—*not* part
of the plan—and said something to Ketrinne that made her
jerk as if stung. Turning to the troopleader, Ketrinne let go

of Pedross, who was immediately dragged away by his two captors.

It was still too soon. There was still too much confusion. Swearing silently to have Ketrinne's spine hot from her back if she'd ruined the timing, Pedross was pulled into the packed dueling ground, buffeted between the cuirasser and the woman, whose fingers bit like talons. They made little progress, indeed were almost separated when a jostled vendor lost a keg that split and splashed right at Rayneth's feet. The guard began shouting and waving, plainly summoning help to clear a path.

It was still too early, but there was no choice.

Pedross snatched the broadknife and gave Rayneth a backward kick which sent her staggering into a tray of food that went flying as Rayneth and the vendor went down together. As the guard looked down at him, Pedross swung a sloppy blow against the chest with the flat of the blade, as though he couldn't reach any higher, and yanked himself back, but the guard's grip held. Pedross could have had the man's hand off at the wrist then, but he just kept twisting and squirming enough to keep the broadknife beyond the man's reach, taking mild pokes at the man's left arm to keep him careful.

He judged Ketrinne should have had time to reach Rayneth by now. He was being shaken around, lifted off his feet half the time, so he couldn't be certain. But the surrounding people were pressing away, fearing the waving broadknife; it gave a little room. Pedross let the guard catch the broadknife—by the blade—and used both his hands to grip the wrist that held him. He ducked under it, yanked, and the man hollered and started to turn to ease the strain on his shoulder. Pedross fell backward, bringing his feet up, and used the leverage to drag the bending guard into the flip. To his credit, the guard kept his hold until he crashed into the ground, flat on his back.

Pedross would have preferred to use an arm flip, which would have left him on his feet, but the weight differential had made that too risky.

Collecting himself, Pedross saw the thicket of legs to his right shifting with the advance of the Crescent reinforcements. He spun and scooted straight away from the hill, where the people were a bit more spread out in the dark and most hadn't yet noticed anything amiss. He battered a twisting passage through the front ranks and then, bent low, had only to avoid stumbling as he weaved among loose clusters of people too intent on finding their way and keeping their footing to notice one more running boy. But a broad woman not much taller than he clapped arms about him, lifting him completely off his feet, hollering, "I got him! I got him!"

Five or six more laid hands on him, so that he was enclosed in the midst of a rotating, unwieldy herd that bore him back toward the light of those cressets still burning. Held securely and pushed along, Pedross just tried to keep from being stepped on. A wad of fabric was pressed against his chest and his compass box, crookedly, into his hands. He'd barely succeeded in stuffing his acquisitions down his shirt front when his captors delivered him into the grasp of a cuirasser who flung him, spinning, into the now-cleared circle.

Falling down gave him the chance to make sure his belt was holding his shirt and its contents securely. Then, through a curtain of hair, he located the two women, who were still arguing, Rayneth standing crookedly and easing her bruises with a hand pressed to the small of her back.

Pedross got his feet under him, choosing which of the outer guards to take out if he had to make a second break for Han Halla—a genuine one, this time, through the solid mass of squat round-faced Innsmiths who'd remained in place after delivering him, to provide him a clear lane out through the crowd if he had to use the fallback after all.

The guard he'd thrown left Rayneth's side and started toward him, wrapping a cloth around the palm which had grabbed the broadknife blade. Pedross backed away at an angle that would bring him within reach of the outer guard he'd selected for a sudden throat-chop. To keep his actual target unsuspecting, he kept his eyes on the advancing man; so when a hand clamped down on the back of his neck, his reaction was startled and violent. Fisting one hand into the other, he drove the point of an elbow backward, producing a pained grunt, and twisted free to find himself confronting Solvig Innsmith.

The Innsmith blinked at him a moment, rubbing his midsection, then brought down a ferocious open-handed slap that knocked Pedross sprawling, feeling as if the whole right side of his head had exploded. Hauled up unceremoniously by the scruff of the neck, trying to find his balance while black blots loomed and faded in his vision, Pedross kept his reactions in check. The blow was good verisimilitude, after all, and the elbow-punch hadn't been pulled or softened either.

"I'll take charge of him now," the Innsmith was declaring in a firm, carrying voice. "The *Obedient's* docked down at Baker Street, under Duke Ashai's banner, and that's on our way home anyhow. Shall I take him off your hands, then, tell me?"

Pedross raged at the wording: they'd worked at it the better part of an hour, choosing phrases that were authoritative, reasonable, and literally true, though both false and misleading in implication. And then the Innsmith had to go and make a question of it, leaving her a choice.

Ketrinne knew. She immediately renewed her threats and maledictions while the lone cuirasser halted a few paces off, silently inquiring as to his Lady's pleasure. Pedross made a show of twisting in the Innsmith's horn-handed grasp and not escaping, raising his eyes to Rayneth only surreptitiously.

The woman looked slowly around the circuit of failing cressets, badgered by Ketrinne's voice, the guard wanting orders, the intimidating bulk of the Innsmith balanced on the edge of motion like a large stone lodged against a shrub—the duke's own factor, as she supposed. No blame to her if Pedross got away, or was roughly handled, in the Innsmith's charge; and she'd just had a demonstration of how hard her own men found him to hold on to.

"Go on, take him, then," she directed and turned her back on Ketrinne, wrapping her mantle more closely about her.

A drawcart was pulled out of the far pavilion to meet her, a broad-faced young man, surely a Smith, leaning to give her a hand in mounting to the seat beside him. Rayneth was saying something about Jannus as the carter wheeled the vehicle about to face the other direction, then braced his feet apart and yanked it into motion, stumbling and sliding the first few paces. The young Smith's bright, speculative gaze rested on Pedross and his captor the whole time, until the cart rolled by.

"Dan knows," Solvig muttered, as the rest of the Innsmiths began moving in around them, an escort and a concealment.

Pedross tenderly touched the side of his face, responding indistinctly, "What of it? He's one of yours."

"Well, he ain't *hers*, anyhow. . . . No matter. Come on,

then. Once we get down to the Crescent, nobody'd notice if
you were naked and painted blue." He gave Pedross a shove,
releasing him, and didn't appear to see the look Pedross gave
him in return.

There were limits to what Pedross would tolerate for the
sake of verisimilitude. But he reminded himself that for
someone unused to playing a part, the Innsmith had done ad-
equately. And Ketrinne. . . .

He glanced back, but she was deep in conversation with
her troopleader. A file of Valde, coming out of the dark, shut
Ketrinne from his view. Well, there'd be plenty of time later,
he reminded himself, to congratulate her more privately on
how well she'd carried out her part.

Following the last few hundred of the dispersing crowd, he
and his Innsmiths passed beyond the reach of fire and torchlight, hugging the hill to keep from losing their way.

The Crescent roared. People who'd been drinking since
midday and stiffening themselves for a general fight were at
last getting it, drunk anew on their victory. They couldn't
wait to hit somebody to celebrate.

Sparrowhawk saw a clapboard fish stall, afire and billowing
smoke. One huge bunch of people were dancing by its light,
reeling and shouting. Another and larger crowd was gathered
just beyond around a knife fight, hollering wagers to each
other because the oddscallers didn't dare show their faces for
fear of being mobbed. The fish stall's awning flapped and
sizzled as the fire contested with the wet, and nobody gave it
two glances.

Most of the ships, he noticed, had pulled in their gang-
planks and had a man or two posted in the bow, watching
the street down the empty length of the piers. They knew the
roar of wildfire when they heard it, knew it could jump a hill
and burn out or flash toward them in a second if the breeze
changed whim. Sparrowhawk hoped the witchwife'd had the
sense to stay with Rayneth and the drawcart: it was getting
very drunk out.

Smiling mirthlessly to himself, Sparrowhawk scanned the
nearest bearded, open-mouthed faces, looking for Jannus. He
was whipped across the cheek by the beads tied into a girl's
hair as she shoved past to join the dancers. Watching the
dancers spin and stagger, Sparrowhawk rubbed his face ab-

sently, irresolute. The wildness had a pull that drew him. Crescent against Circle, Quickmoor itself, meant nothing to him, but Bremneri man against witch, against the ancient authority of a ruling Lady, had the power to blow through him like a wind. He felt the wildfire too and it seemed to him as familiar and natural as breath. But his word and his concern for Jannus held him and finally he eased away as the fish stall collapsed inward, throwing up a cloud of sparks.

It took care to get anywhere near a tavern. Each was ten deep in people outside, with glasses and mugs being handed out through open shutters. One window had a keg poked out, sitting right on the sill, seeming unattended except for the folk blundering over to refill their glasses or saucepans or buckets or whatever else they'd found to drink from. There was a man standing in his socks, using a boot for a beer mug. Another man and a child were staggering along with a kettle between them sloshing half full.

That was just too much to pass by. Sparrowhawk took a bail-handled crock that a fat woman passed out under a drawcart had no further need of, and eventually edged near enough to the keg to hold the crock under the spigot. A man behind him was telling another in a carter's vest about a whipknife fight he'd seen once in Darkstock. Moving aside, Sparrowhawk asked if they'd seen Jannus since the duel.

"Headed down toward High Street, last I saw on 'em," offered the carter. "Past here, anyhow. . . ."

"Obliged t'you," responded Sparrowhawk, and threaded his way out to the riverwall, where it was a bit more open.

He drank just enough to take the worst of the chill off, as he told himself, before resuming his search, leaving the crock on the wall for somebody else to use.

The watchtower bell had already struck its fifteen, and would now be silent until dawn, so Sparrowhawk had no idea of the time except for a brittle midnight feeling in the bones of his face.

Down by High Street, they were chucking people in the river. Sparrowhawk, who'd never learned to swim, stayed wide of that entertainment and looked in windows when he could get near enough. Then, following a new idea, he went out on the nearest dock past the dunking party and called up to the bow watch, "You seen a man—I *say*, you seen a man carried past here about when this hoorah started?"

One waterman turned aside to check with the other, then leaned on the rail and pointed one, two, three times, waggled a hand, then pointed a fourth time and made a pushing motion.

The third or fourth place south from the High Street corner, that seemed to mean, or maybe up Cutter Street. That last seemed likely, since Cutter Street was where duelists hung about. The guards' barracks and two bawdhouses were there too, each handy to the others. Sparrowhawk wigwagged acknowledgment, deciding to try Cutter Street first, then work back. By that time, maybe the dunking party would have broken up or turned to something else.

The Cutter Street taverns were near enough to High Street to have some pretentions. The gambling, whoring, and drinking were at least kept out of each other's sight, and the chokeys who attacked winners in the road were better dressed because in the busy times they doubled as bartenders.

Sparrowhawk first tried the Queen of Night, where Dan had brought him a time or two, then went across to the Cat and Rat which, in spite of the name, was the less rowdy of the pair. In the third place, the Wheel, four or five people were taking turns throwing knives at a straw target against the left wall. The chuckers were leaving them alone because they hadn't hit anybody yet. Their sport created some clear walking space, if you watched your time and leaned away whenever a knife came spinning past.

Among a loud bunch of wildly gesturing 'prentices up by the bar, Sparrowhawk saw one he recognized from the household, a moody fellow called Robie who helped tend the oddscallers' accounts.

"It's our Lisler," Robie remarked to the others, when Sparrowhawk tried to speak to him. "You like the way we do troopmaids here down south? You in funds, Lisler? You happy poor, or happy rich?" Robie began poking at Sparrowhawk's pockets.

"Leave off that," rejoined Sparrowhawk, cuffing Robie's hand away. "Thought you never bedded anybody over twelve."

"*After* twelve," Robie corrected, good humoredly enough. "I need my rest. What do—"

"You seen Jannus?"

"Alan was keeping track of him," said another of the 'prentices, and bawled, "*Al-ann!*"

Robie proposed mournfully, "The chuckers got Alan. Alan is no longer among us."

"Knife chuckers, you mean," commented a 'prentice farther down the bar.

"Saw him just a bit ago. *Al-ann!*"

Sparrowhawk found space to back away from them and started checking the tables and then the booths back against the walls, where the lamps had been removed, a reasonable precaution. In one of the booths was a man asleep or passed out, bent forward onto a table entirely covered with empty mugs and glasses. Sparrowhawk thought he knew the sweater. He slid onto the part of the opposite bench not taken up by the man's outstretched feet and stacked a few of-the glasses to clear a space for his elbows. Reaching across, he tugged lightly at a folded arm, saying, "Jannus . . . ?"

No response.

He joggled the arm again and this time the head started to lift, then stopped, rigidly still. After a minute, stiff careful adjustments began that left Jannus slouched against the bench back, rather than sitting up. Both eyes were ringed with the plum bruising that followed a broken nose, and the left eye was swollen shut, with two stick-welts on the forehead above it.

"It's me—Sparrowhawk. How're you doing? You drunk enough yet t'manage walking?"

The good eye blinked vaguely, the head trying different angles to see better. "Oh, I'm all right," Jannus replied, the words slow but perfectly clear. "Sparrow?"

"Ahuh."

"Would you do a thing for me?"

"I s'pose."

Very gradually Jannus shifted his back against the bench, trying to find some easier angle. "Where's Poli?"

"Back at the Household, by now. Long since."

"Good." Jannus relaxed and sighed. "I was scared she'd try hunting me, with all that going on. . . ."

Sparrowhawk stacked a few more glasses, waiting, then finally asked, "You want me to do something?"

"Where is this?" Jannus responded, trying to make out more of the room.

"The Wheel. Cutter Street."

"Two blocks, then," said Jannus, when he'd worked it out.

To the Household, he meant. "You want a hand, getting back?"

"*No!*" Jannus stiffened and was still a little while. Finally he chanced breathing again and pressed a palm softly against his chest, low on the right. "That's ribs. That's what that is," he remarked to himself.

"Ought to be bound," Sparrowhawk mentioned.

"Not just yet."

To Sparrowhawk the situation was quite plain. Jannus didn't want to go home—Dan had got that right, but the reason wrong. Having beaten one witch, Jannus had another waiting for him. In his place, Sparrowhawk wouldn't have been anxious to budge, either.

"Dan sent some money by me. There're rooms upstairs, where you could stretch out, anyhow. . . ."

Jannus gave him something like a sardonic look. "A crib? No, not just now. I'm fine where I am. Just say I'm fine right here, where I am."

"To her, you mean."

"Right here," Jannus agreed vaguely, and tipped his head to rest in the corner between bench and wall.

Sparrowhawk stood up but remained leaning on the table, undecided. It might take him most of an hour to go the two blocks and get back, the way things were. And meanwhile a brawl could start, or the knife throwers could think what fun it'd be to throw as close to people as they could, or somebody start a fire. He didn't like the notion of leaving Jannus on his own, the way he was, and there was nobody Sparrowhawk dared trust him to—surely not that bunch of 'prentices. . . .

While he was debating, a fight *did* break out, across the room. Glass broke, and the chuckers waded in, and somebody threw a mug that hit the hanging lantern, which swung and spun but didn't break. That decided him. When the fight was finally moved outside and a few score people followed to watch it, Sparrowhawk bought a bottle of the clear grain spirit, the inlander stuff that made incomparable firebombs and wasn't often seen, upriver, for just that reason.

When Sparrowhawk returned to the booth Jannus seemed to think he'd been, and come back already, and Sparrowhawk didn't tell him otherwise.

After a while Jannus seemed to be feeling easier and they started talking about the duel: the crowd, and the public sight of the Circle Lady and the little Andran idiot that was the cause of the whole thing.

"I bet on you," volunteered Sparrowhawk diffidently.

"Then you've got no more sense than me, that's plain. Get good odds?"

"Twenty-three to one."

Jannus winced and laughed, rolling his glass between his palms. "The worst I heard was twenty. Where'd you find twenty-three?"

Sparrowhawk shrugged. "Seen a man. . . ."

"You'd best find him before he flits."

"He won't flit. He was one of Lady Whore's, had her marker."

"He'll catch it, then. Twenty-three!"

Jannus didn't ask how much he'd won, and Sparrowhawk didn't bring up the idea of buying back his bond.

The talk had an easy, offhand impersonality Sparrowhawk felt comfortable with. He thought idly that he liked a man who didn't pry, who knew how to keep a decent distance. Dan was always prying—friendly enough, and likely well-meaning, but sometimes he made Sparrowhawk almost as uneasy as the witchwife, though he supposed she was all right too, in her way. He wouldn't ill-wish her—she'd done *him* no hurt.

And if, under the talk and the unstrained silences, Sparrowhawk remained very much aware that Jannus was hurting and that he himself was staying mainly to protect him, that was just the anchor, out of sight. It didn't have to be dragged up or talked about.

They got to talking about Lisle, which Sparrowhawk called "a scruffy little dump," secretly prepared to defend it to the death and hate its detractors forever. But Jannus offered no criticism, instead talking about the north orchards and a much-married woman Sparrowhawk found they both knew, though Jannus had only been in Lisle the once.

Sparrowhawk recalled the night well, when the Lislers had captured the score of witches off the downriver packet. He'd had to act as his father's prolocutor, reading the terms of the agreement by torchlight, and all those witches looking at him fit to burn him where he stood. " 'Twas the first . . . Valde

I'd seen so close up, don't you see," he explained parenthetically. "Diden' note *her* out specially, though. Happen, they all look about the same till you're used to 'em. Scared me fair to death, they did."

Jannus was quiet so long that Sparrowhawk began to worry whether he'd broken the rules himself and poked into something personal and best left alone.

But while Sparrowhawk hunted anxiously for some safe thing to bring up, to cover his mistake, Jannus tipped his head back and told the ceiling, "They don't belong here. They just make things worse." The tone was flat and bitter and full of trouble. "I should have kept out of it, Hafri. . . . Should have let Rayneth run her mob, and Ketrinne do whatever *she* had to. But I should have kept out. That's what troopmaids do: get in the middle and make things worse. I'm on too many sides at once. Maybe getting beat will finally make me know that, once and for all."

"But you won," objected Sparrowhawk awkwardly.

"I do hear you. Well, you're the one got twenty-three to one on it," commented Jannus, more casually. "I'd suppose you must know."

Much relieved at the teasing, which assured him he hadn't poked too far after all, Sparrowhawk refilled the glasses again, taking great care to get the levels precisely even. He noticed that he didn't feel the burn of the liquor as much as he had. "Going to be shouting whispers, I'll bet," he remarked. "I'm *that* hoarse, what wi' all that hollering. . . . What's that word you called me by?"

Jannus looked puzzled, as if he were trying to recall. "*Hafri*, was it?" he said after a while. "Didn't notice I'd said it."

"What is it?"

"Well, a sort of a call-name. . . . I do believe time's come I have to get outside. Could you . . . ?"

Sparrowhawk helped him slide his feet off the bench and get himself out past the table. Sparrowhawk was still steady enough to be leaned on. And it helped that the place had emptied a lot, and scarcely any who remained were still standing up. They moved slowly around to the alley and found a wall plainly often used for such things.

The cold air bothered Sparrowhawk's balance, but when Jannus made a reach toward the wall, missed it, and fell,

Sparrowhawk's shock of concern sharpened the blurred edges for him again.

"Easy," Jannus warned, with no breath behind the word; reminded about the cracked ribs, Sparrowhawk pulled him up as gently and carefully as he could. Jannus patted out a hand until he found the wall and was able to take most of his own weight. Sparrowhawk tried to keep steady although the cold and the vagueness were coming back.

"I can't tell—is it starting to get light?" Jannus wondered.

"*I* don't know. Looks dark to me."

"Wonder if this alley goes clear through."

He was thinking of the Household again.

"With all this trash underfoot? You want to bust a leg too?" rejoined Sparrowhawk, and Jannus thought that was funny and then nearly choked himself, coughing. Sparrowhawk pushed him back against the wall and held him there, so at least he'd stay on his feet. Sparrowhawk asked, "You been coughing any blood?"

"Not . . . so far. Don't you make me laugh . . . again or I swear . . . I'll die, right here." When he'd caught his breath a bit more, Jannus said, "You figure we can make the Household?" and almost started laughing again, which infected Sparrowhawk.

"You quit that."

"Just thinking what this is going to feel like, when I start feeling it. That motherless witch has near ruined me."

"And that's funny?" demanded Sparrowhawk, and they both exploded. Somehow Sparrowhawk managed to keep them both upright. Blinking his eyes clear, Sparrowhawk finally suggested, "You'd best get a crib till they can send a drawcart—"

Jannus shook his head a few times. "Didn't think I could, before. Go back. But I'm set now."

Sparrowhawk understood perfectly clearly that Jannus wasn't talking about the difficulty of walking.

"I never told her where you were," Sparrowhawk stated and braced himself, feeling he was taking a great risk. When Jannus didn't say anything right away, Sparrowhawk added flatly, "Thought you needed watching worse."

"It was good you stayed," Jannus decided finally. "I guess I needed a Lisler to stay with me just then."

"That's all right, then," rejoined Sparrowhawk curtly, relieved and enormously happy. "We can make a start, any-how. It ain't but two blocks and a little. We ought to make it by noon."

"Don't you start *that* again. . . . You know, this knee's none too good, either. Come 'round this other side."

"That'll hurt your ribs."

"I don't *walk* on my ribs," responded Jannus, and made a choked noise just short of a laugh.

"Now, you quit. Or you'll do us both an injury. It's got pretty drunk out here tonight, or hadn't you seen it?"

"Best thing for them," said Jannus, the hard edge on his voice back again. "Banging around and yelling and filling the air for miles around with the *als'far* of how much they hate troopmaids and how glad they are to see one hurt—"

"Leave off. They got the right—they won."

Jannus made another noise that was *not* a laugh, or any part of one. "Sometimes Bremneri make me sick, that's all."

Unoffended, Sparrowhawk responded sensibly, "I expect sometimes Valde feel the same. About Valde."

"I expect," conceded Jannus, but the anxiety had gone out of his tone.

They'd come as far as the Crescent road, maybe half a block, and two more to go. But Jannus said he had to stop a bit, so Sparrowhawk found him a fuelbox to lean against.

"You certain sure you want to do this?"

Jannus said only, "Look at the stars."

Up above the mast tops, a last trailing scarf of cloud was passing away to northward. Downriver, the winter sky was perfectly black over Is and the sparks in it were hard and bright as beads. By full moonlight they'd have been scarcely visible, like a candle at noonday. Sparrowhawk looked, conscious of the smoke of his breath drifting slowly away.

He said, "That calling-name. What's it mean?"

"Means *little brother*. Valde word."

"Figured it was. . . . You can call me that if you want."

"Your hair's growing out all crooked in the back, you know that?" commented Jannus, after a minute. "If you were an Andran, I'd think you'd sworn feud with the whole world. I should ask Poli to trim it."

"All right," Sparrowhawk responded, accepting that bond too.

"We'd best get home before we freeze," Jannus decided, and Sparrowhawk turned then to help him.

Rising carefully and in silence, Ketrinne lit a taper and roused one of her chambermaids to bring her some warm milk to help her sleep. It was hardly worth it, since dawn could scarcely be an hour away and there'd be the morning audiences to attend to, clearheaded or not.

The trouble was that she *was* clearheaded. Her body ached with weariness and other things—none of the principals to this day's doings seemed to have escaped unscathed—but her thoughts revolved and returned like the blades on a paddle wheel.

The noise from the Crescent seemed to have muted and died down at last, anyway. Slipping her arms into a robe, she drifted over to the window but found it sheathed in ice, inside and out. She touched a finger to the frost and watched the black blot of warmth slowly spread. Then she snatched her hand back and put the chilled fingertip in her mouth.

She wanted the weather cold. She wanted days and days of frost, until the ground was rock hard and the surface of Erth-rimmon gray with drifting slush that one sudden morning would be stiff and immobile for months thereafter. No ships would come upriver then, not till after the thaw floods. She'd have months to decide and prepare, once the river was safely frozen.

The spot of warm she'd made slowly healed itself. The frost was seamless again.

She looked at the boy, Duke Ashai's son, asleep in her bed—stranger, antagonist, bedmate and ally, all within a day's time. One arm and most of his back were uncovered; she imagined his skin would be hot to the touch, as though he contained a tiny private furnace or ran a perpetual fever that wasted him only in invisible ways or perhaps not at all. But she didn't touch him. He was still too new to her for Ketrinne to be careless of his rest, or his waking either—returned safe to her by his own wit and the Innsmiths' aid. *But at what cost,* she asked of herself, for the hundredth time.

Lora, the First Dancer, had deserted: just walked away into Han Halla without forethought or any warning at all. And a full third of the Quickmoor troop had gone with her. It might even be half—Arlanna'd had no definite number when she'd told Ketrinne: only the incomprehensible fact itself.

Ketrinne could scarcely believe it even yet, much less understand it. What the troopleader had said just made no sense. It was something Jannus had done, or felt, or said—Arlanna wasn't even sure of *that*—that'd begun it. But for some reason, certain of the troopmaids felt no further interest in Quickmoor and without a word started to walk home across Han Halla. The rest heard, or felt, the same thing but as inexplicably remained unmoved by it and returned to their usual watch posts and duties as if nothing at all had happened.

All Valde were insane.

Their pledged word, their traditions, her own need of them—none of these meant anything. A change of mood, and they walked away from it all. "But they'll get no bridestones," Ketrinne had protested, and Arlanna had patiently, composedly, explained they didn't need them any more. There were often men remaining unchosen after the Summerfair bridings, these days. The deserting troopmaids could have their choice of those, or next year's, or the year after's. "For them, the Pact is ended," Arlanna had said serenely, as if it made perfectly good sense, except that Ketrinne was too thick to grasp it, although the troopleader wasn't going to say so, right to her face; as if such desertion were commonplace and eight centuries had not passed without such a thing being even imagined.

Arlanna likely thought her Lady odd to feel bitterly betrayed, facing the prospect of holding the Circle against Ashai Rey with perhaps a hundred thirty troopmaids, any of whom might suddenly decide the Pact no longer bound her and stroll off, unconcerned.

It was intolerable!

She wondered if Jannus had any idea of what he'd done, or how he'd done it. Maybe *he* could tell her in some way that would make sense. He'd robbed her of seventy or eighty troopmaids—the *least* he owed her was an explanation.

But she suspected she'd not be able to tempt him to risk coming into the Circle again any time soon.

The chambermaid scratched softly at the door, bringing the milk. Ketrinne thanked her and bade her go back to sleep, but once the door was shut she set the milk aside and settled down before the embers in the hearth with her feet tucked under her, willing it to be cold tomorrow and colder still the day after.

III:

CANDLE AT
NOONDAY

The pigeons which were huddled on the mouths of chimney pots to keep from freezing took fright when Bronh's outspread wings appeared high above them over the crater's rim. The flock eddied and swerved over the rooftops, clapping across the more leisurely flight of some gulls, while Bronh dropped from the icy heights into the perpetually troubled air above Landsend, southernmost of the cities of the Longland Spur.

Buffeted and rolling almost like a pigeon herself, with wings held at a close, sharp-elbowed angle as she fell through the turbulence into the calmer air within the volcanic mountain, Bronh gave the tumbling flock below scarcely a glance.

She could have stooped on a pigeon easily enough, struck and killed it in a midair shock of floating feathers; but she couldn't have eaten it. She was a valkyr only to the eye. Under her keelbone, the body cavity was taken up entirely by brain tissue, lungs, and a fast-beating heart. Instead of crop or stomach, the digestive system was no more than a short tube of undifferentiated intestine designed to assimilate a predigested protein/high-caloric liquid. She carried a supply, powdered, in a small waterproof pouch on her back, between her wings.

She needed to eat soon—the bird's rapid metabolism required food every few hours—but as she drifted above the city and angled toward the harbor she had no thought of breaking her fast before Duke Ashai mixed the meal for her.

167

The swirling pigeons were safe from Bronh. She hunted only information, and men.

Landsend mountain was the last in a chain of volcanic origin that spined the Longlands. At Landsend, the craters stepped out into deep water to become, at intervals, the scattered isles of Andras. A fraction of the Landsend crater was a broad ledge of black crumbly soil, immensely fertile, on which the city and its surrounding fields sheltered from the tidestorm in the lee of southscarp. The rest of the crater was a ladle full of gray-green ocean heaving quietly within a curve of reef, a wet saw-edge of black glass nearly five miles offshore. Guarding and marking the harbor mouth, two Tek-built towers had been tunneled into the reef on either side of a deepwater canyon that gave safe passage between harbor and the Bay of Andras.

Bronh had seen those towers taken, seen Landsend city fuming a pall of smoke that drifted miles, as though the volcano had regained its youth. But that summer eruption had long ago subsided. The only smoke in the air was woodsmoke twirling from chimney pots around which the pigeons were once again settling and trampling with plump urbanity.

Sails furled, twenty-three ships of various shapes and sizes rode at anchor out in the bay. Bronh's long sight easily distinguished the *Rising Sun,* a three-masted galleon of Ismere configuration that served as Ashai's flagship. She read, from the signal banners flying on a slanted line, that the Duke was aboard.

Bronh coasted down a gradient and alighted on the sturdy peg projecting from the sterncastle. Through one of a row of small windows Bronh could see the duke himself in conversation with two sailmasters while two scribes of his personal staff laid out documents the way he liked them, hundreds of sheets placed side by side on a long chart table.

Bronh rapped sharply on the window, which was opened by the elder of the scribes as a matter of routine. The valkyr's comings and goings were never questioned or remarked upon: the duke had let it be known he preferred it that way.

Bronh hopped from the sill to her perch, where she found her meal already mixed in her dish. She alternately dipped and lifted her head, drinking until fresh strength and energy flowed into the body she wore, the latest in a succession of valkyrs that extended more than five hundred years; her rede, her self, was at least six times that old, though she seldom thought back to former times and never idly.

Hers was less than a complete personality, by her own choice. Although the valkyr's capacities had been vastly altered and enhanced, the bird still was inadequate to contain a full human consciousness. There simply wasn't room. A choice had to be made between size, weight, and lift, on the one side, and brain topography and complexity on the other. Choosing to be bodied as a soaring bird capable of raising its own weight from ground-level rather than as some conspicuous roc-monster, such as some Teks had once worn, Bronh had discarded the storage capacity for most long-term memory and the complexity to support many of her former abilities, never worrying whether she'd ever be reconstituted, entire, at some hypothetical future date. Bronh was not protective of her identity or of her life, for that matter, except as either served her purposes. She'd never regretted paring herself down to a will with wings: there was just that much less to distract her.

Having acknowledged her return with a glance, the duke continued his conference. One of Bronh's areas of expertise was the interpretation of minute signals of bodily position and gesture. It was always instructive to watch Ashai perform. He almost never sat when he could stand, with an upright solidity that made his rather ordinary frame shout *authority, authority* on a preverbal level to any watching eye; and yet the silver-handled stick, alternately suggestive of weapon or of crutch, could make him seem violent, a dangerous combatant, or vulnerable, a frail man getting old and in need of the watcher's loyalty and protection, depending on the effect Ashai chose to produce.

In his person, Ashai was all but unchanged from the figure which had emerged from Downbase to meet Bronh almost forty years before. He was of average height, with a striking beauty and strength of countenance designed to make him devastatingly persuasive in small groups and unremarkable, anonymous, at a distance. The face was only lightly lined, the hair a silver that was still short of white, so that his age was mature but indeterminate. His features were sharp-boned and well-defined, habitually mild in expression, control showing only as calm. The voice was an instrument fit for any work, typically soft in delivery to make the auditor attend the harder; the two sailmasters were hunched at the edge of their seats in unconscious anxiety to miss no syllable. And when he let them go at last, each would feel himself confided in, respected, and relied upon in some matter of grave import.

When the cabin was empty, Bronh reported without preamble, "It was a ruse."

"Wait, Bird, let me get through this first." The vocal instrument changed tones slightly, becoming more conversational, the choice of words more colloquial, often with unexpected ironic lifts—no less deliberate or calculated, but Ashai's own voice nonetheless.

He was walking around the table, his eyes passing unfocused over the reports laid out for his inspection. Finishing the circuit in about three minutes, Ashai knocked the tabletop once with his knuckles, as if the correlation of the documents' information, returned to him from the instantaneous assimilation of his larger self, wasn't what he'd hoped.

Like Bronh, Ashai was a diminished self, a fraction of personality suited to the capacity of its container, a human body. But Ashai had the advantage of continuous rapport with his complete dimension. He was an extension, a mobile, of that larger entity whose body was Downbase itself. The link was a neural grid continuously amplifying and transmitting the electrical discharges at the synaptic gaps of the brain—a sort of permanent redecap. Whatever Ashai saw was likewise "seen" in Downbase. All sense data—even to the kinesthetic adjustments of balance required by the lift and roll of the anchored ship in the slow swell—all were simultaneously known and experienced in Downbase. In return, Downbase's correlations and interpretations were as accessible to Ashai as his own memory—which, in a sense, they were.

"Domal's still resupplying the Longlanders from the west shore near Kalin's Cove by little boatloads," Ashai remarked, frowning down at the reports. "A few weapons here, a few hundred-weight of food there. . . . What do I have to do to provoke the man—set his beard afire? He's hired every Fisher and no-name east of Han Halla and them stuffing their faces from his stores for three months, now—when's he going to *move*?"

"Do you want me to go to Ardun," queried Bronh, "or are you being rhetorical again?"

"Bird, you're as literal as a machine," complained Ashai mildly, and, setting his stick aside, he began scooping the documents into one thick pile. Over his shoulder he remarked, "So it was a ruse, was it? Pedross isn't aboard the *Obedient*?"

"Someone's been shrewd enough to predict you'd check on him only by initial on the heliograph. So there's a 'P' on board, all right: an old Crescent hangabout named Persson—"

"A person named Persson," muttered Ashai, then waved Bronh to continue and take no notice of such interruptions.

"This Persson had been hired ostensibly to deliver a cask of documents sealed with your seal."

Ashai stood thinking a moment. "That would make it Solvig Innsmith. Yes, I see. Was Orlengis party to the ruse?"

Bronh, who'd talked to the rivermaster without giving the man any hint anything was amiss, had observed his reactions closely. She gave the opinion that Orlengis appeared unaware of the deception.

Ashai asked, "And Pedross?"

"Still in the Circle of Quickmoor, as far as I could tell. There's a start being made on fortifying the dike that looks like him. But I didn't see him. He didn't stir out of doors while I was watching, and the windows were frosted so I couldn't see inside."

"What does Rayneth say?"

"She thinks he's halfway back, on the *Obedient*."

Ashai nodded, accepting Bronh's professional judgment on such a matter. "And the Valde? Still gone?"

"I counted one hundred seven," replied Bronh, reporting the tally of four days' continuous inspection, "plus the troopleader. Ketrinne's lost nearly half her troop."

That this was welcome news to them both needed no discussion. Ashai didn't want to precipitate immediate war with Bremner by fighting an all-out battle against a lawful Lady and her troopmaids. The more poorly Quickmoor was defended, the less likely such an outcome would be. An afternoon's show of force, an abject surrender, and Pedross received by sunup—that would be Ashai's preference.

As for Bronh, she was well satisfied for other reasons to which Ashai alluded in his next remark. "You're the expert on Valde—what are the chances of still more deserting? Is it worth waiting?"

"The hypersensitives, the *in'marenniath*, are always the catalyst," responded Bronh, her calculations always more labored than his. "And the ratio of *in'marenniath* is getting higher—"

"One in five," supplied Ashai, "in the general population, according to our extrapolations, by this time."

"And what fraction of the whole are Haffa, Brotherless, by now? A quarter?"

"Twenty-two percent and dropping, by your equations."

Those equations and extrapolations were part of what Bronh had lost in taking the valkyr. But the project itself was unfadingly clear to her because it was her sole reason for outliving all of her kind, refusing madness and despair during the trapped centuries, holding fast to the belief that what she'd set in motion was continuing, beyond the prison the High Plain had by that time become.

Segregate the Haffa, the litters with no males among them, and systematically exclude nine in ten from reproducing. Limit that tenth, by late childbearing, to a single litter, further diminishing their numbers and their share in the inheriting generations. To do that, engineer a Great Pact between Bremner and Valde, a pact of healing between allies devastated in the firestorms of the Rebellion.

Bronh had done that.

Before she wore the valkyr, as a Tek of Debern Keep she'd been an ethologist, a studier of cultures specializing in the empathic native humanoids who called themselves Valde, then approaching racial extinction by reason of the deadly imbalance in their ratio of male to female births. The imbalance had been an unforeseen by-product of genetic manipulation undertaken by a Tek of an earlier age to make Valde-human crossbreeding possible. Bronh had set out to reverse that manipulation—to return the Valde to the original condition they'd enjoyed before the first Teks landed. The Great Pact, the Truthtell, the troopservice of the Haffa to win their bridestones, were the earliest fruit of Bronh's efforts. She'd had great influence among Valde in those times because, Tek or not, she'd given considerable numbers of them refuge in Fathori until Fathori itself had felt the firestorm. Now, she supposed, even the memory of her name had been forgotten among them.

And now had come the first sign that her project had
passed the initial phase. Troopmaids had deserted their city.
But Bronh's satisfaction was no more than it would have been
if, flying a long distance over clouds, she'd spied through a
sudden rift a landmark she knew. It confirmed her in her
course.

The next landmark would be the ending of the Summerfair
and its annual intrusion of strangers upon her Valde, an aim
she and Ashai shared, although for different purposes. With
the end of the Troopcalling and of the mass pairing-off of the
bridings, she thought, the Summerfair would wither and die;
and the trade would come to the Longlands, as Ashai
planned.

"Will the rest desert?" Ashai reminded her, without impatience.

"The hypersensitives have already gone," she mused, "gone
beyond reach of the communal link by now. They won't affect the remnant in Quickmoor. The probability of further
desertions there is extremely low."

"What *could* bring about another linked reaction, like the
first?"

"Introduction of another *in'marenniath* into the group,
combined with another duel or similarly traumatic confrontation. Subconsciously, they already know the troopservice to
be both unnecessary and destructive, an emptied ritual serving no further survival purpose. They need not compete for a
disproportionately small pool of available males, now that the
birth ratio is stabilizing. But this fact has to be made
immediate, by some traumatic shock focused through an
in'marenniath, for that low-level awareness to erupt into consciousness with enough force to overcome habit and learned,
artificial, motivations."

Ashai went to tap his primitive barometer, inquiring, "Is
Jannus available for a rematch?"

"No. I didn't see him either. Recuperating, Rayneth reports. Or am I being literal again, Shai?"

"Just the least bit. Though I confess interest in that too.
What do you think of him, Bird, now that you've met him?"

"What *should* I think, a Bremneri mated to a Haffa Valde
eight hundred years too late? Providing a model for a
counter-pattern that could impede the mutual disengagement
of the races?"

"Yes, you *would* see it that way," remarked Ashai thoughtfully. "Don't forget, Bird: leave him alone. You involved him in the knowledge of Pedross's rebellion against my clear intention, and his. Hereafter, there's to be no contact without specific instructions to the contrary. Is that understood?"

"Involving him brought about the desertions you're so pleased about," rejoined Bronh, unawed.

"That's the only reason I haven't disciplined you. But neither of us predicted that result. We were just lucky." Returning to the table, Ashai picked up his stick with every appearance of firm regret, the gesture entirely plain to Bronh's trained eyes, as it was meant to be. "Remember: no contact. He holds the Rule of One and I am bound to accommodate his will in every way the Rule permits."

"And what does the Rule signify, now that you've taken Downbase aloft?" Bronh countered, flexing her talons on the wood of her perch: gesture for gesture. "Kantmorie is extinct."

"As long as Shai, Bird, and King survive together in this world, the old Rule remains. And one part of that equation is dispensable: I'd hate to lose you, Bird," warned Ashai, in the friendliest of voices.

"Sentimentalist," accused Bronh, unmoved. "You're the one proposing to land marines on their front doorstep, not I. If you. . . ."

Ashai was no longer attending. His pose and expression indicated listening and contemplativeness. Bronh fell silent, forbearing to interrupt whatever fresh data Downbase was supplying.

When after a few minutes the abstraction faded, Ashai reported, "Domal's fleet is moving down Arant Dunrimmon. Ten baycraft and thirty-seven barges. At present speed, they ought to reach the sea in seven days, and then they'll probably rendezvous with allies on one of the East Isles. He's *moving*, Bird! Finally! Now, I'll need a check on the fleets at the Keening Isles and at Firstlight Isle. I can't get fine enough definition at this distance to tell if their refitting is finished or how many total ships are seaworthy." As Bronh set talons on a sill, reaching with her beak for the latch, Ashai directed, "Not yet. Tidestorm's due in a little less than two hours, the way this glass is dropping. Wait until it's blown over. There'll be a good moon tonight."

"And Pedross?" inquired Bronh, stepping back onto her perch.

"He'll be safe enough up there, now that the Alliance is making its move. I may have time to make a quick run and fetch him before we have to engage—that will depend on how many baymasters have managed to agree to the alliance, and whether they'll be held up by Timath Rey's refitting. Keening Isles have the largest fleet: the rest won't want to engage without him. And then there's always the question of ice. . . . Can you survey the East Isles and be back before lastlight tomorrow?"

Bronh calculated distances and the available high-level wind streams and their direction in that season. "Barring storms, yes."

"Good."

Ashai whistled up the tube for the sailmaster and directed a change of signal flags to convene a conference of commanders, sub-commanders, and sailmasters in five hours' time: when the tidestorm's daily hurricane would have passed by to exhaust itself punishing the craggy coasts that flanked the mouth of Erth-rimmon and the highlands below Han Halla.

Bronh ruffled and preened her feathers, ignoring the renewed activity in the cabin as new reports were laid out and the old stack removed for filing. Smoothing the interlocking microscopic hooks on the last primary, Bronh tucked her head under her wing and fell asleep.

On the twelfth of the month called Waiting, five days after the duel, Poli returned from a trip to the herbalist's practically spitting with indignation and fury. She'd detoured to the High Street gate to chat with the six troopmaids now assigned there as wardens, and one of them had casually complained about the loneliness and gloom in the troopquarters since the rest had gone.

"They just walked off!" Poli exclaimed to Jannus, flinging her coat in one direction and the wadded scarf in another. "How could they do that? They *chose* to serve, nobody made them answer the Troopcalling. They could have taken the Awiro way, if that's what they wanted. But they just decided it wasn't worth it, just all of a sudden—"

Carefully laying aside the tray of notation slips he'd had

brought down to him because he couldn't manage the stairs, Jannus asked her when all this had happened.

"Right after the duel. They're halfway across Han Halla by now. How could they *do* such a thing?" Poli demanded again, with a suffocated feeling in her chest that threatened to become weeping. She closed her hands hard around a chair back and rattled it against the table because she knew Jannus was still too sore to be hung onto. She felt she must hold onto something.

"Could *I* have done that?" Jannus wondered, in a soft, appalled voice.

"They're grown troopmaids, not fish. They had a choice. Even in Lisle they stood and fought, kept their word. Whatever you threw at them, even in dueltrance, no matter *what* it was, they still had a *choice*, Jannus—"

Flinging up her hands, unable to keep still, she dug the packet of herbs from her coat pocket and went around to the kitchen to ask Arabet to make an infusion. On her way back, as she neared the staircase she could feel, through the soles of her feet, the deliberate heartbeat rhythm of the press. She turned aside and looked in.

Two shirtless boys stood on a box to turn the upright man-high wheel that raised and lowered the upper jaw of the press. One handled the downstroke, and both bent to reverse the wheel into the upstroke. That Poli thought of as the tongue of the press extended and retracted with the stroke of the wheel. Every time it extended, a boy snatched the printed sheet away and a girl slapped a fresh one down with just time to true the corners and snatch her fingers back before the flat frog-mouth of the press clamped down on it. Two older adolescents were laying tiny white cubes—surely the triply-cursed letter slugs—in tiny grooved forms, referring several times a minute to corkboards covered with scraps of paper, fixed to the wall above them. At intervals the Lisler, who seemed to be coordinating things, would go up behind this pair and survey their work without saying anything. Meanwhile Dan, crutches propped against the wall, was straddling a bench and carving away at a thick oarlike piece of wood—fireoak, by the grain—holding it up from time to time to check its trueness of line or laying it upon a triangular braced construction on the floor beside him, of which his oar-piece was evidently to be attached when it was done.

Poli stood watching for quite a while without anyone's taking the least notice of her. It was like being one of what Jannus called Rayneth's invisible bodyguards. She lifted one of the printed sheets from a stack near the door. Oddly, the ink smelled piney: perhaps it was a different sort than Jannus used, which had a tarry smell. She laid the sheet overlapping the one below on the pile and bent forward, comparing them. She could tell they were just exactly the same: the little blocks that were words were just the same length, and there were exactly as many of them, on the first lines of both sheets. She spotted a character she knew—a *p*—and then found it again in three other places, just the same on each sheet. And the whole stack of them hip-high, just alike.

Poli thought how odd it was for anyone to want so many of one thing, or to do the same thing just the same way so many times. But then, Rayneth was an odd Lady. Shrugging mentally, Poli straightened the top sheet again on its pile, making certain the corners were exactly right.

The Lisler noticed her as she was turning to leave and insisted on showing her one of the sheets all over again. To please him she asked why there weren't any little word-blocks for a space three whole fingers wide, down the middle. She wasn't sure she should mention it, thinking it might perhaps be a mistake; but they'd printed a whole hip-high stack already, after all, and surely would have noticed that big empty space themselves by now if it were wrong.

And anyhow the Sparrow had lately been making a real effort to be pleasant and Poli didn't want to discourage him.

The Sparrow seemed delighted to explain that the empty space was so the sheet could be folded, once the other side was printed, and sewn up in little bunches of ten or so. It was going to look like a ledger book, not like a scroll.

Poli said, "Oh," glad that it wasn't a mistake.

The Sparrow wanted to show her how the press worked, but just then Dan hollered her name, adding, "She don't care about our trash, Sparrow, let her be. Poli, can we take midmeal with you?"

Poli tipped her head to catch sight of his foot, but he'd put a sock on it so she couldn't tell if he'd changed the dressing today.

He pulled the foot farther under the bench, saying defensively, "It was cold."

"When did you change it last?"

"Just a few minutes back. Ain't that so, Sparrow?" demanded Dan, a bald-faced lie he invited the Lisler to share.

"Certain sure," confirmed the Lisler, looking sly.

" 'Course, I might have got it dirty since," conceded Dan blandly. "You can see, if you're so minded. If we can come take midmeal with you. Now old Solvig's moved his family into the Circle, and Jannus don't come to daymeal, all the company I got is the Sparrow, and you can guess what a joy *that* is."

The Lisler grinned as if he'd been warmly complimented.

Rather vaguely Poli told them they could come—it hadn't occurred to her they'd suppose they'd need inviting—and went back to the kitchen to make the necessary arrangements with Arabet. The infusion was steeping, so it seemed sensible to wait until it was strained so she could take it back to northwing with her.

Jannus looked up abstractedly when she came in. She needed space to set down the steaming mug, so he took the tray back across his lap. It didn't seem as if he'd done much since she'd left.

From the far side of the room Alis complained loudly that Mallie cheated, that it wasn't her turn.

"Was too," responded Mallie, and hit her.

Alis blew herself up like a bullfrog in a fury and kicked—not Mallie, but Liret, who began to snuffle very softly and pick at a ravel in her sweater sleeve.

"Let's play I Told You So," suggested Alis, deflating abruptly.

"All right. You start," responded Mallie, with entire equanimity.

Poli halted in the middle of the floor, finding her intervention unnecessary, and turned back to face the fire, where Jannus was drinking the infusion without comment and making a slow business of trimming a penpoint.

"Dan and the Sparrow are coming to midmeal," Poli announced. "And afterward I'm going hunting."

She'd just decided. She felt she couldn't stand being shut in any longer, though in fact, since arising, she'd spent less than an hour, altogether, in the northwing rooms.

Jannus said, "Not in Han Halla."

"It's clear today. I could see—"

"Not in Han Halla."

Poli took a breath and held it. Han Halla *was* dangerous, and they both knew it perfectly well. He was only anxious, and that surely was understandable, housebound as he was. "I'll see if any of the troop are free," she offered, as compromise.

Jannus considered the angle of the penpoint. "That's a good notion," he agreed, in a tone of total lack of interest. "Maybe they *are* fish."

"What?"

Instead of answering he leaned around to call, "Sua—I've dropped one of these tiny slips somewhere here. Can you find it?"

Scuttling on all fours, Sua rushed across the room to demonstrate how good she was at finding and retrieving tiny things deliberately dropped from armchairs.

Poli went to dig into a strap-bound trunk for her harness, bowcase, and dagger-darts. Her bowstring she found badly frayed: she'd beg the loan of one from Arlanna until she had time to plait a new one for herself. And she was surprised how dry the leather of her harness had become. But, then, she couldn't remember having it out, or oiling it, since they'd come to Quickmoor. It was past time she attended to it. Locating her jar of sheep-grease and a rag with a half-forgotten, pungent, slightly rancid odor, Poli settled down to put the equipment of a troopmaid in proper repair, humming softly to herself.

It was the simplest defense of all: water. Every day, twice or three times a day, one quadrant of the outer slope of the dike was wetted down with countless buckets of water passed from hand to hand. Each fresh skin of wet thickened the layers beneath and froze in a few minutes' time.

Pedross was turning the Circle into a hill of glass.

Heedless of concealment, because his ruse with the *Obedient* had certainly been discovered by now, Pedross walked the rim to survey the progress, making occasional comments that were taken down by a scribe with a strap desk.

"Southwest quadrant," Pedross said. "There should be ten or twelve smudges set to blanket the hill with smoke from noon to the tenth hour on sunny days. The ice is thinning there."

The scribe nodded acknowledgment, her pen scraping.

To the troopmaid following a few paces behind, Pedross said, "Is the Lady still at audience?"

Having checked through the link, the troopmaid reported that Ketrinne was still occupied. Pedross directed he be informed as soon as the Lady was free.

It was a pity, Pedross mused, to waste Valde as soldiers. Their best use was in communications. The remainder of the Quickmoor troop provided him with the best scouting and signaling corps he'd ever worked with. He could keep in continuous contact with the watchers downriver, his headquarters, and a score of duty posts and task depots at once.

Of course reserving them to such use meant he didn't have any soldiers, but Pedross was confident he'd find a way to remedy that tactical difficulty too.

Above the ice sheath at the crown of the hill, he was having breastworks piled to protect his hypothetical army of archers, when he got them. He judged he'd need about fifteen hundred to cover the hill properly, allowing for the inevitable attrition. The Circle's perimeter was too long for the Valde troopmaids to have defended the half of it, even had the troop remained at full strength. For this reason Pedross was much less agitated about the mass desertion than Ketrinne continued to be.

Leaning on the breastwork and calculating how thick an ice sheathing it would need to become effectively arrow-proof, Pedross continued to take each problem calmly in its turn. Without a protected place to stand, his hypothetical soldiers alone would have been no use. When he got them, they'd have fortifications to man. Each thing in its proper sequence, he thought.

He'd chosen Quickmoor as *his* place to stand, and he would fortify, arm, and man it the best ways he could. Since he'd begun the process, all anxiety seemed to have left him. It was as if he'd been born to such a task, and found even the haste and dread he encountered on every side to be known, predictable forces like time and weather, only factors in his calculations.

Every day's passing bettered his odds and brought the ice nearer. Today, the seventeenth, the river-link reported its progress south beyond Slatefen, and Erth-rimmon was skinning over, some mornings, in Newstock. If the ice arrived before Ashai, all would be well until thaw. If not, then at least

Quickmoor had to face a frontal assault, not a protract-ed siege. Ashai wouldn't withdraw any substantial force from Longlands for any long period—Pedross estimated the attack-ing force he must confront as about five ships carrying fifteen hundred marines at the very most—nor would Ashai risk his ships being iced in here, immobilized for the season and per-haps fired. . . .

Pedross wondered if he'd given sufficient consideration to the uses of fire.

He dictated a reminder to the scribe to find out what sort of combustible liquids could be had in quantity, and bottles of some kind to hold them.

The troopmaid presently reported that the audiences were over. Having directed the scribe to take her notes to Solvig and then report back, Pedross descended the inner slope in long, stiff-legged strides.

In the time he'd been in the Circle of Quickmoor he'd con-structed a mental map of at least the major thoroughfares, checking with his compass and counting intersections; it pleased him to be able to find his way to the audience hall without needing to be led by the hand.

Shoving open the doors, he took two strides inside the hall before he saw what Ketrinne was about. Arms folded, she stood in the center aisle, watching two workers on a ladder decapitate, with mallet and chisel, the Valde sculptured on the walls. The workers were making a methodical business of it: move the ladder, then one would climb, the other bracing the ladder's shafts. Two smart thuds of the chisel biting in, and the head would topple to the floor while the Lady of Quickmoor looked on with bleak, stony satisfaction.

It was not a gesture calculated to improve the morale of the troopmaids who'd remained.

Quickly scanning for Arlanna, Pedross spotted the troop-leader up near the dais in conversation with another Valde, her face no more unreadable than usual.

Pedross felt Ketrinne's gesture unnecessarily savage and melodramatic; but it was, after all, her hall and her city. If she chose to chisel it away in blunt chunks or paint it all over in green stripes, that was her concern.

Schooling his manner to neutrality, Pedross continued down the aisle.

Greeting him with a brief look, Ketrinne remarked needlessly, "They offended me."

"It would appear so," said Pedross, controlling an impulse to flinch as another head thumped down. "Lady, what do the Crescent folk live off in winter, when there's no traffic or trade?"

"What they've put by. And many are birds of passage. They go upriver to Overwater or Aftaban, and then inland, among the farmstead folk, until the thaw comes. Perhaps a third remain through the winter."

"And the Crescent guard: what of them?"

"I don't know. It's never been necessary for me to inform myself what arrangements that woman may make."

Solvig might know. Pedross made a mental note to ask him. Some of the passage-birds might be prepared to stay, and fight, if the pay was right.

Money was fortunately no problem. Ketrinne had opened her treasury to him, allowing whatever sums he required, with minimal interest, against his promissory notes-of-hand; and Solvig Innsmith, by no means a poor man, had put his considerable resources at Pedross's disposal without even that much formality. He had the money to *hire* his army, provided he could locate and recruit them in time.

He asked if the troopmaid sent into Is had yet had any luck locating anyone resembling a leader among the Fishers: someone who might be persuaded to hire out his tribe, or clan, or family—not a lot was known about how Fishers might organize themselves—for a few weeks' training and a bit of fighting thrown in. Ketrinne relayed the question to her troopleader, who returned a negative reply.

The Valde to whom Arlanna had been talking looked around during this exchange, and Pedross was a bit surprised to recognize her as Poli. She was wearing the usual cross-strapped harness of troopmaids, with bowcase and quiver slanted diagonally across her shoulders. Except that the colors she wore were green and silver-gray, he would have taken her for one of the Quickmoor troop; and even the colors hadn't been enough to really rouse his attention.

Curious to learn what she was doing here, Pedross walked nearer, greeting her, "Good morn to you, Mistress Poli."

She looked at him expressionlessly and for a moment

Pedross thought she was going to refuse to reply. Then she said, "Burn bright, Pedross Ashaison," civilly enough.

"What brings you out of the Crescent—more slaves?"

"Hunting."

"How's Jannus?" he asked, trying another tack.

"Mending."

The terse, flat responses sounded less than friendly, but Pedross cautioned himself against judging Valde manners by his own standards. "Could you carry a message to the Lady Rayneth for me?" When she just continued to look at him with that same unnerving blank stare, Pedross continued, "I would like to rent some of her people. I'd be glad to meet her out at the High Street gate at any time she finds convenient. She will, I hope, understand why I don't think it prudent to bring my petition to her personally. . . . Will you carry my word?" he inquired, with some trace of asperity in spite of himself.

She was looking, he belatedly realized, not at him but past him: toward the two workmen. A thump from behind notified Pedross of yet another image beheaded.

"I see little of the Lady," Poli said in a colorless, uninterested voice.

Ketrinne tore herself away from her symbolic massacre and came to join them, inquiring almost casually, "What did he do, Poli?"

The question was ambiguous, but Pedross didn't doubt Ketrinne was referring to Jannus.

"He fought. He did what he could. What did you expect?" responded Poli, with a subtle shift of position: balanced, confronting Ketrinne squarely. Bronh had taught Pedross to understand such things, when he thought to notice them.

"What did he do?" repeated Ketrinne, mild-voiced and relentless. "How did he do it?"

"How should *I* know?"

"Haven't you asked him?"

"We didn't know they'd gone until afterward. . . ."

Judging that to be an evasion, Ketrinne asserted, *"You* didn't know, at least," and Poli didn't dispute it, turning slightly toward Arlanna.

Arlanna's look dropped to the floor: she looked embarrassed. Quietly she gave the confirmation she alone among them could supply: "He did not know."

"Anyway," Poli said, "they had a choice. *In'farioh* or no, he's not a wind, just to blow them away like so many leaves."

"*In'farioh?*" queried Ketrinne.

Arlanna supplied, "A farspeaker. One gifted in the inspeaking, whose *farioh* can reach those far away."

"Far away," mused Ketrinne, and sat down on the dais steps. "Could he bring them back?"

"He didn't send them," replied Poli heatedly. "They broke faith of their own accord."

Feeling increasingly uncomfortable, Pedross put in, "Lady, we don't *need* them. . . ."

"*I* need them!" Ketrinne flashed back at him. "This is a Bremneri riverstock. I require troopmaids, my full troop, to my defense! How are we to endure, if the Valde break faith?"

After a moment's very strained silence Poli demanded, rather plaintively, "Lady what do you want of me?"

"I want my troopmaids back."

"If Arlanna could not hold them, what do you expect from me?" protested Poli—reasonably enough, Pedross thought—but the mood of accusation, defense, and guilt was not to be dispelled by mere logic.

Ketrinne seemed to blame all Valde for the desertions, and Poli, in spite of her protests, to consider herself implicated in either the actions of her mate or of the renegade troopmaids. Pedross saw that plainly enough, even if it didn't make much sense.

Abruptly Poli started down the aisle without any word of parting. Low-voiced, Arlanna remarked to Ketrinne that, on her own authority, she'd given leave for one of the troopmaids to accompany Poli into Han Halla, as she'd done before in the past few days.

"I do *not* give leave," replied Ketrinne harshly.

With an aloof, measuring look, Arlanna said after a moment, "As you will, Lady."

A little cautiously, Pedross settled on the dais beside Ketrinne, who seemed to be inspecting the progress of the workmen, and asked diffidently, "Why blame Poli?"

"Whoever heard of a Bremneri *in'farioh*? It's unnatural, an abomination. How did he learn to focus dueltrance, with no more *marenniath* than a stone, or force troopmaids to break faith, except through *her*?" replied Ketrinne in a rapid, husky mutter. "*She* has brought this on us, pacting with a Bremneri eight hundred years too late, teaching him things no Bremneri has any business knowing. . . . It's *her* fault, Pedross. And she knows it. It's *her* doing."

Seeing that anything he said would only make him a fresh target for her resentment, Pedross postponed the things he'd wanted to discuss with her and went off to confer with Solvig Innsmith instead.

On the morning of the nineteenth, Dan came in with all sorts of excellent pretexts. The writing on one entry slip needed deciphering, and another seemed out of sequence. Tomorrow they'd need more filled corkboards, and were they ready, and how would he know which ones to take?

Jannus deciphered the blotted slip, and confirmed the entry in its order. For the rest, Dan should ask Rayneth. She'd been supervising the two clerks while Jannus wasn't able to get upstairs. Jannus returned his attention to his tray of entry slips, hoping Dan would have the decency to keep still and go away.

"Where's Poli got to, tell me?" inquired Dan, looking around with elaborate casualness.

"I think she said she was going hunting."

It was the fifth time in seven days. What she caught, or what became of it, Jannus had not the slightest idea.

"Into Han Halla?" Dan wanted to know, frowning, and with good reason.

"Likely."

Jannus believed she was now going alone, unaccompanied by any of the troopmaids. But she hadn't said, and he hadn't asked her. There was nothing to be said.

Dan leaned back in the chair he'd drawn up, hands laid on knees. "What's hatching here, tell me?" he asked quietly, as one who had a right to ask such things.

She's going to leave me. Jannus almost said it out loud, the belief that repeated endlessly, every waking hour and sometimes beyond. *She doesn't know it yet, not fully, but she's started to leave already.*

What he said was, "What is it you're talking about?"

"Don't you be cute. You two never did *say* all that much, but there was talk going on all the while, just the same, if a body had eyes to see it. Whatever egg you're hatching now, you'd best look to it: it's gone bad. If it starts to crack, you'd best damn well get clear or you'll get a stink you don't expect."

"Well, now I know what *you* think."

"No you don't because I don't know *what* to think. Figured that first week it was that you was broke up so bad, but that ain't it. And then I figured it was because you beat that troopmaid, that after it was done Poli held it against you some way—"

"Dan. Just go away." That phrase had bad resonances, but Jannus kept them to himself.

"Like you're doing? Just sitting there, you've gone so far I can't hardly see you. And you sure ain't hearing me. Or go off like Poli's done, just drift off with a vague look like she's forgotten— Set still, don't be a bigger fool than you can help."

Jannus continued to force himself erect against the objections of bound ribs, a nearly immobile knee, and enough assorted bruises to make such exercise sufficiently unpleasant to embarrass even Dan, who let his head hang.

"All right, old lad. Have it your own way, then. *Quit*, won't you?" At the last possible second Dan snatched the tray before it slid onto the floor. Jannus left him holding it and worked his way deliberately to the right-bedroom door, leaning against the wall and available furniture. He couldn't use a crutch because the ribs and shoulder wouldn't stand the pressure. Shutting the door behind him, he heard Dan fling the tray onto the table and slam the outside door resoundingly.

What can be lost, will be. He remembered Ketrinne's saying that. Easing with great caution onto the bed, hissing soft breaths unconsciously as a certain angle proved cruel, he managed finally to stretch out.

What can be lost, will be.

Poli's started to leave.

Half the Quickmoor troop have gone. Poli will go next.

Since the duel's ending he'd been lost in a random storm of blame, of shifting obsessive configurations of victims and victimizers who exchanged identities between one hour and the next. Thinking about these configurations only made them more plausible and provided detail. Denying them altogether was impossible: they hurt too much not to be real.

The body's imperative injuries further confused him, so that his perpetual raw headache and his accusatory self-disgust seemed merely alternate ways of feeling the same pain.

He retained just enough perspective to realize he was in no condition to sort out all the guilts of almost nine hundred years of troopmaids or of his fourteen years' contact with Poli. He doubted himself enough to keep his bitter denunciations, whether directed inward or outward, to himself. If that made him appear curt and distant, he thought that better than weeping all over Dan and soliciting pity he alternately felt he didn't deserve or deserved too well.

He had found himself guilty of the deformity of hatred. Therefore in one configuration he believed himself responsible for Poli's becoming and remaining *sa'marenniath*. He believed she could not have tolerated him with what the full inhearing must eventually have revealed to her. So she'd chosen not to hear, not to know. But now the duel had revealed it anyhow: unmistakable, ugly enough to drive away troopmaids against all oaths, all bonds. He couldn't choose, anymore, not to know. She'd leave as the troopmaids had left, and he had no right of complaint.

Yet the deformity was not of his choosing. It'd been done to him by the troopmaids and the Truthtell: and the Truthtell itself was the fault of the Valde disinclination to look ahead to consequences.

He was the injured one.

He'd had the right to fight the duel, strike back.

He was an abomination, with the acquired focusing skills of a Valde conjoined with the furnace-blast of an undisciplined heart.

He should never have seen Poli in Lora and still struck at her.

He could never have struck at Poli *except* by proxy, in a mirror; yet whatever he'd become, whatever skills he'd gained to make of his dark-heartedness a power and a weapon, was because of her alone. She deserved to be struck at and had no right of complaint.

He could not sort or resolve the contradictions and he could not escape them. He could only suffer them and keep them to himself.

But if Poli goes. . . .

That configuration, the intolerable one, came looping back

like a blow. The ugliness and the blame could be endured,
adjusted to, healed, perhaps, if only she would bear with him.
But she was practicing to leave, the trial flights longer and
less mindful of him every day, as if she were trying to become again the Newstock troopmaid uninvolved with anything of Bremner. He saw it, and understood it, and said
nothing because he didn't believe he had the right. He'd seen
her reflection and struck at it. She was leaving. He had no
defense. He could not forgive himself if she could not.

He heard her come in and call for him. He said, "Here,"
pushing the cylinder of bound ribs upright until he was sitting
on the edge of the bed, sweating and slightly dizzy from the
effort. He heard her casting aside her harness and bowcase.
She came into the bedroom, approaching tentatively, wary,
uncertain. Then with a sudden lithe twist she settled on the
floor and leaned against his leg, apologizing indistinctly, "I
don't want to hurt you."

She meant the ribs, or thought she did. Without conscious
intention his right hand settled on her head, fingers spread
and lost among the intricacies of her hair. As though it were
Sua huddled there, Jannus said, "What's wrong?"

"I have to go away."

His unsurprise seemed to him a settling weight of ice.

She went on presently, "I'm going upriver to see Mene.
They know what's happened here, through the river-link. But
it doesn't touch them, not the way it touches me. Troopmaids
cannot break oath, and the rest of us take no account of it.
We're no more than water, or fish, if we cannot keep the
faith we've bound ourselves to."

"You're going to see Mene. She's troopleader to Darkstock. . . ."

"Overwater," she corrected him.

"Overwater," he repeated, trying to pay sane attention. At
least a place was named. That was more tolerable than just
away.

"If the river freezes," she continued, "I'll walk back. The Is
shore is firm enough. . . ." She twisted around to look at
him, moon-eyed, staring. "Will you be all right?"

She wanted reassurance, not an answer.

He said, "I don't know. But go on, if you have to. Come
back as soon as you can. . . ."

She sprang up then, snatching things out of drawers and

wardrobes, stuffing them into a draw-neck sack. He thought of asking if she'd gotten any money, then remembered that Valde had the right of free passage on all river-craft. She'd be welcomed wherever she went.

Tossing the sack over her shoulder, she was out of the room and gone in the space of a few breaths. Jannus sat with his head bent, fighting the pain behind his eyes. She wouldn't mean to. It would just happen, a word or a nearer concern. But she'd be a fish again among the other fish, turning and schooling according to their own nameless imperatives. She would not come back. It seemed he'd always known it. There were many emotions warring in him, but not surprise.

Pedross had requested, and been granted, the top story of the tower for his own use. It was ideal—commanding a view of the whole Circle, the outer ends of the docks, and a considerable stretch of the river—except when the hour bell was struck, just below. Then the reverberation was fit to shake his teeth. Nevertheless he liked the big bare drafty room and had taken it for his command post.

Having invited Goren, Rayneth's guardsmaster, for an interview on the morning of the twenty-first, Pedross deliberately kept him waiting while he conferred with five Innsmiths, Solvig among them, about various phases of weapons production, and with Serlay, the troopmaid assigned him, about the training of his pack of Quickmoor boys.

There were three hundred forty-three boys, grown and strong enough to be worth the training, their ages all within two years of his own. Ketrinne hadn't liked releasing the boys from the custody of their mistresses or authorizing weapons drills, but she was convinced of the city's vulnerability at the desertion of a paltry few score Valde that she'd allowed herself to be persuaded. For their part, the boys took to the training with a sort of sullen enthusiasm. Their chief lack, besides experience, was discipline. That their preferred weapon was unanimously staffs Pedross attributed to the recent rout of the First Dancer. It was just as well. They couldn't shoot, and there weren't enough broadknives yet to have armed the half of them. But the boys weren't shy of being hit, and demolished straw dummies with satisfactory ferocity.

To Ketrinne's condition that a similar number of girls be

trained in slinging, he'd raised no objection, though he doubted they'd be much use unless the attack held off until thaw. Still, downhill or at close range, they might yet hit somebody or, at the worst, use the slings as garrots.

One household was improvising edged shot to be coated with the powerful anesthetic salve to whose effectiveness Pedross could give personal witness. Perhaps the girls might prove useful yet, the salve ran out. The supply had been planned to last the occasional use of troopmaids for a few quiet ice-bound months, not the demands of a full-scale defense of the city.

When Pedross felt he'd demonstrated enough authority to distinguish him from the whining child Goren had chased around the dueling ground, he set about wooing the guardsmaster. Predictably, Goren's keen appreciation of Rayneth was founded on her ability to pay him and her shrewd insight in choosing him as guardsmaster. Pedross offered double wages and increased authority. But Goren continued to decline a commission, also keenly aware, it seemed, of what'd happened to folk who'd offered armed opposition to Duke Ashai in years past. The most service Pedross was able to recruit was Goren's promise to deliver as many as possible of whatever proven fighters and duelists remained among the Crescent folk. He contracted to supply fifty trained, and fifty hale but untrained, men at an agreed price. Pedross had to be satisfied with that.

It still left him desperately short of archers and of experienced fighters of any sort. His patchwork force now consisted of about eight hundred raw adolescents, half of them girls; two hundred ten bewildered Fishers bonded to him for a month for an equal weight in rice; a prospective hundred Crescent men, able perhaps but entirely undisciplined; forty-nine adult Innsmiths, male and female, all worth their weight in anything one could name as construction bosses directing unskilled workers; and one hundred eight Valde he wanted to reserve, if possible, for communications.

If quantity were all that was needed, he had that, barely. Quality was suspect, but was yet to be proven. The breastworks were finished, and the ice sheathing almost so. Pedross felt he'd made reasonable progress, in the fifteen days since he'd first wakened in Quickmoor.

When the bell sounded the first numbing stroke, with five

more to come, Pedross bolted for the stair landing and trotted down the endless turns, Serlay following a few steps behind. There was a firebomb demonstration scheduled in one of the larger courtyards at the sixth hour. Then he had to sit down with his principal officers and get their recommendations for a more formal chain of command. And after that, Ketrinne had promised to release Arlanna for an intensive strategy planning session at about nine. But before he was interrupted by the obligatory daymeal whose leisurely pace and multiple courses drove him frantic with contained impatience, he meant to have his force thoroughly organized, if untrained; equipped, if only for the primary assault; and assigned the place and role on the defense perimeter for which they were best suited, other than hauling water.

Han Halla, he was thinking: all that wonderful fog and ice and quicksand. How could he persuade the attacking force to make Han Halla their primary line of retreat? All splendidly lost and swallowed up?

Serlay's call interrupted his speculation, and Pedross wheeled inquiringly.

"Arlanna says . . ." Serlay began, and then waited some more. Pedross wondered if she couldn't have walked and listened at the same time, but didn't say so. At length, the troopmaid went on, "Arlanna Wir says, sail ships down-river—"

"How many? How far?"

"Many. Still far."

The one disadvantage of Valde, as compared to heliographs, Pedross had already discovered, was their inability to quantify with any precision.

"Which watcher?" he prompted.

"Aria. . . ."

The first. He'd had the six scouts space themselves at a half-day's run apart, just barely in linking distance: that put the ships about a hundred river-miles away. They'd be here by dawn on the twenty-eighth at the latest. He had six or seven days' warning to finish his preparations.

"Are they under Ashai's banner?"

Having checked through the link, Serlay reported that they were.

"Recall Aria. The rest remain in place and report as the ships reach them. I want Solvig, Kevel, Matt, Ketrinne,

Mistress Georgia, and Arlanna, plus two good scribes, in the
green parlor in half an hour. Done?"

"Done," she agreed.

Hurrying on down the passageway, Pedross figured he'd
left himself just enough time before the meeting to fit in the
firebomb demonstration.

Shortly after the midmeal, which Jannus and his two clerks
took inattentively in their upstairs workroom, Jannus was notified that guests were expected. The notification came in the
form of a small procession of pages and hundred-bead
women trudging noisily up the stairs, hauling all his personal
property in large wicker hampers. What actually brought
him, with slow care, off his stool and into the doorway to investigate was an approaching high-pitched howl, unmistakably Sua's.

The front of the procession, children in tow, turned at the
upper landing and bore their burdens away around the corner, heading toward the upper level of northwing. Sua's wail
gained volume through the long corridor behind the Evenhall
gallery, then faded and finally ended as the last of the
column were making the two right turns and passing, with
breathless bursts of conversation, out of sight.

The first thought occurring to him was that Poli never had
liked the garden much anyway.

Distantly, he wondered if he ought to follow to see that the
five were again settled for their nap, which had been interrupted, or find out what had prompted the removal, or do
nothing. Somehow neither of the alternatives that required
moving seemed very urgent. The third option succeeded by
force of inertia.

Jannus was turning back toward his table when Dan came
banging up the stairs—crutches discarded—demanding,
"What's wrong with Sua? I could hear—"

"Seems Rayneth needs the northwing . . . the first level of
it, anyhow."

"What for, tell me?"

"She didn't say."

"Come on," said Dan, and hurried off in pursuit of the
procession.

Dan would see the children settled then: that had been the
proper alternative, Jannus deduced. And now he didn't have

to do it. Dan would find out what was going on too, so that didn't need thinking about either.

Jannus returned to the entry on moonweed he was working on, shifting on the stool until he found a position that wasn't bothersome. The bound ribs were still awkward but his other injuries had eased at least to the point that he wasn't aware of them unless he tried to reach, or do anything quickly or without premeditation.

It was twenty days since the duel, eight since Poli had gone. The Twenty-seventh of Waiting.

He'd finished *moonweed* and was frowning at Rayneth's appallingly thrifty entry on the subject of *moor*, written the length of the paper, then the width, so that the slip was almost entirely black with her tiny script, when Dan's slightly uneven stride announced his return.

Dan reported that the new room—singular—was fifth on the right, next to the chamber with the water heater, and that he'd tucked up the five with the promise their da would be in to wake them when the hourbell struck seven.

Jannus dutifully requested Alan, the more responsible of his clerks, to keep track of the time and tell him when the hour struck.

"When's Poli getting back, tell me?"

Jannus said, "I don't know."

"She's had time to get to Overwater and back twice over. What's she about, to leave the kits alone all this while?"

"Cinda's looking after them."

"That's no answer, fat old body who's asleep half the time," was Dan's definite, disapproving rejoinder. "How could she just off and leave you to manage them, state you was in?"

Inevitably an image of the Quickmoor First Dancer departing the dueling ground as inexplicably flashed into Jannus's mind. But he said only, "Valde don't think ahead much. Whatever is present, right this very minute, that takes all their concern."

"I wonder you let her go, then."

Deliberate, Jannus laid his pen aside and capped the ink. He thought of about five things to say, all comments on the ignorance of Valde which Dan's remark blatantly demonstrated. But the effort of even thinking about arguing, much less explaining to Dan the actual state of things, was more than he could force himself to.

Unbothered by the pause, Dan proceeded to the lesser news that Duke Ashai himself was expected for the daymeal. "And who knows: he might want to stay the night," Dan remarked, with an ironic lift of an eyebrow. "So Rayneth turns you out. What's she think he's here for, tell me: a basket social? 'Course, northwing has a fine view of that ice hill that used to be the Circle—maybe she thinks he'll want to admire it awhile before he cracks it open like an egg."

Jannus picked up the crosswritten entry slip on *moor* and held it before Dan, who frowned at it, trying to catch hold of a horizontal word, then, twisting in search of an identifiable vertical one.

"That's awful," Dan observed fervently, squinting his eyes shut as though the attempt had injured them. "Does she ravel sweaters for knitting wool, too? Better you than me—I'd go blind, or crazy, or both together. All right. I can take a hint when it clubs me. I'll leave you to it. But don't forget: I promised them seven."

Seven what? Jannus wondered, then made the connection and nodded.

"Oh, and did you hear?" Dan said, interrupting his exit just inside the door. "Domal Ai—Old Foureyes—and some of the baymasters are coming out against Ashai, over this Longlands business. Past time, I say, but, then, I was expecting this to happen four, five months ago—"

Jannus held up the entry slip again and, with a half-sour smile, Dan consented to go back downstairs to his work and to leave Jannus to his.

But once free of interruption, Jannus found it impossible to concentrate even on the mechanical business of copying out the slip and standardizing the order and style of the information to match that of the other entries. It wasn't that Dan's news interested him. Rather, it had merely destroyed any interest in learning what history and meaning Rayneth had assigned to the noise *moor*. If he persevered, in three or four days he thought he might reach *mud*. That prospect alone was sufficiently discouraging.

"That's enough," he told his clerks, to their unconcealed delight. "We've been at this three solid days. I'm going to take my five down to the High Street dock to watch Ashai come in. You can come with us, if you want, or do whatever you please so long as Goren or Rayneth don't catch you at it. . . ."

Alan said, "I'll take that risk," and Sann, the other clerk, stretched expressively before bolting for the door.

Jannus capped all the ink, checked to make sure no lamps had been left burning, and then went slowly through frantic corridors full of servants digging into linen presses and arguing, or bursting out of the doorways with bundles of fresh rush matting, or scrubbing down the big Evenhall window, mistrustfully located on an interior wall with a bank of cheap and replaceable windows on the outer wall to slant its colored fires down into the Evenhall whenever the sun fell low in the west.

He found the old woman, Cinda, not merely asleep but missing. The sleeping children, lying crosswise down the length of a bed in their usual fashion, were entirely unattended. But he supposed he should have expected that, with the unseasonal frenzy of cleaning and preparation wracking the Household. He'd decided to take the children out on the assumption that both kitchen and cook would be too occupied for children to be welcome.

It took him a while to locate the children's cold-weather clothes in the haphazard mound of baskets and hampers in the middle of the room. He wasn't in any hurry, and he found shifting the baskets awkward and difficult because of his ribs. Sua, the lightest sleeper, woke while he was working, and helped him dig through the tangled heaps of clothing. Each thing he found that was Poli's he folded with blank meticulousness and laid in a neat pile which, as it grew, became a mute exclamation of order surrounded by carelessness and confusion. When Liret, chasing Alis who'd snatched her scarf, flipped the pile askew, Jannus left it like that and soon located the last mitten.

When they were finally all dressed it was past the eighth hour, midafternoon, but there was still time to get down to High Street; had Ashai arrived, Jannus was sure he'd have heard the uproar.

Going downstairs wasn't nearly as hard as going up, though he had to get both feet on each stair before stepping toward the next. "Mallie, you keep track of the three," he directed, as Jacko opened the outside door for them. "Sua, you keep track of Mallie. And you three, you keep track of me so I don't get lost or rolled on by a drawcart."

In fact, he didn't see a single drawcart moving. Dan had remarked how the Crescent had been thinning out lately, only one shop in three still open. The rest, Dan had reported, had loaded whatever remained of their stock onto a barge or two and had been towed upriver to some more profitable wintering ground. If their sheds and stalls, that now gaped vacant, survived the scouring of the thaw flood, they'd return to take possession when the season changed. If not, they'd collect usable debris, buy a bit of canvas, and build a new stall only slightly more ramshackle than the one it replaced.

The docks, too, were all but empty, with not a single baycraft to bar the opposing shore with its masts or rigging. Several blocks south he could see a late-departing barge being piled and lashed, and, beyond that, a lone packet tied close to the riverwall, the tideswell being high enough today to cover a stretch of each dock above and below its fixed hinge, so that only the crooked, tarred pilings marked its middle portion.

High Street, though, was never abandoned. The merchants and innkeepers there fought every inch of flood rise, sometimes ending up on the rooftops, he'd heard, in especially bad years, to maintain ownership of their sites and begin cleaning and repair of the establishments the instant the water began to go down. That was what happened in Rayneth's Household too. There was still a line, seemingly ineradicable, at head height on the second level, left by the flood of '68 which had lasted most of a month and reached nearly two-thirds of the way up the dike.

Hearing his name called, Jannus looked back to find Sparrowhawk just reaching the Crescent road, waving as he hurried to catch up.

"Alan said where you were bound," the Lisler explained, tossing a dangling scarf end back over his shoulder and falling into step. "Wanted me to go drinking wi' him, but I said no. I'd as soon see Ashai my own self, that held my bond, and not from the fat-meat end of the daymeal table. Ain't too cold out, is it? Wonder how their ice is holding out?"

Over the rooftops the hill glittered wetly, topped by its new wall over which Jannus could see an apparently unbroken line of heads and torsos, like turned dark posts against the sky, looking down.

"*They* know," commented Sparrowhawk, nodding toward the levee. "What'll happen, do you s'pose?"

Jannus noticed Sparrowhawk had caught Dan's tribal habit of ending most things in a question. He caught Alis's eye, recalling her from investigating a dead gull, and replied, "Well, first there'll be a talk, I imagine. Pedross and Ashai trading threats to see if one can scare the other one out. That will come to nothing. That'll probably be tonight, unless they try a night fight. . . . What is it, the twenty-eighth?"

"Twenty-seventh. Two months yesterday, that you bought my bond," commented Sparrowhawk, with a sudden grin.

"So the moon will be just past the full a good three days yet. Enough light for fighting, if it stays clear. . . ." Only slightly interested, Jannus looked south, where most of their weather came from, and found the sky unmarked.

Or nearly so. Almost motionless, poised on some upper wind, was a hanging dot Jannus thought he could have put a name to.

Jannus found a seat in the riverwall, counting the children with a glance, and continued, "But poor light would favor the Circle. Shooting down, they'd be pretty sure to hit somebody, plain against the ice, while staying bad targets themselves. So I'd guess Ashai would wait until morning."

The children had started a game of touch-me-last in the broad open space where High Street met the Crescent road. Looking beyond them, up to the head of the street, Jannus noticed only a solid darkness where the gate usually stood open. Ketrinne had put in the flood panels. Jannus wondered if they'd do her any good, and how she and Pedross might be getting on.

It had bothered him to learn Pedross was back in the Circle in spite of the duel, whose only effect now seemed to have been to drive Valde from Jannus's immediate vicinity. But now Jannus found he really didn't care. Dispassionately, he supposed Pedross hadn't been the aim of the duel, only its occasion. There'd been Rayneth's conscripted mob ready to make its dash at the Circle, and Ketrinne's troopmaids making ready to receive them, and that had been averted. Anybody who could take any joy in that, including Pedross, was welcome to, for all Jannus cared.

"Will it be safe in the household, do you think?" Sparrowhawk asked, breaking in on Jannus's abstraction.

"Watch Rayneth. She won't stay any longer than she figures it's safe."

"I s'pose that's true, too. . . . Dan says *he* thinks that *you* think she ain't coming back." Sparrowhawk didn't mean Rayneth.

"Dan's got enough sense not to say so to *me*," rejoined Jannus harshly. Then he saw how stricken the young Lisler looked and felt very tired. "Hafri, you're the *touchiest* person I think I ever—what is it?"

Sparrowhawk controlled his twitch of a grin and looked off downriver. "Just that that's what Dan says. About you. Says a lot, Dan does. . . ."

It was a sort of apology. Jannus agreed, "That he does."

Sparrowhawk nodded solemnly and continued to look downriver while Jannus watched the progress of the game of touch-me-last just to be sure the children didn't start investigating any of the vacant shops and get into something they oughtn't.

The hourbell struck nine and the game ended as if on signal. Huffing and red-faced, the children submitted to having their buttons rebuttoned and their mufflers retied. Sparrowhawk had collected a little pile of flat stones, the remains of some past thaw flood caught behind the riverwall as the water had receded; without saying anything, he began skipping stones as far out on the surface of the river as he could throw. The children instantly pounced on his pile, hurling the stones in tiny arcs that plopped when they hit, a scant rod or two out. Sua was the only one strong and coordinated enough to achieve even one bounce, though Liret, with increasing ill-temper, refused to stop trying to match her feat.

The game was too old for them.

Jannus looked around until he spotted an empty bottle and had Mallie fetch it to him, then had Alis push the tiniest stones down the neck until it was about a quarter full. He dropped the bottle very gently onto the water, where it steadied and bobbed just beyond arm's reach. All the children pelted it gleefully with pebbles and assorted trash, trying to sink it, occasionally hitting it, until it floated underneath a dock and didn't reappear. Then the children scattered to hunt another bottle, Jannus reminding them to keep out of the shops.

"I see them," remarked Sparrowhawk quietly, and Jannus turned too suddenly and hurt himself. Pressing an arm close against the offended ribs, he stood up, looking south.

Over the stretch of reeds behind which the river curved, masts, sails, and banners showed, some superimposed on the others so it was impossible to determine how many ships there were. The sails were all but slack. The baycraft were riding the tidelift, with just enough following breeze to give them steerage way. Presently the first rounded the curve, having to tack across the current a bit to keep the breeze. Mallie had found a bottle and jammed it into Jannus's hands for filling, a chore which he managed without having to look down more than once.

As the second ship emerged from the cover of the intervening reeds, a crowd of the Crescent guard came trotting out of Cutter Street with their pikes on their shoulders, leather body-armor dark and shiny with fresh grease. Jannus called the children to him and they all moved one dock farther north while the guardsmen took up positions beside the head of High Street pier under the almost continuous orders of the two tenners present, identified by rosettes of blue and yellow streamers attached at their left shoulders.

Three ships were in view when Rayneth herself arrived in a drawcart decorated with inlaid enamelwork, four more guardsmen and Goren accompanying her on foot. The High Street and Cutter Street taverns started to empty then, producing a fairly sizeable crowd.

Two more ships came into view, and a set of masts was still visible beyond the brown reeds. Six ships, altogether, then. Jannus told the children, "Time to get back now."

Sparrowhawk goggled at him, demanding incredulously, "You're *leaving?*"

"I've seen Ashai before this," responded Jannus, checking for missing mittens or scarves. Finding, miraculously, all accounted for, he started around the back of the crowd, the children keeping close without needing to be told. After one indecisive look to either side, Sparrowhawk apparently decided not to miss the grand reception and Jannus lost sight of him.

They passed Cutter Street as the leading ship came level

with the first of the docks and began its turn, the sails being hauled toward the mast's crossarms, voices shouting orders that carried clearly across the water. The near railing was solidly packed with armed men—a hundred or more, Jannus guessed, just on the one side. With their dark helmets it was hard to be certain, but Jannus thought quite a lot of them looked like Bremneri. Well, he'd predicted it, though not quite the fashion of it.

He said, "Alis, let the cat be, It doesn't want to meet you. Let it go its ways."

Alis, refusing to be warned, made a snatch at the large rail-ribbed stray which had been investigating a pile of frozen refuse. The cat grabbed back with both sudden forepaws before bounding away. Alis howled, more from startlement and disappointment than hurt, as bundled as she was; but Jannus sat her down on a doorstep and rolled up her sleeve to inspect the tiny claw dots, only one of which seemed to have broken the skin.

"Spit on it?" Mallie offered, pulling off a mitten to prepare her fingers for the procedure. Given permission, Mallie spat with great intentness onto two fingers and applied them to the dots while Alis demanded to be told why he'd *done* that, she hadn't hurt *him*.

"Da *tol'* you," Sua reminded her smugly.

Two of the ships were in the process of tying up, hard against the riverwall; a third, presumably Ashai's own by the extra bannerwork in back, was throwing cables to be caught by the nearest guardsmen. The last three ships were completing their turns and approaching docks farther along. A hinged walkway was being let down from Ashai's ship and fastened by two guardsmen to the slant of the pier above the waterline. Rayneth had left her drawcart and taken a place at the end of the double file of guardsmen to do her patron full honor.

The minute the walkway was secured, a man in a long blue coat began descending, hanging onto its rope sideguard. The ship's crews and the marines set up a shout, the latter hammering on the rail with the butt ends of their broadknives. Into this tumult fell Bronh, opening wings in the last instant to check her stoop, hurtling directly into the man in the blue coat who toppled off the steep walkway into the river with the alver clutched against his chest.

Then the arrows hailed down.

Nearly all the guardsmen were struck at once. The crowd exploded back toward the buildings for shelter, many hit as they retreated. The ships were casting loose in great haste, but those moored on the south side of their piers were held briefly in place by the current, long enough for a few small men to run from vacant buildings where they'd been hidden and hurl bottles with rags aflame in the necks. Three ships backed clear with smoke beginning to rise on their bow decks, the other three already past the docks' ends, so that the renewed deluge of arrows fell short.

Watching utterly stunned, Jannus saw a blot of blue clinging to the hanging walkway as Ashai's ship drifted broadside toward the Is shore. A line was thrown down and Ashai was hauled up over the rail, still holding Bronh like a bunch of wet rags against his chest.

All the ships were in open water now, approaching midriver. Anchors were rattling out, and the smoke still eddied and swirled from the bows of the three craft that'd been firebombed.

The arrows had stopped falling. They littered the street stones, practically in piles, looking harmless as haystalks.

Jannus snatched the nearest children and shoved them into the doorway beside Alis, then sat the last pair forceably on the bottom step. "You stay here and don't move one step, do you hear me? You could be hurt. Do you understand? Stay right here and don't move."

Getting a few frightened nods—they'd been more upset by his rough handling of them than by the attack—Jannus ran back toward High Street, glancing around twice to make sure they were still safe in the doorway's shelter.

The chief slaughter had been among those closest to the river: the targets had been the ships, and Ashai himself, not the crowd. Except for Bronh's last-second warning, the archers would have held off longer, until the Andran troops had landed; as it was, the victims seemed mainly guardsmen, but there were many huddled lumps without body armor fallen by the low wall where a few minutes before his children had been gathering tiny stones.

Jannus moved among the bodies, then looked toward the middle of the road where those only wounded, or knocked down in the panic retreat, were stirring, giving vent to confused cries of either pain or alarm. One was Rayneth, lurching upright with another howling woman clinging to her arm. Past the rising people Jannus saw Sparrowhawk waving at him from an empty doorspace, not daring yet to venture into the open road.

Relieved, then shocked all over by the bodies fallen into poses of ungainly immobility, Jannus became aware of a sound that had been going on for some time—a wordless, eerie keening that wandered and shifted, finding strange harmonies and strange discords: the sound of a Valde troop in full cry, louder and more ominous than he'd ever heard it. He looked slowly up toward the dike. Every single torso now visible was tabarded, the sun falling on color combinations of many different riverstocks. Some he didn't even recognize. He could see the dark dots of opened mouths as hundreds upon hundreds of troopmaids sang their peculiar melodies at the ships of Ashai Rey.

"No," replied Ashai definitively, "I won't risk you, Bird. Pedross will have alerted the Valde. They can't hear you, but they're not blind and they're wicked shots. It'd be too ironic for you to be skewered by a Valde after all this while."

He was making a pool on the floorboards and shivering convulsively from his submersion in the frigid water of Erthrimmon, but stood studying a map unrolled on his chart table. Bronh, more attentive to her condition, spread her immense waterlogged wings alternately above a small stove, too soaked even to begin preening and still suffering from the bodily shock of the chill.

"Then what are you going to do?" she asked, while wet from her spread primaries bounced and hissed on the stovetop.

"Nothing," Ashai responded abstractedly, reaching for a distance-rule, then squeezed water out of a sleeve end as he realized he was dripping on the map. "An hour or so before moonset is soon enough. Give them time to get tired and worried."

"Pedross knows that trick."

"That's because it works. What colors did you see, Bronh? Which riverstocks?"

Bronh half shut one wing and cupped the other over the stove's radiance. There wasn't room in the cabin for her to extend both wings at once. Reviewing what she'd seen in the long moment of her dive, she listed slowly, "Overwater. They were the most numerous. That's to be expected, since it's nearest. Then Aftaban, perhaps a hundred fifty. Dark, scarcely less. Hillstock, no more than thirty."

Frowning and shivering, Ashai began making measurements, pausing occasionally to wring out a cuff or shake drops from his fingers. "Why the variation in number, Bird? Why thirty from one place and a full troop from another?"

"Farther into their service," Bronh began, meaning to state the obvious, that most troops were diminished to two or three dozen by the time their service was done: after all, that was the whole idea. But Darkstock's troop was five years into its term whereas Hillstock's had been replaced only last spring. Bronh kept track of such things, even when they were of no obvious use, if they involved Valde. So the older troop was the better represented, though fewer in available numbers. She described this discrepancy, then continued, "It might depend on how many the various Ladies were willing to cede to Quickmoor's defense, leaving themselves correspondingly vulnerable."

"Possibly. . . . There's a correlation between numbers and distance here that's strange—the ratio fits actual land miles, not traveling distance by river. Notice. Numbers drop off sharply between Dark and Hillstock. And Hillstock is the farthest north, and farthest in its overland interval, though the river distances are roughly comparable for all four. It looks like one arc of an impact crater, Bird," remarked Ashai, walking spread fingertips from one marked city to the next. "Overwater and Aftaban affected equally, Dark slightly less, then no more than a slight stir when it hit Hillstock."

"When *what* hit Hillstock?"

"Overwater was the epicenter, to change metaphors," Ashai remarked, ignoring her question. "If it weren't, there'd have been more variation between there and Aftaban, and there isn't. And a really strong blast might . . . *might* reach as far as Dark direct, before it was muted into the usual relay of the river-link. An arc of direct impact from Overwater that reached as far as Dark; and then, diminishing effect through the link. That fits the correlation. . . ." Ashai laid aside the distance-rule and looked up. "Bronh, could we be dealing with volunteers? Desertion *to* Quickmoor, instead of away?"

Bronh shook herself, every quill coming erect so that she seemed twice her size. "Impossible. What would be their motivation—abstract loyalty? Ridiculous. Sympathy for Ketrinne? Twice as ridiculous. If that kind of empathic bond couldn't hold her own troopmaids, how would it so affect total strangers? Impossible."

"But the correlation is still to be accounted for. It would be nice to know whether I'm at war with Bremner yet or not. If they're volunteers. . . ."

Still obviously pondering the question, Ashai called in one of his bodyservants and allowed himself to be stripped of the sodden clothes. The attire he chose to have as a replacement was white, shirt, jacket, and trousers alike, resplendent with gold stitchery at collar and cuffs.

Bronh, jabbing at her underlayer of insulating fluff, took small notice, still reacting to the outrageous suggestion that Haffa troopmaids could have been capable of volunteering for a battle in which they had absolutely nothing to gain. It was unthinkable that her Valde could so disregard the dictates of their survival-drives: race-specific rather than self-specific, the same irresistible Troopcalling and then remain at their posts, even to the wasting of their lives, ten whole years to gain collective sanction and acceptance as adults with the right to choose mates and bear young. Bronh found even the suggestion intolerable.

As if aware of her thought—and probably he *was* aware: they'd known each other so very long—Ashai broke the long silence enforced by the bodyservant's presence by quietly quoting her to herself: " 'There's always an alternative.' "

"Not for my Valde," rejoined Bronh implacably. "They will live and be whole. As they were before. The harm shall be undone. There is *no* alternative."

"May it be as you will," commented Ashai gravely. Wrapping a blanket around his shoulders like an outsize shawl, he began mixing nutrient powder with water in her bowl. "You stay here tonight, Bird. Downbase is too far, and I'll be occupied."

Bronh turned a steady, unblinking eye at the snowy jacket between the hanging folds of blanket, the trousers beneath its trailing points: wonderfully visible by moonlight. Bronh understood then why Ashai had taken so few pains to amend this body's chill and shaking. He didn't plan to be wearing it much longer.

Ashai set the dish on its perch tray and then summoned his principal commanders and the six sailmasters to confirm the final plan for the assault.

Informing Ketrinne that Quickmoor could no longer afford the luxury of measuring only daylit hours, Pedross had devised a system of his own. He'd lit candles of various lengths and diameters at noon precisely and determined how far each had burned in three hours. Choosing one of these for reasons Ketrinne didn't bother to discover, he'd had a few score made up, all from the same mold and the same melt batch of wax, and marked them with notches. The dark was now officially divided into three watches.

Ketrinne's head timekeeper had been offended. An ancient sundial supplemented by an even more ancient water clock had sufficed since the Circle's founding, and the timekeeper resented the intrusion on her art and her prerogatives.

Ketrinne had placated her by giving the candles into her charge and instructing her to mark the beginning of second-watch and thirdwatch by a single stroke of the tower bell—firstwatch, of course, being announced by the bell's sounding fifteen. Ketrinne had learned that half a leader's task was keeping her subordinates sweet and effective. Her will had prevailed over Pedross's intention to trust his timekeeping to the Innsmiths.

Unless he was actively courting or being forced to deal with someone, Ketrinne had discovered, Pedross tended to forget about people. They had no separate reality for him apart from whatever task was at hand.

Once she had thought him hot. Now she believed that he was indifferent to cold because he shared it. Cold was his element, like air to a bird. But even that analogy wouldn't serve: another blackbird had fallen down the chimney today, drugged with smoke, and had roasted in the flue just above her chamber with a terrible smell of burnt feathers. Even air, warm or cold, could betray a bird. Ketrinne reminded herself to have that chimney seen to as soon as this all was over and life returned to normal.

She was wide awake, musing on candles and chimney pots, because the thrice-cursed bell had startled her out of the first

shallows of sleep. She had the scant satisfaction of knowing
secondwatch had begun, attested and approved by the newest
methods.

Pedross could sleep right through the bell. She might never
forgive him that ability. The bell was practically right under
his cot, up where he'd insisted on camping tonight, up at the
top of the tower. She hoped it'd blasted him straight into the
air. She wanted the reassurances of his presence right now,
beside her; but to him, touch-loving and sleep were activities
properly kept separate. She had been more likely to receive
him after brisk breakfast, or to celebrate an opportunity in
midafternoon, than to have him spend the nightwatches with
her when they both demonstrably needed whatever uninter-
rupted sleep they could manage before the attack commenced,
when sleep would be scarce and touch-loving well-nigh
impossible.

Though she could not doubt the sense of that estimate,
Ketrinne was not entirely happy that he could face the prospect of such a fast with such equanimity.

She was frightened. She'd seen executions which she herself
had ordered; but she'd never seen random slaughter like that
wrought by the Valde archers against the folk at the riverside
this afternoon. She'd never heard a sound like the troopmaids' cry, fierce and vast as bitter wind moaning around the
eaves. Had her confidence not had the buttressing of the
massed troopmaids, come from as far as Hillstock to her defense, Ketrinne would have cast Pedross out there and then,
unable to tolerate the real cost of keeping him any longer.
But with thirty score troopmaids, more than had ever stood
to a riverstock's defense before, Ketrinne felt honored and
hopeful against any threat.

She just couldn't sleep, and was terrified. That was all.

Therefore she was awake when the attack began.

One of her chambermaids burst in, followed by a troopmaid bringing the news that Ashai's forces were attempting
the slope from the Han Halla side while a catapult-mount
was being assembled on the solid stones of the Crescent, the
workers protected by a roof of planking wrested from the
walls of abandoned buildings.

Dressing hastily, Ketrinne demanded, "Where's Arlanna?"

"In the tower, Lady."

Ketrinne discarded her first impulse, to summon the

troopleader to her, as both needless and unwise. Quickmoor had a total of five troopleaders now, an unwieldy number; four had taken each one quadrant of the Circle under her charge, with a shifting flow of troopmaids moving from one to another as need dictated. Arlanna was serving to coordinate among them, with the tower's view and Pedross's instructions to aid her. The troopleader had enough to occupy her without adding her Lady's ignorant interference.

It occurred to Ketrinne then that every particular quarter of Quickmoor had almost its own full troop of Valde to guard it. *That* was a thing to ponder—a wonder and a gift.

Tying her sash, Ketrinne asked abruptly, "Does the Lord Pedross request my presence, there above?"

"No, Lady," replied the troopmaid. "He thought you would wish to know battle had been joined."

Well, that was blunt enough, Ketrinne reflected, and likely reasonable, as well. Pedross had set himself to stand here, in the Circle of Quickmoor, and she with him. She would leave him to do so as he judged fit. She herself would never even have thought of using ice as a defense, she knew. Her trust might well be more support than her presence. She'd leave him to his own singular skills.

She had another task to do.

She gave directions for a cold meal to be taken to the tower immediately—things which could be snatched and devoured without thought—and ordered that two woodcrafters of the green rank—judged fit to practice in her own household—and their chief apprentices be roused at once and sent to her in the audience hall.

There, during the second watch of the night and on into the third, while the battle went on unheard and unknown, Ketrinne smoothed pegs and tended the small fire heating a crock of glue while the yawning master woodcrafters undertook the delicate task of drilling small holes without cracking the ancient wood. Then Ketrinne mounted a ladder and set the first of the heads on the torso from which it had been so roughly struck. The woodcrafters' apprentices followed her, tapping, clamping, and gently sanding; but Ketrinne alone, with her own hands, restored each of the sculpted Valde to integrity and honor.

It was the perfect way to direct a battle. By merely

crossing the room, Pedross could overlook the whole confused tumult of attackers and defenders struggling as on a game board, diminished, manageable, responding as quickly to his direction as though he'd put out a hand and moved a piece or two to put the pattern more to his advantage. By leaning on the recess of the north window he could see Ashai's six ships anchored upriver, their masts dark stick shapes against the dull silver of the water, and know whether reinforcements were being sent out.

The quiet center of his shuttling from one open window to another was Arlanna, mentioning facts, reporting, like some wonderful talking heliograph. He replied through her, as he would have spoken through a tube on shipboard. Valde were marvelous. He couldn't imagine himself ever doing without them again. They were a hundred times better than Bronh.

On level ground his patch-quilt force wouldn't have lasted an hour, but the game board had been well prepared. The greatest effort of the attacking force was simply to get up the slope of solid ice to a place where they could fight. Not two out of ten made it, and often no more than a hearty shove was needed to send them barreling back into the climbers below.

The attack was from the Han Halla side, from within the shadow of the levee itself which the falling moon cast to eastward like a second, darker, Crescent. The archers below and the climbing marines were poor targets in the utter black, whereas the defenders, above, were silhouetted against the pale sky. Pedross had lost some people on that account, but not enough to matter yet.

The angle of attack was a good short-term tactic, Pedross judged, but could prove dangerous to Ashai if Pedross could cut the marines off from the ships and drive them into Han Halla. But such a sortie could itself be endangered, trapped between the present enemy force and any fresh troops advancing from the ships: Ashai had not yet committed the half of his people.

The thought of sending such a sortie, a hundred or so from two directions, was a temptation Pedross was continually thrusting away from him. Ashai was a past master of outwaiting an opponent and then tempting him into just that sort of rash action. Pedross had seen him do so, time and time again, in the Longlands campaign. It had protracted the contest more than a season, but Ashai had kept his own losses light while encouraging his opponents to waste their resources until the balance and the ground were finally to his liking. Pedross didn't forget that Ashai had undertaken the conquest of the Longland Spur with a force originally numbering less than five thousand.

The economics of battle dictated that Pedross content himself with a defensive battle, keeping within his strength and letting time, ice, and weather work for him.

Arlanna reported in her quiet monotone that the catapult at the foot of High Street had begun to fling pried-up paving stones completely over the Circle into the Inner Households, to the ruin of their roofs. Pedross, going to look out toward the west, found it impossible to see the falling stone itself, but the explosion of slates where it struck was plain enough.

The siege engine was superfluous to the present battle. Pedross wondered if it were just bait, if Ashai imagined him silly enough to rush out to destroy a catapult capable only of cracking a few slates and making a frightening noise. The Crescent wasn't broad enough to permit the catapult to hurl at the reinforced gates, and the river was *too* broad to make its mounting on the Is shore worthwhile.

"Ignore it," he directed through Arlanna. "The ladies minor should be warned, though, that they'll be getting flaming pitch-balls through their roofs and windows next. The walls won't burn, nor the roofs, but they'll have some scorched carpets. Keep part of the southwest quadrant as fire-spotters and relay warning to the households if any flame is seen."

Returning to the east window that overlooked the fighting, Pedross noted that the marines were resorting to grapples on long lines and that some rough scaling ladders had been brought into play. He directed the lines be cut faster and a few firebombs be tried against the ladders. That was when he learned all the firebombs on two quadrants had been drunk by the defenders—mostly the Crescent men, whose erratic responses Pedross had until then ascribed to simple ineptitude.

He thought of having *them* lit and thrown over to singe the ladders, but restrained himself short of actually giving the order. It would have been bad for morale and probably done the ladders little harm.

Instead he went to his fallback, sacks of grain wetted thoroughly this afternoon and now frozen solid as stone. A few of these, slid off the breastwork at intervals, kept the enemy from moving more marines onto the hilltop than his defenders could easily handle, four or five to one. Their limp forms, unconscious from dart hits or staffs or wounds, supplemented the grain sacks in knocking climbers off the ladders and keeping the outer line of archers skipping to keep their legs from being cut out from under them.

"Fire in Lesilla's household," reported Arlanna.

"Have Lesilla see to it, then. If she lets it spread, I'll have her ears. Don't *say* that," Pedross amended hastily. "Just warn Lesilla and see she gets help from southwest quadrant if she needs it. Nothing's happening over there."

Still watching the shadowy fight on the east, Pedross saw perhaps thirty of the marines come over the breastworks together where his collection of Fishers was posted. The larger marines were battering the Fishers in all directions, upraised hands glinting with broadknives. The Fishers were giving way, jumping and tumbling down the inside of the hill. Pedross's order brought a line of troopmaids running from the right on the inner slope, flinging darts, forcing the marines around the curve of the hill. After a few minutes the marines were mere weights sliding down on the climbers, that part of the quadrant again under control, a mixed collection of Quickmoor youngsters replacing the routed Fishers whom three troopmaids were detailed to collect. But the slingers were running short of stones. Pedross demanded to know what was delaying the resupply.

"The stones are coming. The delivery was hit by a falling paving block and the stones scattered. The Innsmiths are collecting them. . . . They've stopped now, and have sent a runner to bring what they have."

"Good. Any more fires?"

"Two. Known, contained. . . ."

"Keep southwest quad watching. Is the sortie by the drain ready?"

Those firebombs, at least, should have remained intact.

Arlanna said the fifteen, mixed Innsmiths and reliable Crescent men, with two troopmaids to scout, were in place in the central courtyard beside the big storm drain. The stone grate was being winched clear.

He couldn't see it. The corner of a building intervened. He directed, "Tell them *go*. Tell them to keep to the dark when they reach the riverside." Blast Bronh, he thought; he had about as much chance of firebombing a longboat, when the reinforcements were sent, with Bronh aloft, as Ashai'd had of surprising him with a night attack when he had Valde as sentries.

But he could afford at least a small sortie, he'd decided.

"Water," he said, voicing a sudden thought. "Tell Solvig to get as many buckets of good cold water up to northeast quad as he can spare the people to carry them. Get those Fishers, they're no use for anything else. Wet the climbers down a bit. Give my lord duke a few score cases of frostburn to treat. A man's a fool to fight a winter war. . . ."

Pedross wondered how Ashai had enjoyed his frantic plunge into Erth-rimmon. If Bronh had been just two minutes slower noticing the tabarded Valde—Ketrinne and the four strange troopleaders had all insisted the Valde continue to wear their own cities' colors; so it was civic pride which had been the ruin of *that* ambush—Ashai would have been skewered a few dozen times over, and a good third of the marines besides. But the dunking alone should have been enough to give a man that age the agues . . . unless agues went the way of smashed legs and cut throats. . . .

"Get those folk from southwest quad around—half, one in two—get them around to back the Quickmoor youngsters, it's getting too thick on their side. And now that we've made their archers back off a bit, our archers should be concentrating on them, not on the climbers. And get that water moving. Where is—"

"Marines in the drain," interrupted Arlanna suddenly. "Coming on. They're fighting, with no room . . . they're trying to turn now, they're—"

"Get anybody near there to the grate right *now*, whatever they're doing. Get torches, bring everybody off northwest quadrant—" Unable to see the drain itself, Pedross could spot running figures streaming down the inner side of the northwest curve of the dike and hear closer cries rising.

It was the worst quarter hour of the battle. There were fully fifty men in the drain, advancing from the riverside—trust Bronh, Pedross thought savagely, to have spotted the exit hole of the drain all buried in weeds and brush—and they managed to cut their way through the sortie Pedross had sent down, killing both the Valde scouts so that Pedross had no idea what was going on down there. Twice he almost ordered the drain grate dropped back into place, though it would have trapped his people too without any retreat. Then smoke began rising—*somebody* had gotten a firebomb alight—and the marines began springing out of the drain. Though surrounded, the marines were better armed, and the fire cut off their retreat. Many got past the crowd around the grate, whose numbers impeded their own effectiveness, and had to be hunted down by a second line of troopmaids Pedross hastily threw around the inner one. When the frantic fighting stopped, twenty of the marines were dead and the rest captured, most with wounds. Seven of the sortie squad had survived, two with severe burns. As the last of these was being hauled out of the drain, the catapult, which had been idle a while, tossed a blazing ball of tar and tow into the area and the defenders scattered.

Pedross ordered the stone grate lowered immediately. He'd been foolish to leave the winch in plain sight: it told its own tale of drain and sortie to anybody who saw it. But after all it was rather hard to *hide* a winch fit to lift such a weight. The sortie, Pedross concluded, hadn't been one of his better ideas.

The catapult loads were still coming. Looking casually toward the gates, Pedross was shocked to find only the catapult's arm visible, the rest close enough to the gate to be hidden behind it. They'd been moving it forward a bit each time the arm's momentum at release made an uphill push possible. They'd brought it nearly the length of High Street without his noticing it.

Therefore he wasn't surprised to see a swarm of longboats drifting free of the ships. The second assault was to be on the gates, the catapult equally as useful as battering tool or as scaling-tower.

Pedross instantly ordered all available archers to the west dike overlooking the gate, together with the remainder of his firebombs and a resupply crew hauling a cart full of baled rush stalks, cut in the autumn and kept to weave matting with.

Wood, or fuelbricks, the marines below the gate could have tossed away as quickly as it was dropped; but not mounds of fiercely burning reeds, with a firebomb flung on for good measure every few minutes. The marines pulled out the wheel blocks and let the catapult roll backward, probably intending to extinguish the fire beyond reach of the firebombs, themselves protected from the rain of arrows by a wooden roof they carried over them; but the roof was ignited too, and the momentum of the groaning, flaming catapult made it lurch right over the blocks they tried to halt it with. Tipping and swaying, threatening to topple on one or another of the buildings, the catapult reeled drunkenly all the way back down High Street and burst right through the riverwall, which nevertheless checked it a moment, so that it plunged as neatly as a diver headlong into Erth-rimmon in the space between two piers.

The marines skulked along shop fronts to get back to their longboats and retreated in a scramble of arrows, catcalls, and flailing oar blades lifting out of rhythm. The five boats of reinforcements turned in midriver and began pulling back toward the ships.

The attack from Han Halla was also slackening. The ladders were being carried off, leaving a number of the enemy stranded on top of the dike. Some simply turned and slid down on their backs and hotfooted after the rest, ducking arrows. Others threw down their weapons and raised their hands, owning themselves fairly caught. One of these stranded folk was odd, Arlanna reported slowly, as if puzzled. The troopmaids couldn't hear him—it was as if nobody were there, yet there he stood, propped on his stick.

Pedross, elated at having won his first actual engagement, caught the word *stick* and spun, staring at Arlanna. He directed curtly, "More."

One of those captured, Arlanna repeated, was strange, *sa'farioh*. An older man, dressed all in white—

Pedross stared down from the east window. He had no difficulty discerning which man was meant, for the figure, tiny as a toy, shone in his white attire among the dark forms surrounding him.

Such luck was beyond hoping for.

Pedross asked, "Where is the Lady Ketrinne?"

"In the audience hall."

"Have him brought there, that one. Thirdwatch sentries remain on duty, resupply inventory within an hour, the rest retire to . . . to wherever they're being housed, I don't know. Casualty report as soon as it's ready. . . ."

Pedross called the last of his orders over his shoulder, already racing around the first turn of staircase, in haste to reach the audience hall to inspect this strange man, the *sa'farioh* with his stick, so fortuitously fallen into his hands.

The old man walked a half pace ahead of his guard of Valde. He limped, tilting his upper body and leaning just perceptibly into the act of trusting his weight to his right leg. The cane was a tool, not an affectation, moving in its own stride like a third leg. From descriptions she'd heard, Ketrinne recognized Ashai, Duke of Ismere and Camarr, Regent of Blackrock, Sailmaster and Lord of the Windward Isles, so-called Master of Andras. She felt mild surprise that he wasn't a taller man: he was scarcely bigger than Pedross, who stood by the Guest Seat to receive him.

Her work of restoration had brought Ketrinne up the south wall, across the east wall with its great round window, and halfway down the north wall. She stood by the ladder, wiping her hands on a cloth and conscious of her hair hanging loose about her shoulders, uncovered like a wanton's or a child's, as the duke passed by her. He sent her a look compounded of interest, curiosity, and a disquietingly knowing amusement, as though he were perfectly aware of her discomfiture to be receiving even a prisoner in such dishabille, himself immaculate and composed with his deliberate, tilting, three-legged stride. After a decorous nod, his head turned, inspecting the line of restored effigies as though he comprehended perfectly her rage, and her amends, to which they bore mute testimony.

Having indicated that the duke was to take the Guest Seat, which Ashai did without comment, Pedross dragged around one of the audience benches and sat down on it, tensely leaning forward and looking for all the world like a schoolboy attending to his instructor with great earnestness.

"So this is a Bremneri audience hall," remarked the duke, still looking about him with that same blend of curiosity and amusement. "I've never seen a functional one before. Lisle's is merely a shell. Will the Lady favor us with the honor of her lovely countenance, or must she retire behind the Stranger Screen for the proprieties to be maintained?"

Ketrinne felt herself coloring even while she registered the odd timbre of Ashai's voice. For a moment she was confused,

because his voice was of middle range, deeper than that of
Pedross, with a decided Andran intonation, but in no way re-
markable. Then she identified the lack: there was no under-
hum of conviction resonating in the words, nor the jagged
discord of falsehood either. The words merely entered the air,
naked as characters on a page, with no additional burden of
human attitude to carry to the Truthtell.

This was what the troopmaid had meant, then: *sa'farioh*.
The Unheard, the Unhearable—silent to their senses as the
stone in which he sat. Ketrinne noticed that his guard of
troopmaids had retired the instant they'd delivered this civil
monstrosity into her charge and Pedross's, as though they
found the awareness of his physical presence, when the
marenniath insisted that air was empty, too uncanny to tolerate—as though he were a lurking ghost which reason could
not exorcise.

To Ashai's question, Pedross was responding, "The Lady
does as she chooses. But I would not meet with you except in
her presence. She is my honorable ally and entitled to know
all that passes between us."

"As you will," replied the musical, timbreless voice of the
man in the Guest Seat.

After that, Ketrinne felt that hiding behind the Stranger
Screen would have been transparently just that: hiding. She
laid down the cloth and quietly dismissed the woodcrafters
and apprentices, then went up the side aisle to the front and
took a place beside Pedross, thinking, *Now we are two
schoolchildren, to demonstrate how well we have learned our
sums. . . .*

She said, with a grave nod, "My lord duke."

"My Lady Ketrinne," he responded, as courteously. "What
are we to do about this child of mine? It's a pity you had to
be involved in this family disagreement, Lady: for myself, I
have always regarded Quickmoor with a certain fondness, as
perhaps you know."

"I am aware of your interest in a *part* of it," rejoined
Ketrinne dryly. "We have enjoyed your more especial notice
these last few hours. We would prefer you to take *all* your interest elsewhere."

Pedross stirred, as if to contradict, and a look passed between him and Ashai which Ketrinne couldn't interpret.

Nevertheless Ketrinne continued, "If you agree to take

your folk away and leave us alone in future, you will be allowed to return to your ships."

"It's not quite that simple, Lady," responded Ashai, and
crossed his left leg over his right. "I cannot contract in a way
the Truthtell can confirm for you, as you have noticed. My
infirmity also prevents me from swearing a binding oath on
which you could safely reply—"

"He's not leaving," Pedross cut in harshly. "He's a captive
who's brought unlawful war on a Bremneri riverstock, the patron of Lisle as well as the Crescent. Tomorrow Quickmoor's
Lady will give judgment in public audience and publicly, before all the folk of Circle and Crescent alike, and all the folk
aboard his ships, execution will be done upon him in the full
sight of all."

Ashai nodded meditatively, as though this grim declaration
confirmed some point about which he'd been curious. "You
handled your battle fairly well, Pedross. You should have had
torches on the east hill, and the matter of the drain was
poorly handled, but you dealt with the catapult with com-
mendable dispatch. Marco wagered he could take the gate before you could find a way of dislodging the engine. He
underestimated the effect of excellent communications and
the ingenuity of the Innsmiths. I'll confine my reprisals for
their disloyalty to Solvig himself: Innsmiths are too valuable
to waste. Which reminds me: how did you come to be
honored with such a myriad of troopmaids, Pedross? Surely
not *all* were motivated by affection for your person."

Flushing, Pedross replied, "They came to the Lady's need."

"Do riverstock Ladies then take such alarm at a little
family dispute among Andrans, in which the Lady Ketrinne
has unfortunately interposed herself, that they cede whole
troops to each other? Strange that the Lisle folk have never
had such altruism inflicted upon *them*."

"They came of themselves," Ketrinne put in haughtily, in
spite of Pedross's squeezing her hand in request that she be
still. "To repair the fault of those who left, and to honor the
Great Pact."

"Indeed, indeed. I feared I might be at war with all southern Bremner at once, a prospect I have in nowise sought. I
have quite enough to occupy me with the Longlands and my
envious countrymen. But the Valde volunteered, to your

need. Most interesting. It must have been a powerful appeal you sent, so to move them, even as far as Hillstock."

"I sent no appeal," rejoined Ketrinne, refusing to be shushed, determined to do the troopmaids their full honor. "They came of themselves, I say."

"Indeed a tribute, if they came unlooked-for. Pedross would have found it difficult to devise such a startling reception for me at the harbor without them. Not to mention the ingenious use he made of them during this first skirmish."

"*Final* skirmish," broke in Pedross. Plainly he didn't like the way Duke Ashai was talking past him. "Didn't you hear? After a public execution, in front of several thousand reliable witnesses, few will doubt that I am the sole claimant to the title of Master of Andras."

Pedross put some special emphasis in his declaration which Ashai seemed to understand. Ketrinne recalled Pedross's absurd conviction, drawn out during his interrogation, that he'd killed his father; for the first time, Ketrinne wondered whether there could be any truth at all to the claim. Certainly the Andran before her was not alive, not in any way that Valde would acknowledge. He was unable to conceal his unnaturalness from even *her* lesser senses. Ketrinne unconsciously slid farther back on the bench, feeling the impulse to shiver gathering at the nape of her neck.

"Do you seriously consider yourself ready, at barely sixteen, to formally claim that title?" Ashai inquired of his son gravely. "Do you consider youself competent, with one minor skirmish to your credit, to wage the sea battle that will be joined in less than a month? Do you think my commanders will entrust their ships and their men to the wit of an untried boy?"

"If I can defeat the great Duke Ashai Rey in formal battle, and even catch and execute him, they'll reserve judgment," declared Pedross heatedly; and though his voice rang with conviction for Ketrinne, she also knew the sound of one who'd persuaded himself of what he wished to believe. "They'll give me at least a chance to prove myself, which is more than you were ever willing to do."

"A facile word, *ever*," observed Ashai calmly. "Last spring I took you into the Longlands campaign and kept you at my right hand nearly every waking hour, and ignored the general opinion that you were too young for even that much involvement. There are no 'chances' now, Pedross. Longlands must be won, or it will be lost, and claimed, and fortified against us. The Eastern Alliance must be defeated, once and for all, or our own allies will go scuttling for protection to one or another of the baymasters with less far-reaching ambitions, one who's satisfied to rule his isle and skirmish against his rivals for occasional entertainment, and trade spies and hostages about, as he's always done. There can be *no* mistakes, Pedross. They'll unite against you and bring you down, less even than they—if they let you live at all, which I'd doubt. And who is *your* heir, Pedross: who will protect the Five Isles—Ismere and Camarr and beautiful Blackrock, or the insubordinate Windwards—if you are brought down? I've made pledges to those folk to keep them under my hand, as my own people, as long as my line and theirs shall last. These pledges I have been prepared to entrust to you, in time. You know that. I have never disputed that you are my sole and acknowledged heir. But who is yours, Pedross? Who will keep faith with those folk if I carelessly hand over my faith to you to keep, and you fail? An empire that lasts less than twenty years works more hurt in its collapse than one that lasts millennia. And consider my commanders and sailmasters, which would be yours: they'd immediately turn to intriguing for power under any new administration, wasting their energies when they were most needed, united. Can you claim otherwise? If you do, I need no Truthsayer to confirm my disbelief. Wait five years, six at most. The balance will be stabilized then, and you can be brought into power gradually, your authority unquestioned. I will make you a sub-commander in what remains of the Longlands campaign: *that,* at least, you've proved yourself capable of, tonight, though you're young for even that much power and you'll have envy, resentment, and rivalry among our own folk to contend with, as well as the enemy. If you will accept these terms, I'll accept you back and cease to trouble Quickmoor's rest."

Ketrinne looked to discover what Pedross would make of this offer, which to her seemed both responsible and reasonable. And, looking, it struck her anew just how *very* young Pedross was, how callow and bony and downright hungry he seemed, especially beside his father's steady-eyed authority, which was such that Ketrinne found it difficult to remember he had not come here of his own will specifically to name the terms on which he'd accept Pedross's return.

Pedross's face was set and pale, his workman's hands locked into each other as if to keep them from some sudden act. He said, "If words won battles, we'd all be scribes. I've heard you out. Now you hear me. First, I'll have this one chance to stand, and no other. If I surrender now, nobody would trust me not to do the same another time. Second. Once I am in your hands, I have no recourse. One can negotiate only from power, and I'd have none except what you chose to grant me; and since I've stood against you once, you'll never trust me with enough power to do so again. I won't stand second to you, but lower even than your commanders, as long as you live. Thirdly, this talk of five or six years is a silly fiction. There'll be another war, or some crisis then, and myself still untested, still without the unquestioned authority you say I must have to rule. I'll just be older, and that much deeper in your shadow. You'd find some reason to put off the time, and I'd be less able and maybe less willing to dispute that in arms than I am right now. Fourthly, you will never willingly abdicate in my favor. You'll always be older and more experienced, and you'll convince yourself *younger* means *too young*. Other men grow old, Ashai, and they *die*, Ashai—but we both know you are not as other men. You've not aged a day in thirty *years*, Ashai: men who were your apparent contemporaries when you arrived and worked yourself into the rule of Ismere are eighty or more now, and most of them are *dead*, Ashai, while you go on unchanged. When I'm fifty, how will you look then? Will your hair be one bit nearer white, or your *limp* improved, after all that time? Bronh says you're not a Tek: what sort of creature *are* you, then, Sa'farioh? What am I kin to? I have my mother's word that you fathered me, in the manner of men—but I'm told my mother was unreliable, and imagined things, like killing you up on the rimwalk one night and casting the body into the sea. What do you say, Sa'farioh: shall I take my poor silly mother's word that you're my father?"

"You are my son and will, in time, be the Master of Andras when I have prepared it for you," replied Ashai steadily.

"In *whose* time? And what Truthsayer can call you to account if you lie? No. I will not give up that leverage I have gained, by my own efforts, to rest on the mercy of your unsupported and unenforceable word. If even Valde faith can fail, how should I entrust all my hope to such as you? No. Whatever *you* may be, *I* am an Andran. I've sworn feud and I will not leave it until I am satisfied. I will see you dead, with as much of the green world watching as I can gather to see it too, for the sake of my mother's sanity and truth. And if you come back afterward I will declare you an imposter, and your commanders will support, if not me, then *their* sanity and their eyes' own memory. A duke who never ages, they can tolerate; one who returns from the dead, never. So if you come back, do not come to me. I am capable of watching you die once a month. if need be. I could do it. I proved that, I think, at our last meeting. I knew it would all hinge on that, at the last. You've been dead by my hand once already, *Sa'farioh*: twice wouldn't be any harder for me to bear."

Turning casually from Pedross's rigid glare, Ashai seemed to be inspecting the surrounding statues, images of trust broken and restored almost to original unity. To Ketrinne's eye, he looked both weary and sad. "Lady. Surrender him to me, or I'll raze your city to the mud."

Just that, a stark declaration, undecorated by reasons or arguments. In spite of herself, Ketrinne was shocked and uneasy. She said, "You cannot."

"Perhaps. But remember it, all the same. What I have said, I will do. Even with no Truthsayers or Valde to Witness for me, I am not known as a man who has ever declared and yet not done." Ashai's somber glance left the walls and returned to Pedross. "Since I was young, a very long while ago and in another place, there have been four people with both the power and the will to do me hurt. Of these, one lost the will, and the rest, the power. You are not one of those four, Pedross. I wish you well, for my own sole self; but I fear little good will come to you from me hereafter."

As he spoke he had taken his cane lightly into both hands, as though he were preparing to leave. As he finished speaking he moved one hand with a gesture like shaking out a handkerchief. He and the chair disappeared in a towering column of flame that scorched the cement ceiling and charred the beams, all in a moment, with an unspeakable smell of burning.

Ketrinne had fallen as Pedross upset the bench in springing away. He dragged her across the floor and shoved her huddled against the baseboards, keeping the heat from her with his own body. When he released her she did not move immediately; he had to take her arm and lift her before she would gather her legs beneath her and attempt to stand. Her eyes felt scorched, as much by the sight as by the heat.

As she slowly approached the Guest Seat she could feel the stone radiating like a furnace, with the chunks of charred beam dropping on it and collapsing into ash. In places the stone had run like wax; in others, it was cracked through, as though no more than a hammer blow would suffice to shatter it completely. On the seat and the floor were little melted blobs of metal, copper colored or gray; coins, or buttons, or the head of the cane. There was nothing else in the chair.

"Is he a demon, then?" Ketrinne found herself asking, slowly weeping with the stinging of her eyes.

Pedross, staring at the Guest Seat with most of his brows and lashes crisped away, and the fringe of hair over his forehead no more than scorched ash, made her no reply.

Ashai had escaped them.

Jannus stood waiting in the long shadow of the levee a little farther into Han Halla than was safe, but he wanted no encounters with wandering marines. It was becoming perceptibly darker as the moon fell. Very soon now, the stars would hold the sky alone. Jannus stuffed his hands deeper into his coat pockets and walked the little tussock of land he was willing to trust, keeping warm. He didn't think he'd be waiting too much longer.

The destruction of the catapult had brought most of the Household out of doors to watch, carefully keeping the front of the building between themselves and the levee. The principal fighting seemed to be on the far side of the Circle, which Rayneth, still fully dressed, remarked was thoughtful of the duke. Jannus suspected the welfare of the Crescent was not among Ashai's major concerns just now, but then Jannus hadn't thought Ashai would trouble himself about the letter cubes, or attack by night either. So Rayneth might have the right of it for all he knew.

Because of Ashai's consideration, if that was what it was, the slowly advancing and then thunderously retreating bucket of the catapult moving above the roofs was the household's own personal view of the battle, and they watched it with interest, making comments and laying bets on when, or whether, young Pedross would act against it, and what the result would be if he did. When the catapult smashed, flaming, into the riverwall and took its ponderous dive, people around Jannus were clamorous or glum, depending on which way their wagers lay.

Jannus wasn't very interested. He hadn't been sleeping much anyhow, of late, and had come downstairs chiefly because he was tired of staring at the wall. As people started moving around him, declaring their intention to get back inside and get warm, Jannus moved nearer the wall to escape being jostled. That was how he came to notice the falling star.

It fell from almost directly overhead, from the cluster known locally as the Dragon. The odd thing was that he'd noticed that same star the night he'd been returning with Sparrowhawk after the duel. He'd noticed it because it was new. It'd been in the cluster called the Kite—four stars arranged in a diamond. Only there had been five that night, one, brighter than the rest, beside the right corner but quite distinct from it. Since, he'd noticed the star other times—before moonrise or after moonset, when he'd sometimes stepped into the frozen garden to think or clear his head, while everybody else was asleep. Sometimes it'd been in the Dragon, and sometimes in the Kite, depending on which was overhead at that hour. The star's position did not vary. The constellations moved past or around it.

And now it was falling.

He'd backed down the alley, watching its fall, then turned and crossed Mason Street and followed another alley. Moving in this zigzag fashion he came clear of the Crescent and began following the south curve of the levee. The star had sprouted a tail. He'd looked up every few paces to discover if it'd changed direction, then hurried on. When he'd reached the shadow of the dike the sounds of battle seemed to be diminishing before him, but he'd nevertheless swung wide, out to the very edge of the shadow, until he'd come to the farthest limit of its curve. Now the shadow had overtaken him again, but he was satisfied with the place he'd chosen. The seeing wasn't very good, but it had become a still night and the hearing was excellent.

Presently he heard what he'd been expecting: the crunch and rustle of a lone man walking toward him out of Han

Halla. Jannus moved toward the sound without particular care for his own noise, and the walking stopped. Jannus said, "Don't worry. It's only me."

The steps, cautious but regular, resumed and Jannus saw the outline of a man silhouetted against the paler surface of a frozen pond. Jannus stood waiting and then fell in beside the walker.

"I thought you wanted to be kept out of it," remarked Ashai Rey, flicking at dry rush stalks with his stick.

"So Downbase is a star now," mused Jannus, letting the question slide by. "I'd figured it must be somewhere about. You've been getting rebodied so fast—between night and the next morning, according to Pedross. You couldn't be doing that if Downbase were still in Kantmorie. And there's nothing, now, to hold you to the High Plain. . . . But until I saw it coming down, I didn't think of its looking like a star."

"Reflected sunlight," commented Ashai absently. "At that altitude I catch all but a few hours' light. But the glitter off my sails shows here below at some angles. What do you want, Jannus?"

The question was blunt but not unfriendly—rather, the privileged directness of long or intimate acquaintance.

Jannus replied, "I've got something to trade. I can tell you where the troopmaids came from, if you want to know."

" 'News for a copper?' " Jannus missed a step, and Ashai changed hands on his cane to reach out and steady him, then continued, "I know where they came from: Overwater, Aftaban, Dark, and Hillstock."

"All right, *how* they came, then. What brought them."

"Did you do it? I know you've shown unexpected talent as a farspeaker, but that's a little beyond even you."

"No. Not me. Interested?"

"Perhaps. What were you thinking of trading for?"

"How did you come to be based this time?" rejoined Jannus, once more evading an immediate answer. "Pedross again?"

"Indirectly." Ashai paused, seeking the best way around a solid sheet of ice. Choosing a right-hand detour, Ashai said, "He was planning a very public execution. I declined."

Jannus thought about that, finally nodding. "He knows just enough to bother him, not enough to forget it and go on.

You let him know about Bronh—why not the rest? It nags at him, not knowing."

"Why didn't you tell him?"

"Didn't seem up to me. But I could see it bothers him."

"And you think the bald truth would be an improvement over safe uncertainty? You *are* optimistic, aren't you? Besides, his fearing the worst has its uses too. Did you know there's a high correlation, historically, between young men becoming successful military conquerors and their hating their fathers?" The remark was calm, conversational. "Hating one's elders and betters seems to supply some useful motivation."

"If there'd been a high correlation between being a good conqueror and being a dwarf, would you have raised him in a box?" rejoined Jannus acidly.

"As a matter of fact, there's a height correlation, too—on the whole, statistically less significant, but measurable. But there was no need to use a box. I just made certain his mother was a short woman. But the point's not worth arguing. He won't come to terms. He won't believe I'll ever step aside, and he's fairly sure I'm immortal, though he hasn't figured out the mechanics of it yet. . . . So he won't compromise. And I can't just leave him. I've made him too dangerous to be able to afford to have him as an enemy. I'll have to scrap him and start over."

From Teks, Jannus had learned not to let such casually chilling pronouncements shock him. There was no use in indignation—only in offering some acceptable alternative.

"I could talk to him . . ." he suggested diffidently.

"Play arbiter? I see you've not lost your odd attraction toward threatened freaks—the stranger, the better." Ashai could say that without offense, because he was one of those freaks. He added, "I'd think you would have outgrown that habit. It's uncomfortable and probably dangerous."

"I don't guess I can. However it started, I seem to be used to it now." Jannus tightened his arm against the bound ribs which that habit had won him. This was the farthest he'd walked since the duel, and his whole side ached. "I'll play arbiter, if you'll have me. It isn't just Pedross. You could have killed him ten times over. Fact?"

"Fact," conceded Ashai, a bit warily.

"You're punishing Ketrinne for taking him in. Fact?"

"I have a reputation to uphold," responded Ashai, with a certain austerity. "It saves trouble in the long run. I made an exception for you, and look what's come of *that*."

"*I* never asked for those stinking letter cubes."

"I apologize. I *have* apologized. Does that make it all better?" was Ashai's sour rejoinder.

"I really don't care a whole lot, if you want to know. I want you out of here, back hacking away at the poor Longlanders, if that's what the Rule of One dictates you be occupied with these days. I'm not altogether overjoyed about *that*, but at least I don't have to watch, and I've never met a Longlander."

"You wouldn't like them. They're ordinary enough folk—not nearly strange enough to engage your seemingly limitless sympathies."

"I know what I am. I don't need you to tell me I'm on four sides at once. As long as I'm the one who gets cut, I don't see that you have any complaint."

"I don't want you cut at all," pointed out Ashai quietly, finding a way to walk among the exposed roots of a tree, and waited until Jannus more slowly managed to cross. Ashai said, "Don't put me into a corner, Jannus. I have no discretion about some things. But I *do* have preferences. In anything that doesn't touch the Rule of One, I'll gladly . . . but, no. You're right. It's better if I leave you alone. Safer. . . . You'd have to pass a few thousand years among Teks, as I have, to value yourself properly, Jannus. Teks are obsessional and fanatic. They always have been. To them, I'm just a tool, a means. Your blind, compulsive, universal sympathy makes you rarer than any Tek. But it makes you correspondingly vulnerable. And one of the things I am is a weapon. If you push, I'll cut you to the bone. I'll have no choice. Let's talk trading," Ashai requested, with an abrupt change of tone. "It's safer."

But Jannus persisted, "What's the use of my holding the Rule of One, if anything I try to do with it gets me killed?"

"No use. The Rule's passed beyond you and Kantmorie, in all but name. It was never more than a formality, to authorize my ending the bases."

"Yet I hold it."

"Nominally."

"Nominally, Solvig was sworn to Pedross instead of to you.

A formality. But Pedross took him up on it, formality or no. The words matter, Shai. I *do* hold the Rule of One, and if you give me no option, I'll use it."

"You'll *try*."

"To Pedross, through me. To the Circle of Quickmoor, through me," summarized Jannus tersely.

"If you give me an order contravening the proper use of the Rule of One, I have to execute you. So you *threaten* to give that order. And the threat, alone, does not merit execution. A nice point," commented Ashai, and slashed at some more reeds, letting that express both his frustration and his threat. "I wish I had a new rede of yours, to know if you're bluffing."

"Get a Truthsayer. Flip a coin. I don't care. I don't even *believe* in the Rule of One. Why can't there be a Rule of Two? A balance?"

"Because balances always tip, sooner or later, and each side must stand alone . . . Where's Poli, Jannus?"

Jannus hadn't realized he was that transparent. But then, with the capacities of Downbase, Ashai'd had plenty of time to work that out, who commonly juggled probabilities infinitely more complex. Quietly, he admitted, "I don't know."

"So. It would have to be something like that. All right, I'll play your Rule of Two: double or nothing. You bring Pedross out of the Circle, alone, before morning and I'll forego further punishment of Quickmoor. I'll attribute it to my great awe of Valde troopmaids. It shouldn't do too much future damage that way. Agreed?"

"If I bring Pedross out, what becomes of him?"

"That depends. Let me think a little. The chief problem is that he doesn't command enough respect yet. The commanders would fall to intriguing for influence, or try to actually supplant him, probably by assassination. High probability," Ashai commented, to himself. "He'd need two things: a prestigious victory, and a regent who can keep the commanders occupied with maneuvering against *him*, rather than against Pedross. There's a naval battle coming in a few weeks against Domal Ai and the Eastern Isles. *That* would do, for the victory. And for the regent . . . Secolo."

"Who's he?"

"My chief of security. Spymaster and chief of assassins. Frighteningly stupid man, in some ways. But the profession encourages a limited viewpoint. He's to be promoted to chief strategist, and his plan for the naval battle is to be followed without deviation. Those are my conditions, then. Pedross must accept Secolo as his regent for five years, and retain him in his present duties as well as making him chief strategist, with absolute authority for planning the engagement with the Eastern Alliance's fleet. If you can get him to agree to that, I'll accept him as Master of Andras. Otherwise he's no use to me. I'd lose Longlands and the Five Isles, and not even you would like what would come of that. I've always found it effective to be viewed as the lesser of two evils. And, usually, it's true. . . ."

They'd reached the first stones of the Crescent road, on the north end of the city. Finally on level footing, Jannus tried to ease the soreness in his side. Ashai was looking upriver toward his ships anchored out in the current well beyond bowshot from the shore.

Ashai said, "If he won't take my terms, stand aside, Jannus. It's his only alternative. If I didn't kill him, his own commanders would; and you have no call on *their* forbearance. I doubt they have any. I've barely succeeded in breaking them of their quaint habit of impaling their enemies. . . ."

"*You* skin people."

"It's expected," rejoined Ashai calmly. "I conform to the local standards. I expect Pedross will skin people, too. It's the custom. They didn't ask my opinion when they evolved it. At least mine are dead before they're subjected to that repulsive bit of folklore—the primary effect is on the living, not on those who suffer it. Eventually I'll substitute something more humane, like public flogging—but look how long it took the Masters of Ardun to ban public dueling. In Quickmoor, nobody's even tried to stop it yet. For the time being, I'll skin people whenever it seems necessary to provide an example and secure obedience. Which is more brutal: fifty floggings, or one skinning? That's the sort of alternatives I have to work with."

"The lesser of two evils."

"Precisely. Stand aside. Be content with the rescue of Quickmoor, if you can manage even that much. You can't rescue a drowning man without his consent. He'll only drown you both. I'd hate to lose you, Jannus."

"I expect I'd hate it worse."

"It would relieve me to think so," responded Ashai gravely. As Jannus started away, Ashai called after him, "As a bonus, between friends: what brought the Valde?"

Jannus paused and looked slowly back. "Poli did."

"*Poli* did? How?"

"I'd like to know that myself. Maybe Arlann' will tell me, or Mene—I think I saw her, this afternoon. . . . But I'll tell you what I think. I think maybe once she was away from me, her *marenniath* waked again. Wouldn't that be funny?"

Receiving no reply, Jannus turned his back on Ashai and went on toward High Street.

As soon as the scorched, warped stone of the Guest Seat could be touched, Pedross sat down in it and saw Ketrinne wince from the image he presented. But it was a true and accurate image and Pedross refused to flinch from it. His life rested under her judgment more truly than Ashai's had.

"Pedross . . ." she began, reaching toward him, but he bent away from her hand, gripping the chair's arms as he'd done once before.

"Lady, take your place and do judgment," he directed flatly.

Slowly Ketrinne mounted the dais, mutely asking that she not be required to confront this thing. He wondered if she'd really have preferred the ugliness of doubt and vacillation, the humiliating bedroom hypocrisies which were the only other alternative. He at least did not so prefer. He would do as he'd been taught: strike clean, and to the bone. Reading this in his face, Ketrinne turned away at last and took her place behind the Stranger Screen.

Pedross frowned, ordering his thoughts. "First, the argument for keeping me. I've, we've, beaten off the first attack. That's a fact, for all his patronizing remarks. Our losses were light, and we're as well armed and well prepared as ever. Morale and discipline are better. And we have to hold only five days, perhaps six, until the ice reaches us and drives him south. His threat to raze the city to the mud is so much rhetoric, just noise, to frighten you. Quickmoor's not worth that much time or trouble to him. The worst that could come is death, Lady; the city would stand. Now say against it."

Ketrinne's voice, hesitant and low, replied from behind the

screen. "Against it, I say he attacked tonight only lightly, to get himself captured and brought safely inside to offer terms and treat with you face to face. I say tonight proves nothing. I say, *my* morale and discipline are poor. Now that I have seen him, Pedross, I fear him as I never thought to fear anyone living. I believe if you are not surrendered before battle is joined again, he will do the word of his threat to the letter and mark. Who has the will to burn himself in such a fire, who can then return from death itself, what can be beyond him? Jannus warned me, and I thought him a superstitious fool. I have been made wiser, to my hurt. Whether the sky will rain fire on us or the earth open and swallow us, the city will not stand."

Pedross had braced himself against the reply and nevertheless felt his confidence gravely wounded and bleeding its strength away. The chair's heat felt raw and feverish under his touch. "Second, the argument for surrendering me. Ashai may keep the letter and mark of his word to give way in my favor after a certain time, and I shall not be forgetful of you then. And if he does not, or if he and I again fall out, at least it won't be here. You are answerable for your city's health. I am none of your kin or your necessary concern. If you give me up, you, and your gift of Valde, and your city will all endure. It is expedient and wise to let go of a candle when the wax begins to burn your fingers. A candle is not much light to lose; and morning always comes. Now speak against it."

"I would not break the faith I have promised. You chose this place to stand on my promise to support you, freely given. . . . I would not be humbled before this creature, Ashai, if I might stand instead. I would not be parted from you, Pedross—and not in such a fashion!"

Pedross heard in the brevity and regret of that reply what answer she would make, at the last. Nevertheless he would not take it off her shoulders onto his own. "Lady, I tell you that I will never break my oath of feud, or return to him of my own will, whatever the cost. I will fight until I am prevented. Now, Lady, do judgment on the question as you may see fit."

The minutes passed and still she could not make up her mind to it, or, having done so, could not speak it to him openly. Pedross was about to demand her answer when she appeared around the screen, looking past him, and ran down the aisle as if to the hope of hope, or at least of a fresh excuse to delay. But it was only Arlanna, Pedross discovered; and no news, short of the arrival of the ice or the departure of the ships, could affect anything that mattered.

Pedross faced the screen again, impatient to have the matter settled, ended.

Ketrinne spoke and was answered by a man's voice. Pedross jerked around to find out what this new interruption might be. The man was dark and sullen-looking, maybe one of Rayneth's guards. Pedross gave him only a cursory glance. Then the man looked at him, a cold stare that noted him and returned to Ketrinne, and Pedross recognized Jannus.

It wasn't the man he'd seen in the dueling ring stubbornly trying to hold his own against a First Dancer, though the signs of that night were on him yet, in the way he stood and the broken-nosed profile; even less was it the man Pedross had seen combing his daughters' hair with such casual tenderness while using them as Truthsayers against his uninvited guest, or arguing hopefully with the Valde, his wife. This man looked like one named Voss, Secolo's principal executioner.

As they came up the aisle followed by two Valde, Arlanna and one of the stranger troopleaders, Ketrinne reported, "He's seen *him*. Ashai."

It wasn't the reprieve she'd hoped for—rather, the confirmation of her fears. She looked pale, twisting one fist self-consciously into her unbound hair.

Pedross sneered, "How *is* my lord duke? Slightly singed?"

Jannus regarded him favorlessly. "Under certain conditions Ashai will accept you as Master of Andras—"

"In five years, or was it fifteen? That's stale news, not worth the copper."

"He'll take you for Master of Andras *now*. Witness for me, Mene."

The strange troopleader—from Overwater, he seemed to recall—declared to Pedross, "It is truth. I stand witness."

But Pedross looked to Ketrinne, whom he knew. She also assented, though adding more cautiously, "*He* believes it. . . ." The emphatic word now meant Jannus.

Pedross looked away disgustedly. "Stale bait for stale fish. It's still not worth a copper."

"You silly kit," rejoined Jannus with a withering dispassion, "I'm trying to keep you breathing. I've walked the better part of eight miles to get you that much, and not for the fun of it. Will you hear the conditions or not?"

"Not. If I wouldn't trust Ashai's word out of his own mouth, why should I trust it from yours?" countered Pedross succinctly. "You're free to believe what you please. Your life doesn't hang on it."

Jannus looked around the walls as if forcibly holding his temper. "Forget that, then. Trade with me, for what *I* have. I can tell you exactly who and what Ashai is."

It was, Pedross thought, almost equally offer and threat. Almost imperceptibly, Ketrinne nodded, confirming it. Pedross said, "In return for what?"

"Come into the Crescent. That's all. Come clear of the Circle. I'll hold you myself, if I can."

Pedross understood he was at last being offered the protection he'd come north seeking. Puzzled at why Jannus was willing to try to be walls and troopmaids to him, when he wouldn't before, Pedross scanned the man's dark, bearded face; but it gave him no answer except tiredness and a kind of stubborn attention.

Perhaps responding to some silent request, the troopleader named Mene volunteered, "I stand witness to the intent."

Ketrinne said anxiously to Jannus, "But *can* you?"

"I don't know. He's not a keg of letter cubes. But I've told Ashai he cannot come at him except through me. It's all I can do."

Pedross said simply, "Wait. I'll get a coat."

Ketrinne moved with him toward the door, her eyes asking permission. Pedross hesitated an instant, then put an arm around her waist.

Presently they approached a place where the ways divided. A stair climbed toward the tower; the level way led toward Ketrinne's own chambers. Ketrinne walked more slowly, forcing no decision on him. The corridors, the situation, did that. Pedross tightened his arm, and her weight settled more warmly against his side. The stair was left behind.

There was a pressure on their intimacy, a sadness, and the sense of many things unsaid—but nothing withheld. It was not the acrimonious encounter he'd dreaded: only a leavetaking, with regret and fondness on both sides.

She said to him softly, "If a child comes of us, and if it is

a boy, I shall nevertheless keep him by me and he will have
Quickmoor after me: the first legitimate Lord of a Bremneri
riverstock. I swear it."

He replied, "Enough talk of heirs," and silenced her in a
way he knew. All the same, he was touched, and was still
thinking about that possibility when he left her, apparently
sleeping, and went to the tower for his things. He had no
children, that he knew of; but then, he'd started late.

With his compass in one coat pocket and his sling and shot
in the other, he returned to the audience hall, where he found
Jannus waiting alone—a mark of singular favor, since
Pedross knew well that no men, and certainly no outsiders,
were ever permitted abroad in the household without an escort.

Hearing him approach, Jannus turned to him a face full of
the impact of grievous news, so that Pedross asked at once,
"What is it?"

"Nothing that concerns you," rejoined the man curtly.

Pedross said, "I do hear you," and Jannus's look lightened
fractionally at the Watertalk phrase, so incongruous in
Pedross's mouth.

Pedross led the way to the main doors, choosing the route
with the fewest stairs after he saw what work Jannus made of
the first set. At High Street, the sentries dragged aside a
heavy panel in the left watch-post to let them edge through a
narrow slit in the stone.

Pedross noticed all the inns and taverns had put up their
flood doors and shutters, hoping to avoid being caught between Circle and duke. There was no warm place to sit and
hear what was to be said. Pedross turned his collar up and
wished for a muffler, discovering that his tiredness had made
him vulnerable to the cold.

They turned onto the Crescent road, where morning fogs
had begun drifting above the river like flat smoke, so that the
Is shore opposite seemed to hang suspended above a layer of
dim emptiness. The only light anywhere was the tiny dots of
lanterns hung from Ashai's ships anchored upriver—that, and
the stars, still undimmed by any approach of dawn.

Having gone north about three blocks, Jannus rummaged
in a bin beside a boarded-up tavern and came up with two
broken chunks of firebrick—compressed straw and saw-
dust—and a handful of twigs. Saying, "You bend easier than

I do," he dropped these gleanings on the stones before a broad doorstep. It wouldn't have occurred to Pedross to make a fire right in the street, but it was perfectly reasonable. After all, who was there to object? With a fire-striker Jannus handed down to him when he was ready Pedross got the kindling alight and soon the pieces of firebrick caught, propped against an upended paving stone probably intended for the catapult.

Jannus apparently found it more comfortable to stand. While Pedross sat on the doorstep, turning his hands to the fire, Jannus set one shoulder against the building's front—which creaked—and began quietly, "Once a long time ago, the Teks needed a pilot. Their ways had got them into trouble with the rulers and laws of the place where they lived then, and they'd made up their minds to leave. That place where they were was a world like this, circling a sun, a star, so far off we can't even see it from here. I was told once it's in *that* direction." His arm lifted in the firelight, pointing at a declension just past the nooning place. "Through the left-hand corner of the Kite. But such a journey would take several lifetimes and besides, they didn't know where they were going, except away.

"They say air is a layer, like water. And beyond the top of where the air ends is an emptiness as much thinner than air, as air is than water. Empty and dark it is, out past the air, with every once in a while a sun and its worlds, like little islands in the whole of the sea. And it was to the sea the Teks went to get their pilot."

"Did Bronh tell you this?" Pedross inquired.

"No. Another Tek I knew once." Jannus waited to see if Pedross wanted to ask anything more, but Pedross was content to listen, twirling a tiny flame on the end of a crooked twig. Jannus went on, "Imagine a fish, Pedross, nearly as big as all of Quickmoor. Imagine it living on a world where no land was, only water. Clever, it was, and wise about water and the deeps, the things it knew, but without hands or tools or any made thing. And by means they knew, the Teks took the brain of that fish and gave it a new body even huger than the one it'd lost. A body that ate light and never wearied or aged. A body that was a ship, with room for all the Teks and their tools and the unborn eggs to hatch out cats and fleas and goats and birds . . . and people, too, to be their servants

and helpers when they came to a place where the air and
water and warmth and all were right for them. The ship was
called *Sunfire*. And the pilot, whose body *Sunfire* was, was
called sometimes Deepfish and sometimes Pilot. The word for
pilot, in the pilot's own language, was something that sounded most like *Shai*. So that was what he named himself.

"The pilot was alone on the whole of that journey, with the
sleeping and the unborn. But he was used to being alone,
with only far voices to talk to, and this was much the same.
The deeps beyond the air were not so different from the
deeps of water he'd known. So he wasn't unhappy, and tasted
the light and the new sorts of fish that passed him; and he
learned, Pedross—learned everything the Teks had known or
done, and the knowledge and deeds of the folk that were before the Teks, back to the very beginnings of words and
records. And he became very wise. He thought about all he'd
learned about how people got along together the most easily,
with the fewest upheavals and upsets and wars, and he called
the pattern he saw the *Rule of One*. He came to believe, as
the Teks did, that all power was finally single and the best
form of government was one in which all available power
was given into the hands of one person who was then held
absolutely accountable for its use. And because he was well-
disposed toward people, it seemed right to him that he should
serve the Rule of One, which lasted, rather than ordinary human people—even if they *were* Teks—with lives as brief as
sparks. Because in his new body, there was no natural reason
why the pilot should ever die.

"Eventually the ship came here. The pilot tasted at the air
and the water, and watched the seasons pass, from out beyond the moon. He'd done it before, countless times, but the
tastes or the light or the seasons had never been quite right.
But this time, they were near enough right to make him wake
some of the sleeping Teks so they could decide if they liked
this world or not.

"It had a lot of sea, they thought, compared to the amount
of land. And the moon was large and nearer in than most, so
the tides were the worst any of them had ever seen. And
there were already people of a sort living here, though not
quite human. But the Teks decided, all in all, they liked this
world and told the pilot to come down in the middle of a
huge tableland with steep cliffs on the west and mountains to

the east and south, bare as a brick, but with plenty of room and safe from the worst of the weather: the High Plain. And where they landed, they called Down. The ship became Downbase, the first and chief of the Tek bases on the High Plain. But the pilot was still called Deepfish, or the Shai. And the Teks began hatching out all the creatures and people they'd brought, and making new ones, and tinkering with the ones that were here before they came, and began the Empire of Kantmorie that lasted almost three thousand years, until the Rebellion . . . and didn't really end until four years ago, when the Shai and I ended all the bases but Downbase itself. . . ."

Pedross found a fresh twig to light, wondering when Jannus was going to get to his father, who was certainly not a Tek or a fish with a ship for a body. But he didn't interrupt. Besides, he was in no particular hurry to go before Ashai with only Jannus, the scribe and tale-teller, as walls, weapons, and troops.

"The part that Bronh maybe told you," Jannus went on, shifting his shoulder against the boards and seeming to watch the rising fog, "the redes and the deathlessness and the founding of the lowland nations, that all followed, and what was done to the Valde. And meanwhile there was the pilot, landbound and stuck in one place, knowing more now than any single man could ever learn or keep, already immensely old and shrewd but still learning because he served the Teks, who always have wanted to understand everything about how things worked. After a while the Teks devised a way for the Shai to move among them as a man, to do their bidding and find out things they wanted to know: a mobile. A human body with a rede, a self-record, of the pilot awake in it, with hands and two eyes, and all that a man has. A mobile couldn't hold *all* the pilot's rede, any more than you could empty a full pitcher into a glass. The mobile could hold only what a man can hold. But sometimes the mobile would take new redes and share what he'd learned with Downbase, and spill the water back into the pitcher and pour it out fresh."

"The mobile," said Pedross. "What was it called?"

"Nothing, then. I'm coming to that. After the Rebellion and the setting of the Barrier, the pilot was trapped for a long while on the High Plain, as the Teks were. They fell into madness, but the pilot was only bored, a little. He was used to waiting much longer than that, with nothing to do but think and listen to voices far away. When the Barrier failed in one place on account of an earthquake, he sent out a mobile to see what had been happening in the lowlands. The mobile had trouble climbing down the west cliffs of the High Plain—"

Pedross said softly, "He broke his right leg in fifteen places and swam Erth-rimmon to Lisle."

The mists had reached the rooftops, cutting off all view of the stars or Ashai's ships. There were visible only this little fire, the cold cement of the doorway, and Jannus's leaning figure turned half-away and motionless.

"He healed eventually, and followed Erth-rimmon down to the sea. He understood the sea, and sea-people, the best of any he'd met in the lowlands. He decided to shape Andras into a unity to fill the hole left by Kantmorie's passing. He became duke of Ismere, and conquered Camarr. That's when I first saw him. Meanwhile he'd married and had a son, to hold the Rule of One. But there came a time when the mobile was badly injured, or had reason to think he might be killed; and Downbase was a very long way off. He'd have been missed, in the time it would take a new mobile to travel all that way. So the pilot took Downbase out of the ground, where it'd been since the first landing, and went back into the emptiness above the air, eating light with great sails the way he had during the journey. That was about four years ago."

"When my mother killed him," said Pedross. "That's when it happened."

"Seems likely. I'd been onto the High Plain by then, and taken the Rule of One onto myself to give the pilot the authority he had to have to end the bases and the Barrier altogether. His responsibilities in maintaining the High Plain were ended. He could leave. So thereafter, if a mobile was killed, he could send out a new one between night and morning: water from the same pitcher, the Shai of Downbase. The mobile sired you, but your father is the pilot who began life as a fish, whose body is a building, a ship, and a machine."

Into the silence, Pedross spoke his first thought: "My mother would never have understood. She couldn't bear even Bronh."

"He mistrusted the effects of telling you. It's a personal

sort of thing, after all. I'd guess he thought there was no need for you to know, no need to risk confusing you when all he wanted for a son was a sort of superior pirate chief. A knife, pure and simple—not a force-sword, such as Teks made. A broadknife, maybe, that would be easy to keep honed and to use. But you cut at him before he was ready, and you wouldn't make terms. So he decided to scrap you, like a knife flawed in the forging, and no more than that. Generally, he values people according to how useful they are to the Rule of One."

"Except you," said Pedross, and poked the last of his twig into the fire.

"I did him a service once that he didn't expect. I didn't want such a treasure of knowledge, such a person, lost if there were any other way the bases could be ended. He hadn't expected anybody would side with him. So as long as I don't get seriously in his way, he likes me enough to walk around me as much as he can," replied Jannus, without inflection. "But I'm square in his way now, and what comes of that depends on you."

The new terms. Trying to evaluate what he'd been told, Pedross found he had no particular feeling toward the unhuman pilot-mobile he'd known as his father. Revenge against such a being seemed pointless, an inherited duty completed, fulfilled, that night in Landsend harbor. For his own part, Pedross felt no need to hate the fractional part of something larger which was forever beyond his reach.

Pedross took his sling out of his pocket and used it to bind back as much of his hair as he could. It would be months before it was long enough to braid again. But the feud was finished, complete.

He asked, "What are the terms? I'll listen now."

"First, that you accept a five-year regency under somebody named Secolo. Second, that in addition to his present duties, you appoint Secolo your chief strategist and give him complete authority over planning the battle Ashai says is due in about a halfmonth. *That* plan, you must agree to follow absolutely. Afterward, I guess you can take whatever of his advice seems sensible and ignore the rest."

"What battle is it?"

"Domal Ai of Ardun, my city, and the dukes of the East

Isles have gotten a fleet together, it seems. That storm's been brewing up for years."

Pedross nodded absently; he'd heard Ashai fuming time and time again how slow the other baymasters were in rousing, how he wanted that inevitable confrontation over and done with so he could get down to the serious business of organizing Longlands. "But why Secolo? Ashai barely tolerates the man."

"I don't know. I'd suppose his likes or dislikes don't matter much to him, if the man's useful. He seems to think Secolo can keep your commanders away from each other's throats. And yours."

"Yes, I suppose so. . . . The only man feared more would be Ashai himself. Yes, I suppose that makes sense. . . ." Pedross began thinking about what enticement he could offer Valde to serve him on shipboard the way they had tonight. Sea battles were clumsy enough at best, with ships separated and signals all but useless once battle was joined. Immediate and reliable communications would give him an enormous advantage. And with his compass, a ship could ride out a tidestorm out of sight of land and still find its way home. If they engaged near tidestorm, the enemy fleet would be scattered over a hundred leagues of ocean while his own could quickly regroup and hunt them down one at a time, locate them even over the horizon by means of his Valde signal corps. . . .

He noticed Jannus watching him rather tensely and realized the Bremneri was waiting for his response to the conditions.

"Oh, that's fine," he said briskly. "But a halfmonth's not much time to get my commanders used to using compasses. I'd better get under way before the tidelift arrives, or I'll lose half a day. Jannus, how could I go about recruiting maybe a score of Valde? Men or women, I don't care which." Pedross stamped on the embers of the firebricks and started upriver at an impatient pace, explaining to Jannus how he'd use the Valde once he had them, cutting the fog with wide, quick gestures.

The body of Ashai Rey was laid out on the chart table, looking remarkably serene considering that a gnarly man was busy going through the pockets. Pedross, discovering him, was clearly more taken aback than was the gnarly man, being discovered. Jannus sidled along the way by the cabin door, ducking the exceedingly low rafters, too tired to be surprised at much of anything.

The gnarly man threw Pedross an unfriendly, heavy-lidded glance, remarking provocatively, "Well, are you satisfied now?" Under the weight of Pedross's waiting, the man added, "My lord duke," giving the last word an emphasis scarcely short of insult.

He looked, Jannus thought, like something from a pocket himself—wrinkled and lined and wadded up, with gray streaks like lint in his tied-back hair.

Choosing to ignore the tone, Pedross gestured toward the body. "How did this happen, Secolo?"

"My lord instructed me to wait for him with a lantern at the north end of the Crescent. But the time passed, and he hadn't come. So I looked around the area myself to find out what was wrong. I found my lord stark at the base of the dike, without any sort of a mark on him—struck down by a curse."

Pedross made a rude noise. "If curses could have such power, he'd have been dead twenty times over before this. Don't be absurd."

"What's this, then?" snapped the gnarly man, Secolo, and flung what seemed a bit of twine onto the boy's chest. "How is it I found a string of witch knots pinned right over his heart?"

"You and your witches." Pedross picked up the bit of cord and lowered it into the flame of a candle burning at the body's head. "My father was an old man—past eighty, by all accounts. Old men die every day without the aid of witches. Especially when they try to charge up hills of solid ice in the middle of the night after being dunked in Erth-rimmon. My father overtaxed himself, and the cold and the weariness took him. That is what you will say, because that's what happened. Isn't that so?"

"My lord duke would never allow Valde into his presence, fearing one of those witches might just try such a thing against him," declared Secolo stubbornly.

"I will hear no more of that. Valde will serve aboard my ships, if I can persuade them to do so, and no man of mine will so much as make a wardsign against them, under pain of

flogging. See the sailmasters are informed of my wish in this
matter. . . . Is that quite clear, Secolo?"

"Yes . . . my lord *duke*."

Again Pedross chose to ignore the tone. Glancing around
the cabin, he asked, "Where is my father's valkyr?"

"Gone, my lord duke. The perch was empty when I came.
She knew . . ." suggested Secolo meaningfully, nodding.

Jannus was beginning to wonder about the purpose of this
charade, with the body for public display and all this silly
talk of witches from a man who certainly couldn't be a total
fool, if he'd been Ashai's chief of security. Jannus listened to
Pedross giving directions for a meeting with the sailmasters
and commanders of marines, and for disposing of the body,
suitably weighted, into Erth-rimmon. And then it occurred to
Jannus that not a single word had been said about a regency
nor about appointing the disagreeable, superstitious Secolo as
chief strategist.

It wasn't surprising if Pedross found the prospect distaste-
ful, but it was certainly better than the alternative. And
besides, Pedross had accepted the terms.

Jannus watched, with indefinite unease, the fair boy and
the sallow gnarly man facing each other across the stiff furniture of the corpse, the boy blithely giving orders and the man
steadily retreating, grudgingly deferential, never once looking
toward Jannus.

"Master Secolo," said Jannus-suddenly. "The sailmaster of
the *Rising Sun* said only that Ashai had been brought back ill
and fainting. Who knows Ashai's dead, besides you?"

Still without sparing him a glance, Secolo looked to
Pedross as if to inquire whether he was obliged to notice this
interloper. Directed to answer by Pedross's careless wave,
Secolo replied gruffly, "Nobody."

"But he was dead when you found him."

"That's right."

"Why pretend otherwise, then?"

Pedross conjectured, "He didn't want the news to get out
before he'd decided what to do about it. Master Secolo is not
so generally loved as he perhaps deserves. Without the duke's
hand over him, he'd want time to choose the safest course."

"I'd like to hear Secolo's answer," said Jannus mildly.

Secolo cleared his throat and spat on the floor. "That's

about it. Information's a treasure, not to be tossed about blind, nor to beggars."

That seemed reasonable enough. Nothing there but an unpopular subordinate's caution, faced with the end of his lord's protection. Yet it bothered Jannus that, should a new mobile arrive on shore an hour hence, there'd be nobody to find the fact anything more than passing odd except Secolo himself: a man with apparent and persuasive reasons for keeping silent.

And it bothered Jannus that, in spite of appearances, nothing irrevocable had happened yet, though Secolo addressed Pedross as "my lord duke" and seemed to give assent to everything he said. So far, for all his deference, Secolo had in fact done nothing at all *but* agree. None of Pedross's directions had yet resulted in any action whatever on Secolo's part. Secolo would merely bring up some fresh matter for Pedross to pronounce on, which Pedross seemed more than willing to do: ordering the world more to his liking, as if it were that easy, just a matter of deciding.

Jannus noticed Ashai's stick leaned against the foot of the bunk, and bent carefully to pick it up. From Ketrinne's description of Ashai's spectacular method of departing the audience hall, Jannus had concluded it must contain a fuser. The bands around the handle should be the controlling rings, to set the heat beam's dispersion and strength. But when Jannus tried to realign them, they proved merely decorative, part of the substance of the head. The cane was a useless fraud, a model identical only to an uninformed eye—like the rigid calm corpse on the chart table, something supplied for show.

But again, that seemed reasonable enough. The Shai wouldn't let a functioning fuser drop into ignorant hands for mere verisimilitude. And *some* cane had to be there, he supposed. It went with Ashai, alive or dead.

It occurred to Jannus to wonder for whose benefit this elaborate show had been contrived—its potential audience of marines and sailmasters and Quickmoor folk, or its immediate audience of two? Or Secolo alone, since he presumably was the only one who didn't know the mobile for what it was, or realize that the Shai could supply a practically endless succession of live dukes or dead ones with equal ease.

Or was it for Pedross, to give him the public corpse he'd wanted and reassure him that Ashai had really retired from the scene?

And Pedross still hadn't brought up the terms he'd agreed to. It occurred to Jannus then that Ashai had "died" without communicating his conditions to Secolo, and that Pedross didn't mean to enlighten him, now or ever: as if Ashai's death ended all conditions, all oaths, and Pedross could inherit everything without paying the price.

That thought had a very dangerous feel about it. There was always a price.

A bit diffidently, still holding the cane, Jannus interrupted Secolo's report on the progress of the Longlands campaign to prompt, "Pedross, about the conditions. . . ."

Secolo broke off, and Pedross looked around, both with undisguised annoyance. Pedross remarked, "I'm busy now, Jannus, and tired. I expect you are too. I'll have a longboat ordered to take you back to the dock nearest to Rayneth's place."

"My lord duke," cut in Secolo smoothly, "what's to be done about that Rayneth woman, who's called Lady of the Crescent?"

After a moment's consideration, Pedross decided, "Tell her she has until thaw to order her affairs. Then she has to get out. There is only one Lady in Quickmoor."

Secolo said, "But my . . . my former lord promised to support her as long as she was faithful. She's been that."

"Ashai's dead," declared Pedross, as bluntly as though he believed it. "I will not prop a gaudy goods-bolt, that Lady Ketrinne wishes so ardently to be rid of. *I* say, there is only one Lady in Quickmoor, and it's not Rayneth."

"As you say, my lord duke," replied Secolo, with a glitter of what looked like satisfaction in his heavy-lidded eyes. "I'll see she's told."

"Pedross. You are bound to honor Ashai's commitments for at least five years," Jannus reminded him. "That means to Rayneth too, no matter *what* Ketrinne wants. Ketrinne's put up with Rayneth *this* long—"

"Jannus, I'm grateful for your taking my part in my feud, even if it *was* a bit late and wasn't needed, after all. But you can't tell me what I can and can't do. That's for—"

"I shouldn't *have* to tell you," snapped Jannus. "Those were the conditions. You agreed to them. Will you face a Truthsayer—Ketrinne herself, say—and claim otherwise?"

"Nobody sets foot on *Rising Sun* without my consent. Not even Ketrinne. And I don't have to *claim* anything."

"I *got* you those terms. You'll swear to them, or deny them, right here, to my face."

"Why?" rejoined Pedross coolly. "Who are you?"

"Listen to my lord duke, Bremneri," Secolo warned. "Listen, and avoid displeasure. It's the lesser of two evils. *No*," directed the gnarly, wrinkled man sharply, meeting Jannus's comprehending look directly, *"don't interfere.* Our young duke knows best how to manage his own affairs."

It was a new mobile, a counterfeit of Secolo good enough to fool even Pedross, who knew the man well. That was where Bronh was, then: speeding to eliminate the original Secolo, lest there be any notable discrepancies.

But unless Pedross openly acknowledged the conditions, Ashai Rey would make an abrupt recovery—publicly—and sail south, mourning his intransigent and very dead son.

It was a trap, a test, a trial, with the new mobile as both judge and executioner.

"I'd advise you to *stand aside*," continued the mobile meaningfully, talking past the oblivious Pedross. "Or if you stay, be silent. That, *I* require. Shall I have the longboat manned for you, Bremneri?"

"Yes," said Pedross.

"No," said Jannus.

Intuitively he knew that if he unmasked the mobile, the trial was ended. The whole foundation of the regency, he now realized, had been the mobile's continuing authority and influence in a form Pedross would accept.

If Secolo was exposed, the offered terms would be withdrawn and Pedross would die.

And if it came to that, or if Pedross was found wanting, Jannus would have no option but to try to protect him, as he'd threatened to do, even with a direct order in contravention of the Rule of One. Then the mobile would scrap them both and choose new tools less troublesome.

A tidy trap, fully big enough for two.

Not even Ketrinne's inquisition had inspired Jannus to try to weigh words with such desperate exactitude.

He whacked the cane down on the rigid torso of the corpse, startling even Pedross, and exclaimed, "Pedross, you utter and incredible fool, think what you're doing. Think what I've told you. *I* didn't make the conditions. Who did? It wasn't to *me* you swore. Who holds your oath? In honor of *Ashai's memory,* think what you're doing!"

Pedross's angry flush faded as he stared down at the cane and the corpse, the public corpse he'd wanted and now gotten, thinking that was all he needed to free him of all restraint. Visibly pale, Pedross said, "Of course. He's not . . ." and, glancing cautiously at the impassive Secolo, became awkwardly circumspect. "I'd forgotten my father's *memory* was still . . . with us. The glass is broken but the pitcher remains. I hear, but I don't always listen. I do beg your pardon. . . ."

Meeting Secolo's shadowed, sly eyes, Jannus said, "Do you object to my cautioning the young duke to take care? Some of us are very tired."

Secolo said blandly, "Our young duke can't be told too often to take care. *So much* depends on his good judgment."

"I do hear you," rejoined Jannus, understanding the threat perfectly.

"We are all concerned for his wise choices. I'm a poor substitute for his father's shrewdness and experience."

"I'm sure you underestimate your gifts, Master Secolo," responded Jannus, with perhaps equal bland pointedness. "I'm sure you'll be as a second father to the young duke while he learns his powers and his duties."

"I wouldn't be rash enough even to suggest such a thing." Secolo's frown gave warning that the exchange was reaching the limit of permissible hinting.

"Secolo," said Pedross slowly, emerging from apparent meditation, "I have thought again of what I said concerning the woman Rayneth. In honor of my father's memory, her loyalty should be rewarded. I say therefore that support to her shall continue exactly as before for the time being—at least five years. And all commitments my father made in his lifetime shall be likewise honored, the people rewarded or punished according to their worth and faithfulness. Except Solvig Innsmith. He's mine. I don't care. I'm not going to punish him for siding with me, and that's flat."

Secolo said, "I'm sure your father would understand that the Innsmith followed the word of his oath, if not its intent. And the word, after all, does matter."

"All right, then." Pedross sighed, then continued, "Master

Secolo, you know my father's thinking concerning the coming battle against the East Isles."

"My lord, I do. We planned it together."

"Then I will rely on you to be my chief strategist, especially in the matter of this first battle. I have some ideas about the use of compasses and Valde that perhaps you might consider . . . but you will have the planning of it, entirely," Pedross ended in a burst.

"I'm honored by your trust, my lord. I won't fail you."

"And. . . ." There was a long pause, but Pedross was merely bracing himself to get the last, worst, acceptance said. "Secolo, you have been my tutor and my armsmaster, and there have been hard words between us at times. Now that I must rule in my father's place, it cannot be between us as it was before. But neither am I my father, a man of mature years, whom nobody ever feared or trusted without reason. I will ask you to act as my regent for . . . for five years—" Plainly, that had been a real effort. "To have the final say, without fear of punishment, over all I do, lest inexperience lead me into hazard, and others who rely on my protection and leadership. Will you accept this charge?"

"My lord duke, what wisdom and experience I have are at your disposal already. Why have a regency?" asked Secolo, which Jannus thought a bit much.

"Because I wish it." Pedross almost choked, but he said it.

"Then of course I will obey you in that wish, as in all things. . . . Bremneri, shall I see to that longboat for you now?"

"Oh, I suppose." Jannus tipped the fraudulent cane back into the corner, responding vaguely to Pedross's remarks of leavetaking. There were stairs up to the deck, scarcely better than a ladder, and there was the descent to the longboat to look forward to. And then, if he were extremely diligent and persevering, he might today reach the entry for *mud*.

Poli descended the gully sidewise, balancing, to learn whether the peeled willow whips she'd left soaking were pliable enough yet to be worked. The stream at the bottom of the gully was no more than a series of clear pools, still and numbingly cold to her dipping hands, but the shaggy south bank was low enough to let the sun in and thaw each night's skin of ice by midday.

There were even a few fish still to be had, in the deeper pools. One day soon she'd try hooking a couple with her fingers—not to eat, although she was hungry, but to trade. There was a small Fisher encampment probably no more than a few hours' walk inland. She thought in a few days more she'd be able to stand getting that close to people without the risk of losing herself into the confusion of their *fariohe*, self-singings. She might trade the fish for some rice, and maybe some salt. She'd been missing salt.

It'd only been a few days since the *als'far* of the encampment had been a continual pressure even at that distance. Willing or unwilling, she'd known the rhythms of the Fisher's sleeping and walking as clearly as her own, known the adults from the children and even from the erratic flaring moods of the adolescents, known all the relationships and attitudes of each to the others. She'd known the manic intentness of their poultry, and the waiting of every chick within its shell had intruded on her dreams.

But today her world had become narrower and quieter. The farthest life she sensed was that of a badger whose digs were under the roots of the willow which was the source of the whips, a little way along the bank. The circle of her *marenniath* had drawn in again, encompassing less than she could see. Maybe tomorrow she'd catch the fish and trade, or the day after that.

The whips were still too stiff. She wedged the bundle back underneath a rock and climbed back up to the hollow in the south-facing bank where she'd made her shelter—only boughs and some bundles of rushes, as yet. With the willow, she could weave mats to support a coating of clay to keep the wind out.

The only food she had left was a small pile of lily bulbs. At first she hadn't been able to hunt at all—every fear, every hurt, had felt as if she were suffering it herself. But now she had a line of snares set, out beyond the retreating ebb-line of her *marenniath*. She had hopes of a rabbit. She reminded herself to check the snares. She'd be needing more branchwood anyway, to keep her fire going through the night.

As she picked up a handful of twigs, debating whether to use up the rest of her branchwood to get thoroughly warm before setting out to collect more, the thought came, *Kindling burns first, and brightest.*

That was a saying, among troopmaids, about First Dancers.

Well, she'd been kindling of a sort, it occurred to her. She'd blazed through the river-link, self-forgetful in the intensity of her desire that the careless ones, the deserters, be replaced tenfold, that Valde have a word to give and, having given it, the will to keep it. Otherwise they were no more than fish, leaves on a breeze.

With the heedless openness of her deafness, she'd thrown herself into a sort of Troopcalling—wilder and more extravagant than that which divided young Haffa into troopmaids and Awiro at the Summerfair. And either in that unreserved reaching out, or in the gathering resonance of the reply from, first, Mene's troop, then link after link as the Troopcalling strengthened, magnified, *reached*, her *marenniath* had waked, unexpected, so that the challenge and the answer had seemed to her only one vast voice. . . .

Poli weighed the little bunch of remaining sticks for a moment, then let them fall. Walking would warm her. There was no need for a fire.

Taking with her only a twine of woven grass to bind the branchwood she found, she went up onto the bank and among the thin, scattered coppices of bushwillow, yellowwood, and ash.

The Is marshes were not true swamp, like Han Halla. There was more solid ground than water, and the dense reedbeds kept mostly to the immediate margin of Erth-rimmon. From the higher ground where she walked, Poli could look past their dun screen to the river and see, beyond, the rise of the Kantmorie escarpment topped by the arching blue talon of the Broken Bridge.

To the south, the land flattened; but Quickmoor was too far away to be seen or felt.

The daysinging of the Is marshes was at this season scarcely more than what was known to her own ears and eyes. The fundamental drone of plant life had gone with the green, leaving only the continuance of trees and the indefinable sense of waiting which was the voices of seeds. The complex intertwined urgency of summer's insects was also thinned, diminished to a few dazed flies clutching grass tops in the sun. The birds within her radius were fretful, yearning south, aware of the slow pursuit of ice. Beasts, hungry and wary, wove their separate *fariohe* like folk crying each from his own hilltop and afraid of a reply.

Poli could not have tolerated more. She'd been altogether open, unprepared, unbraced. She'd lost herself into the link and still hadn't found her way completely back to single identity. The boundary between outer and inner, other and self, had been ruptured and was slow to heal.

In her seasons as First Dancer she'd known the feeling of confusion and loss that followed the breaking of dueltrance: how one fell for a time into the communal *als'far* of the troop as water into water, slack, passive. This reaction had been similar, but magnified manyfold—as though she'd been in separate trance-link with each of the multitude of troopmaids responding to the Troopcalling. Stretched, locked in that incredible multiple rapport, she'd lost herself completely.

It'd been as if she'd sent her whole self blazing outward into the linkage; and when the linkage broke, there'd been nothing left of her but a vortex, an insatiable hunger without a center. The hunger had snatched out, impossibly trying to *become* what it heard, to echo the whole daysinging because it had no voice of its own, yet could not bear the silence.

She had no clear recollection of what had happened after that. Her first memory was of seeing her own reflection in a pool and wondering what it was. The cold of the water, as her hand stretched to touch the image, had roused a more particular awareness of the thirst, hunger, and cold of this single body, separate from the trees or from the beasts' unending cycles of pursuit, hunger, and comfort. Her *marenniath* began to withdraw from the outer awareness toward the inner. There was again a center, a single being who could name itself *I*. The scattered daysinging of Is was weak enough to be tasted in tiny sips, without any overwhelmingly strong or concentrated *fariohe*, self-singings, to pull her out of identity while she had so little strength to resist them. She no longer easily confused herself with the trees or field mice.

As she stopped to tie up the bundle of dead branches she'd accumulated, someone inspoke to her a question of meeting, an offer of food/comfort, these images overlaid upon a turbulence of lack, concern, and anger, though only the concern was directed toward her. Startled, she looked all about her, assuming the person must be almost close enough to touch, the way her range had been diminishing. But she was alone.

The inspeaking replied with the nearness of the river, the feel of something overhead, blue, unwilling willingness to leave/remain farther off. . . .

Jannus. It'd been so long since she'd heard his *farioh*, and it'd changed meanwhile—more definiteness and clarity, and the volume of a shout.

Assuming he must be able to see her, she clapped her hands over her ears. The inspeaking stopped. Much more muted, the unfocused currents of his *farioh* were within bearable limits. She removed her hands from her ears in a slow broad gesture, then made a wide wave of beckoning.

Presently she could see him moving on the near side of the reed-curtain, tipped right by the weight of something he carried on that side. Cautiously, she went a few paces forward and found the pressure of his *farioh* no greater than before. So she went on, still hesitantly, while he slowly approached.

When the distance was near enough for breathtalk, he called, "Are you all right? I can't just leave this," lifting the hamper he carried.

Poli crossed the distance in about ten running strides and grabbed him in a confusion of reunion, greeting, gladness whose origins she could not have separated. Breaking away finally, she tried to recover a coherent sense of her own *farioh* while he nursed his sore ribs and tried to right the dropped hamper.

He said, "I came as soon as I could. Mene told me. . . ." The anger gathered like thunder. "They did it again. Went off and left you—"

"No, don't," responded Poli, wincing away and patting vaguely at the air.

Jannus turned his back, focusing on the Broken Bridge until that image displaced his rage at the troopmaids. He remarked, "There were no paddle-wheelers in the Crescent—I guess they're gone till thaw, now. The Sparrow brought me in a dinghy. I could no more have rowed this far, or walked, than I could have flown. Can you hear him? Sparrowhawk?"

Relaxing, Poli sat on her heels to open the hamper, replying, "No, he's too far. My range is down to about ten or twenty paces. When no farspeaker is shouting at me. . . ."

She found the hamper full of cooking pot, which in turn was full of food—baked chicken, two apples, a thick loaf of bread, a huge wedge of cheese, and a mix of nuts and raisins tied up in a cloth.

Jannus said, "There's blankets and a weatherproof tent in the dinghy, and some firebricks, but I couldn't carry it all at once, and I thought maybe the last thing you'd need after a bad mood-echo recoil would be a Lisler. . . ." Almost shy, he added, "Am *I* bothering you? I can go after the blankets, leave you alone for a bit. . . ."

She shook her head vehemently, her mouth full of nuts and raisins. Swallowing, she exclaimed, "Oh, it's *good* to hear you! It's been so *long*—"

The response was unbearable for only an instant before he managed to damp it down with reflections on how awkward bodies were, lasping midway into breathtalk, "—can't on the *ground*. . . . Can you haul that thing over there?"

He gestured toward a dead ash whose top was wedged into a neighboring tree, its slanted trunk thick enough to serve as a seat. Poli pulled the hamper over and sat on the ground, using the ash as a backrest, while Jannus sat on the trunk beside her.

He remarked, "Well, at least the whole winter wasn't wasted. I finally got to see the Broken Bridge after all, and Fathori—what's left of it."

Cracking a chicken wing, she responded, "How are the five?"

"Oh, fairly well, considering. I . . . haven't been much help—" He stopped short on the edge of that sinkpool, found safe ground. "Dan's trying to teach Sua how to knit, you can imagine what a time *he's* having. But it's been hard for them, changing rooms twice, and me, and you. . . ." Another check, retreat, and sidestep. His hand glanced off her neck and settled on her shoulder. "I'm so out of practice. . . . It's so strange to be trying to keep the inspeaking still around you, after all this while. I don't—" He pulled the hand back, prisoned it in the other, meanwhile hunting outward for safe neutral things he could control better. He said, "Even now, Fathori's more to my liking than Han Halla, you know? It's solider than it looks, from the Quickmoor side, where all you can see are more reeds. . . . We could come over here sometimes. Let the girls loose without anybody drowning or getting lost, and not need any troopmaids to tend us. . . . Will it stay this way, do you think? The *marenniath*?"

"It'll be the way it was, I think." Poli licked at her fingers meditatively. "All the fresh second-growth has been burned off again, scorched down to the bare ground. I feel scalded all over on the inside of my skin—does that make sense? I never thought I'd be caught like that, pulled in all directions, turned inside out like a glove. . . ."

"Once burned, twice shy?"

"Twice burned, now. And shy . . . ?" She glanced around at him, making a wry face. "Worse than any *in'marenniath* now—no screens or control at all, raw edges all over. *You're* all right," she said, reacting to his inspoken concern, "I can get lost in you and it doesn't matter, but anybody else, like the Sparrow. . . ."

Less tentatively, he put his arm around her back and, leaning into that comfort, Poli discovered within herself, unsuspected, a starvation so profound it had numbed even hunger.

"Anyhow, you did it," he commended her presently. "They came—about five hundred of them, some from as far off as Hillstock."

"No. It wasn't me. All I did was share what I knew and cared about. But they chose. I didn't make them, any more than you made Lora and the rest leave, sharing the truth that you knew and cared about—of the hurt Valde do here."

"Was that what I did?" he responded softly, wonderingly. "Was that all it was? I thought . . . I thought it was just *me*. . . ." She felt him adjusting, settling. "Just the same, for once somebody told them so that they had to hear. I did that. *We* did that. Between us, we've disrupted the troops of five riverstocks, did you think of that?"

He was proud of that, and pleased, and Poli shared inspoken laughter contemplating what a notable confusion they had wrought. She rummaged through the food in the hamper to find another piece of chicken.

"But I'll tell you something," he added, to a lunging counterpoint of brooding anger breaking free of controls. "Sometimes I wonder if Valde are fit to live. That's twice they've gone off and left you—no, this one time, let me get it said—and if Ketrinne's forgiven them, *I* haven't. Mene said you went *sa'farioh*, like a Tek, when the echo broke, and they couldn't find you. *I* say, they didn't *try* very hard. . . ." Again checked, again blazing, the focus of the anger shifted and became more immediate, changing, its target ambiguous. "That they could just go off and leave you lost, and not care—"

Although the tight, focused anger was painful, Poli did not retreat from it, accepting its ambiguous resentments and hurts. She offered no answer but that of her presence, the contact carrying its own message of acceptance and warmth.

Some things could be shared only by indirection, and obliquely; and the *marenniath* made no difference at all.

The accusing focus faded by degree into the random background, becoming no more than a mutual awareness of presence, quiet and intimate as breathing.

With his foot he nudged away the piece of food she'd dropped and, bending with stiff care, found another in the hamper to offer her. She took it, gazing up at him steadily, exchanging the gestures of a third language that was neither the breathtalk nor the inspeaking—the language of the rapport itself.

They smiled at the same time and comfortably, casually, looked away, full of contentment.

She asked presently, "Do you have to go back?"

He thought about that, the currents of his *farioh* flashing into sudden turns, bright colors, warmth. Smiling again, he said, "Someday. . . ."

"No, really. Maybe a tenday . . . ?"

"You sure you wouldn't be better just by yourself?" he asked, though his *farioh* said plainly that he'd already decided and wouldn't have budged.

That remembered disparity between what he felt and said was all she'd needed to be perfectly happy in his company again. "I'm sure," she said, and reached up to stroke the side of his face. "Tell the Sparrow to bring some more firebrick and things with him tomorrow, what we'll need. Sing out when he's gone and I'll come help carry the blankets and all. It gets cold here at night," she added, and grinned.

Pushing to his feet, he said, "Who'll notice?" and started back toward the river while Poli set aside the piece of chicken and broke the loaf.